Forgive and Forget

Born in Gainsborough, Lincolnshire, Margaret Dickinson moved to the coast at the age of seven and so began her love for the sea and the Lincolnshire landscape.

Her ambition to be a writer began early and she had her first novel published at the age of twenty-five. This was followed by twenty-four further titles including *Plough the Furrow*, *Sow the Seed* and *Reap the Harvest*, which make up her Lincolnshire Fleethaven trilogy. Many of her novels are set in the heart of her home county, but in *Tangled Threads* and *Twisted Strands* the stories included not only Lincolnshire but also the framework knitting and lace industries of Nottingham. The Workhouse Museum at Southwell in Nottinghamshire inspired *Without Sin* and the magnificent countryside of Derbyshire and the fascinating town of Macclesfield in Cheshire formed the backdrop for the story of *Pauper's Gold*. *Wish Me Luck* returned to Lincolnshire once more and the county was also the setting for *Sing as We Go*. Part of the story in *Suffragette Girl* took place in Davos, Switzerland, but *Sons and Daughters* was set solely in the flat marshlands near the East Coast. *Forgive and Forget* centres on the rich history of the beautiful city of Lincoln.

www.margaret-dickinson.co.uk

ALSO BY MARGARET DICKINSON

Plough the Furrow

Sow the Seed

Reap the Harvest

The Miller's Daughter

Chaff upon the Wind

The Fisher Lass

The Tulip Girl

The River Folk

Tangled Threads

Twisted Strands

Red Sky in the Morning

Without Sin

Pauper's Gold

Wish Me Luck

Sing as We Go

Suffragette Girl

Sons and Daughters

Margaret Dickinson

Forgive and Forget

PAN BOOKS

First published 2011 by Pan Books
an imprint of Pan Macmillan, a division of Macmillan Publishers Limited
Pan Macmillan, 20 New Wharf Road, London N1 9RR
Basingstoke and Oxford
Associated companies throughout the world
www.panmacmillan.com

ISBN 978-0-330-51623-5

1 3 5 7 9 8 6 4 2

A CIP catalogue record for this book is available from
the British Library.

Typeset by SetSystems Ltd, Saffron Walden, Essex
Printed in the UK by CPI Mackays, Chatham ME5 8TD

Visit www.panmacmillan.com to read more about all our books
and to buy them. You will also find features, author interviews and
news of any author events, and you can sign up for e-newsletters
so that you're always first to hear about our new releases.

For my beautiful granddaughter
Zara Elizabeth Robena Jean

Acknowledgements

The characters in my story are entirely fictitious, but I do like to place them in real events. The research for this novel has been fascinating and I have learned so much more about the city I have always loved.

My grateful thanks to Ann Yeates-Langley (formerly Wright) for all her wonderful help with some of the background material for this story. Ann is the co-author, along with Christopher Bray and Kirsty Grantham, of *The Enemy in Our Midst, the Story of Lincoln's Typhoid Epidemic*.

I am also indebted to the *Lincolnshire Chronicle* newspapers of the time, which gave a wealth of factual information on all the events.

I would also like to thank the staff of the Museum of Lincolnshire Life in Lincoln, Lincoln Central Library, Lincolnshire Archives and Skegness Library for their wonderful help with my research. Thank you all.

And last, but never least, my love and thanks to those members of my family and friends who read and comment on the scripts. Your help is invaluable and always appreciated.

One

'Poll, get the doctor.'

Polly turned to stare at her father, her green eyes widening.

'The – the doctor?' she stammered.

Calling the doctor was unheard of in the Longdens' terraced house. Doctors had to be paid for and money was short for the family of seven.

'It's yar mam. She's badly.'

'I know that,' Polly countered. 'She's been badly ever since the babby was born. Can't Mrs Halliday see to her?'

William Longden ran his hand through his springy auburn hair. 'This hasn't owt to do wi' having the babby. She's got steadily worse these last two weeks. You know that.'

'But . . .' Polly began to argue, but her father's next words cut her short and brought dread to her heart.

'I reckon she's got the fever.'

The young girl gasped. 'Typhoid? You mean the typhoid?'

Rumour – like the disease itself – had been spreading through Lincoln since the beginning of December and now, in early February, word was that an epidemic was rife in the city.

1

'But how?' the girl asked, anxious yet puzzled. 'Like they told us to in the *Chronicle*, we boil all our water. An' I scrub the privy every day.' She wrinkled her nose in disgust. The standpipe and the lavatory in the backyard were shared by three families and each household was supposed to take its share in the cleaning, but Sarah Longden, Polly's mother, didn't trust the slovenly standards of her neighbours and cleaned the wooden seat of the privy every day. Since she'd given birth to the latest addition to the family just before Christmas – a baby girl they'd named Miriam – the unenviable task had fallen upon Polly's thirteen-year-old shoulders.

'I know you do, love.' Her father's tone softened a little, yet the dreadful fear never left his eyes. 'And,' he was pleading now, 'you'll have to stay off work a bit longer.'

'Stay off?' Polly's eyes blazed. '*Again?*'

'I'm sorry, Poll, but—'

'I'll get the sack,' she reminded him grimly. 'Mr Spicer's warned me once already when Mam had Miriam and I stayed off to look after her.'

'I know, I know,' William said distractedly. 'But what else can I do, love? Yar mam's sick and getting worse by the day. And now—'. He broke off and glanced away from Polly's glare.

'What?'

'She's got the rash.'

Cold fear ran through the girl's slim body. 'Rash?' she whispered hoarsely. 'Is it – is it pink?'

The symptoms of typhoid were now the main topic of conversation in every street throughout the beleaguered city. They all recognized the first signs: headaches, stomach pains and a dry cough. As the days progressed, a pinkish rash appeared, then vomiting and severe diarrhoea confirmed their worst fears.

'Aye.' William nodded hopelessly. 'So that's why I say, lass, you'll have to fetch the doctor. Best go to Mrs Halliday's. She'll know what we've to do.'

Polly couldn't remember them ever seeking the services of a doctor and so neither she nor her father knew where the nearest one lived. But Mrs Halliday would know.

'Yes, Dad,' Polly said meekly now and reached for her coat from the peg behind the door. 'I'll be as quick as I can.'

As she ran down the street, her heart was thumping with fear for her mother – for all the family. Yet part of her railed against the unfairness of it all. She'd left school the previous summer to work in the glue factory. She'd wanted to stay on and become a teacher one day, like Miss Broughton, but her father had insisted she leave and find work. They needed the money, he'd said, and though her mother's troubled eyes had sent her a silent apology, Sarah had made no attempt to side with her daughter. Only Polly, green eyes flashing with indignation, her wild auburn hair flying free, had faced her father.

'I want to stay on. You said I could. I want to be a teacher, I want—'

'Enough,' her father had boomed. 'It's not about what you want. It's about what this family needs.'

William Longden, tall, thin and slightly stooping and with the red-hair colouring that Polly had inherited, was normally a reasonable man, but he was quick-tempered and when roused to anger he was fearsome. He raised his arm and for a brief moment Polly thought he was going to strike her. He'd never hit any of his children, not like the other fathers in the street, who took their belts to their kids at the slightest excuse. He'd never even leathered their Eddie, who, at eleven, was fast becoming a tearaway. At least, not yet. But as Polly had faced him, her determined little chin jutting out obstinately, her tangle of red hair framing a mutinous face, her small feet planted firmly on the floor and her arms folded across her chest, she'd trembled inwardly. For the first time in her young life she knew she'd driven her father too far with her answering back. To her surprise, William had let his arm fall, his hot anger dying as swiftly as it had come. But he was still not about to give way.

'You've got your certificate from the school so you can leave. You'll start at the factory on Monday,' William had said heavily. 'I've seen Spicer and it's all arranged.'

Now, as she sped along the street, Polly was wishing fervently that she'd not worked so hard at her lessons and become Miss Broughton's star pupil. Maybe if she'd been lazy and messy in her work instead of being attentive and neat, she'd not have been given the certificate that said she'd reached the required standard in her education as set out by the local by-laws. She kicked herself mentally – that way she could have stayed on at school. She wouldn't be working in the glue factory or be kept at home to nurse her mother and look after a tiny baby. She'd still be in class, sitting in the front row, drinking in every word that the teacher said, revelling in the knowledge and the skills being imparted.

And she wouldn't have been kept off school because

the one thing her father had feared was the arrival of the school attendance officer at his door.

It had all been her own stupid fault, she reproached herself, for trying to be so clever, and now she was paying the price of sinful pride.

Two

The Longdens lived in a two-up, two-down terraced house in one of the streets set at right angles to the long High Street. The River Witham meandered past the bottom end of their street, but Sarah forbade her children to play near it, even though some folk swam there in warm weather or boated on it.

It was a friendly street, though the youngsters would rough and tumble with one another, which usually resulted in scraped knees, bleeding noses and torn clothes. A shouting match between the mothers as to who had started the fight often followed, but a week or two of frostiness between the women involved would eventually thaw – until the next altercation. With the men, it was simple. They went off together to the football matches on a Saturday afternoon at Sincil Bank, ending up in the local pub after the game either to celebrate or to drown their sorrows. Either way, most of them came home drunk. Sometimes there were fisticuffs in the streets, but by next morning the cause was forgotten. The bruises and bloody noses took longer to heal than did the friendships. But visits to the racecourse, where the highlight of the year was the Lincoln Handicap, were what their wives feared the most. Strong-willed Sarah Longden dreaded that time, for even she could not stop William joining the other men in spending their week's wages on the 'gee-gees'.

Polly banged on the door of the house at the end of the street near the river and shouted at the same time. 'Mrs Halliday, Mrs Halliday. Come quick.'

The house was just the same as her own home; the front door opening straight into the best front room, leading through a small area at the foot of the stairs into the kitchen, which was the main family living room where the range dominated one wall. Beyond that was the scullery with a shallow sink, where the washing of crockery and of clothes was done. All the family's meals were prepared here and the copper bricked into the corner provided hot water on bath nights.

'Now, now,' came a voice from beyond the door in answer to Polly's frantic knocking. 'If 'tis a babby comin', it'll tek its time an' if someone's died, there's no rush.'

The door flew open and Polly looked up into the motherly round face of the local midwife and layer-out, the woman to whom everyone came in times of trouble for help and advice.

'We need the doctor, Mrs Halliday,' Polly panted. 'Me mam's real bad.'

Mrs Halliday's ready smile faded. 'What's 'er symptoms, lass?' she asked and then, beneath her breath added, 'As if I didn't know.'

'She's bein' sick.'

'And the lax? Has she got the lax?'

The girl shuddered as she thought of the foul-smelling diarrhoea in the chamber pot that she was obliged to empty several times a day. She nodded. 'Ever so bad and now – ' she pulled in a shuddering breath – 'there's a rash.'

'Oh dear. Then you do need the doctor to see her. It'll 'ave to be notified, love, won't it?' A ghost of a

7

smile lit Bertha Halliday's eyes briefly as she added, 'We must abide by the law, specially now our Leo's a policeman.'

Bertha Halliday's son, Leo, had joined the city police force a few months earlier at the age of eighteen. Fair-haired and blue-eyed with a cheeky grin that belied his chosen profession, Leo was the apple of his mother's eye. And all the unattached young girls in the neighbourhood would make sure they were wearing a clean pinafore or their best coat when stepping out of their front doors just in case he should be striding up the street. Even at thirteen, Polly was unusually tongue-tied when she ran into him unexpectedly. But this morning the handsome young man was not occupying her thoughts.

'Please, Mrs Halliday, will you—?'

''Course I will, lass. I'll get the doctor to call. You leave it to me and get yarsen back home to look after yar mam and the bairns.'

Polly retraced her steps more slowly. She paused briefly outside her own house, but then she ran swiftly to the end of the street where it joined the High Street. She stood on the corner and gazed up at the cathedral sitting proudly on the top of the hill. She loved the huge building, but she'd never had the chance to attend services there; in fact she'd never seen the inside. One day, she'd always promised herself, I'll walk all the way up the High Street, up Steep Hill and I'll go and see it for mesen. Their own church was smaller but much nearer – only a few hundred yards away. Polly bit her lip. Come Sunday, she thought, she'd really have something to pray about.

By the time she returned home, her father had left for work, afraid too that he would lose his job on the nearby railway if he stayed away. The baby was howling, four-year-old Stevie was sitting wide-eyed beside the drawer that doubled as a cradle sucking his thumb anxiously and Sarah was calling weakly from the bedroom upstairs. Polly sighed, took off her coat and hung it behind the door. Then she patted Stevie's dark curls, promising, 'I'll be down in a minute, love.'

The boy removed his thumb and nodded towards the baby. 'I fink she's hungry.'

'No doubt she is,' Polly remarked dryly and could have added, 'we all are.' But she turned away and climbed the dark stairway to the bedrooms above feeling as if she carried the troubles of the whole city on her slight shoulders.

She entered the front bedroom, the smell of vomit hitting her so forcibly that she retched. Her parents occupied this room, whilst the back bedroom had been partitioned by their father into two, so that Polly and her younger sister, Violet, slept on one side and the boys, Eddie and Stevie, on the other. The house was crowded enough now, Polly had thought resentfully when she'd first heard that there was to be yet another addition to the family. But Miriam was a sweet little thing, whom she'd adored at once. For the last few days since her mother had been taken worse, Polly had done everything for the tiny baby. She loved caring for the mite, but she didn't want to do it for ever; she wanted to get back to work, to save enough money so that she could train to be a teacher. Despite being obliged to obey her father, she still hadn't given up her dream, even though, so far, all her wages had been handed over to Sarah to help feed and clothe the family. Now, with all the missed days at work, she feared she'd even lose that job.

'It's typhoid right enough.'

The doctor confirmed their worst fears.

'Now,' he went on, turning to Polly standing fearfully beside the bed, 'keep her warm and give her only fluids. Nothing solid. And make sure you boil all drinking water because that's where this disease is coming from. The supply's been contaminated somehow. And you must boil milk, too. You understand, child?'

Polly nodded, looking up into the man's solemn face. Behind the round spectacles, his eyes were tired with a weariness caused by the weight of responsibility that rested on his shoulders. Dr Fenwick was in his early fifties, of portly build, with a balding pate and a bristling white moustache, which he stroked thoughtfully when considering his patients' ailments. But there was no need to ponder today; sadly, the diagnosis was all too easy. Though highly respected, he was something of a figure of fun amongst his patients, for he always wore a black jacket and pinstriped trousers, with a brightly coloured waistcoat and bow tie. A gold chain attached to the watch hidden in his waistcoat pocket was looped across his broad chest.

Dr Fenwick struggled down the narrow stairs. He paused in the kitchen, eyeing the young boy and the crying baby. He nodded towards them and raised his voice above the noise to say, 'If they fall ill, child, send for me at once. You hear me? At once.'

*

By nightfall Polly was exhausted. Though she was willing and capable, caring for a sick mother, a demanding baby and the rest of the family was a heavy burden. Her father tried to help when he came home, but never having been used to household chores he was less than useless, as Bertha Halliday would have put it.

At last, Polly got baby Miriam to sleep for the night and Stevie into bed. Violet argued with her sister that, at ten, she was old enough to help her and shouldn't be sent to bed with the babies.

'You'll do as I say,' Polly snapped, gripping the younger girl's shoulder and marching her towards the stairs. 'Till Mam's better I'm in charge, so there.'

Violet paused and looked up into her sister's face. 'Is she going to get better?'

Polly blinked. 'Course she is.' But the slight hesitation had spoken volumes. Young as they both were, they knew that typhoid was a killer. Two people in their immediate neighbourhood had died and the funeral of a man further down their own street had taken place the previous day. And he hadn't been old or infirm or already weakened by childbirth like their mam.

Polly bent forward, her face close to Violet's, as she whispered, 'We've just all got to do what we can and be good.'

Violet pursed her lips and glowered, but then she muttered, 'All right. You win. *This* time.'

Then she stomped up the stairs until Polly called after her, 'Quietly, Vi. Mam might be asleep. And don't wake Baby. She's in with us tonight.'

The footsteps quietened and Violet disappeared into the part of the bedroom they shared.

Polly went back into the scullery to finish washing

the pots and to make a warm, milky drink to take up to her mother. Now there was only Eddie to deal with when he came in. He was late already and the girl knew that her brother, only fifteen months younger than her, was taking advantage of their mother's illness to stay out playing with his mates. And he was banking on his father, in his anxiety, not noticing.

But Polly was not about to let Eddie get away with it. He might already be as tall as she was, and stronger, but she'd show him who was boss.

Oh no, Eddie wasn't going to get away with anything, not while she was in charge of the household.

Three

Eddie came in at ten o'clock, two hours after he'd been told to be home.

Polly was waiting for him. She grabbed him by the shoulder as he sneaked in.

'What d'you think you're doing staying out till all hours when our mam's ill?'

'Geroff. You're hurting.'

'I'll hurt you, you little tyke. I'll tell me dad an' he'll give you a leathering.'

Eddie smirked. 'Him? He won't raise a finger to any of us. You know that, Pol.'

'More's the pity where you're concerned. Look, Eddie, if you don't care about Dad or me, then think about Mam. If she gets to know you're staying out, she'll worry.' Polly was pulling no punches as she added deliberately, 'An' it'll make her worse.'

Eddie thrust his face close to hers. 'It's only while she's ill that I can get away with it. Don't you see?'

Their mother was the driving force in the household. Sarah was the one who administered the punishments and kept her children in line. And now that she was ill Eddie, and even Violet, were quick to misbehave. But they'd both reckoned without their fiery elder sister.

Through gritted teeth, Polly said, 'I see all right, but you're not going to get away with it, Eddie Longden, so you start coming in at the proper time, or else—'

13

'Or else what?' he sneered. 'What d'you think you can do? You're only thirteen.'

'Fourteen in a couple of months. And as for what I can do – ' she narrowed her eyes – 'just try me.'

For a brief moment doubt flickered in the boy's eyes, then he pulled himself free of her grasp and swaggered towards the inner door. 'Go on, then, do your worst.'

Grimly, Polly watched him go, but she smiled to herself as she heard him tiptoeing up the stairs, his bravado giving way to thoughts of his mother's wrath when she recovered.

Polly banked down the fire and followed her brother. Creeping into their half of the bedroom, she was relieved to see both Violet and the baby sleeping. Quietly, she undressed and slipped into bed beside Violet. An hour or two's sleep was the most she could hope for before the baby woke to be fed . . .

But to her surprise and relief, Miriam slept until five o'clock, waking with what seemed to the bleary-eyed Polly to be an apologetic whimper. 'There, there, little love,' she whispered as she plucked the baby out of her cradle and carried her downstairs. Violet burrowed beneath the bedclothes and went back to sleep.

Shivering in the early morning air, Polly roused the fire and prepared the baby's bottle. Just as she'd finished feeding and changing her, William appeared. Polly looked up at once.

'How's Mam?'

William yawned and stretched. 'I reckon she's a bit better, Polly. She's asking for some breakfast. Tek 'er some toast up, eh?'

'Doctor said only fluids, Dad.'

'She's hungry. That's a good sign, in't it?'

'I suppose so,' Polly agreed reluctantly, the doctor's instructions still ringing in her ears. 'Anyway, I'll go up an' see her and ask her what she fancies.'

The young girl bit her lip, debating whether to tell her father about Eddie's lateness the previous night. She didn't like telling tales and maybe her brother would mend his ways when he heard that their mother was improving. It wouldn't be many days now before Sarah regained her strength and he'd feel the back of her hand if he was late home.

Polly decided against saying anything and bustled about the scullery and kitchen preparing her father's breakfast; bacon, eggs and fried bread. The children had porridge, but William's job in the railway goods department was a cold one in winter. So, however short money was, Sarah always minded the man of the house was well fed. And Polly knew she must do the same.

With the baby quiet and her father tucking into his meal, Polly went upstairs.

''Morning, Mam. How're you feeling?'

Sarah lay weakly against the pillows. Her face was blotchy, her eyes dark hollows, her lips dry and cracked.

'Better this morning, love.' She sniffed the air. 'My, yar dad's breakfast smells good. I could just eat a plateful.'

'Doctor said no solids, Mam. You heard him. I don't think you should—'

'I'm hungry, love. Ravenous. You make me bacon and eggs. There's a good girl. And don't forget the fried bread. I love a bit of fried bread.'

Polly bit her lip, but didn't like to argue. It must be a good sign that her mother wanted to eat, she argued with herself. After days of being sick and having nothing but water, no wonder she was hungry. But the doctor had said . . .

Resolutely, she pushed his words out of her mind and hurried downstairs. Mam was on the mend. She'd soon be up and about and she, Polly, could go back to work.

Not that her work at the glue factory was so wonderful, but to the young girl it was a start. After a year or so, she fully intended to look for something better.

Oh yes, Polly promised herself, once her mother was better, she'd never miss a day's work. She'd build up a good reputation for being a reliable worker. And perhaps when she was older – she hardly dared to hope – she could even become a teacher just as she'd always wanted.

And then, maybe, Leo Halliday would notice her too.

'That was lovely, Polly.'

Her mother almost smacked her lips as she finished the breakfast Polly had cooked for her. Sarah lay back against the pillows and sighed. 'I think I'll have a little nap now, love. Can you see to the baby?'

As if I haven't been doing for the past week or more, Polly wanted to shout, but instead she picked up the tray and said meekly, 'Yes, Mam. She's a good little thing.'

But already Sarah's eyes were closed.

The baby had been fed, washed and dressed and was back in her cradle sleeping. Eddie and Violet, after much protesting, had gone to school. Stevie played quietly with his wooden bricks, building towers and then knocking them down, smiling happily to himself as he did so. Polly washed up the breakfast pots, mended the fire, swept the floors and sorted out the washing. Several times she crept upstairs to check on her mother, but Sarah was sleeping peacefully.

As she peeled potatoes for her father's meal when he got home in the evening and prepared dinner for herself and Stevie, Polly was humming softly to herself.

Everything was going to be all right. Her mam was getting better and no one else in the family had got the disease. Soon she'd be able to go back to work. Though she knew Mr Spicer's warnings were not idle ones, she didn't think he'd sack her. Not now, not whilst the city was so badly hit by this dreadful disease.

Roland Spicer was a kindly man who still lived with his widowed mother. Polly couldn't understand why he'd never married. Admittedly, with mousy hair and pale, hazel eyes he wasn't handsome, not like Leo Halliday, but he was – now what was the word her mother had used to describe him? Personable. That was it – personable. Maybe Mr Spicer was shy when it came to women. Polly smiled to herself. But he wasn't shy with the women and the girls who worked at the glue factory. He laughed and joked with them, yet he still managed to maintain his foreman's position if firmness was needed or there were orders to be given.

And he was always very nice to her. Some of the other women teased her. 'I reckon our Roland's sweet on little Miss Polly.'

Polly would find herself blushing even as she argued fiercely, 'He's old enough to be me dad.'

'Ee, lass, better to be an old man's darling than a young man's slave,' was always the answer. 'Besides, he's only in his mid-twenties. That's not old.'

It is to me, Polly would think, but would hold her

tongue. A lot of the women who worked at the glue factory were well beyond their twenties and wouldn't take kindly to being thought of as 'old'.

A sudden noise from the bedroom above interrupted Polly's thoughts and she heard her mother calling frantically. 'Polly! Oh, Polly, come quick.'

The girl ran upstairs and into her parents' bedroom. Her mother was sitting up in bed, leaning forward and holding her stomach. 'Oh, Polly, the pain. It's terrible – like nothing I've had before. Fetch Mrs Halliday. Fetch the doctor—' Her demands ended in a cry of agony.

'Oh no, no,' Polly muttered as she ran downstairs again and out of the house without even stopping to put her coat on. 'I shouldn't've let her have that breakfast. Doctor said only fluids.'

Mrs Halliday came at once, heaving her heavy frame up the stairs and into the front bedroom. 'Now, Sarah, what's to do?'

For a moment, she watched the woman writhing in agony, then turned to the anxious girl standing behind her.

'Run back to our house, love. Leo's at home. He'll fetch the doc. Hurry now, yar mam's bad.'

I can see that, Polly thought as she retraced her steps, still at a run. And it's all my fault. I should have been stronger – stood up to them both – made them understand what the doctor had said. And now . . .

Dr Fenwick was angry. He didn't shout, but she could tell by the look on his face. 'What have you been eating, Mrs Longden?'

Her mother still thrashed about the bed in pain, sweat glistening on her forehead. 'Polly cooked me a lovely breakfast. I expect it's 'cos I haven't eaten much for a week.' Again her words ended in a groan as the doctor glanced at Polly. The girl withered beneath his glare.

'You should have stayed on fluids, Mrs Longden, until I told you otherwise. Now I think we'd better get you to hospital.'

'No, oh no, I can't go. Who'll look after the family? The children?'

'As long as the youngsters stay well, your girl here can manage. And I'm sure your neighbours will lend a hand.'

'I don't want—' Sarah began, but again whatever she'd been going to say was cut short by pain-ridden cries.

Dr Fenwick turned to Polly. 'Get her some night-clothes and washing things together,' he said shortly. 'I'll send an ambulance at once.'

Four

Polly was waiting nervously for her father to come home from work. As he sat down heavily in his chair and she placed the steaming plate of food before him, his first question was, 'How's yar mam?'

Polly took a deep breath. 'She – she's in hospital, Dad. The ambulance came to fetch her.'

It had caused quite a stir when the horse-drawn ambulance had clattered into the street. Now everyone knew just how ill poor Sarah Longden was.

His knife and fork poised above the plate, William looked up at Polly, his dark eyes boring into her. 'Hospital? When did this happen?'

Polly bit her lip. 'This afternoon. She got so bad, I fetched Mrs Halliday and she said to get the doctor. He – he was cross.'

'Cross? Why?'

'Because – because Mam'd eaten that breakfast. He'd said to keep her on fluids and—'

William's face darkened. 'I didn't know that. You should have said, Poll.'

'I did – I told you . . .'

His knife and fork clattered onto the plate. 'Don't you answer me back, girl. I said, I didn't know.'

Polly stared at her father, her mouth dropping open. She'd told him. She had, she had. But now he was denying it and placing all the blame on her.

He pointed his finger at her. 'If yar mam dies, it'll be your fault. You should have told us what the doctor said.'

He sat down again, picked up his knife and fork and began to eat, but his hands were shaking and he avoided looking at his daughter again. Polly turned away, tears stinging her eyes. How could her father lie?

And if her mother died, he didn't need to blame her for she would blame herself. And that was far worse.

'I'm going out,' William said shortly.

'Are you going to the hospital? She's in the new one on Long Leys Road.'

'I aren't going anywhere near there,' William snapped as he pulled on his cap. 'There's a full Council meeting at the Guildhall tonight and me, Seth Halliday and Bert Fowler are going. We want to know what our precious councillors are doing about all this.'

Wordlessly, Polly stared after him as he slammed the door behind him.

As the councillors, led by the Mayor, entered the Council Chamber and sat down around the huge table, the murmuring from the packed public-seating area rose. One or two men shook their fists and several shouted.

'When are you goin' to start telling us the truth?'

'All we've got is rumour an' scaremongering. We want facts.'

'We want to know how bad it is and what you're going to do about it.'

'It's all right for you sat up in your high and mighty seats and livin' in yar posh houses with yar running water and yar hot baths at the turn of a tap.' William was on his feet, shouting and thumping the air with his fist. 'What about us poor folk? We have to share a standpipe and a privy in the backyard. What about us?'

'I can assure you, sir,' one of the councillors began, standing up, 'that this disease is no respecter of persons. It is hitting all and sundry.'

'Aye, mebbe so, but I reckon it's the sundry that's worst hit.'

A snigger, swiftly stifled, ran through the onlookers.

'Sit down, William, and listen.' Seth Halliday, Bertha's husband and Leo's father, pulled on his arm. William grunted but subsided into his seat. Whilst William was quick-tempered, Seth was a reasonable man. 'Let's hear what they've got to say, eh?'

The meeting began with the Mayor making a statement about how the situation stood at the moment. He was frequently interrupted by shouts and jeers from the public, but at the end of the speech, in which he declared that the members of the Council were deeply sorry for the epidemic, there was silence, except for a little applause for his words.

But as the three neighbours walked home side by side, William was still incensed and Bert Fowler demanded, 'How can they put the blame on us having a hot summer last year followed by a cold winter. What's that got to do with the water supply? They more or less admit that's where the infection's coming from.' He paused and added, 'Don't they?'

'It would seem it's what they suspect,' Seth agreed.

'So what are they going to do about it?' William put in. 'Are either of you any the wiser after listening to 'em, 'cos I aren't?'

'They're doing their best,' Seth said mildly. 'They're trying to get a new supply.'

William gave a wry, humourless laugh. 'Aye and a right pig's ear of it they seem to be making. What was that he said, they've lost a boring tool at Boultham more'n a year ago?'

'Er, yes, I believe so.'

'And drilling there's been stopped ever since,' Bert added.

'So, in the meantime, we all go on getting typhoid. You know my Sarah's in hospital, don't you?'

'Yes, Bertha said. I'm sorry to hear that, Will.' Seth paused and then added, 'But they're certainly doing their best to provide extra hospital accommodation.'

'Aye, makeshift wards in halls around the city. How can they be proper hospitals?'

'Well, it was said that they think the number of cases is decreasing.'

'I don't believe them an' I bet your Bertha won't. And I don't think they're doing everything that could be done either. Fancy saying that the number of deaths that have occurred is "highly satisfactory". It might only be twenty-odd, but it's not highly satisfactory if it's one of your family, now is it?'

And here Seth was obliged to agree. 'No, William,' he said soberly, 'it isn't.'

'And how dare they hand out instructions about hygiene? If my Sarah'd been there, she'd've given 'em what for, I can tell you.'

'Not everyone's as clean in their ways as Sarah, William,' Seth put in quietly. 'They just want to be sure everyone follows whatever precautions they can.'

'Poll boils all the water and milk and she's washing and scrubbing from morning till night.'

Poor little lass, Seth thought, but he said nothing.

The three of them walked on in silence until they came to the end of the road where they lived.

'I'm going for a pint,' William said. 'You coming?'

'No, if you don't mind,' Seth said. 'I'll get along home. It's late now.'

'Suit yarsen,' William flung over his shoulder as he headed towards the George and Dragon.

But Bert was always ready for an excuse to go to the pub. 'I'll come wi' ya, Will. Wait on.'

By the time William staggered home his children were all in bed and, mostly, asleep. Only Polly lay awake, rigid with guilt and fear. She heard the door slam and her father crashing into the furniture as he wove his way through the front room. The girl closed her eyes and groaned inwardly.

Obviously, the Council meeting was not the only place he'd been that night. She heard him climbing the stairs, cursing, and making no effort to be quiet. In the darkness Polly winced, expecting any moment to hear the wails from the wooden drawer beside her bed. But the baby slept soundly and only Violet stirred, wriggled, and then snuggled closer to Polly for warmth.

At last Polly heard the creak of the bedsprings from her parents' bedroom and, after only a few moments, her father's snoring. But even though he was home and the house fell quiet, Polly could not sleep.

She lay awake far into the night, thinking of her mother and what might be happening in the hospital. Tomorrow, she promised herself, she'd put Baby in the battered old perambulator and walk there. It wasn't far and even Stevie would be able to walk that distance.

Tomorrow, she'd find out.

William ate the breakfast she prepared for him without speaking to her. In fact, he hardly acknowledged her presence. She longed to ask him what had happened at the meeting, but this morning for the first time in her young life she felt afraid of her father.

When he'd left the house, she got the other children up and ready for school. For once, they were subdued and worryingly obedient.

Polly washed and fed the baby and placed a blanket in the bottom of the old pram. Then she wrapped Miriam in a warm shawl and put her in it.

'Get yar coat, our Stevie. We're going out.'

Stevie removed his thumb from his mouth long enough to ask, 'Where to?'

'See how Mam is, that's where. Now, come on. Look sharp.'

A sudden knock sounded on the door. Polly opened it to find a solemn-faced Dr Fenwick standing there.

'Is your father at home?'

'N-no, sir. He – he's at work.'

'I see.' The doctor pondered for a moment. Then he gave a heavy sigh. 'May I come in for a moment, my dear?'

Wordlessly, Polly pulled the door wider and ushered him inside. Standing with his back to the fire in the range, the doctor regarded her gravely.

'None of your family visited the hospital last night, I understand.'

Polly shook her head.

'I thought I should come myself,' he went on gently. 'I'm sorry to tell you, my dear, that your mother passed away early this morning.'

The young girl's eyes widened and her mouth dropped open in a horrified gasp. She clutched her throat as she uttered hoarsely, 'No, oh no!'

She felt herself swaying and felt the doctor's strong hands steadying her and then lowering her into a chair.

Now the tears flowed and she cried out in anguish. 'It's my fault. It's my fault.'

'My dear child, why ever should you think that?'

She raised tear-filled eyes. 'You know. You were angry with me.'

'I? Angry with you? When?'

Had he forgotten already? Or was he, like her father, denying it?

'When you came to see my mother,' she stammered. 'When you sent her to the hospital. I'd made her a breakfast.'

'Ah yes,' Dr Fenwick said heavily, frowning now. 'I remember now. Forgive me, child. I've seen so many patients over the last few days.' He sighed and sat down slowly in the chair beside her. Taking her hand in his, he leant towards her. 'Tell me, my dear, what actually happened.'

'You'd said she was only to have fluids, but she was asking and asking for breakfast – like I'd cooked for me dad.' The words tumbled out with a sense of relief. Perhaps, after all, this kindly man would understand. 'She smelt it from upstairs, see, and – and Dad said I was to make it for her. I told him what you'd said . . .' She hiccuped and scrubbed her tear-streaked face with the back of her hand. 'But he said she must be feeling better if she was asking for something to eat. That it must be a good sign.'

The doctor sighed again and shook his head slowly, but he was still listening intently to what Polly was saying. 'And then I reminded Mam what you'd said. She'd heard you herself – you was standing by the bed when you said it – but – she wouldn't listen neither and – and then . . .' Her voice petered out in a fresh wave of grief and guilt.

'Hunger can be one of the symptoms, but, sadly, solid food can cause the bowel to perforate. That's what happened with your mother, I'm afraid.'

'So it was my fault,' Polly whispered.

The doctor was silent. He was unable to deny it. He was a truthful man and even though he realized a lie now would lift a lifetime's burden from this child's shoulders, he couldn't do it. All he could say was, 'You were doing what your parents told you, my dear.'

She lifted her head and looked straight into his eyes; hers were clear and honest yet at this moment filled with suffering. 'But I should have done what *you* told me to do. Not them.'

'Ah well, ah well,' was all Dr Fenwick could say as he patted her hand. But neither his words nor his actions brought Polly any comfort.

'I must go,' he said at last. 'I'll call in on Mrs Halliday. Let her know . . .'

As the door closed quietly behind him, Miriam began to wail.

Five

Bertha and Seth Halliday had come to live at the end of the street when they'd married. Bertha had done a little nursing at the County Hospital, though she'd never qualified. She'd met Seth when he'd been a patient for a few days following an injury at work. Seth worked at one of the engineering firms and lived in the streets to the south of the city. But Bertha lived up-hill. Her father had died when she was very young and she and her mother had lived with her maternal grandparents. Her grandfather, a retired bank clerk, had not approved of his own daughter's choice of husband and neither did he take to Bertha's choice, Seth.

'You can do better for yourself, Bertha,' he told her bluntly. 'You're a pretty lass. Don't tell me you're not capable of catching the eye of an up-and-coming young doctor at the hospital.'

Bertha had smiled to herself but hadn't argued; her grandfather had no concept of the ratio of nurses to doctors. And the marriageable ones were in even shorter supply. She'd continued to meet Seth in secret, but when she fell pregnant the romance could no longer be kept hidden. Her grandfather, with his Victorian ideals, was incensed and had forbidden her to 'darken his door again'. Her grandmother sided with her husband and Bertha's gentle mother had been torn between her love for her daughter and obedience to her own parents. She could not afford to fall out with them. Suffering ill health, she was unable to work and was totally dependent on them. So Bertha left the only home she could remember in tearful disgrace. She never saw her grandparents again, although, greatly daring, her mother visited Bertha in secret or met her by prior arrangement in the city. Though on these occasions the little woman was nervous in case someone who knew them should see them together.

Bertha's mother lived long enough to see her grandson, Leo, born and to hold him in her arms, but six months later she contracted pneumonia and died. Bertha tried to make peace with her grandparents, but they were adamant they didn't want to see her or their great-grandson. Two years later they were both dead and Bertha had no near relatives left. Her world became Seth and her baby, but she was a friendly, outgoing soul and her early nursing training, though incomplete, equipped her to offer help to her friends and neighbours when they needed it. Respected by the local doctors and qualified nurses alike, she was soon assisting at births and was always on hand to undertake the less appealing job of laying out the dead. Her no-nonsense approach, tempered with an innate kindness and understanding of the foibles and weaknesses of human nature, endeared her to everyone. The little house at the end of the street became a refuge for those who needed help or a comforting word.

Though both Bertha and Seth would dearly have loved more children – 'a whole barrowload of 'em' – no more appeared and their boundless love became focused on Leo. And he did not disappoint them. He was a lovable child, did well at school and, though an early apprenticeship at Robey's engineering works alongside his father didn't suit him, his ambition to join the police force was achieved as soon as he reached the right age. The whole family, whilst not being looked upon as 'do-gooders', nevertheless did a lot of good in their community. Bertha never turned anyone in distress away from her door and she was backed and encouraged by her husband and son.

And Bertha had never been in such demand as she was when typhoid struck the city.

'There, there lovey, don't take on so.' Bertha Halliday's plump arms were holding Polly tightly as she sobbed against the woman's soft bosom.

'How am I going to tell me dad? He'll – he'll – '

'Yar not to blame yarsen, Polly,' Bertha said firmly. She held the girl away from her and looked down into her face. Placing strong fingers beneath Polly's chin, she lifted the girl's face to look up at her. 'You hear me? Yar dad should have listened to you – and yar mam. She heard the doctor say it. You said so.'

Polly nodded.

'Well, then. It's not your fault. And Dr Fenwick should have spelt it out to you. Just saying "only fluids" to a slip of a lass. How was you to know what he meant, specially when your mam started demanding you cook her a breakfast? Oh no, me lass, I won't have you blaming yarsen. D'you hear me?'

It warmed Polly's frozen heart to hear Mrs Halliday defending her, but it didn't help her. Not really. She knew that she would always blame herself and that the guilt would stay with her for the rest of her life.

*

The Longden family was devastated: the hub of their home was gone. William sank into a deep depression, refusing to leave his chair by the fire to go to work even after the funeral was over and Polly was trying desperately to get the family back to something like normality. Even Eddie and Violet were subdued.

Only Stevie and the baby, both too young to understand fully what had happened, were the same as always. But when the four-year-old little boy tried to climb onto his father's lap and was rebuffed, even Stevie began to realize that something was very wrong.

'Leave me alone,' William said heavily. 'There's a good chap. I've got a headache.'

Polly glanced at her father, a sudden fear clutching her heart. That was the first symptom her mother had complained about when she'd started with the dreadful disease. Polly watched him for a moment as he sat huddled in the chair in front of the fire. Then she saw him shiver and hold his hands out to the warmth.

She bit her lip. 'Dad, have you got a fever?'

He glanced up, his eyes haunted by the loss his family had suffered. But there was something more there too. An unnatural brightness.

Polly moved closer. 'Have – have you any pain?'

William considered. 'A bit. Me stomach feels sort of – unsettled, but I wouldn't call it pain. Not really.' He seemed about to say more, but a fit of coughing overtook him as Polly looked on anxiously.

'Mam had a cough, Dad,' she said softly when the fit had subsided.

William shook his head irritably. 'Do stop fussing, girl. Haven't I enough to worry about without you wishing the disease on me?'

Polly gasped. 'Dad, how can you say such a thing? I'd never—'

He glared at her. 'If you hadn't given your mam that breakfast, she'd still be here.'

Polly felt the colour drain from her face and she clutched at the nearest chair. Her heart began to thump painfully. To blame herself was one thing, but to keep hearing from her father that he blamed her too was unbearable.

But then her fiery temper came to her rescue. She pulled in a deep breath and pointed an accusing finger at him. 'I told you what the doctor had said and Mam heard him 'ersen. You wouldn't listen – neither of you – and now you're trying to put all the blame on me. You're as good as saying I killed her. Well, you listen to me, Dad.' She bent closer. 'I'll always blame mesen, but don't you dare say it's all my fault, 'cos it ain't. And if you do, then I'm off. I'll leave and then where will you be? The kids'll all be in the workhouse up the hill, that's where.'

William groaned and dropped his head into his hands. 'Don't, Poll, don't say such things. What would yar mam say if she could hear you?'

Polly felt the anger still rising within her and before she could stop herself, she said, 'And what would she say to you if she could see you sat in front of the fire all day while your family go hungry?'

As he raised his head to look at her, she could see the beads of sweat on his forehead, see his shoulders shaking. Her anger died as swiftly as it had come. 'Dad, you are ill, aren't you? This is more than – more than grievin', in't it?'

William groaned and rested his head against the back of his chair. His eyes were closed and his breathing rapid.

'I'm fetching the doctor.'

'No,' he argued, but his voice was weak and lacked conviction. 'We can't afford no more doctor's bills.'

Polly leant close, unafraid of contracting the disease. 'Dr Fenwick told me to get him if anyone else fell ill. And I aren't about to disobey him. Not again. Besides, if you have got the typhoid, we'll be breaking the law if we don't notify it, won't we?'

Again, a deep, guttural groan escaped his lips. 'I don't know, Poll. Don't bother me. Just look after the bairns and don't bother me, there's a good girl.'

Polly had been down the street to the Hallidays' house and was back home waiting anxiously for the doctor to call. When the knock came at the front door, she ran to it, flinging it open in her haste to get the medical man into the house to help her father.

'Oh!' She gaped up at the tall, handsome figure of Leo Halliday standing there with a huge tureen in his hands.

'Me ma's sent this, Polly. She ses your dad's taken badly and you could likely do with a bit of help.' He thrust the tureen towards her. 'Mind, it's hot. Tek hold of it with the cloth.'

Tears sprang to Polly's eyes not only at Bertha Halliday's kindness but also at the gentle concern in Leo's voice.

Polly had grown up knowing Leo. Her earliest memories had been of him kicking a ball about in the street with lads of his own age. But despite being lavished with love and whatever his hardworking parents could give him, Leo was surprisingly unspoilt. He was well liked amongst his peers and popular at school, and even when he joined the police force he still retained the friends he'd always had.

'By heck,' they teased him, 'we'll have to mind our Ps and Qs now he's to be a copper. He'll run us in soon as look at us.'

'That's true.' Leo would grin, giving back as good as he got. 'I've warned me mam, if she dun't toe the line, I'll run her in an' all.'

They'd all laughed, but there was a grain of truth in Leo's threat – or rather promise. If he became an upholder of the law, he meant to carry it out to the letter, no matter what.

But now he was a police constable, albeit still in his probationary period, he saw his job as something more than just apprehending criminals. He meant to be a help to the community. And so he was happy to stand on the doorstep with a bowl of hot stew in his hands to help his neighbours.

As little Polly Longden reached out to take the bowl, he noticed for the first time how she was growing up. To him she'd always been just the kid from up their street, the eldest of a family whose older son had the makings of a real tearaway.

'You'll have to watch that Eddie of theirs,' his mother had always warned him. 'He's a bad 'un. He'll be the death of his poor mam, if I'm not mistaken.'

Well, the poor mother had died. It had not been young Eddie who'd caused it but the disease that was bringing such heartache and suffering to their lovely city, a city Leo now felt responsible for.

Now, close to, Leo noticed Polly's eyes for the first time – green and sparkling and her pretty little face surrounded by that glorious cloud of red curling hair.

He saw too that there was a blush to her cheeks that he hoped wasn't the start of the fever.

'Thank you,' she was saying shyly. As she took the bowl, he saw her hands tremble.

'Careful.' Leo laughed. 'Don't spill it.'

'It's very kind of your mam. Please thank her.'

Leo nodded and his expression sobered. 'She said you reckon your dad might be starting with the fever?'

Polly bit her lip and nodded. 'We're waiting for the doctor now. I – I thought you were him. When you knocked, I mean.'

'Is there anything else I can do for you? D'you want me to come in and wait with you?'

'No, no – I wouldn't want you to catch it. I mean – I don't know if you can catch it exactly . . .' Her voice trailed away.

Leo shrugged. 'Me neither, but I've been amongst it enough just lately that if I'm going to get it, well, I will. And me ma's helping folks out all the time.'

Polly nodded. 'I know. She's been very good to us.'

There was a brief pause whilst they looked at each other; Polly with the bowl of stew in her hands that was becoming almost too hot to hold. But she wasn't going to admit it – not whilst there was chance of talking to Leo for a few minutes longer.

'There's something else,' Leo said. 'Mam's got chance of an old cot going begging. It wants doing up a bit, but she thought you might be glad of it.'

'Ooo yes, please, Leo. Mebbe Dad could—'

'That's all right. I'll have a go at it. Paint it up and that.'

'That'd be grand.' She felt herself close to tears at his kindness. 'Baby's sleeping in a drawer at the moment.'

Margaret Dickinson

Leo smiled briefly. 'I'd best be off. Don't forget, if you need any help, just you let us know.'

Polly gave a watery smile in response. As he turned away, she called, 'Please thank yar mam.'

He did not look back but raised his hand in acknowledgement.

Six

'I can't be one hundred per cent sure yet, but I think it could be the typhoid, Mr Longden.' Dr Fenwick turned to Polly. 'Now, my dear, just keep him on fluids. Even if he protests he wants more, you take no notice.'

Polly nodded vigorously.

William, still sitting in the chair, looking hotter by the minute and yet shivering violently, muttered, 'Her mam'll be down soon. She'll look after me. Sarah'll look after us all . . .'

Polly let out a startled cry and then clapped her hand over her mouth to stifle the noise. Dr Fenwick's face was grim. 'Mm. Mental confusion.' He sighed. 'That's another sign.' He watched the patient for another moment before saying, 'Perhaps it would be best if I arranged for him to go into hospital now, before he gets any worse.' He glanced at the young girl standing beside him. 'At least it would be one less burden for you, child. Can you manage the rest of the family or do you want me to – ?'

'We'll be fine, sir. Honest. Mrs Halliday will help us. I know she will.'

'And your other neighbours? Will they lend a hand?'

There was a brief hesitation before Polly answered. She was not a good liar. Sarah had not been on particularly good terms with her immediate neighbours – the ones who shared the water tap and the privy. They

37

regarded Sarah's efforts to be hygienic as high-handed and offensive and there'd been many a row in the backyard. Polly didn't think she could count on them now.

Instead, she said again that Mrs Halliday would look out for them.

Seeming satisfied, Dr Fenwick said, 'Then I'll arrange for him to be taken in. It'll most likely be the Drill Hall, child. They've opened up several places to take patients and the Drill Hall's one of them. The Infectious Diseases Hospital, where your mother went, is full, as I believe is the ward at the County Hospital.' He fastened his bag. 'So get a few things ready for him and I'll arrange for the ambulance to fetch him. Meanwhile, like I said before, if any of the youngsters – or you – feel ill, let me know. At once, mind.'

As the doctor had said, things were a little easier for Polly once her father had been taken to the temporary hospital accommodation. Now she had only the young ones to look after. But it didn't stop her worrying about her father too.

The baby and Stevie were easy. Though Miriam cried when she was hungry or needed changing, she was a placid little thing and the little boy played quietly on the hearthrug with his bricks. It was Violet and even more so, Eddie, who caused Polly her biggest headaches. Violet was obstinate and difficult, refusing to do anything about the house to help. There were little jobs that the ten-year-old could have managed, but no, Violet took the absence of both parents as an opportunity to do just what she liked. She even refused to go to school until Polly threatened to seek out the attendance officer herself.

'You wouldn't?' Violet blinked in the face of her sister's anger.

'Try me,' Polly flashed back. 'What'll Dad say when he comes home? And – and what would Mam have said?'

For a while those words subdued the rebellious girl, but they didn't work on the tougher Eddie.

'You'll be in at eight o'clock and no later,' Polly ordered.

'Fat chance,' the boy sneered. 'Gonner make me, are ya?'

'No, I can't make you, I know that.' Polly's eyes narrowed. 'But there's those that can.'

Eddie laughed. 'Oh aye. Who?'

Polly pursed her lips. 'You'll see, if you try it, Edward Longden. You'll see.'

And, of course, Eddie did try it.

By half-past nine on the very same evening that Polly had issued her warning, there was still no sign of her brother.

'Right, he's asked for it,' she muttered reaching for her coat from behind the door.

Violet's eyes were wide. 'What are you going to do, Poll?'

'Never you mind. The less you know, the better.' As she pulled on her coat and wrapped a scarf around her neck, she glared at her sister. 'I wouldn't put it past you to take his side.'

Violet grinned and her dark eyes were full of mischief. 'Oh, I would.' The younger girl stood up, stretched and yawned. 'I'm off to bed, if little squealer doesn't keep me awake.'

'And about time. You should have been in bed hours ago. And don't call Baby that. She's a good little thing.'

Polly pulled her coat closely around her as she closed the door quietly and set off down the street towards the Hallidays' house.

''Ello, love. What brings you out this late?' Seth asked as he peered at her through the darkness.

'Is Leo at home, Mr Halliday?'

'He is, lass. Come away in.' He ushered the shivering girl into the kitchen. 'Bertha – Leo, mek room by the fire. This little lass is freezing.'

'Aw, Polly, love. Whatever's the matter? Is it your dad?'

Polly shook her head. 'No. He's all right, as far as I know.' She glanced at Leo, who'd risen from his chair and was gesturing for her to sit down in it.

She gave him a wan smile and sat down. 'I – I've come to ask for some advice. From – from Leo really, I suppose.'

Polly glanced around the three kindly, concerned faces, her gaze coming to rest on Leo's. She drank in the sight of him; his curly fair hair, his bright blue eyes and his generous mouth that was nearly always smiling. For a brief moment, she allowed herself to dream, but then she pulled herself back to the reason for her visit.

'It's our Eddie. He's playing me up summat rotten. It started a bit when Mam was first ill.' At the thought of her mother, her voice broke a little but she carried on bravely. 'You know, staying out late if he thought Dad was out and wouldn't notice. But since Mam died and – and Dad got ill, Eddie's got worse. He's stopping out until all hours. I don't even know where he is – or who he's with.' Polly's head dropped as she strove to hold back the tears.

She felt Leo's hand on her shoulder as his mother

said, 'Aw, Polly love, don't cry. We'll see what we can do.' She looked up at Leo 'Have you heard owt?'

Polly looked up to see Leo shaking his head. 'No, but I'll go down the station this minute and make enquiries.'

'Oh – I don't want to get him into trouble. I mean, not with the coppers.'

'He already is,' Leo said, but he was laughing.

Polly gasped and clutched her throat. 'What d'you mean?'

'He's in trouble with me for upsetting you. And I'm a copper, aren't I?'

Polly relaxed and smiled too. 'Oh yes. Just for a moment, I thought you meant . . .'

He patted her shoulder. 'You go back to the little ones, Poll, and I'll go out and see if I can track that rascal down.'

As she stood up to leave, Bertha asked bluntly, 'And what about young Violet? Is she behaving herself?'

Polly pulled a wry face. 'Yes – and no. I have a job to get her to go to school, but she's going at the moment ever since I threatened to tell the attendance officer mesen if she didn't.'

'I know she's only ten, but she's a little madam, that one. You'll have to watch her, Polly.'

'I assume Eddie's not been going to school either?' Leo asked quietly.

Polly shook her head. 'Not since Mam died.'

The three Hallidays exchanged a worried glance.

'You know, this could all be to do with losing your mam, love. Kids deal with trouble in different ways and maybe this is Eddie's way. He's trying to block it all out of his mind and mebbe, by staying out with his mates, he can forget it for a while. Though it's not fair on you, lass.'

'I just – I just don't want the authorities to put us in the workhouse.' Polly covered her face with her hands.

Bertha reached out towards her and Leo put his arm round her shoulders. Even Seth said at once, 'Don't you worry about that. We'll see that doesn't happen. Now let me see you home and Leo'll see what he can find out.'

'I'll come in with you. Just to make sure he's not come home since you left,' Leo added, pulling on his overcoat.

The three of them walked up the icy street and entered the Longdens' home. There was no one in the kitchen or the scullery.

'Just nip upstairs, Polly, and see that he's not sneaked straight up to bed,' Leo suggested.

When she came downstairs a few moments later, Polly shook her head. 'No, he's not there. He must still be out. Oh, where can he be? It's nearly ten o'clock now.'

At that moment, the thin wailing of a hungry baby sounded upstairs.

'You stay here, Polly,' Seth said at once. 'See to the little ones. I'll go with Leo.'

'I don't know how to thank you,' she began as she moved towards the stairs, but both men waved aside her thanks as they left by the front door.

Outside, Leo muttered to his father. 'That little bugger. I'll knock his head off if I catch him. Worrying young Polly like this. Teking advantage, that's what he's doing.'

'Aye well, don't be too tough on the lad. He's just lost his mam and his dad's in the hospital. He's frightened. They all are.'

'But he's not being fair to Polly. She's a star the way

she's trying to cope and he's just a little . . .' His tirade
tailed off into an expletive.

'Let's get him found first and then we'll see what we
can do.'

Seven

It was almost midnight when Polly, sitting huddled in front of a dying fire, heard a soft knock on the front door. Her heart in her mouth, she rushed to open it hoping that it was Eddie. But Leo stood there alone.

In the shadows, she couldn't read his expression, but there was sorrow in his voice as he said softly, 'Can I come in a minute, Polly?'

Wordlessly, she pulled the door wider. 'You haven't found him?'

'Actually,' Leo said, stepping across the threshold and following her through the front room into the kitchen, 'I have, but it's not good news, I'm afraid.'

Polly's hand flew to cover her mouth. 'He's not hurt, is he? What's happened?'

'No, nothing like that. He's at the police station.'

'The police— Oh no! Is he in trouble?'

''Fraid so. He was caught stealing in the market this afternoon. He was arrested and taken to the police station, but he was refusing to say anything. He wouldn't even give his name and address. It wasn't until I turned up tonight that they found out who he was. I'm sorry, Polly, but I had to tell them.'

'Of course you did. You couldn't do anything else.' Polly was forced to agree, but a tiny part of her wished Leo hadn't told them.

'I've told them about your mam and how your dad's

ill too and they're going to let him go with a caution. This time. The stallholder, Albert Thorpe – I don't know if you know him?'

'I might,' Polly murmured. 'I go to the market a lot, but I don't know names.'

'When Mr Thorpe heard about what's happened to your family, he decided, in the circumstances, that he wouldn't press charges.'

'Then where is Eddie? Why hasn't he come home?'

Leo gave a wry laugh. 'The custody sergeant thought it would be a good idea to keep him in a cell just for the night. Give him a sharpener, he called it. A taste of what he could expect if he breaks the law again.'

Polly pursed her lips and nodded. 'And when he does come home, he'll have me to face, an' all.'

Leo watched her little face harden and her green eyes glitter.

He wouldn't want to be in Eddie Longden's shoes when he got home the following morning.

Eddie had hardly stepped through the door before he felt the flat of Polly's hand smack his cheek.

'Oi, what's that for?'

'What d'you think it's for? Ending up in a police cell. That's what it's for. Wait till our dad hears about this.'

Eddie gripped her arms so firmly that his fingers dug into her flesh. 'Don't you dare say a word to Dad. Or else . . .'

Though he was stronger than she was, Polly was not going to let him beat her. She thrust her face close to his, her spittle raining on his face. 'Or what, Eddie Longden? You don't frighten me and – if I have to – I will tell Dad. When he's better.'

Eddie's face twisted in a sneer. '*If* he gets better.'

'Oh, don't you worry, Dad'll get better. He's not weak from childbirth like poor Mam was. I'm going to see him today.'

His grip tightened and Polly pressed her lips together to stop herself crying out in pain. She wouldn't give him the satisfaction of knowing he was hurting her.

'And you're planning on telling him? About me?'

Polly put her head on one side, considering. 'That depends.'

'On what?'

'On if you get yourself to school every day until he comes home and you're in by – let's say half-past eight.'

Eddie grimaced. 'I'm leaving school in the summer when I'm twelve. What difference does a few days or weeks make now?'

'All the difference. You need that certificate, don't you? Look, Eddie, you might not think it, but you're bright. If only you'd work a bit harder – be more reliable – you might get a decent job when you leave school.'

'D'you know summat, our Poll, you're beginning to sound more like me mam every day. Quite the mother hen, aren't you?'

'Someone's got to look after the bairns,' she countered. 'Don't you think I'd rather be out working than looking after you lot and doing housework?'

'At the glue factory? Some job that is.'

'I don't – ' she hesitated and then changed it to – 'didn't intend to be there all me life. I'd got plans, see. But now . . .' She sighed, lost for a moment in her own broken dreams. Then, more briskly, she added, 'But you could do anything you liked, Eddie. You could really make something of yourself, if only you'd try.'

'Huh! You really think the likes of us can "make

something of ourselves"? Fat chance, Poll.' He loosened his grip and stepped away. 'But if you promise not to tell Dad about last night, then I will go to school. At least until he's back home.'

Surreptitiously, Polly rubbed the place where his strong fingers had bruised her arms.

'All right, but just mind you keep your side of the bargain then.'

Polly did not go to see her father the following afternoon, nor the next.

'I wouldn't go yet, me love,' Bertha advised. 'He's in good hands but he'll be in the worst stages of it now. Best leave it another week or so, at least, eh? I'll ask our Leo to call and ask after him? All right?'

Polly nodded and despite the awful reason for it, she couldn't quell the little thrill of pleasure she felt at the thought of an excuse to see Leo again.

'He's going on nicely,' Leo told her when, removing his policeman's helmet, he stepped into the Longdens' home two days later. 'One of the nurses said it should be all right for you to visit him, if you want to, early next week. And me ma says she'll mind the bairns for you while you go. She says to tell you not to think of taking the little 'uns there.'

Polly shook her head vigorously. 'No, I wouldn't.'

And so it wasn't until the first Monday in March that Polly knocked on the door of the house at the end of the street.

'Mrs Halliday, could you look after Baby and Stevie for me for an hour or so this afternoon? I want to go to the Drill Hall to see how me dad's going on.'

'Course I can, lovey. You bring them down here,

47

though, 'cos then I can get on with me own work while I keep an eye on them.'

It was quite a walk from where the Longdens lived to the Drill Hall, which had been turned into a temporary hospital for typhoid victims. Polly put on her warm winter coat and hat and walked up the street. At the end, she turned left into the long High Street, passing St Peter at Gowts Church on her right, then the two railway level crossings. Soon she was passing shops and the market. At the Stonebow she paused a moment and glanced up at the huge archway across the road. It was a Tudor building she'd learnt about at school and stood where once the southern gate had guarded the Roman city of Lincoln. Its frontage was decorated with stone carvings and above it was the Guildhall, where only a few weeks ago her father had attended a Council meeting. And now he was in hospital. With a little sigh she turned right into the newly widened Saltergate and came at last to Broadgate and the Drill Hall. As Polly stepped into the building, a nurse came forward. Wearing a pale pink dress with a long, starched white apron and bib, and a white cap holding her hair in place, the nurse smiled at the nervous young girl.

'Is it all right to see me dad?'

The nurse was friendly, but Polly could see the dark shadows of weariness under the young woman's eyes. 'And who might that be?'

'Mr Longden. Mr William Longden.'

'Ah yes. Follow me. We can only allow you a few minutes, Miss Longden. As you will see – ' she opened a door and gestured Polly inside – 'we are very cramped for space and if everyone had several visitors, well, you can imagine it would be rather chaotic. Mind you – ' she pulled a face – 'our poor patients aren't actually getting

many visitors. I think people are afraid they might catch
it by just being near them. You can't get it like that, by
the way.'

Polly nodded. 'I know. I nursed me mam. If I'd been
going to catch it from someone, I'd've got it by now.'

The nurse's face was suddenly full of sympathy.
'Your father told us, my dear. About your mother.
We're very sorry. And now he has it too; it must be
difficult for you. Are the rest of the family still well?'

'So far.' Polly held up crossed fingers. 'The doctor's
been very good to us. He says if any of the bairns get it,
I'm to get him at once. And he hasn't even sent us a bill
yet.'

The nurse smiled. 'A lot of the doctors around the
city aren't sending their bills out yet. If they ever do.'

'We couldn't pay it if he did,' Polly said dryly. 'With
me dad not working now and me off work to look after
the little 'uns, there's no money coming in.'

'I'm sorry to hear that. How are you managing?'

Polly shrugged. 'As long as I've enough money to get
food for us. Me mam always had a bit put by, but when
that's gone . . .' She pulled a face.

As the nurse opened the door into the main hall,
Polly gasped in surprise. The large room was filled with
beds set in rows down its full length and along the end
wall. They were close together and though screens stood
about, ready to be put around a bed when needed, there
was no privacy whatsoever. The patients could reach
out and touch the bed next to them.

'Not ideal.' The nurse sighed. 'But what can we do?
By the way, we're very short of blankets. Could you
spare one or two from home?'

'I could bring the ones off me – me mam and dad's
bed.' Her voice broke a little.

'That'd be wonderful. Wash them first, won't you, and we'll make sure they stay on your father's bed and he can take them home with him when he—'

Polly looked at her sharply. 'Is he ever going to come home? Is he going to get better?'

The nurse's smile broadened. 'We hope so, Miss Long-den.'

'Polly.'

The nurse nodded. 'Very well. We hope so, Polly. He's showing signs of improvement already.'

'Is he?' Polly's face brightened. 'Is he really?'

'Come. You shall see for yourself.'

The nurse led her down the room. 'By the way, you'll need to bring some clothes in for him. We had to burn those he arrived in, I'm afraid.'

Polly's heart sank. There were only her father's Sunday best clothes left.

'Here he is,' the nurse was saying. 'Sitting up and drinking beef tea. Now, isn't that good?'

'Dad?' Polly approached the bed tentatively, rather fearing another tirade for having caused Sarah's death.

But William looked up and smiled. He was much thinner in the face and unshaven, his growth of beard hiding the lower part of his face. But his eyes were bright – a more natural brightness now – and he was smiling at her.

'Polly, lass, I've missed you. Are you all right? And the bairns?'

'We're fine, Dad. None of us have got ill.'

'Good. That's good. A' ya coping, lass? What about Eddie? Is he behaving?'

'You know Eddie, Dad.' She pulled a wry face, but neatly avoided going into more detail. 'He's going to school, but he's talking about leaving as soon as he can.'

Forgive and Forget

'Aye well, mebbe he'll have to, lass. We'll need the money. Talking of money – are you managing? Did you know about yar mam's little stash in the tea caddy?'

Polly nodded. 'There's still a bit left. We're all right,' she said, forcing a cheerfulness she didn't feel inside. She was feeling so very tired now. The strain of caring for the family, of grieving for her mother and yet trying to keep cheerful for everyone else was becoming harder and harder each day. And the guilt. Oh, the guilt was the hardest to bear. 'Just you get better, Dad. Nurse has asked me to bring you a blanket or two and some clothes. I'll bring them in a day or two, but I won't come in 'cos I'll have Baby and Stevie with me.'

The nurse was coming towards them. 'I'm sorry, Polly, but I'll have to ask you to go now. There are more visitors and—'

'It's all right. I must go anyway. 'Bye for now, Dad.' She made no move to kiss him, but gave a cheery wave and followed the nurse out.

'He does look a lot better. If only me mam had gone into hospital earlier . . .'

The nurse put a comforting hand on the girl's shoulder, but could think of no words to say. She didn't know the circumstances of the family, nor what had actually happened to the mother other than that she'd given birth recently, had contracted the dreaded disease and died soon after being admitted to hospital. When William Longden had been brought to the Drill Hall, one of her colleagues had entered on his medical record that he'd been rambling about 'Sarah', 'breakfast' and 'Polly's fault'. The nurse could only guess what might have happened, but she was not going to question this poor girl. William was safe here and would be given dietary advice when he left. If there had been a problem

51

with what the mother had eaten, the nurse believed that such burdens should not have been put on the slight shoulders of this young girl.

As the nurse saw Polly out of the door, the ambulance was bringing yet another patient to the building.

Eight

'Where is it, you bloody little thief?'

Once more, Polly was waiting for her brother when he sauntered in at nine o'clock on the Friday night of that same week.

'Gerroff,' he shouted, trying to twist free of her grasp, but Polly's outrage was lending her strength.

'Where's the money from the tea caddy?'

Eddie blinked and gaped at her. 'What money? I don't know what you're talking about.'

For a brief moment doubt entered her mind. He looked – and sounded – innocent. But the next moment her eyes narrowed and she gripped his arm even harder. 'Oh, you're a good liar, Eddie Longden, I'll give you that. But don't try to tell me you don't know that Mam kept her housekeeping money in the tea caddy on the mantelpiece. And don't tell me you haven't taken the last bit of money we had left, 'cos I know you have.'

With one final wriggle Eddie freed himself, but instead of turning away he stood and faced her, toe to toe. 'I didn't take any money from the tea caddy or from anywhere else in this house. I wouldn't steal from me own family.'

'But you'd steal from a shop, wouldn't you? Or a market stall,' she added pointedly.

Eddie glowered. 'That's different.'

'No, it isn't. It's still stealing.'

'But I was stealing *for* the family.'

'That doesn't make it right. We're not *that* poor we have to steal from folks that's probably not much better off than ourselves.'

'It was only a couple of measly buns,' Eddie muttered. 'And it was almost packing-up time. They weren't going to sell 'em and they'd've been stale by next day.'

'That's still no excuse, Eddie.' Despite her anger, her tone softened a little.

'So – ' Eddie was meeting her gaze – 'if I haven't taken your precious money, who has then?'

'I don't know.'

'You sure there was some left? A' you sure you haven't spent it?'

Polly shook her head firmly. 'No, there was two shillings and fourpence left.'

'Blimey! An' it's all gone?'

To the boy who had a penny on a Saturday, and only then if he was lucky, the amount of money their mother had managed to put by sounded like a fortune.

Polly bit her lip and nodded, worried to death now about how she was to feed the family for the next week or two until her father came home. And even then he probably wouldn't be fit enough to go back to work straight away.

'You get to bed, Eddie.'

As he turned to go, he said over his shoulder. 'Wake me up at six in the morning, Poll. I'm starting as a delivery lad for a greengrocer in the High Street. I even get a bike.'

Polly's mouth dropped open but before she could ask him any more questions, he was creeping up the stairs and she couldn't call him back for fear of waking the others. A few moments later Polly followed him up and slipped into bed beside Violet, shivering in the icy bedroom. Despite her overwhelming weariness, it was some time before she fell asleep.

The baby woke at half-past five crying hungrily. Polly pulled herself up feeling little rested since the night before. She dressed quickly and pulled on her outdoor coat for extra warmth. Carrying the baby in a shawl, she crept downstairs, lying Miriam in the big battered armchair by the range whilst she roused the fire and made the infant's bottle. She made a bowl of hot porridge for Eddie and, having fed the baby and changed her, she woke her brother.

As he spooned the thick creamy porridge into his mouth, Polly asked, 'How did you get the job? With Mr Wilmott, is it?'

Eddie answered between mouthfuls. 'His usual lad's got the typhoid.'

'Does he know about our mam and dad?'

Eddie nodded. 'Yeah. I reckon everyone knows now.'

'And he doesn't mind? That – that you might be – well – mixed up with it?'

Eddie shook his head. 'Leo put a good word in for me yesterday and told me to go and see Mr Wilmott last night after he shut the shop.' He grinned up at her cheekily. 'That's why I was late home.'

Polly blinked and smiled ruefully. 'Oh, well then. I'll let you off.' She wagged her finger at him. 'Just this once, mind.'

He stood up. 'It won't be much, Poll. Only pennies, but you can have whatever I get. Leo said some of the customers are quite generous with tips.'

Polly's face brightened. Now she remembered. Leo had worked for Mr Wilmott, the greengrocer just round the corner on the High Street, at nights and weekends in his last year at school. 'It was good of Leo to recommend you, Eddie. Mind you don't let him down.'

'I won't, Poll.'

He pulled on his cap and his shabby overcoat. 'I'll be off then.'

That night, when Eddie came home, he was dragging a bag bursting with vegetables.

'Oh, Eddie . . .' Polly began, but he reassured her quickly. 'I ain't stolen it, Poll. Mr Wilmott clears out all his fruit and veg on a Saturday night that won't keep till Monday morning. He's given me all this.'

As Polly peered into the sack and pulled out fruit and vegetables, she saw that they were indeed past their best. Yet, when she'd discarded withering outer leaves on the cabbages, cut out the squashy pieces on the potatoes and the brown spots from apples that had been stored since the previous autumn and dealt with all the other items in the sack, there was still a lot she could use.

She grinned up at Eddie. 'Things is looking up, Eddie.'

On the following Monday morning, Polly opened the front door to find the foreman from the glue factory standing there.

'Oh, Mr Spicer – come in, please.'

'I – er – won't if you don't mind, Polly. I – um . . .'

The man was ill at ease, twisting his cap between nervous fingers.

'Of course,' Polly said, understanding at once. No one – except perhaps the doctors and nurses – understood just how the disease spread and no one wanted to take unnecessary risks.

'I just came to ask if you'd be coming back to work,

Polly. I've managed to keep your job open for you so far, but – but Mr Wainwright's pressing me . . .' His voice trailed away.

Mr Wainwright was the manager of the glue factory and Roland Spicer's boss. A strict, dour man with no sense of humour, Mr Wainwright had little kindness or understanding in his soul.

'I'm sorry, but I don't think I'll be able to come back at all. I've got the little ones to look after now that me mam – me mam . . .' Her voice broke and she dipped her head.

Roland bit his lip. He ran his hand nervously through his mousy hair and his hazel eyes were full of sympathy. 'I'm so sorry to come like this, Polly, but Mr Wainwright insisted.'

Polly looked up again and brushed a stray tear away with an impatient gesture. Most of the time, she was coping well, but just now and again, when someone showed concern, the loss of the woman who had been at the heart of their home hit her hard.

'An' me dad's in the hospital – well, the Drill Hall. He's getting better, but I don't know when he'll be home.'

'Oh, I'm sorry. I didn't know that.'

Polly's voice trembled as she said, 'But you'd better tell Mr Wainwright I won't be coming back.'

'I'm sorry, real sorry. You're a good little worker and – ' he smiled shyly – 'I'll miss your cheery smile. We – we all will.'

'That's nice of you, Mr Spicer.'

'Oh please – call me Roland. And if there's anything I can do to help, you will let me know, won't you? And if you find you can come back, then you come and see me. Promise?'

Polly nodded and smiled, but as she closed the door after him, she was thoughtful.

Call him Roland, she thought. Now what was all that about?

Nine

'Where did you get that, Violet?'

'What?'

'That pink ribbon in your hair. Where did you get it?'

Violet faced her sister insolently. 'I bought it.'

'*Bought* it? What with?'

'Money, stupid. What d'you usually buy things with?'

'And where, might I ask, did you get the money from to spend on fripperies when I've scarcely enough to buy food for us all?'

Now Violet was avoiding Polly's stern gaze. The older girl was standing with her arms folded, her eyes blazing. 'Where, Violet?'

Violet shrugged. 'Eddie gave me threepence from his wages for me birthday next week.'

'No, he didn't. He's giving everything to me. At least Eddie's *trying* to help.'

'Oh yes?' Violet laughed sarcastically. 'Nicking half Mr Wilmott's stuff. That's really trying, that is.'

'He's not nicking anything. On a Saturday night Mr Wilmott always sells stuff off cheap – fruit and veg that won't be fresh enough to sell by Monday morning. You know he does. Mam often used to go down late on a Saturday to the shops and the market just to pick up cheaper food. And he only gives Eddie what he couldn't sell.'

'You really think,' Violet persisted, 'that Mr Wilmott gives him *all* that?'

Polly blinked. 'Maybe it's instead of money.'

'Huh!'

Violet was deflecting the questions from herself, but Polly was sharper than that. 'We weren't talking about Eddie. I'm asking you where you got the money to buy ribbon.'

'I told you—'

Polly gripped Violet's arm. 'So it was you, was it? You took the money, didn't you? It wasn't Eddie at all.'

'Let go. You're hurting.'

'I'll hurt you all right. Have you spent it all?'

'I never took—'

'Don't make it worse by lying. Where's the rest of the money? Surely you haven't spent it all on yourself, you greedy little girl. A whole two and fourpence. Me mam could have fed us for a week on that.'

It was perhaps an exaggeration, but the younger girl wasn't to know.

Violet glared into her sister's eyes. 'I never touched the tea caddy—'

Polly's eyes narrowed and her voice was quiet now but all the more menacing as she said slowly, 'Who said anything about the tea caddy?'

The two girls stared at each other for a moment before Polly, holding the smaller girl with one hand, delved into Violet's apron pocket. Her hand closed over a few coins and she pulled them out and thrust them under the girl's nose. 'You little liar! You're a thief and a liar, Violet. Aren't you ashamed, with our mam scarcely cold in her grave and Dad—?'

With a cry, Violet twisted free of Polly's grasp and ran towards the door. Pausing briefly, she turned back and spat, 'And what are you going to do about it? Get your precious Leo onto me?'

With that she ran out of the house, slamming the door behind her, leaving Polly gazing down at the one shilling and five coppers in her hand. A piece of ribbon hadn't cost that much, she thought, and wondered what else Violet had spent their precious money on. Sighing, she slipped the coins into her own apron pocket.

No more putting money in the tea caddy, she thought. At least, not until Dad gets home.

Polly's world was now bound up with housework, caring for the little ones and praying that her father survived; if he didn't it would be the workhouse for them all, for sure. The responsibility for the family lay heavily on her. She had no free time, no time to read or to play; she'd had to grow up very quickly. Outside the family circle, there was only Bertha in whom she could confide. She'd even lost touch with her schoolfriends. How she yearned to be back at school, sitting in the classroom or playing in the schoolyard. Such happy carefree days that she hadn't appreciated at the time.

But one afternoon after school had finished, Miss Broughton, her former teacher, knocked on the door.

'Oh, please come in, come in. That's if you're not afraid of catching—'

'Goodness me, no.' Miss Broughton smiled as she peeled off her gloves and sat down in the chair near the range. 'I just came to see how you were coping, Polly. I heard about your mother, my dear. I'm so sorry. Is there anything I can do?'

Polly shook her head, biting her lip. Then the words she'd held back for so long came bursting out. 'I don't want to sound disloyal to my dad, specially not while he's in hospital. Miss Broughton, I did so want to stay on at school, but he made me leave. Said being a teacher wasn't for the likes of us.'

'Oh dear, I'm sorry to hear he said that and, I have to say, I don't agree with him. You'd have made an excellent pupil teacher, Polly, my dear. I'd already spoken to the head about you and he was willing to give you a trial. And I was ready to give you whatever extra tuition you needed out of school hours.' She sighed. 'But you had to leave and now, I suppose . . .' Her voice faded away.

'No,' Polly said dully. 'There's no chance now. With Mam gone, there's only me to look after the little ones.'

'And you're so young too,' Miss Broughton murmured. 'But don't give up hope, Polly. You never know, perhaps when you're older, when Stevie and the baby are both at school, perhaps then . . .'

But to the young girl that seemed an age away; she couldn't even imagine such a time.

'And in the meantime, Polly, keep up your reading. I'll lend you some books, if you like. And read the newspapers if you can. Newspapers are a great source of education.'

'I will,' Polly promised, but the promise was made half-heartedly. When on earth would she have time to read? But she did not voice the thought to her former teacher. Miss Broughton meant it kindly.

William was discharged from hospital, but he was still not strong enough to return to his labouring job on the railway.

He came home the day before Violet's birthday, but

there were no celebrations for the eleven-year-old as William sat huddled by the range, weakened by the illness and feeling the cold more than normal. But he was getting better, Polly told herself. Soon their little family could return to normal. Well, not as they'd known it before, of course. Life would never be 'normal' again, not since they'd lost their mother. But at least, if her dad got back to work, she'd be able to manage better.

As Polly bustled about the kitchen and the scullery, Eddie came to stand on the hearth in front of William. 'Dad – Mr Hopkins ses I can leave school at Easter instead of waiting till summer. He ses if I work hard from now till then I can get me certificate, an' Mr Wilmott ses I can work for him full-time.'

William looked up slowly. His voice was dull and lifeless as he said, 'That's good, Eddie. But what about the lad that works for Mr Wilmott usually?'

Eddie hesitated a moment before saying, 'He got the typhoid. He – he's not coming back.'

Polly, overhearing, moved closer. 'Little Benny? Don't tell me he died, Eddie.'

Eddie nodded. 'Last week, Mr Wilmott said. They took him to the County, but it was too late. Bit like—' He broke off and looked down at the floor, but they all knew what he'd been going to say. 'Bit like our mam.'

William glanced at Polly, bitterness in his eyes. 'Mebbe his mam cooked him a nice breakfast, did she?'

Polly swallowed the lump that rose in her throat. She opened her mouth to speak, but already William had turned back to Eddie.

With the thought of his Sarah still on his mind, William said, 'Is it what you want, lad? It's not what your mam would have wanted for you. She had high hopes you'd stay on at school. Mebbe get an apprentice-ship.'

Polly turned away, feeling a shaft of jealousy. She couldn't help it. Why was it always boys who got the chances? She'd been forced to leave school when she'd *wanted* to stay on, forced to work in a smelly glue factory. And now, at thirteen – nearly fourteen, she reminded herself – her life for the next few years was mapped out for her and she'd have no say in the matter. She'd be expected to stay at home and run the house-hold; trapped in a life of drudgery that was none of her making.

She stalked back into the scullery and plunged her hands into the sink, not trying, for once, to stem the flow of tears that plopped into the hot washing-up water.

Ten

William was improving. Even the doctor said he was ready to go back to work whenever he liked. But no one could pull him from his lethargy. He was content to sit gazing into the fire, letting Polly wait on him hand and foot.

At last the girl could stand it no longer. She stood on the hearth looking down at her father as he sat slumped in his chair. 'Dad, this won't do. We've no money left at all.' In fact, there'd been no money for weeks and they were existing on the half-rotten fruit and vegetables that Eddie brought home on a Saturday night, and the few pence Mr Wilmott paid him. Even if he started full-time work after Easter as had been promised, the young boy's wage would not stretch to feeding the whole family.

William raised soulful eyes. 'I can't seem to get going, Poll. If only yar mam was still here . . .'

Polly bit back the rising anger and tried valiantly to sound sympathetic. In truth, she was becoming increasingly impatient with her father's apathy. She felt as if the whole weight of responsibility for the family rested on her slight shoulders, though she had to admit that Eddie was doing his bit now, even if it was to ensure he got his own way. He was going to school every day and working in the evenings and at weekends for Mr Wilmott. And, as far as she knew, he was handing over every penny he earned. He was certainly bringing home the only food they had. Now Polly hadn't even any money to buy flour to make bread.

As she trudged up to the goods yard at the railway station carrying two buckets to collect their share of the drinking water that was now being brought in by train from Newark, Polly was still worrying. Soon water – allegedly the cause of the epidemic – would be all they had left.

And on Monday, she realized with a fresh wave of panic, the rent man was due to call. She'd avoided his last visit by hiding in the backyard until he'd given up knocking at the front door and gone away. Now they owed him for two months.

The Hallidays had been wonderful. Mrs Halliday had brought pies, scones and a loaf of bread and Leo, as he'd promised, had told her that he was keeping an eye on young Eddie, but Polly couldn't expect them to pay the rent the Longdens owed.

And she'd tried everything she could think of to stir her father: pleading, getting angry, even forcing a light-hearted teasing. Anything to cajole William out of his chair. But nothing was working.

Help came from a very unexpected quarter on the last Sunday afternoon in March.

'I just wondered how you all were.' Once more Roland Spicer was standing nervously on the doorstep, clutching his cap in white-knuckled fingers.

Polly smiled at him and opened the door wider. 'Please come in, Mr Spicer. I'm sure it's safe now. Dad's home and no one else in the family has the disease.'

'Roland,' he prompted, smiling and stepping over the threshold. 'I'd heard your father was out of hospital. How is he?'

Standing close beside him just inside the front door, Polly lowered her voice. 'Better. Much better. In fact, the doctor said he can go back to work, but I can't get him to budge. I – I suppose he's still mourning Mam, we all are, but I'm getting desperate. The rent man comes on Monday and—' She stopped, appalled at herself for spilling out such private matters to a comparative stranger. And yet Mr Spicer – Roland – didn't seem like a stranger. True, he had been her boss at the factory, but he'd always been so friendly, so kind to her, even stepping in on more than one occasion when the raucous teasing of the older women had got hurtful.

He needn't have done; young though she was, Polly was an equal match for any of the women at the glue factory, giving back as good as she got. In time, as with all teasing – even that which bordered on bullying – once their prey stood up to them, the bullies' fun was spoiled and they turned their attention to more sensitive souls. But Polly had remained one of Roland's favourites, a fact not lost on the other women, whose teasing had then turned to spite.

'She's a bit young for a man of his age to be eyeing up.' Ida Norton was malicious, hinting at something improper.

Nelly Rawdon had rounded on her. 'You wash yar mouth out, Ida. There's not a bad bone in Roland's body. He's only looking out for a young lass who has to deal wi' the likes of you.'

Nelly became Polly's one real friend at the factory. She reminded Polly of Bertha; a big woman with a heart to match who'd taken the young girl under her wing from Polly's first day. And when the teasing about Roland Spicer had started, Nelly told her, 'They're only jealous. You stick with me, duck, and I'll see you right.

Don't let them buggers get to you with their nasty tongues, specially that Ida Norton. She's a cow and a half.' Nelly had laughed loudly. 'An' that's insulting cows!'

And Bertha Halliday had agreed with her when Polly had confided in her. 'Pretty young lass like you working at the glue factory? Stands to reason they're envious. The sooner you get out of that place the better. In the meantime, you stick with Nelly. She's a good sort even if she is a bit rough round the edges.'

Well, Polly was out of the factory now, but not of her own choice.

And here was Roland Spicer still concerned about her. She smiled ruefully at him. 'I shouldn't be telling you all this. I'm sorry.'

'Of course you should.' Suddenly, she found her hand being clasped in his slightly sweaty one. 'Polly – I want to help you. You can trust me, you know. Whatever you tell me will go no further.'

'You're very kind,' she murmured, pulling her hand away. 'Please, come and talk to Dad. I – I'm sure he'll be pleased to see you.'

Roland sat down in the chair on the opposite side of the range. 'There's a bit of good news,' he began cheerfully. As she moved about the kitchen and scullery, Polly listened in.

'They've started a water train running daily from a well at Willoughby. It'll bring in thousands of gallons, so they say, and they've promised to do it completely free of charge for at least three months.'

'That's good,' was all William could muster.

'That's wonderful,' Polly added, trying to make up for William's lack of enthusiasm.

'Are you getting water all right, Polly?' Roland turned to ask.

She forced a smile and pushed aside her other worries. 'Yes, thank you, Roland. Me or Eddie fetch it from the station. T'aint far.'

'Yes, me too,' he nodded. 'Though with only mother and me, it's no hardship. If you ever want any help, Polly, you've only to say.'

'It tastes horrible, though, doesn't it? But I suppose we're lucky to get any.'

'I think they're putting something in the water to purify it,' Roland explained. 'We've certainly a lot to be grateful to the people of Newark for. And now Willoughby too.'

'Did you bring me a newspaper, Mr Spicer?' William asked suddenly.

'Er – no. I'm sorry.' Roland gave a wry laugh. 'But you don't want to be reading them at the moment. All full of doom and gloom, I'm afraid.'

'They were saying in the hospital – just before I left – that the death column is getting longer and longer every day.' William paused, as if waiting for confirmation of his statement.

'Er – well, to tell you the truth, Mr Longden, they say the epidemic is widespread now, but surely,' Roland added hastily, trying to instil some optimism into this sad household, 'things will get better very soon.'

'Or worse,' William muttered morosely. He seemed determined to wallow in gloom and self-pity. Though still feeling the loss of her mother keenly, Polly was fast losing patience with her father; he should be thinking about the living, especially his children. There were hundreds of folks throughout their poor, beleaguered city who were grieving just like the Longdens. Their family wasn't the only one suffering.

Polly turned away and busied herself in the scullery, cutting out the eyes in the potatoes that Eddie had brought home last night and peeling speckled apples. They'd already managed a Sunday dinner of a kind and there was enough left to make a meal tomorrow, though rather a strange one. She sighed as she sorted out one or two good leaves from a rotting cabbage. Perhaps she could make soup . . .

She could still hear Roland's voice from the other room, rising and falling as he tried to steer the conversation onto happier topics. He stayed all afternoon and even when it began to grow dusk, he still sat there.

At last he rose and said with the kind of firmness in his tone that Polly had only heard him use at work, 'Now, Mr Longden, how about you and me take a little walk whilst your lass gets your evening meal ready. The fresh air'd do you good.'

Polly held her breath as she watched her father look up and smile wanly. Then he began to lever himself out of the chair – the only time he'd risen, except to go outside to the privy or up to bed, since he'd come home from the hospital. 'D'you know, I think it might, young feller. Polly, get me coat an' me muffler.'

'That's right. Wrap up warm,' Roland advised. 'It's still very cold out and you must feel it more than ever since your illness.'

Eagerly, Polly ran to fetch her father's coat and scarf. With a silent 'thank you' in her eyes as she met Roland's glance, she ushered them out of the house.

It wasn't until the door had closed behind them that she saw a pound note lying on the kitchen table and knew that Roland Spicer had left it for the rent.

Eleven

William and Sarah had been childhood sweethearts. Born only a street apart in the same area of the city where the family still lived and with only a month between them, they'd grown up with their two families knowing each other. They'd started school on the same day and played along the banks of the river flowing past the end of their streets. As youngsters they'd played with all the other children but, as they all grew older, a natural separation between the groups of girls and boys occurred. Embarrassment and teasing followed as the growing adolescents became aware of each other in a totally different way. The girls giggled and simpered, the boys swaggered and postured. But away from the others, William and Sarah began a quiet friendship that blossomed into an early love. By sixteen, they were no longer interested in anyone else other than each other and other friendships fell away. By nineteen, they were married and a year later Polly was born.

William was a hard worker; no one would ever deny that. For the most part he was an even-tempered, kindly man. But just occasionally, if he felt an injustice was being done, his temper would flare. And it was worse when he'd had a pint or two. Drink affected him quickly and badly. In one of his recalcitrant moods, Sarah was the only one who could deal with him. At such times the children scuttled out of sight; they went out to play in the street or kept to their bedroom until the shouting and the swearing had ceased and he was snoring loudly, sleeping off the effects of alcohol. Sarah knew just how to cope. She would quietly and patiently guide him upstairs, tuck him into bed and leave him there. In the morning she would make no reference to the previous night and carry on as if nothing had happened.

The worst occasions to deal with were when something angered him but he was coldly sober. But even then Sarah would sit him down near the fire when the children were in bed and would let him tell her his troubles. His voice would rise in anger and he would shake his fist in the telling of his tale, until his wife said, 'William, the children are asleep.' For a moment, he would grumble under his breath and then gradually his voice would rise again until another warning was required. It was doubtful whether or not the children were asleep with all the noise he made, but it was Sarah's way of trying to calm him down.

The causes of his bouts of bad temper varied little. He rarely had quarrels with his neighbours or drinking mates – only perhaps with Bert Fowler now and again as they staggered home together. But his place of work was another matter. William worked in the goods yard on the railway and, sadly, he did not get along with the foreman. Against anything he saw as a miscarriage of justice William was quick – and often the first – to raise his voice in protest. And it was not only on his own behalf. If he saw a workmate being unfairly treated, he would leap to that man's defence, often to his own detriment. He'd already received two warnings from the foreman and one from the boss.

'We don't want troublemakers here, Longden. If you don't like the work, you know what you can do.'

But work for a poorly educated man with few skills was not easily found and his employment with the railway was steady and reasonably well paid.

'You'll not find another job like this one, William,' Sarah had told him often. 'Bite your tongue, why don't you? 'Tis no concern of yours. Do your work and come home to your family.'

''Tis all very well for you to talk, Sarah. You're your own mistress, free to do what you like.'

Sarah had laughed wryly. 'Free, am I? Looking after you, your children and this house. Cooking, washing and cleaning. That's freedom, is it?'

William had had the grace to look ashamed and his fit of temper had died under her calm persuasion. Seeing it, Sarah had touched his arm. 'You're a wonderful husband and father, William. Don't throw it away and see us all in the workhouse just because of your pride. Life isn't fair; it never has been and it never will be. We all just have to do our best in our own little corner of the world.'

But now Sarah was gone and there was no one to reason with William, no one who could pacify him.

Since Sarah's death and his own illness, he'd become docile. Yet sometimes Polly wished she could see some of the old fire and vigour he'd once had. At least that would be better than this terrible apathy that kept him rooted in his chair by the fire.

But Roland Spicer's visits were the turning point for her father. He came again the very next night and took William out again, this time to the George and Dragon. Polly heard later that William's cronies at the local pub had made him welcome, pitching their sympathy just right; not too gushing, but with a few sincere words at first and then changing the subject to other matters, they broke the ice for him to return to some kind of normal life. And the following Monday, William, by his own choice returned to work. His fellow workmates were pleased to see him back, his employers perhaps less so. But they all soon noticed a change in him.

Now he was peaceable, grateful to be still in work and thankful to be well enough to do it. And the thought that his children relied even more on the money he brought home was enough for the moment to make him bite his tongue, as Sarah had always advised, and turn his back on trouble. He carried her words with him and tried his hardest to do what she'd always wanted; to look after his own little corner of the world. Even on his trips to the pub once or twice a week, he restricted himself to two pints, knowing that more would tip him over the edge. He marvelled at the men who could drink nine or ten pints and still seem reasonably sober or who were 'happy drunks'. He was not, and he had to accept it. Drink – even a relatively small amount – made him nasty and now there was no Sarah to chide him gently and keep him out of trouble.

'I've missed the races then, have I?' William asked Roland when he visited the following week.

'The meeting was very poorly attended. The worst on record, they say. And the hotels and eating houses have suffered dreadfully.' Roland grimaced. 'The racegoers who did come brought their own food and drink.'

'Can't say I blame 'em,' William murmured. After a pause he asked, 'What won the Handicap? D'you know?'

'Sansovino at a hundred to nine.'

'No! Really?'

Roland nodded.

'Huh! Wish I'd had a bet. First time I've ever missed having a little flutter on that race.' The Lincolnshire Handicap was renowned amongst racegoers. William looked up and caught Polly's eye. 'But yar mam wouldn't have wanted me to be wasting money on betting when things is tight.' He smiled ruefully. 'I never win anyway. Mind you,' he added, with some of his old spirit, 'I aren't promising I won't have a bet another year.'

In April the typhoid epidemic began to subside. Life for the Longdens and for the city folk settled into a new routine. Things could never be quite the same as they had been before, either in the family circle or in the wider community. The city had been cruelly hit by the tragedy. Over one thousand people of all ages and from all walks of life had suffered with the disease and there had been more than a hundred deaths. The Council promised to take steps to improve the water supply but, whatever they did, it would take some time to achieve. There was still a lot of wrangling between those in authority and the public, but now, thankfully, William did not involve himself with it.

Polly could not concern herself with the wider issues; her daily life was difficult enough. She worked from early morning until last thing at night, cooking for the family, washing, cleaning the house and caring for the baby. Thankfully, no one else in the family had contracted the disease and though, eventually, the citizens of Lincoln were assured that their water supply was now safe, Polly – no doubt along with many others – continued to boil all the water they used for drinking and cooking.

Polly Longden wasn't going to take any chances.

Twelve

Polly had no heart to take the younger ones to the annual horse fair that came to Lincoln in April. The previous year William and Sarah had taken them, Stevie, just turned four, riding on his father's shoulders to get a better view and Violet holding her mother's hand. Only Polly and Eddie had been thought old enough to be trusted to wander about on their own. Horses lined both sides of the High Street, being trotted up and down when a buyer seemed interested. And then there was the sheep fair, and the pleasure fair that came around the same time, with all manner of stalls and rides. Polly's favourite was the helter-skelter – climbing to the very top and then whizzing round and round and down and down, the view around flashing by in a blur. And a huge treat had been a toffee apple each. As she remembered, she could almost taste the sweet sticky toffee with the tangy apple beneath. Violet had dropped hers and cried floods of tears until Sarah, relenting for once, had bought her another.

Tears filled Polly's eyes as she thought about the carefree happiness of that day and knew it could never come again.

'I can't afford for us to go to the fair this year,' she told a tearful Stevie, 'but we can go and watch the horses if you like.'

So, on the day the horses were due to arrive, pushing

the unwieldy perambulator carrying Miriam, she took him into the centre of the city to watch the horse-trading.

'Why, there's hardly anyone here,' she gasped in surprise. Only a few horses and their dealers had gathered in the High Street. 'Where is everybody?'

Overhearing her, a man at her side said glumly, 'Staying away, that's what. Frightened of catching the typhoid, they are. It was the same a few weeks back at the races.' He nodded towards the horses. 'There's just not the people about. Neither traders nor buyers. I reckon the sheep fair'll be the same.'

'What about the pleasure fair? Will it still come?' Polly asked.

The man shrugged. 'I dunno. It clashes with Easter this year and several of the fairground folk have regular places for Easter.' He sniffed. 'Still, it probably dun't mek any diff'rence. They might not come anyway.'

But on the Wednesday after Easter Eddie came home to say that the roundabouts and shows were arriving on Monks Road. Polly had no pennies for rides and toffee apples this year. Stevie was an amiable little boy and never whined for what he couldn't have. Somehow, young as he was, he seemed to understand their plight. Not so Violet. She tossed her curls and wheedled a penny out of her father when he came home with his wage packet at the end of each week.

On the Thursday morning Eddie and Violet disappeared soon after breakfast. Polly sighed. Instead of being able to run to the local shops and back without the hindrance of the two little ones, she had to take them with her.

'Can we just go and *look* at the fair?' Stevie was five now and would soon be starting school. Miss Broughton had said they'd have a place for him when the summer term started after Easter.

'Maybe next year,' Polly promised. 'Things might be better then and we can all go. Now let's go home. I'll have to get the dinner ready.'

When they turned off the High Street towards their home, the street was strangely quiet. There was no sign of any children playing; no hopscotch, no skipping, no games of tag, no sound of laughing and shouting as they chased each other.

'They've all gone to the fair,' a voice floated up the street and Polly saw Mrs Fowler waving from her doorway. The Fowlers lived right at the far end of the street, near the river.

Polly parked the pram outside their own door. 'Mind the baby for a minute, Stevie,' she murmured and then she hurried down the street towards Hetty Fowler.

'The fair? What d'you mean? They've gone to the fair?'

'All the kids from the street. My lot.' The Fowlers had so many children crammed into the small terraced house that was no bigger than the Longdens Polly wondered where they all slept. The Fowlers hadn't exactly been Sarah's favourite family in the street and Bert Fowler and William – both quick-tempered – were drinking pals one minute and bitter enemies the next. 'They've been planning it for weeks,' Hetty was saying, 'and saving their pennies. I thought you knew, Polly. Violet said you'd been giving her a penny each week.'

Polly gasped at the cheek of her sister. Violet knew how poor the whole family were now, even pennies were precious. She knew, too, that Polly had been refusing to take them this year, though she'd taken Stevie to see the horses. That cost nothing.

Violet, just turned eleven and now thinking herself very grown up, had tossed her curls defiantly. 'Well, I aren't going just to look. If I go, I'm going to enjoy mesen.'

Polly had hardly listened to the girl, never thinking that Violet was secretly planning such an escapade.

'They'll be all right,' Hetty was saying, smiling her toothless grin. 'Your Eddie's with them and our Micky said he'd look after 'em all.'

'Oh, that's all right then,' Polly said, turned on her heel and marched back up the street, hoping that Mrs Fowler hadn't noticed the sarcasm in her tone. She hadn't been able to stop herself. Micky Fowler was the last person she'd trust to look after a cat, let alone several excitable children let loose on the busy city streets.

She sighed as she manoeuvred the pram into the house and pushed it through into the back scullery. Now Stevie would feel aggrieved that he'd not been allowed to go, but Violet had.

'Violet's been a very naughty girl,' Polly told him as she set his dinner before him. 'But you're a very good boy and this afternoon we'll go to the fair and I'll buy you a toffee apple.'

She was rewarded by the most loving smile from her little brother.

Bother Violet! she thought. And if Dad complains there's not enough meat for him later in the week, this time I *will* tell him why.

But Violet, with her saucy, coquettish smile, won over the whole family – except Polly. She brought home little gifts she'd won or bought for each of them. A piece of green ribbon for Polly. 'I thought it'd look lovely with your red hair.'

A tiny doll for Miriam and a paper flag for Stevie. 'You can put it on top of your brick towers.'

The final gift was for them all. 'Micky won it for me,' she said proudly, holding out a real coconut.

Stevie, waving his flag, asked, 'Did you have a toffee apple, Vi? Polly bought me one.'

Violet frowned. 'I thought you said you weren't going to the fair? That you couldn't afford to take us all.'

'I couldn't, but it didn't seem right when you and Eddie had gone with the rest of the kids. So I took him and Miriam this afternoon,' Polly told her, trying to quell the laughter that was bubbling up inside her.

For once she seemed to have got the better of her scheming little sister. William, busily trying to crack open the coconut for them all to share, didn't seem to notice the sisters glaring at each other.

Violet turned away with the familiar toss of the curls that said, 'See if I care.' Inwardly, Polly sighed. She wasn't sure which one of them was turning out to be the most difficult to handle – Eddie or Violet.

Thirteen

The fair had helped to cheer people's spirits a little and by autumn folks were trying to put the sorrow of the previous winter and spring firmly behind them, but the tragedy had left a gaping hole in the lives of many families who'd lost loved ones. None more so than in the Longden family.

Though Polly did her best, she could never take Sarah's place or have a mother's authority over the family. For the first few months everyone had seemed to be trying to help, determined to unite the family in Sarah's memory. But as the weeks passed Polly could see that their resolutions were fading and old ways were beginning to emerge once more; William began to grumble again about the working conditions on the railway and in particular the unfairness of his boss. Eddie, though working full-time for the greengrocer now, stayed out later and later each night. And Violet, as Bertha Halliday put it so succinctly, was becoming 'a right little madam'.

'Hello, Polly. My, but you're growing up.' Leo stood on the doorstep, handsome in his dark uniform.

Polly smiled and couldn't stop herself blushing a little.

Then Leo's face sobered as he said, 'May I come in for a moment?'

He sat down, placing his helmet carefully on the table

and waited whilst Polly made a cup of tea. When they were both seated, Polly said, 'You look very serious, Leo. Is something wrong?'

'I hope not, but I thought I'd better come and have a word.'

Polly waited, her heart pounding so loudly she was sure he must hear it. Though whether it was from fear of what he might be about to say or from his nearness, even she could not have said.

'It's about Eddie.'

Her eyes widened. 'Eddie? Why – what's he done?'

'I'm not sure he's *done* anything. Not yet.' He paused, whilst he stirred his tea, not meeting her questioning gaze. 'It's just – he's mixing with a bad crowd. They roam the streets at night, shouting and generally making a disturbance. We've had a few complaints from residents and the lads have been warned. But, as yet, they've done nothing criminal. I suppose I really shouldn't be telling you this, but I don't want to see Eddie in trouble. You've got enough to cope with.' He raised his eyes and looked into hers. 'You're a lovely girl, Polly, and doing such a great job looking after all the family.'

Now it was Polly who dropped her head in embarrassment. 'I'll have a word with him,' she said softly. 'And I won't mention that it was you who told me. No one need know you even called.'

Leo rose and picked up his helmet. Polly got up too and for a moment they stood looking at each other. Then Leo seemed to shake himself, murmuring, 'I must go. I'm on duty at two. Thanks for the tea.'

'Thank *you* for coming.'

Polly wondered how she could broach the subject without letting Leo down, but the matter was made easier for her by another knock at the door as the family was having tea that evening.

'I'll go,' Eddie said, scrambling up from the table and knocking against it in his haste.

'Careful,' Polly scolded. 'You'll have the teapot over.'

'What's the hurry?' William looked up from his meal.

'It'll be Micky for me.'

'Who's Micky when he's at home?' He paused and then snapped, 'I hope it's not that Micky Fowler from the end of the street. You know we don't get on with the Fowlers. I aren't havin' him in here.' Polly hid her smile; Bert and William must have had another of their spats. Only last week they'd rolled home from the pub late at night, their arms about each other's shoulders, holding one another up. But now . . .

'He's just a mate, Dad,' Eddie shouted back over his shoulder. 'Anyway, we're off out.'

Polly saw her chance. 'Bring him in for a cuppa, Eddie. He can wait while you get ready.'

William glowered at her, but Polly leant closer and whispered, 'It's what Mam would have said. She liked us to bring friends home so she could see what company we were keeping. And, be fair, Dad, just because you don't get on with the father now and again dun't mean we should bar the son, an' all.'

William glared at her, grunted and then went back to his meal, jabbing a piece of meat viciously with his fork.

The Fowlers lived opposite the Hallidays and the difference between the two families was extreme. Whilst Seth Halliday was a peace-loving, law-abiding man, the Fowlers were trouble with a capital T. There was a brood of children – Polly had lost count, but she never seemed to see Hetty Fowler when she wasn't pregnant. Hetty was a mousy, plain little woman, who seemed to spend most of her time standing in the doorway of her home, watching the comings and goings of her neighbours.

Micky was the second eldest, a year older than Polly and he'd gone to the same school. As a youngster he'd pulled her pigtails and called after her on the way home, but all that had stopped one winter evening when the children in their street had been having a friendly snowball fight. Polly threw a snowball that hit Micky on the forehead. For a moment he stood still, stunned to think that a mere girl would dare to throw one at him. Then he scooped up a handful of snow and bore down on Polly. She squealed, half in fun, half afraid, and began to run. But Micky was older and bigger and soon caught up with her. He grabbed her and rubbed the snow in her face and pushed it down her neck.

Incensed and smaller though she was, Polly turned on him with a fury that lent her strength. She hurled her wiry little body at him. Caught of balance, he fell flat on his back into the snow, with Polly sitting astride him and heaping the snow on top of him. At last, her revenge complete, she got up, laughing. 'Don't you ever do that to me again, Micky Fowler.'

He'd got up and, soaking wet and humiliated in front of the other children, including his younger brothers and sisters, he'd slunk home.

Next day, Polly's right eye was red and swollen so much that it was almost closed.

'Who did that to you, Poll?' William had demanded and even Sarah had tried to get her to name her assailant. But Polly had kept her mouth firmly closed; she was no telltale. She'd fight her own battles.

She fully expected retaliation and kept a wary eye out for Micky Fowler at school. She saw him in the distance in the playground, but he seemed to be avoiding her. At home time her heart was pounding. Now he'll get me, she thought. Polly walked home through the gloom, trying to keep her footing in the freezing snow and ice. She heard footsteps trudging through the snow and glanced over her shoulder. It was Micky Fowler following her. She pulled in a deep breath and turned to face him. Whatever was coming to her, she thought, better get it over with.

Micky sauntered towards her, whistling, his hands in his pockets.

'All right, Poll?' he greeted her. He stopped in front of her, but made no move to touch her. Softly, he said, 'Sorry about your eye, Poll. I didn't mean to hurt you. It was only a bit of fun.'

Now, closer to, she could see that he had a red scratch on his left cheek running from the corner of his eye right down almost to his chin. He touched it gently. 'Reckon we're quits, though, eh?'

'Did – did I do that to you?'

'Yeah. Reckon there must have been a bit of grit or a pebble in the snow when you pushed it in my face.'

'Then I'm sorry too, Micky.'

Through the deepening darkness she saw the flash of his white teeth as he grinned. 'You're a little firebrand, Polly Longden. I won't be crossing you again in a hurry.'

She'd laughed and then they'd turned and walked together to her front door, she to step into the house, he to walk on to the end of the street. And from that day she'd never had any bother with Micky or with any of the other lads.

Any trouble between the two families had been between the two men. Bert Fowler was as quick-tempered as her own father was and even more ready to get into a real fisticuffs. He worked on the railway too and was a big union man. Bert and her father should have been bosom pals, Polly had always thought, seeing as how they were so alike. They were both quick to grumble about working conditions, rates of pay and so on. They even fought for the same causes, so why did they keep falling out? Perhaps, she thought, with sudden insight, it was because they *were* so alike. At times the very name of Bert Fowler was like a red rag to a bull for William. And now, it seemed, was one of those times.

In an effort to pour oil on troubled waters, she suggested, 'Mek the lad welcome, Dad, why don't you? Mebbe he's not like his dad. Let's give him a chance, eh?'

William growled but said no more.

'I can go now, Poll.' Eddie paused in the doorway. 'I'm ready. He dun't need to come in.'

But Polly followed him to the door and, as he opened it, she plastered her most winning smile on her face. Peering over Eddie's shoulder she said, 'Hello, Micky? Come on in and 'ave a cup of tea.'

For a moment the boy blinked in surprise then he grinned. 'Don't mind if I do, Poll.' And without waiting for further invitation, he stepped inside.

Deliberately, Polly ignored the look of thunder on her brother's face.

Of course, Polly saw Micky often; she could scarcely avoid it, living in the same street, but she'd not seen him close to for months. He'd grown and filled out from the skinny urchin she remembered at school. He was a little taller than she was – though not as tall as Leo – and his shoulders were broad. He still had the same wide, cheeky grin and his black hair was slicked back beneath the cap that he now pulled off his head.

'So, what a' you doing' these days, young Micky?' William asked and Polly knew he was trying to be civil. But he couldn't prevent the edge in his tone.

'Oh, this and that,' he said and winked at William.

The older man stared at him for a moment. His tone was even sharper as he said, 'I mean, where do you work?'

Before Micky could reply, Eddie butted in. 'Time we was off, if we don't want to miss the beginning.'

Micky got up. 'Going to the theatre, we are. Ain't we posh all of a sudden?'

Polly felt a flash of envy. How she'd love a night out at the theatre or just a walk into town without having to push the unwieldy perambulator; just a bit of time to herself to do anything she wanted would be nice. The words 'It's all right for some' sprang to her lips, but she bit them back and instead forced a smile and said, 'Have a good time. Tell us all about it when you get back.'

As she saw them to the door, she said lightly, 'See you again, Micky.'

She felt his eyes on her, appraising her, and suddenly she felt uncomfortable. His glance was nothing like Leo's – or even Roland Spicer's. There was something unnerving about Micky Fowler's glance and his 'You certainly will, Polly.'

Fourteen

'So, what d'you think to Micky Fowler now, Dad?'
Polly asked when she returned to the kitchen.

William wrinkled his brow. 'I didn't like the way
he winked when I asked him what he did. As if I was
in cahoots with him.' He glanced at Polly. 'And he was
eyeing you up – I didn't like that. You want to watch
yourself. You're growing up.' For a brief moment his
glance rested on her developing bosom, but he looked
away swiftly. 'Lads'll be starting to notice you. Eh, dear
me – ' he shook his head sadly – 'this is when I miss yar
mam the most. How am I supposed to guide lasses?'

Polly put her hand on his shoulder and said softly.
'I know what's what. And I'll mek sure Violet does very
soon, 'cos she's growing up an' all. Don't you worry
about us. It's Eddie you need to keep an eye on.'

'I thought he'd been a lot better just lately. Since he
started working full-time for Mr Wilmott, he's seemed
steadier.'

'Oh, he works hard and the stuff he still brings home
on a Saturday night is a boon, but—'

'But what lass,' William prompted. 'Out with it, 'cos
I know you're not one to find fault with others unless
there's a good reason.'

Polly was thinking fast. How could she get the message across to her father without bringing Leo into it?
'It's just – it's just – well – he goes out nearly every night

now with his mates. We don't know where he is or what he's doing.'

'He doesn't sound to be getting into mischief if he's going to the theatre.' William smiled. 'Very grand, I'd call that.'

Polly eyed him sceptically. 'If he really *is* going to the theatre.'

William raised his eyebrows.

'Don't you believe him?'

'There was a funny sort of look that passed between them when Micky said that's where they were going. I just wondered if he – Micky, I mean – was showing off, like. Trying to impress.'

William was thoughtful. 'You could be right,' he said slowly. 'We'll keep an eye on him. On both of them.'

Polly went to bed satisfied. She'd got the seed of doubt sown in her father's mind without revealing that Leo had given her the first warning.

Long before Eddie came home, Polly fell asleep dreaming of the handsome young policeman in his dark uniform, his lopsided smile and his blue eyes, but her lovely dream was spoiled by Micky Fowler throwing snowballs and knocking Leo's helmet off.

The next time Micky Fowler knocked on their door Violet answered it.

'My, my, another pretty sister,' Polly heard Micky's saucy greeting and pursed her lips. But she was obliged to make the boy welcome; if they were to keep an eye on him and Eddie, then they must all appear friendly and welcoming.

'Come away in, Micky,' she called. 'I reckon you must've smelt me baking.'

Bread, scones and a sponge cake lay on the table cooling. Money, though still tight, was a lot easier now both William and Eddie were earning, and just now and again Polly managed to make a special treat for the family. As he came into the kitchen, Micky's eyes lit up.

'By heck, have you made all this?' Micky winked at her. 'You'll mek someone a grand wife one day.'

Violet sidled up to him. 'I helped. I kneaded the dough and then put it in the hearth to let it prove.' She put her head on one side coquettishly and simpered, 'Won't I make someone a good wife too?'

Micky laughed. 'Of course you will, pretty Violet.'

Polly bit the end of her tongue to stop it making some sharp retort. It was bad enough if he was leading her brother astray, but now watching Violet looking up at him with adoring eyes, a new anxiety crept into Polly's heart. Maybe it wasn't such a good idea to make him so welcome in their home.

At that moment, there was wail from upstairs and Polly was obliged to leave them and go to see to the baby, though Miriam was no longer a baby really. She was almost a year old and already pulling herself up in the cot – the cot that Leo had repaired and painted.

Polly smiled as she remembered the day – it had been whilst her father was still in hospital – that Leo had knocked on the door. She'd opened it to find him and his father carrying the cot between them.

Amidst all the anxiety and sadness, Leo's kind gesture had brought tears to her eyes.

'We'll put it up for you, if you like. Where d'you want it?'

'In – in the bedroom – with me an' Vi. But there's not much room.'

The two men had carried the pieces upstairs, moved

the bed that Polly and Violet shared to one corner of the divided room and put the cot up in the other corner behind the door.

'It's wonderful,' Polly had said gratefully. 'Thank you so much – both of you.'

And now Miriam was standing up in it and soon she'd be walking. How the time had flown.

Whilst she was changing the little girl, Polly heard Eddie clatter down the stairs and the two boys leave by the front door. When she carried Miriam down, it was to find Violet still sitting at the table, a dreamy expression on her face.

'Which do you want to do, Vi? Look after Miriam or put the baking away?'

With a sigh, Violet got up and held out her arms for the child. Handing her over, Polly thought: Always opting for the easy job, is our Vi. But then she castigated herself for her uncharitable thought. It was a great help to her when someone would mind the baby whilst she got on with the household chores. But Violet was good with the little one. She never lost patience and always seemed to have Miriam smiling and gurgling happily in moments. Stevie was at school now and though Violet was still there too, she'd be twelve in the coming March and already she was fidgeting to leave and start working. She was growing up so fast; too fast, to Polly's mind. Already the girl went into town on a Saturday with her friends – with or without Polly's permission. And Polly's worries over Eddie were nothing beside her anxieties for her younger sister. She wished she could talk to her father about her fears for them both, but he'd never been the easiest man to confide in. Despite her brave assertion that she'd be able to guide her younger sister, Polly still felt the need for an older woman's counsel.

Violet was going to be a handful, Polly could see that already by the way the young girl had flirted – and yes, there was no other word for it – Violet had flirted quite brazenly with Micky Fowler.

If only their mother was still here . . .

Mrs Halliday, Polly thought with a sudden smile. I can talk to Leo's mam about anything. She'll understand.

'Come away in, lass, and sit yarsen down. Eee, let's have a look at this little one,' she added, her eyes softening as she reached to take Miriam from Polly's arms. 'My, she's growing. She'll be walking before you know it and then you'll have your hands full.'

'I reckon I've got my hands full now, Mrs Halliday,' Polly blurted out, almost before she'd got into the kitchen and sat down.

Bertha Halliday's shrewd glance raked the young girl's face. 'Summat wrong, lass? Out wi' it then.'

Polly sighed.

'Mebbe I'm making summat out of nothing, but I'm not sure I like the company our Eddie's keeping.' Once again, she made no reference to Leo's warning.

'Ah.' Bertha placed a fireguard in front of the open fire and then set Miriam down on the hearthrug where they could both watch her. She tipped some battered toy bricks onto the floor for the baby to play with.

'I take it you're talking about Micky Fowler?'

Polly nodded.

'Well, his family's a bit rough, I grant you, and his older brother's been in a bit of bother with the police. Oh, it's common knowledge,' she added swiftly, anxious not to let Polly think she was breaking any of her son's confidences. 'Leo doesn't tell me about his work and I never ask. It wouldn't do.'

Polly hoped Bertha would think the redness in her cheeks was caused by the fire's heat. But the woman's words had told her just what a risk Leo had taken in warning her about Eddie and his cronies. The thought warmed her.

'He's never been in prison,' Bertha went on. 'The brother, I mean, but he ended up in court once and was – what do they call it? – bound over.'

'So, what do you think of Micky?'

Bertha wrinkled her forehead before answering. 'Not much, if I'm honest. He's a cheeky little varmint, an' he's already eyeing up the lasses, young though he is.'

'I reckon he's about a year older than me, isn't he?'

'He's fifteen,' Bertha replied promptly. 'I know, 'cos I delivered him and I keep a diary with all the birthdays of the kiddies I've helped bring into the world.' Now the older woman met Polly's gaze. 'It's you I'd be more worried about than your brother. Falling for the young rascal's charms.'

Polly laughed aloud. 'Oh, you've no need to worry about *me*, Mrs Halliday.' Then her laughter died. 'But I tell you who I am worried about. Our Violet. Her face lights up when he comes to call for Eddie and, if she knows he's coming, she puts a clean pinafore on and a pink ribbon in her hair.' At the mention of the ribbon, Polly was reminded of what Violet was capable of, and her anxiety deepened.

Bertha nodded. 'Violet's getting to the age when she'll start being aware of boys – I mean in a romantic way.'

'But she's so much younger than him. Too young to be thinking about – well – that sort of thing.'

'Girls grow up quicker than boys.' Bertha sighed and

nodded towards her. 'Look how you've had to grow up sudden, after your poor mam died. No one thinks of you as a child any more.'

Far from making Polly feel sad because her childhood had been snatched away from her, Bertha's words brought a warm glow to her heart.

If only Leo would see me as a grown-up too, she thought.

Fifteen

In November, there was great excitement in the city when an electrified tramway replaced the old horse-drawn one.

'Let's go on the new tram, *please*,' Violet begged and even quiet little Stevie looked hopeful.

Polly shook her head, 'We'll go and see it, but I've no pennies to spare to take you on it. You can watch though.'

Violet pouted and Stevie looked disappointed, but it was all Polly could offer. On the day the new tram was to run for the first time, Polly wrapped the children warmly and pushed Miriam in the pram with the other two walking beside her up the High Street to where the tram was to make its very first trip. The streets were crowded, the people buzzing with excitement as the dignitaries climbed aboard. The tram was bedecked with flags and bunting and crammed with as many people as it would hold. There were so many on the top deck that Polly was afraid it would topple over.

'There's Leo,' Violet cried and began to wave.

Two or three constables were standing near the tram, keeping order, Polly supposed.

'He's not waving back.' Violet was disappointed.

'He can't. He's on duty.'

'He could. He could at least *wave*.'

As Polly watched him, her heart beat faster. He

looked so handsome in his uniform and so solemn. No cheeky grin today. Then, as the crowd moved and he saw them, he met Polly's gaze. He didn't smile, he didn't wave, but very slowly and deliberately, he winked at her.

Polly stifled a giggle and gave him a little wave in return to show that she had noticed. Then the milling crowd moved in front of her once more, blocking her view, as they surged forward when the tram began to move. A cheer went up and men and boys threw their caps in the air.

As it moved away down the High Street, the crowd began to disperse, either to follow its route or to go home.

'Come on, we'd best get home,' Polly said.

'I wish we could have ridden on it,' Violet whined. 'It'd've taken us home.'

'So it would,' Polly said brightly. 'But unless you want to go without your dinner for the rest of the week, we can't afford it.'

Violet pouted but said no more.

Miriam's first birthday, four days before Christmas, was marked by a very quiet celebration; the day brought poignant memories back for them all. Polly baked a special cake and iced it and the family clubbed together and bought a second-hand teddy bear. It had seen better days, but the little girl loved it.

And the first Christmas without Sarah was always going to be difficult for the whole family, but Polly was determined to make the best of it for the sake of the youngsters. Each week she saved a few pennies so that she could buy little gifts. There'd only be one each with perhaps an apple or some chocolate as a special treat in the bottom of their stockings.

'D'you think Mr Wilmott will give you some veg on Saturday night as usual?' Polly asked anxiously. Christmas Day fell on the Monday and if she hadn't got everything she needed for the day by Saturday night, she doubted she'd find a shop open on a Sunday.

'I dunno.' Eddie shrugged. 'He might 'ave sold out by then. He ses it's always hectic at Christmas. Best time of the year for trade, he ses.'

'Oh dear.' Polly chewed her lip.

'Look, Poll, I'll ask him—'

'No, no, don't do that. I don't want him to think we're beggars. We're very grateful for all he lets you bring home every week. I don't know where we'd've been without it, specially when Dad was ill.'

'Union Workhouse, most likely,' Eddie said cheerfully, but Polly shuddered. Thoughts of ending up in the workhouse overshadowed the lives of all those who struggled to make ends meet.

But on the Friday night Eddie arrived home tottering under the weight of a box full of vegetables. Breathless, but grinning from ear to ear, he dumped it on the table with a flourish.

'There's the usual stuff that's going off a bit, but he's given us some good stuff an' all. Mr Wilmott ses I'm such a good worker I deserve a bonus at Christmas. There's even a bit of holly for you to decorate the house.'

'How wonderful.' Polly unpacked the box carefully. 'Oh, I must call in tomorrow and thank Mr Wilmott myself.'

'No, don't do that,' Eddie said swiftly. 'He – it'd embarrass him.'

'Would it? Because I don't like not to say thank you for all this.'

'I'll tell him you said "Ta".'

'I hope you'll thank him properly, Eddie,' Polly said primly. 'From all of us.'

'Course I will. Right, where's me tea, 'cos I'm off out?'

Polly hurried to get it ready, anxious that her brother should be ready when Micky arrived. He seemed to be calling earlier and earlier for Eddie these days and spent the time whilst he was waiting chatting to Polly.

Tonight was no exception and whilst Eddie washed in the back scullery, Micky sat near the fire and watched Polly clearing away the tea things.

'Yar dad gone out already, has he, Poll?'

'He's not home from work yet.'

'Nor's my dad.' He grinned. 'It'll be some union meeting. Big union men are my dad and yourn.'

Polly looked up with worried eyes. 'Is there trouble?'

Micky grinned. 'More'n likely if them two's involved. It's the only time they agree – and then not always.'

Polly stacked the crockery carefully and was about to carry it through to the back scullery when Micky said, 'Poll, would you go out with me one night? Just for a walk or – or summat? We could go to the theatre, if you'd like that.'

'It's – it's very kind of you, Micky, but I can't leave the little ones. Violet's not old enough to look after them.'

'Wouldn't your dad or Eddie stay in? Just one night?' He rose and went to stand close to her. From his pocket he pulled out a sprig of mistletoe and waved it above their heads. 'Just a little kiss, Poll. It's nearly Christmas.'

Polly shuddered. How she'd longed to hear these

words said to her by Leo. But it wasn't Leo saying them
– it was Micky.

'You'll be lucky, Micky Fowler.' But she forced a
smile as she said the words and managed to make them
sound teasing, almost as if she was playing hard to get.
She didn't want to fall out with him.

His face fell but then he grinned and shrugged. 'Oh
well, it's your loss. I've got 'em queuing up for me,
y'know.'

'I'm sure you have, Micky, you're a good-looking
lad. And thanks for asking me out, but I can't. Not yet
awhile.'

'Then I'll just have to keep on asking, won't I, until
you say yes.'

After Eddie and Micky had gone, Polly sat down by
the fire and let out a huge sigh of relief. She hoped that
that was the end of it. But she rather feared it wouldn't
be.

As Polly was banking down the fire that night and
preparing for bed, she was still anxious, but now it was
not about Micky and his advances but more about her
father; he still hadn't come home after work.

When there was a knock at the door, her heart leapt
and she flew to open it. When she saw Leo standing
there she felt both a thrill of delight and stab of fear.
But then she realized that he wasn't in uniform. So this
wasn't an official visit and he was carrying a huge
parcel.

'H-hello,' she stammered and felt the colour rise in
her face.

'Hello, Poll. Mam's sent this down for you. Can I
come in? It's a bit heavy.'

Flustered, she said, 'Oh – sorry, yes of course.'

He set the parcel on the table and unwrapped it to reveal a large goose. 'Mam gets given all sorts of gifts at Christmas, you know,' Leo explained. 'From grateful folks she's helped. Delivered their babies or helped 'em out when they've lost someone. And this year she got given two geese, would you believe?'

Polly bit her lip; she didn't know whether she did believe it or not. Was it just the Hallidays being kind to the Longdens, who'd had such a dreadful year? But she did know that what Leo said was right; Bertha did get given all sorts of presents by those who could afford to be generous with their thanks for her help.

Leo was watching her face and must have guessed at some of the thoughts troubling her. Casually, he said, 'But of course, if you've already got something—'

Polly shook her head. 'No, no, we haven't. Eddie's brought a lot of vegetables and fruit home that Mr Wilmott's kindly given him.' Polly's eyes were on the plump goose so she didn't see Leo's sceptical glance, though he said nothing. 'But – no,' she went on. 'I haven't got anything to go with them. I – I was going to go out tomorrow and see if I could . . .'

Her voice trailed away. She didn't want to admit that she'd been planning to hang around the market the following day until the very last minute to see what she could pick up cheaply for the family's Christmas dinner.

'Then please have it,' Leo said gently. 'We've got more than the three of us can eat if we sat at the table from morning until night.'

Polly giggled at the mental picture of the Hallidays sitting round their table the whole day stuffing themselves with food.

'And Mam said to ask you: have you got a Christmas pudding?'

'Oh yes. I made one in November.'

Leo grinned. 'On Stir-up Sunday?'

Polly blinked and stared at him. 'Eh?'

'Stir-up Sunday, Mam calls it. It's a Sunday in November. It's the Sunday before Advent, she says. It's when she always makes her puddings.'

'I've never heard that,' Polly murmured, still entranced by the sight of the lovely goose and picturing in her mind's eye the dinner table loaded with wonderful food on Christmas Day. She was going to be so busy for the next two days she'd have to get Violet to lend a hand for once.

'I hope you got everyone in the family to have a stir when you were making it and make a wish?'

'Oh yes,' she murmured. At the memory of her own secret wish, which had involved the person standing beside her at this very minute, she blushed again.

As she fell asleep that night Polly couldn't help wishing – if only it had been Leo who'd brought the sprig of mistletoe with him.

Sixteen

'Where on earth did you get to last night, Dad?' Polly demanded the next morning as she cooked his breakfast. It was Saturday and two days before Christmas, but the railway was still running and her father was on duty.

'We had a union meeting and then we went to the pub. It carried on a bit.'

Polly eyed him sharply as she set the plate before him. 'Was there any trouble?'

William shook his head. His mouth full, he muttered, 'Me and Bert Fowler, we actually agree for once.'

'About what?'

'Oh, you wouldn't understand. You're only a girl.'

Polly's green eyes sparkled with fire. 'Is that because I'm fourteen or because I'm female?' she snapped.

'Bit o' both. What do women want to worry their heads with politics and stuff like that? They'd be better looking after their husbands and bairns.'

'What was it about?' Polly persisted.

'We want the vote for everybody, old age pensions and an eight-hour working day.'

Polly stared at him in disbelief. She'd heard about unions – of course she had – but she hadn't known they could demand such things. 'Don't want much, do you?' she muttered.

Her father glared at her. 'I told you, you wouldn't understand.'

'Oh, I understand all right. You're fighting for a fair day's pay for a fair day's work and something to look after you in your old age when you've given a lifetime of service instead of ending up in the workhouse. And as for the vote, well I reckon it's high time women had the vote an' all.'

William stared at her, his fork suspended halfway between the plate and his mouth, but Polly was not done yet. She'd followed Miss Broughton's advice and whenever she could get hold of a newspaper – even if it was a few days old – she read it avidly.

'One of Mrs Pankhurst's daughters, Christabel, went to prison in October for her beliefs. Aye,' she added, standing up to fetch the teapot from the hearth, 'and if I had the time, I'd be marching alongside 'em, an' all. Brave women, they are.'

'Well, I never, our Poll. You *do* understand, don't you?'

Polly sat down again with a sigh. 'Not all of it, no, I don't, but I'd like to. That's why I wanted to stay on at school and become a pupil teacher, like Miss Broughton said I might be able to.' Softly, she added, 'But it didn't work out that way, did it? And now it's too late.'

William said nothing. It was not in his nature to give praise or thanks, even when it was due, and Polly didn't expect any.

'I'll tell you this, young Poll, and don't you ever forget it. Working folks have got to fight to get a fair deal in life. That's what the unions are fighting for and that's why I'll always back 'em, see?'

Polly wasn't sure she did see, not all of it, but she'd make it her business to find out. She'd start reading the newspapers more regularly. Although her family couldn't afford to buy a daily newspaper, she knew the Hallidays took one. Maybe Bertha would let her have their copy instead of throwing it out when they'd finished with it.

After Christmas was over, Polly promised herself, she'd ask Bertha.

But today there was a lot of work for Polly to get through . . .

By nightfall the young girl was exhausted, but when she saw Stevie holding out his well-darned sock for her to hang up on the mantelpiece for Father Christmas, she knew all her scrimping and saving and hard work had been worthwhile. First she pinned up Miriam's tiny sock and then, beside it, Stevie's.

'There, now Father Christmas can't miss those, can he? He'll see them the minute he comes down the chimney.'

Stevie looked doubtfully at the fire still burning brightly in the grate. 'Won't he burn his feet if he lands in the fire?'

'Oh, I'll see it's out 'afore I go to bed,' Polly promised. She saw Violet's mouth twitching and raised a warning finger. 'Now, Vi, where's your stocking?'

Violet opened her mouth but seeing the glint in Polly's eye, she smiled and said, 'Well, I'll hang it up, but I don't reckon Father Christmas will be able to get *my* present in a stocking this year. It'll be too big.'

'Now you, Eddie. Come on.'

With a roguish grin, Eddie took off one of the socks he was wearing and held it out to Polly.

'Ugh!' She pulled a face. 'I don't think he'll leave you anything if he catches a whiff of *that*! Wait a minute . . .' She hurried to her mending basket and fished out a pair of Eddie's socks she'd been darning. 'Here's a clean pair. Use one of these, Eddie.'

Eddie pinned his on the edge of the mantelpiece and Polly followed suit with one of her own woollen stockings. 'Now you, Dad.'

William grunted, his glance running along the line of socks and stockings hanging there, each getting bigger and bigger towards the space left for him to hang his. Huskily, he said, 'There's one missing. There should be one for your mam.'

There was a dreadful silence in the room. Eddie shuffled his feet and Violet bit her lip and hung her head. Tears welled in Stevie's eyes. Only Miriam gurgled happily and pointed at her own little sock.

Polly touched her father's arm and said quietly, 'It's what Mam would have wanted us to do. She'll be watching over us and wishing us a happy Christmas. You know she will, Dad, so come on, hang your sock up with the rest of us. I'll get the little 'uns to bed and then I'm going to Midnight Mass. Vi's said she'll look after the bairns just for half an hour or so. She'll be all right. A' you an' Eddie coming with me?'

Slowly, William held out his well-worn sock and Polly pinned it at the end of the row. She stood back and smiled. 'Won't Father Christmas have a busy time filling all them?'

'Now, little one, it's your bedtime.' She picked Miriam up and then turned to Stevie. 'You, too, 'cos he won't come till you're fast asleep.'

By the time she came back downstairs after putting the two youngest children to bed, only Violet was sitting by the fire.

'Where's Dad and Eddie?'

'Gone out. Said to tell you they won't be coming to church with you.'

Polly pursed her lips. 'Well, I'm still going. I'm only

going to the local church, so I won't be long. You go to bed, Vi, but keep your ear up for the little 'uns.'

As Polly put on her warm coat and pulled a shawl over her hair and around her shoulders, she expected a lonely walk through the cold night to church. How she wished just one of her family was coming with her. But when she stepped out into the street, she saw several of their neighbours walking up the street carrying lanterns.

'Hello, lass, you off to church, then?'

'Hello, Mrs Halliday. Yes, I am.' Behind Bertha, she saw Seth and Leo.

'On yar own, a' ya?'

'Mm.'

Bertha tucked her arm through Polly's. 'Then you can come along with us. And afterwards you can step into ours for a glass of mulled wine, 'cos if I know that church on a Christmas Eve, we'll need summat warming when we come out.'

Polly hadn't expected to enjoy Christmas Eve half so much. There was a festive feeling through the congregation and as they left, the night air was filled with calls of 'Merry Christmas' and 'Happy New Year'.

'I ought to get home really,' Polly demurred when Bertha repeated her invitation to join them. 'Dad and Eddie are out and there's only Vi to mind the bairns.'

'Just pop in as we go past and see if everything's all right. If it is, come on down to our house. Ten minutes won't hurt and Leo will see you home after, won't you, son?'

'Course.'

And now there was no way Polly was going to refuse such an invitation.

Seventeen

Despite their inner sadness, the Longden family enjoyed their Christmas Day. Polly had returned home in the early hours of the morning walking on air. William and Eddie were already in bed and the little ones had not stirred. Before she went to bed herself, she put fruit and nuts and chocolate into each of the stockings hanging above the fire. Then she put a gift in each of them. Woollen gloves and scarves she'd knitted for each member of the family; Miriam had a little pink hat to match too. Polly'd even knitted a set for herself to keep up the pretence that Father Christmas had brought them.

But her best Christmas present had been the precious few moments alone with Leo in the darkness when he'd walked home with her.

'Happy Christmas, little Polly,' he'd murmured and given her a swift hug. As she lay in bed that night next to Violet, she could still feel the warmth of his arms around her and sleep was a long time coming . . .

But her Christmas pudding wish did not really come true until the day of her fifteenth birthday the following April. It fell on a Wednesday and, apart from her family wishing her a happy birthday, the day was little different from any other – until evening. Polly had cleared away the pots after tea and Violet, possibly as the only birthday present Polly was likely to get, had helped with the washing up.

'I'll put the bairns to bed,' she volunteered as the last plate was dried.

Polly raised her eyebrows. 'What's got into you, Vi? I know it's me birthday, but . . .'

The words came out in a rush. 'I can leave school next week. At Easter. Miss Broughton ses so. I'm going to get me certificate and . . .'

'Oh, Vi, no. You're a bright girl – clever. You – you could be anything you want to be. Didn't – didn't –' the words came haltingly for it was like handing over her own hopes and dreams – 'Miss Broughton say you could be a pupil teacher?'

Violet screwed up her face. 'What – spend the rest of me life as if I've never left school? Wiping a lot of snotty noses? No, thanks! Besides, I've got a job.'

'You have? Without even talking it over with me – or Dad?'

'And what good would that have done? I know what you'd've wanted me to do. You've just said as much. And as for Dad –' her tone was scathing – 'all he'd think about would be how much would I be bringing home so's he can be sure of his pint in the George and Dragon.'

Polly bit her lip; she couldn't argue with Violet's statement for there was more than a grain of truth in it.

'So,' she said brightly, trying to instil some enthusiasm into her tone. She wasn't quite sure whether she was pleased or sorry that Violet had no inclination to follow Polly's own dreams, for now they could remain just that, her own ambitions.

Violet smiled smugly. 'I've got a nice little job in the big store beyond the Stonebow.'

'Mawer and Collingham's? You're not serious.'

'I am. Miss Broughton's got a friend who's worked there years and she gave me such a good reference that

109

her friend, Miss Marshall, said she'd see what she could do. She had a word with somebody and I went for an interview yesterday.'

'So that's why you went out in your Sunday best clothes,' Polly murmured. She'd wondered at the time what Violet had been up to but, as she'd been about to ask her, Miriam, just finding her feet, had taken a tumble and begun to cry. Hurrying to pick her up, Polly had missed her chance. But now she knew she was genuinely pleased for her sister.

She put her arms around the startled girl and hugged her. 'Oh, Vi, that's wonderful. It'll be such a lovely job.'

'I'm on trial for a month.'

'But if you work hard, they'll likely keep you on. Oh, Vi, I'm so proud of you. The likes of us don't often get the chance to get such a good job. Wait till Dad hears.'

'Do you think we should tell him yet?'

'Of course we must tell him. He'll be thrilled.'

'Thrilled' wasn't exactly the word Violet would have used when they told William the news; she'd been nearer the mark when she'd said William's only thought would be what money she would be bringing home. His actual words were, 'Huh, cost us a penny to speak to ya soon, then, will it? Working in one o' them posh shops. Just you mind you don't get above yarsen, m'girl.'

'It's just his way,' Polly said to placate an angry Violet. 'At least you've got a chance, Vi. Take it and make something of yourself.'

'Oh, I will, Polly, don't you worry about that.'

Polly's birthday was almost over when a knock came at the door. Polly caught her breath. It couldn't be Micky

– not on a Wednesday night, surely? She hoped not; she didn't want to have to fend off his advances again.

But the breath almost left her body when she opened the door to Leo.

'Happy birthday, Poll. It's a fine evening, I wondered if you'd like to come for a little walk? Sorry I couldn't come earlier – we could have taken the little 'un to the park this afternoon – but I've only just come off duty.'

'Oh – er – yes, that'd be lovely. I – I'll just ask Dad or – or Violet if they'd stay in.'

William was sitting in the chair by the hearth reading the newspaper that Polly now fetched from the Hallidays every day.

'Dad, can I go out for a little walk? The little 'uns are in bed. I – I won't be long.'

'Aye, off you go, love.' He glanced up and gave her a rare smile. 'It is your birthday, after all.' He gestured towards the door. 'Who's that? Micky?'

'No – no, it's – ' She ran her tongue nervously around her lips. 'It's Leo.'

'Oh, brought me another paper, has he?'

'No, he – I – ' Against her will, she began to blush.

'Ah, I see.' To Polly's surprise, William actually chuckled and nodded his head. 'Get on wi' ya, then. Don't keep the lad waiting.'

They walked up the High Street, keeping a distance between them, and then along Silver Street and across Broadgate. As they passed the Drill Hall, where her father had lain so ill, Polly shuddered. But determinedly, she put her mind to happier times. The typhoid epidemic was behind them and with the authorities fully aware now that they must not allow such a thing to happen again, the city was almost back to normal. But families like the Longdens, who had lost someone dear, would never forget.

And then they were walking along Monks Road towards the city's park, the Arboretum.

'I thought you said we were going for a little walk,' she teased him.

Leo chuckled. 'The longer we walk, the longer we'll be walking back. Besides, I like the Arboretum.'

'So do I and it's so pretty at this time of the year when everything's just starting to come into bud.'

When they had passed through the park gates, Leo moved a little closer and took her hand in his. Polly said nothing, but her heart began to thump and her knees trembled so much she began to be afraid she wouldn't be able to walk another step. But of course she did and they walked on, not speaking now, but just enjoying being together and the feel of each other's nearness.

It was dark by the time they reached the corner of their street again and just before they reached the door of Polly's home, Leo stopped and pulled her gently towards him. He circled her in his arms. 'We'll go again to the park. One weekend when one of the bands might be playing. And will you come to the fair with me, Poll? I shall be on extra duty a lot of the time when it's here, but I should get an evening off.'

'I – I'll try,' she said breathlessly.

'I know it's difficult for you,' he said soberly. 'But you're a grand lass to care for your family the way you do. You deserve a bit of fun now and again.'

She thought for one blissful moment that he was going to bend his head and kiss her, but then, he loosened his hold on her with a little sigh and said, 'And now you must go in. 'Night, night, pretty little Polly.'

Polly hated being teased and called 'pretty Polly'. 'Makes me sound like a parrot,' she'd always snapped.

But not the way Leo said it – oh, not the way Leo said it, it didn't.

Eighteen

'Can I go to the fair tonight, Dad? Violet's old enough to see to Miriam for one night and as long as you're here . . .'

Before William could even open his mouth to answer, Violet said pertly, 'But I'm going out. I'm going to the fair.'

Polly rounded on her. 'Who with? You've not asked. And besides you're only twelve. You're too young to be staying out late.'

'I don't have to ask. I'm working. I give you money for my keep. I don't have to ask.'

'Yes, you do,' William put in. 'You have to ask me. You're still a child, Violet, even if you are working. Your sister has looked after us all since your mother died with never a word of complaint. Now, for once, she's asking for a night out and I think she should be able to go. If she was in a union, she'd be allowed some time off every week, so just think about that.'

It was the first time Polly had heard her father say anything that was close to appreciation for all that she'd done – all that she'd given up – for the family.

As Violet opened her mouth to protest, William held up his hand. 'Not another word. You'll stay home and mind the young ones.'

Polly felt her excitement rising as she got ready to go out. She put on her best black dress and the delicate white

114

lace tippet that had been her mother's. But all the time she was aware of Violet's expression as black as thunder. She sat huddled in the chair by the fire, glowering first at Polly and then at her father. William took no notice and Polly was far too happy at the thought that Leo had asked her out again, and that she was going to spend the whole evening with him, to let Violet's resentment trouble her.

Though she resolved silently that the following night, before the fair ended, she would see if she could let Violet go for an hour or so.

Polly had never known such carefree happiness. Leo took her on all the rides; on the helter-skelter they slid down together with Leo's arms wrapped tightly around her waist. She squealed with pretended fear so that he would hold her even closer. He bought toffee apples for them both and won her a prize on one of the stalls.

Laughter filled the night air all around them and Polly was moved to say, 'Folks are getting back to normal after – after—' She couldn't say the words for the lump that rose in her throat, but Leo understood.

He squeezed her arm tucked through his own. 'I know,' he said gently. 'But you know, whatever our lovely city has to suffer, it'll always survive. Oh, Poll, I do love being a policeman.' He chuckled softly. 'A copper, as your Eddie would call me. I love being on the beat – meeting people, trying to help them. It's not all about catching criminals, y'know.'

'I do know,' she said softly. 'You were wonderful at the time of the epidemic. Like your mam, not thinking of yourself – just trying to help others.'

They were walking home now through the streets still busy with people, even so late at night. The fair always brought people out of their houses for a few hours' pleasure.

115

'But the trouble is, if I do know of – of some wrong doing, then I am obliged to report it. You do understand that, don't you, Poll?'

Filled with the happiness of the evening, of his closeness, Polly didn't understand the gentle warning behind his words.

Instead, she made light of it. 'You mean, if your mam was caught stealing so much as an apple from the market, you'd have to arrest her?'

But Leo wasn't joking as he said softly, 'Exactly.'

As they paused outside the door to her home, Polly lifted her face. Now, surely, tonight, he would kiss her. But Leo touched her forehead with his lips and brushed her cheek gently with the tip of his fingers.

'Night, night, my pretty little Polly. Thank you for a wonderful evening. Now in you go and make sure those bairns are all right in Violet's tender care.'

Without another word he walked jauntily down the street, whistling softly under his breath.

Polly watched him all the way down to the bottom of the street until she could scarcely see him through the gloom. But she was sure he turned at the last moment and waved to her.

'Night, night, Leo. My love . . .' she whispered to the bright stars and the empty street.

As she opened the door, she heard the screaming at once. Not just the wails of a hungry or thirsty infant, but desperate, terror-stricken shrieks. Miriam and Stevie were both howling.

Polly tore off her coat and ran up the stairs. 'I'm coming, I'm coming. Oh, whatever's the matter?'

She flung open the door to the bedroom she still

116

shared with Violet and Miriam. The little girl was standing up in the cot, tears running down her face. She was crying and hiccuping and stretching out her chubby little hands towards Polly.

'Oh, darling, darling,' Polly cried, scooping her up and holding her close. The warm little body was shaking and her nightdress was soaking. As her sobs began to subside now that familiar, comforting arms were holding her, Polly moved into the part of the room the two boys shared. Stevie was sitting up in bed, crying and shivering. There was no sign of Eddie – which she hadn't expected – but where was Violet?

'There, there, it's all right. I'm home now.' She sat on the side of Stevie's bed. He snuggled up to her and she sat with the infant on her lap and her little brother with his head buried against her shoulder. As his tears dried, he whispered, 'Polly, I wet the bed.'

Gently, she said, 'Didn't you get out of bed and use the pot?'

'I – I was frightened.'

This was not the first time that Stevie had had a 'little accident' as she always referred to it. Since starting school, he'd sometimes wet the bed at night. It caused more washing, but Bertha Halliday's advice had been, 'Mek nothing of it, lass. It'll stop of it's own accord as he grows. And if you mek a fuss, it'll likely mek him worse.'

So Polly had kept her patience with the sensitive little boy and merely found him clean bed linen, though she put a waterproof sheet underneath so that the mattress should not be spoiled.

Although money was a little easier now that William was in full-time work again and both Eddie and Violet were also employed, one thing the Longden family still

117

could not afford was an expensive item like a new mattress.

'Didn't you shout for Vi?'

'Yes.' The little boy's voice still quivered with the residual fear. 'But – but she didn't come.'

Swiftly and competently, Polly changed Miriam and put her back in her cot. The child fell asleep at once, happy and safe now that Polly was home. Stevie took a little longer to settle, but at last he too fell asleep.

Polly peeked into her father's room, knowing before she even looked that he wouldn't be there. No one could have slept through that racket and she knew he would have at least gone to the children if he'd heard them crying.

There was no one downstairs and Polly realized grimly that the two little ones had been left alone in the house and, worse still, the fire had been left unguarded. She shuddered as she realized what a tragedy might have occurred.

And once more she would have blamed herself.

Violet scarcely knew what hit her as she crept in the back door at a quarter to midnight. William had come home from the pub at just after ten and even Eddie had been home by eleven. This time, Polly told them both at once what she had found on her return home.

'Those two bairns were left alone in this house with an unguarded fire and the back door unlocked. I'll skelp the livin' daylights out of that girl when she gets home. One night – that's all I asked for – one night and not one of you could stay in and mind the little ones.'

Her father shook his head, trying to clear his mind befuddled by the beer he'd consumed in the George and

Dragon. 'I'm sorry, love. I thought Violet was here. She was when I left.'

'And me.' Even Eddie had the grace to look abashed. 'She was here when I went out. I didn't know she'd sneak out. Honest, Poll.'

For once, Polly believed him.

Her anger at the gross unfairness of it all was making her emotional, but she brushed away her tears with an angry, impatient movement.

'Just wait till I get me hands on her. You two go on up. I'll wait up for her, though I warn you, there'll be a ruckus when she does come in.'

And now as the door creaked open and Violet tiptoed into the house, Polly pounced on her and grabbed hold of the girl's hair, dragging her into the kitchen and shaking her. 'How could you, you dirty little stop-out?'

The torrent of abuse hurled about Violet's ears mingled with the girl's cries of pain and alarm. She was suddenly frightened of her sister. Whilst William, even in one of his fits of temper, had never hit his children, Violet knew Polly had no such compunction. She covered her face with her hands as the blows rained about her.

'Leave – them – bairns, would you? And with an unguarded fire? You 'aven't the sense you were born with. Well, you won't be going out again in a hurry, let me tell you.'

At last even Polly ran out of steam and stepped back from her sister, panting, her red hair flying and her green eyes spitting fire. Warily, Violet dropped her hands from her tear-streaked face and looked at Polly.

'They was all right. They was asleep, Poll. I—'

'They weren't when I came in.' Polly lunged at her again, but Violet nimbly avoided her grasp this time.

119

'Miriam was screaming the place down and poor little Stevie had wet the bed. You know he's had trouble since he started school and 'e needs a cuddle if he wakes up in the night. He doesn't –' she stepped menacingly closer – 'need leaving alone in a dark house.'

Violet flung her hair back over her shoulders. Her scalp was still smarting from where Polly had almost pulled her hair out by its roots. 'Well,' she said defiantly, 'you'd better mind you stop in and look after them then, hadn't you?' Bolder now, she thrust her face close to her sister's. 'Instead of flirting with Leo Halliday.'

The slap that Polly gave her resounded through the silence of the house and left a red mark that would not disappear for days. 'Get to bed,' she muttered through gritted teeth. 'And remember, no going out for you until I say so.'

The two girls hardly spoke to each other for several days. Eddie revelled in the tense atmosphere in the house.

'Meks a change for someone else to be getting the rough edge of Poll's tongue,' he quipped as the family sat down to tea about a week after the incident.

'Now then, lad. It wasn't right what Violet did,' William said gruffly. 'She promised to stay in and mind the bairns and she didn't. She not only broke her promise – something I can't and won't abide – but she left the little ones in danger. No, our Poll does a grand job. Where would we all be without her, eh? Just think on for a minute. She deserves a night out now an' again.' He waved his fork at them all. 'And I reckon that we should pull together as a family. If we all agree to take it in turns to mind the young ones when Poll wants to go out, then it's not asking too much of any of us, now is it?'

There was silence until Eddie, his mouth full of potato pie, agreed, 'Well, I'm game. Just so long as our Poll don't think she's going to marry a copper.'

That had all the family laughing. All except for Polly, who scurried to the scullery, blushing furiously.

Nineteen

To Polly's joy, even though he'd heard about the events of the night he'd taken her to the fair, Leo did not stop paying a gentle courtship to her. His shift work as a city policeman prevented regular meetings, but on his days off he'd walk with her to the Arboretum, even helping to push the pram up the inclines.

'There's not many fellers'd be seen pushing a pram,' she said. 'Doesn't it bother you?'

Leo chuckled. 'I'm a copper – remember. Nobody'd dare poke fun at me.'

Polly smiled and walked proudly at his side. 'Everybody seems to like you, don't they?' she remarked. Whenever they walked through the streets and the park, even though he was out of uniform, people recognized him, smiled and greeted him.

'Like I said before,' Leo said, 'a copper's job is not just to run the miscreants in.' He chuckled softly. 'Though I'm quite good at doing that an' all. No, I see it as a way of helping my community. Of putting a bit back. I lock the bad 'uns up to keep them away from the good folk and, at the same time, I try to help those that need it.' His face sobered. 'There's times when I don't like it, of course. I hate it when we have to go to some poor folk's house when the bailiffs are banging on their door. Or even – ' he bit his lip and Polly could see that he was deeply moved – 'having to take some poor

122

old soul to the workhouse and I know full well they'll never come out of there again. It fair breaks my heart at times, Poll, I don't mind telling you.'

Greatly daring, Polly linked her arm through his and squeezed it to her side. 'You're a good sort, Leo. All your family are. You'll always do what's right. I know you will.'

They walked on side by side, acutely aware of each other's nearness, and Leo made no effort to release her arm. In fact, he hugged it closer to him. True to his promise, when he wasn't on duty at the weekend, he would take Polly, and Miriam and Stevie too, to the park to hear the band or to the Brayford to see the boats. He even took Stevie on a rowing boat on the river. Polly was anxious the whole time they were out on the water and flatly refused to go too. Even Leo could not persuade her to go out on a boat, she was so terrified of falling in. 'If I fall in that mucky lot, I won't drown, I'll suffocate.'

Leo had only laughed. 'Whatever would our councillors say if they heard you criticizing their waterways when they're doing so much to clean everything up?'

But still Polly would not give in. And so she and Miriam watched from the bank as Leo rowed strongly, taking the excited little boy for a trip.

The summer of 1906 was wonderful for Polly as she fell deeper and deeper in love with Leo.

'Micky!' Polly hoped the disappointment she felt inside didn't sound in her tone. 'Eddie's not home yet. Can you come back later?'

''S'all right, Polly. I'm not doing owt. I'll wait wi' you.'

It was just what Polly didn't want, but she had no alternative as Micky put his foot in the door before she could close it. With an inward sigh, she turned back to the kitchen. 'Mek yarsen at home, then, but you'll excuse me if I get on with Dad's tea. And Eddie's.'

'I haven't eaten. Me mam's got one of her huffs on and she's not cooking tea tonight. Is there enough for me an' all?'

Polly was surprised. She hadn't thought Hetty Fowler had it in her to refuse to cook tea for her family. Maybe there was more to the dowdy little woman than Polly had realized. And no, there wasn't really enough food to share, but Polly wasn't going to admit to Micky Fowler just how hard-pressed for money the Longden family still were at times. It was especially difficult when William kept more back for his beer than normal and, for some reason, Eddie hadn't been giving her as much lately as he once had.

'Of course there is,' she answered Micky brightly. 'Eddie's friends are always welcome.'

He came to the doorway of the scullery and leant again the frame, watching her peel potatoes. 'I'd much rather be *your* friend, Polly. Will you come out with me one night?'

'Sorry. I'm seeing someone.'

Micky's mouth curved in a sneer. 'Our upstanding, pillar-of-society copper, eh?'

There was silence between them. Polly was determined not to rise to his goading, so she carried on peeling the potatoes, but inside she was churning with anger.

'Well, I don't reckon he'll ever want to marry into a family where there's a thief.'

Polly's hands trembled. How on earth did Micky

know about Violet taking the money from the tea caddy that time? Had Eddie told him?

Slowly, she turned to face him, making her face expressionless. 'I don't know what you're talking about.'

'Oh, come off it, Poll. You must know that Eddie got the sack from Wilmott's for pinching.'

The potato she was holding slipped out of her fingers and splashed into the water. Now she couldn't hide the shock from showing on her face.

'You didn't know?' Micky said softly, but he was still grinning. 'He's been left there nearly a month.'

Polly said nothing and just continued to stare at him. But her mind was working fast. That was about the time when his contribution to the housekeeping each week had dropped.

She found her voice at last. 'Pinching what, exactly?'

Micky shrugged. 'Veg, fruit, owt, I suppose.'

'Not money? He didn't take money?'

'How should I know?'

'Well, you seem to think you *do* know. But let me tell you summat, Micky Fowler. On a Saturday night Mr Wilmott *gave* our Eddie any fruit and veg that wouldn't be good enough to sell by the Monday. He's been good to us. Very good. If it hadn't been for the stuff he gave us at the time of the typhoid, I don't reckon we'd've survived.'

'So, why's Eddie left there then, if it was such a brilliant job?'

For a moment, Polly was flustered, then she made herself shrug nonchalantly. 'Mebbe he's found a better job.' The suggestion didn't ring true, even to her own ears, but it was all she could think of to say.

There was a pause before Polly couldn't help asking,

'So where's he working now then, if you know so much?'

'In the market. With me. We both work for a bloke called Vince Norton. He runs one or two stalls on the market.'

'Not Ida Norton's husband?' Ida Norton worked at the glue factory; Polly knew her from the time she'd worked there. She couldn't stand the woman; Ida was a spiteful cow and a telltale to the management. She'd tried to wheedle her way into Roland Spicer's good books, but, credit due to him, he'd seen right through her tactics. The other workers universally disliked her and it was rumoured that her husband – a market trader – wasn't above bending the law to his advantage. A lot of shady deals went on behind the scenes, according to the other women.

'Don't buy owt from his stall, Polly lass,' her friend at the glue factory, Nelly Rawdon, had warned. 'You don't know where it's come from.' Nelly, a big, jolly woman, had befriended the young girl on her first day at work and had told her many a titbit of gossip. But there was no malice in Nelly; she always 'told the truth and shamed the Devil', as she said herself.

Polly felt her heart plummet. If it was true that he was now working for Vince Norton, there was no knowing what trouble Eddie might get himself into.

And, she thought, just as Micky had gleefully predicted, Leo wouldn't want to be associated with such a family.

Polly worried through the night and, as dawn filtered through the thin curtains, she made up her mind to visit Mr Wilmott and find out exactly what had happened.

Although Miriam, at just over eighteen months old, was walking well, she couldn't manage long distances and the greengrocer's was too far for the toddler to manage. So when she'd taken Stevie across the High Street to school, Polly set off with the perambulator in the opposite direction.

'Morning, miss, what can I get you this fine morning?'

Polly had never had occasion to meet Mr Wilmott in person, always relying on Eddie to bring home whatever they needed – or had been able to afford – in the way of vegetables and fruit.

Now, facing the tall, thin man, who was peering at her benignly over steel-rimmed spectacles, she licked her lips nervously. She glanced around to make sure there were no other customers to overhear what she had to ask. 'Mr Wilmott, I – I'm Polly Longden, Eddie's sister.'

The smile faded from Mr Wilmott's face. 'Ah.'

'Is it true?' Polly blurted out, her sleepless night making her rash. All her carefully rehearsed questions flew out of her head.

The man sighed. 'I don't know what he's told you.'

'*He's* told me nowt. I didn't even know Eddie wasn't still working here until Micky Fowler told me last night that – that you'd sacked him.'

Softly, Mr Wilmott asked, 'And did young Micky tell you why?'

Mutely, Polly nodded, tears springing to her eyes as the last vestige of hope died. Oh, Eddie, Eddie, she was crying inside. Haven't we had enough trouble in our family without something like this?

Mr Wilmott sighed heavily. 'I didn't want to do it, lass, and I didn't want to mek trouble for him. I just said I thought it'd be better if he found somewhere else to work. But I did warn him that he should keep his nose clean in future. Other employers might not be so lenient.'

'What – what exactly did he do? Did he take money?'

'No. Just fruit and veg.'

'I see. So you didn't ever give him stuff that was going off on a Saturday night, then?'

'Oh yes, that. Yes, I did, but then I noticed he was taking the good stuff. And I never *gave* him that. I can't afford to, lass. Only wish I could.'

'So – so you didn't give him some extra at Christmas as a – a bonus?'

'Is that what he told you?'

Dumbly, she nodded and her reply elicited another sigh from Mr Wilmott as he said heavily, 'That's when I noticed that some of the good stuff was going an' all. After that, I kept an eye on him and, yes, I'm afraid he was taking things he shouldn't have.'

'I knew he was bringing some good veg and that home, but I thought he was paying for it. If I'd thought for one moment . . .' She stopped and bit down on her lip to stop the tears from spilling down her cheeks.

'Aw, lass, don't upset yarsen. It's done with now and by what I hear he's working on the market, so he's all right. There's some good fellers on the market. Straight as a die, most of 'em are. They'll keep him in line.'

'Will they, Mr Wilmott?' Polly said grimly. 'Even Vince Norton? Will he "keep him in line"?'

Mr Wilmott blinked behind his spectacles. 'Is that who he's working for?'

When Polly nodded, all he said was, 'Oh dear.'

Twenty

As she walked home, Polly pondered what she could do about Eddie. She didn't want their father to know and she certainly didn't want Leo to find out, but she knew she had to make Eddie aware that *she* knew.

'But Dad'll have to know Eddie's working at the market now,' she murmured.

Miriam, hearing her soft voice, gurgled and smiled beatifically at her. 'Oh, Baby, what would I do without you and little Stevie?'

When she arrived home, Polly picked the little girl up from the pram and gave her an extra special hug and that afternoon she had a special treat for Stevie when she met him from school.

'A whole bar of chocolate just for me?' he asked with wide eyes.

She ruffled his hair. 'You're a good boy, Stevie. Mind you always stay that way, won't you?'

Stevie nodded as he broke off a piece of the chocolate and put it in his mouth, but the next piece, Polly noticed, he put in Miriam's chubby hand.

He was such a good, kind little boy. The two younger children she cared for never gave her a moment's trouble, but she couldn't say the same for the older pair.

To Polly's relief, William took the news that Eddie was working in the market now with a disinterested shrug. 'As long as he's earning, Poll,' was all he said.

She didn't want him to know why Eddie had left the greengrocer's shop; she didn't want a blazing row between father and son. But she resolved to have a quiet word with her brother when she could get him on his own sometime.

The opportunity came the following week.

'What are you doing home?' Polly demanded when Eddie walked in, whistling jauntily, just after dinner-time.

'Got the afternoon off.'

'Oh aye, and what does Mr Wilmott say about you taking time off work in the middle of the week, eh?'

Eddie frowned at her and she returned his gaze steadily.

'I – don't work for him any more,' he said glancing away.

'I know that,' she snapped. '*And* I know why.'

Eddie's head shot up. 'How—?'

'Ne'er mind how. I just do. And I hear you're work-ing for Vince Norton.'

'That's right. What of it?'

'He's got a reputation, that's "What of it?"'

'He wheels and deals a bit. They all do, them market traders.'

'Not like Vince Norton, they don't. They're straight. He's not, from what I've heard.'

Eddie shrugged. 'Well, you heard wrong, didn't you? He's all right is Vince. And Micky too. He got me the job, so just you be nice to Micky. He's more our sort than your precious copper. Run one of us in as soon as look at us, he would.'

'Aye,' Polly said. 'And from what I've heard, he might have good reason.'

'Oh, going to tell him, are we? Going to snitch on your own brother?'

She stepped forward and thrust her face close to his. 'I'm no snitch, as you put it. I'd never deliberately tell on you, Eddie. We're family, but never, ever expect me to lie for you either, if it comes to it. Understood?'

For a moment they glared into each other's eyes in a battle of wills, but it was Eddie's glance that fell away first. 'Fair enough. You've made your point.' As he turned away, he flung over his shoulder, 'Just have to make sure you never find out what I'm up to, then, won't I?'

Polly didn't like the sound of that – not one bit. But there was nothing else she could do, short of telling Leo.

And she'd never do that.

Whenever Polly opened the door to a knock it was in the hopes of seeing Leo, especially if it was on a night when her father was staying in and there was a chance she could go for a walk with Leo. She hadn't dared to leave the little ones with Violet again, but she so longed to have some time alone with him. He was very good about it; he never complained but would come and sit in the Longdens' kitchen with her when the rest of the family – apart from Miriam – were at school or at work. With his pattern of shift work, this was quite easy and on fine days they would walk in the park or stroll around the shops or the market, though Polly did her best to steer him away from the market. She didn't want Leo to find out that Eddie was now working there, though she guessed he'd know anyway. Policemen knew everything: it was their job.

But one Wednesday afternoon just before the family were to spend their second Christmas without Sarah, it was Roland Spicer who stood on the doorstep, twisting his cap nervously through agitated fingers. He'd become a regular visitor to the Longdens' home, usually on Friday or Saturday nights when he would have tea with the family and then go to the pub with William.

'Hello, Roland, what are you doing here? It's only Wednesday.' Then she caught his worried expression. 'Is summat wrong? Is it yar mam? Is she worse?' It was well known that poor Roland led a dog's life at the beck and call of his invalid mother. His only respite seemed to be his work at the glue factory. Polly felt sorry for him and encouraged his weekly visits. In a roundabout way, it helped her too; William never came home drunk when he'd been with Roland.

Now, Roland shook his head. 'Could – could I have a word, Polly? In – in private, like.'

'Of course. Come in. There's no one home yet, 'cept Miriam. Stevie's out playing with a mate in the next street, I think.'

Roland nodded. 'I know, I saw them. That's why I – I thought the coast'd be clear.'

Polly opened her mouth to say, 'Oooh, Roland, what's all the cloak and dagger stuff?' but seeing he was genuinely anxious about something, she bit back the jovial remark and ushered him into the warm kitchen.

'Cold, isn't it? But then, it is December.' She tried to make light conversation, but it wasn't working. So she used Bertha's tried and trusted remedy for all ills. 'Cup o' tea, Roland?'

'Thank you, Polly. That would be nice.' He sat down at the table and waited until the tea was made and she joined him.

Always straight to the point, Polly said, 'What is it, Roland? 'Cos I can see summat's bothering you. If it's not your mam, then is it summat at your work? At the glue factory?'

He raised soulful eyes to look into hers. 'Not really, Polly, but that's where I heard about it.'

'Heard what?'

'Ida Norton's off work because – because her husband's been arrested for receiving stolen goods and the two lads that work for him are at the police station an' all.'

Polly gave a gasp and her hand flew to cover her mouth as she stared at him with wide, frightened eyes.

'Oh no! You mean Micky and – and Eddie?'

Solemnly, Roland nodded.

Twenty-One

'When I get me hands on the little tyke, I won't half give him what for.'

She was pushing Miriam into her coat and hat and thrusting her into the pram with such unaccustomed roughness that the little girl began to cry.

'Here, let me,' Roland said, getting up. 'You get your coat on and I'll see to her. There, there, pet,' he soothed the child. 'Polly's not shouting at you. She's just upset about something. Come on, dry those tears now.'

Roland took a clean white handkerchief from his pocket and dabbed tenderly at Miriam's cheeks. But Polly was far too agitated to notice; it wasn't until much later that she would recall his kind action.

'Now,' he said, straightening up, 'do you want me to come with you?'

Polly pursed her lips and shook her head. 'No, I'm going to ask Bertha to have Miriam for an hour or so and I'll tell Stevie to go there too. Dad and Violet will have to fend for themselves for once if I'm not back.'

'Mrs – Mrs Halliday? Leo's mother?'

'That's right. She'll look after the bairns and if Leo's at home, he'll help me.'

'But he's in an awkward position, Polly. I mean . . .' Roland's voice faded away.

'You mean, if he's been involved with the arrest?'

Miserably, Roland nodded. 'I – I know you're walking out with him, but—'

'He'll help me, I know he will.'

Roland gave a wan smile and didn't argue any more.

'Course I'll have em, duck,' Bertha said readily. 'I don't reckon anyone's going to call for my services this afternoon.' She chuckled. 'Though you can never be sure with either those coming into the world or going out of it just when they're going to decide to do it.'

'Has Leo said owt?'

'Eh? What about?'

'Oh – nothing. I just wondered.'

'You look a bit flustered, lass. Is owt wrong?'

'I don't know yet,' Polly said grimly, 'but our Eddie's at the police station and I'm about to go and find out why.'

Bertha's mouth formed a round 'Oh', but she said no more.

When Polly arrived at the station, it was to meet both Eddie and Micky just coming out.

She stood near the entrance, her arms folded and tapping her foot on the ground. 'They've not thrown you in a cell, then? More's the pity.'

To give him his due, Eddie looked white and more than a little shamefaced, but Micky was walking jauntily towards her as if he hadn't a care in the world. Perhaps he hadn't. Maybe – for once – she'd misjudged them both, for surely if they'd been under suspicion they wouldn't be walking out of the station.

'All been a big mistake. They're still questioning Vince, but he'll be out before nightfall,' Micky told her and put his arm about her waist. She slapped his hand away and his pretended look of hurt incensed her even more. She turned to her brother.

'Eddie . . . ?'

'Leave it, Poll. I don't want to talk about it.'

'There's nowt to talk about, Eddie,' Micky said swiftly and Polly was quick to see the warning glance he gave her brother. So, she thought, not everything's as hunky-dory as Micky would have her believe.

Well, when she got Eddie on his own at home she'd soon get at the truth.

But Polly could get nothing out of Eddie.

'I can't get a word out of him, Leo. Will *you* tell me?'

Leo regarded her solemnly. 'I can't say much, Poll.'

'But you know, don't you?'

'A bit.'

'Then tell me. Please.'

'Polly, lass, Leo can't talk about police matters,' Bertha cut in. 'You should understand that.'

Polly rounded on her. 'But it's my *brother*. How can I keep him out of trouble if I don't know what's going on?' She turned back to Leo, pleading with her eyes. 'Is it this Vince he's working for? Is he a wrong 'un?'

Leo sighed and shook his head. 'He's helping us with our enquiries, but more than that I can't tell you.'

'But Eddie – and Micky – are they involved? Are they in trouble?'

'I don't think so, but they might be called as witnesses if charges are made against Vince Norton.'

Polly bit her lip. 'And that's all you're going to tell me?'

Leo glanced away, not wanting to meet her eyes,

as he said stiffly, 'I'm sorry, Polly, but it's all I can tell you.'

She stared at him. There was more he *could* tell her, she was sure, but it was obvious he wasn't going to do so.

'I'll go and ask Ida Norton, then,' she muttered and made to rise, but Leo grabbed her arm and pulled her back.

'No, don't do that. Leave it, Polly. Stay out of it.'

'Leo – it's my *brother*.'

'I know, I know, but you could make things worse for him if you try to interfere.' He was silent a moment, seeming to struggle with his conscience before saying haltingly, 'Look, I will say this. Vince will try to wriggle out of – of whatever he's being accused of and he'll try to lay the blame at someone else's door. *Anyone* else.' Now he met her gaze fully and held it. 'Do you understand what I'm saying?'

'I do,' Bertha chipped in again. 'He means, lass, that if you start asking too many questions, Vince'll likely turn on the lads and put the blame on them.' With a shrewd guess, she added, 'Receiving stolen goods, that's what he'll have been doing. Do as Leo ses, love, an' keep out of it.'

Polly stared at him for another long moment before she nodded slowly, but as she walked home, pushing the pram, she felt that Leo – and to a certain extent Bertha too – had let her down.

Once more, Polly was torn between telling their father and keeping the matter quiet. She decided – for the moment – on the latter course. If there was trouble, William would find out soon enough. But the days went by; Eddie and Micky went to work as usual and, at the end of the week when he handed over part of his wages to her, all Eddie said was, 'Everything's OK now, Poll. You needn't worry any more.'

'Needn't worry?' she snapped, her anxiety of the past few days making her short-tempered. 'When you're working for that – that crook?'

Eddie grinned, seeming more relaxed than he had been for the past week. Even he'd seemed on edge. 'He's all right is Vince. They're not charging him.'

'Not this time, maybe,' Polly said grimly. 'But you – and him – might not be so lucky next time.'

Eddie frowned. 'What do you mean "next time"?'

Polly leaned closer. 'A man like Vince Norton isn't going to give up, specially if he's got away with whatever he's up to once – or more than once, for all I know.'

Eddie's lip curled. 'Oh, lover boy been giving you the lowdown on all the criminals in Lincoln, has he?'

'No, he wouldn't say a word. He wouldn't even tell me what you were being accused of.' The memory of Leo's unwillingness to help her family still hurt.

Eddie looked surprised. 'Really? He didn't say owt?'

Polly pressed her lips together and shook her head.

'Well, I wasn't *accused*, as you put it, of anything. Me and Micky were just questioned about Vince. That's all.'

'What about?'

'Ah, now Poll, that I can't tell you, but just take my word for it, everything's OK now.'

'Your word,' Polly muttered. 'And what's that worth, might I ask?'

Eddie glared at her for a moment, but then turned away without answering.

Twenty-Two

Polly's head and heart were at war with one another. With her head, she knew that Leo was only doing his job, as he never failed to remind her, but her heart told her that he could have bent the rules – just a little – to help the family of the girl he loved.

'You've got to understand he can't talk about anything that happens in his job. He doesn't say a word, even to us,' Bertha tried to explain gently. She gave a wry laugh. 'He warned us when he first joined up that if we was caught doing anything wrong, he'd run us in himself. I don't suppose he meant it literally, but you know what I mean. He couldn't pull any strings.' Her expression sobered as she added softly, 'And the same goes for your family, lass. If your Eddie gets himself into trouble, there won't be anything that Leo can do to help him. That doesn't mean he wouldn't *like* to, but it'd be his own job on the line. You do see that, don't you?'

'I – suppose so,' Polly agreed reluctantly. 'But I thought policemen were supposed to help the community. That's what Leo told me.'

'Ah yes, but not when they've done summat wrong. So just you tell that brother of yours to keep his nose clean.'

And there the subject was closed and though, for a week or two, there was a constraint between Polly and Leo, eventually the matter faded from the forefront of their minds. But Polly was never quite able to forget it and when something brought it back to her, she still felt that little twinge of unease that Leo had not been more willing to help Eddie.

Polly and Leo continued to walk out together, and for the next two or three years life seemed to settle into a pattern. Polly still stayed at home to care for the family, though she was concerned for her friends when a disastrous fire destroyed Cannon's glue factory one Bonfire Night. But it was rebuilt and Roland, Nelly and the other women were reinstated as soon as it reopened. William was in full-time employment on the railway and Eddie continued to work for Vince Norton alongside Micky Fowler. There was no more trouble, though rumours about the man still circulated. Violet enjoyed her job and was doing well, though Polly despaired of her sister's grand ideas.

'Getting above herself,' she moaned to Bertha, but the older woman only laughed and said, 'Tis the folks she's mixing with at work, lass.'

Only Stevie, the quiet one of the family, and little Miriam caused Polly no worry. Stevie was growing fast and Polly could hardly keep pace with clothes for him. 'He's grown out of his trousers and his shoes *again*.'

'I can help you with some decent trousers, duck,' Bertha promised. 'But shoes you'll have to buy.'

And soon, it would be time for Miriam to start school. 'I can't believe where the time's gone.'

Miriam was a sunny child, rather like Stevie in nature, but she chattered non-stop from morning until night.

'Does that child ever shut up?' Violet would mutter.

'After a day dealing with awkward customers, she gives me a headache.'

But Polly liked the little girl's liveliness.

Roland was still a regular visitor to the Longdens' home and though he came ostensibly to accompany William to the pub on a Saturday night, Polly was acutely conscious that his glance frequently rested on her and followed her about the room.

'Have you heard?'

Bertha Halliday was brimming over with the news, her eyes shining and her ample chest puffed out in pride.

Polly smiled as she led Miriam into Bertha's kitchen one May morning. Their weekly visit on a Monday morning when the washing was done and hanging on the line in the backyard would soon be at an end. Miriam would be five just before Christmas and could start school when the autumn term began in September. Polly had mixed feelings; she relished the thought of a little more freedom, yet she would miss the child's company. Though she would always find a warm welcome in Bertha's kitchen, she knew.

'I don't know till you tell me.'

'About the lion in the Arboretum?'

'No. What about it?'

'It's been daubed with paint by some – some, well, vandals, I suppose you'd call them. At least – ' her chest swelled even more – 'that's what my Leo's calling them. All colours they've used.' She chuckled in spite of herself. 'I shouldn't,' she whispered almost like a naughty schoolchild and covered her mouth with her hand, 'but 'e looks more like a tiger now, they say.'

Polly smiled thinly, but she was unable to see the

funny side as a worrying thought came into her head. Eddie's shirt that she had washed that very morning had streaks of black paint on it and even splashes of red and yellow. Surely . . . ?

Polly swallowed the fear rising in her throat. 'Have they any idea who's done it?'

'No, the rascals got clean away. The park keeper's livid. You know how proud he is of the Arboretum. I wouldn't like to be in their shoes if he catches up with them.'

'Are the – are the police involved?'

'Oh yes. Leo reckons he knows who might've done it. But proving it's another matter.'

Polly avoided looking at the older woman and busied herself finding something to occupy Miriam, but her heart was pounding in her chest. Just wait till she got hold of Eddie.

Despite her affection for Leo – a fondness that had grown into real love on both sides – Polly was no telltale and certainly not on her own family. If the law came knocking, then Eddie and his cronies would have to face up to whatever they'd done and take their punishment. She would never lie for them, but she wasn't going to be the one to bring Leo or any of his fellow officers to their door.

But she meant to find out the truth, even if only for herself.

After tea that night whilst William sat dozing by the fire with his pipe and the younger ones were in bed, Polly pulled Eddie into the back scullery. Of Violet there was no sign.

'Was it you?'

'Was what me?'

'The lion in the park? Everyone's talking about it. Was it you?'

'Everyone? Who's everyone? Your precious Leo, I s'pose.'

'There was paint on that shirt of yours I washed this morning.'

'So? Me an' Micky have been painting the stall for Vince.' He grinned. 'Very smart it looks.'

'Is that where you and your cronies got the paint from then? 'Cos they reckon there was a gang of them.' She paused and tightened her grip on his lapel. 'Or was it just you and your friend Micky?'

He glared at her. 'What if it was? What are you going to do? Tell the copper?'

Grimly, she thrust her face close to his and her whispered threat was far more menacing than if she'd shouted. 'No, but I tell you this, Eddie Longden, if they do find out some other way that it was you and they question me, I'll not lie for you. I've told you that before. I'll not split on you, but, if I'm asked, I won't lie neither.'

Eddie nodded. 'Fair enough. We both know where we stand then, don't we?'

'Aye,' Polly nodded. 'I reckon we do. And that goes for the future, Eddie, an' all. Me an' Leo are walking out proper now and if he should ask me to marry him one day, then I mean to say yes.'

For a moment he stared at her and then he threw back his head and laughed. 'Leo Halliday marry you? I wouldn't hold your breath, Sis. He'd never take on all this brood you 'ave to look after.'

If he had punched her in the stomach, he couldn't have wounded her more. She felt as if he had, indeed, knocked the breath out of her. She gave a gasp of shock and hurt and her grip on him loosened. He shook himself free and swaggered to the back door.

'An' I'll tell you summat else an' all, for what it's worth. It's not me you need to keep your beady eye on. I can tek care of mesen. But you watch out for our Violet.'

'What do you mean? Eddie? Eddie . . . ?'

But he was gone, slamming the back door behind him.

Twenty-Three

When Violet came home a little later, Polly eyed her closely.

Since her sister had begun working at the department store and mixing with girls who were not only considerably older than Violet, but also more worldly-wise, Polly had been unable to control her. Violet had fast become what Bertha Halliday called 'a little madam'. The younger girl did nothing to help about the house and only with a great deal of persuasion and William's backing did she babysit the younger ones whilst Polly enjoyed an all too rare evening out. To her relief, though, Violet had never again left the children alone in the house, but every time Polly had been out with Leo, she'd been on tenterhooks all the time, wondering what was happening at home.

But tonight, for once, Violet was in a good mood. When she'd changed out of the smart costume she wore for work, she even carried some of the dishes from the scullery into the kitchen and laid them on the table.

'Going out later, Vi?' Polly tried to make her tone sound friendly and not as if she was interrogating the girl.

'No. I want to wash my hair. Would you help me, Poll?'

Polly turned away, hiding her wry smile. So that was the reason for Violet's sudden helpfulness: she wanted something. Over her shoulder, she said, with deliberate casualness, 'Course I will.' Then, mischievously, she added, 'And then you can help me do mine.'

Washing their long hair was quite an operation for the two girls. Hot water had to be carried in jugs from the tap at the side of the range into the deep sink in the scullery. Then soaping and rinsing took several more jugs, before sitting on the pegged hearthrug to dry their hair in front of the fire. But tonight Polly took the opportunity of the shared intimacy to chat to her sister.

'So are you still enjoying your job, Vi?' she asked as they sat in front of the glowing coals, taking it in turns to rub each other's hair dry with a towel.

'Yes, it's great – most of the time.'

Since she'd started working in the store, Polly had noticed that Violet was deliberately trying to speak better, to iron out the Lincolnshire dialect from her speech. She wondered if it was the girl's own choice or whether her superiors at the store had suggested it. She didn't like to ask Violet outright; such a question might spoil the closeness of the moment.

'I suppose there's things you don't like about every job, but it really seems to suit you, Vi. You look so smart in the costume and wearing your hair up makes you look so much older.'

'I'm fifteen,' Violet reminded her.

Polly smiled wistfully. 'I can hardly believe it and little Miriam nearly five already.'

There was a silence between them before Polly asked, 'Do they let you serve the posh folk yet?'

'Oh yes. I'm no longer the youngest assistant there. I'm still a junior, of course, but they let me do a lot more now. Miss Carr says I've a natural sales technique. I encourage the customers without being pushy.'

'That's a nice compliment. Who's Miss Carr?'

'The head of our department.'

'And – and which department's that?'

'Oh, didn't I tell you? I've moved to millinery. I sell the most marvellous creations to all the posh women.' She giggled. 'You should see some of them, Poll. Faces like the back end of a bus, but they're the ones with the money.'

'I'd love to see you in action.'

Violet stopped rubbing Polly's long, tangled locks. 'Don't you dare, Poll. I don't want you coming into the shop and showing me up.'

Slowly, Polly raised her head and looked into her sister's eyes. 'What – what d'you mean?'

Violet shrugged. 'I know it's not your fault, and you're quite pretty, but you haven't the first idea how to dress or do your hair. You leave it flowing free most of the time and it's halfway down your back now. It's a lovely colour but it's so untidy. I mean, you're eighteen now. You ought to put your hair up. And as for your clothes – ' Now Violet actually rolled her eyes.

Polly bit back the angry retort that sprang to her lips. When did she ever have money to spare to spend on fancy clothes? Maybe if Violet gave her a bit more of her wages towards the housekeeping rather than keeping most of it for herself, then Polly would be able to afford a new frock now and again. But she held her tongue; she didn't want to antagonize her sister.

With pretended meekness she said, 'Perhaps you could show me how to put my hair up.'

Violet let a strand of Polly's hair slide through her fingers. Then she smiled. 'I'll get you some combs and pins tomorrow and when you next go out with darling Leo he won't recognize you.'

That was not quite what Polly had in mind, but perhaps Leo would like her to look a little more grown up. Perhaps it was high time she thought about herself for once instead of always worrying about the family.

But that was easier said than done. On the following Friday evening Violet dressed Polly's hair for her in a smart chignon. And, to Polly's surprise, she also agreed to stay in and mind the younger children without any argument, but Polly could still not quell the anxiety that was constantly at the back of her mind even when she was sitting in the Palace with her hand in Leo's.

'Come on, let's take you home,' Leo said as they came out of the music hall entertainment where they'd laughed and clapped and even joined in the singing. 'You've not enjoyed this evening, have you?'

'Oh, I have, I have,' Polly cried. She hugged his arm close to her. '*And* you liked my hair up. Violet did it for me.'

Leo chuckled. 'It makes you look very sophisticated.'

Polly giggled. 'I'll never be that.'

'I wouldn't want you to be.' Leo traced the line of her jaw with a gentle finger. 'I love you just the way you are.'

'Oh, Leo,' she breathed and might have said more, if a deep voice had not interrupted them.

'Now then, young feller me lad. A' you caught them little devils that des'crated yon lion in the park?'

Leo's hand dropped away and Polly felt him stiffen. 'Mr Soper,' Leo greeted the man politely. 'Our enquiries are continuing.'

'Aye, mebbe so, but have you caught the rascals?'

'Not yet, but—'

The man gave a grunt of exasperation. 'Then you never will. You needed to catch 'em red-handed.' He

148

wagged a forefinger in Leo's face. 'And that's not meant to be a pun on the colour of the paint they used neither.'

With her arm still through his, Polly felt Leo shaking. She glanced up at his face and saw that he was having difficulty in keeping his expression serious. Leo's shaking was not with anger, but with laughter. He raised his hat to the man and bade him goodnight, promising that he and his colleagues would do everything they could to apprehend the culprits. Then he turned and hurried Polly away.

It wasn't until they were some distance away and had turned a corner that he allowed his laughter to bubble up. He clung to Polly. 'Oh, oh dear. I shouldn't laugh. It was wrong of whoever did it, but I'll never forget the look of righteous indignation on the park keeper's face the following morning. You'd've thought they'd robbed him of all his possessions.'

As their laughter subsided, Polly said seriously, 'The Arboretum keeper's very proud of his park. I expect he did take it very personal.'

Leo nodded. 'He did and we shall go on looking for them.'

Polly shuddered at the thought but said nothing. Misinterpreting her shiver, Leo put his arm round her. 'Come on, let's get you home. It's getting late and, if I'm not mistaken, you're still fretting over the young ones left in Violet's tender care.'

Polly sighed as they turned and began to walk a little more quickly in the direction of their street. 'I know I should learn to trust her. It was only that one time – she's never done it since – but somehow I just can't help worrying. I'm so sorry.'

'You silly goose, why didn't you say? We needn't have gone out. I could have come round to yours. I mean, if we'd've had the place to ourselves . . .' He hugged her to him, leaving the suggestion hanging between them.

Polly chuckled softly and rested her cheek against his shoulder.

He stopped and, in the shadows of an alleyway, took her into his arms. 'I thought perhaps you were getting tired of me, Poll.'

'Never!' she breathed and raised her face for his kiss.

It was several minutes before the breathless couple moved out of the shadows and resumed their way home. Taking her hand, Leo said, 'Come on, we'd better run now.'

Laughing, they ran through the streets, their footsteps echoing on the pavements and people side-stepping the running pair to avoid being knocked over. But they smiled to see the young courting couple enjoying life.

As they turned from the High Street into the street where they both lived, Leo said, 'I'll see you safely in.'

'You don't need to—' she began, but Leo laughed softly. 'Indeed, I do. I might be able to steal another kiss.'

In the darkness, Polly whispered, 'You don't need to steal them Leo. I give them willingly.'

'Oho, do you indeed, Miss Polly,' he teased. 'But only to me, I hope.'

'Of course only to you, Leo. You know that.'

He was serious at once as he said softly, 'Of course I do, Poll.' As they stopped outside her front door, he added softly, 'You – you do know I love you, don't you, Polly?'

She reached up and planted a swift kiss on the end of his nose. 'I hope you do, Mr Halliday, because I've loved you for years.'

He hugged her to him and buried his face in her neck. 'Oh, Polly, Polly . . .'

At that moment a door banged across the street and they sprang apart, giggling like two naughty school-children caught out making mischief.

'I'd better go,' Leo whispered, 'before my sergeant hears I've been disturbing the peace.'

'I'd better go in too – but I don't want to.'

'I know, I know, but you must.' He kissed her cheek swiftly and then turned and sauntered down the street, his merry whistling echoing through the night air.

As Polly let herself into the dark front room of the house, she was humming softly to herself. She was feeling her way carefully through to the kitchen, when she heard a noise from the direction of the sofa; a startled gasp and a rustling.

'Who . . . ?' She began and then felt suddenly afraid. Had someone broken into their house to steal what meagre possessions the family had?

She scurried through the room towards the door leading into the kitchen, knocking her leg on a chair in her haste, and into the light. Rushing across the room, she picked up the poker and turned to face the intruder.

Her mouth dropped open as Violet appeared, her face bright red, her hair wild and tangled and her clothes in disarray. At that moment, Polly heard the front door close.

'What . . . ?'

Still brandishing the poker, she pushed past her sister and flung open the front door. Glancing down the street, she saw a fleeing figure and heard running footsteps. There was no point in giving chase for whoever it was had a head start on her. She lowered her weapon and went back into the house, shutting and bolting the door.

She returned the poker to its rightful place and then turned to face her sister. 'What's going on, Vi? Who was that?'

'No one,' the girl replied sullenly.

Polly stood on the hearthrug with her hands on her hips. 'Don't lie. I'm not stupid. Was it some boy?'

Violet's head came up and her boldness returned. She fastened the buttons of her blouse and straightened her skirt. 'That's none of your business.'

'It is my business if you're up to no good.'

Violet laughed, a hard, humourless sound. 'Up to no good? Me? What about you and the wonderful Leo? I saw you outside the window, kissing and cuddling.'

'And what were you doing in there then?' Polly jabbed an angry finger towards the front room. 'The same? All right, mebbe you were, but I want to know who with and why he has scuttled off as if he's ashamed.' She took a step towards Violet. 'What's he got to be ashamed of, I'd like to know?'

'Polly, it's nothing to do with you. I'm fifteen. I've got a good job and I give you money towards the housekeeping. But you're not my mother. I'll do what I like.' She turned to flounce up the stairs, but Polly lunged forward and clutched her arm. 'No, I'm not Mam, but what would she have said, if she'd still been here?' She saw Violet falter and some of the belligerence in her face softened. Polly drove home her final weapon. 'And what will Dad say?'

The anger flashed again in Violet's eyes and her mouth curled. 'You're nothing but a telltale, Polly Longden. You think you know it all, don't you, you and your holier-than-thou copper?' Violet thrust her face close to Polly's. 'Well, you don't know nothing. D'you really think the high and mighty Leo Halliday will marry you? He'll not take us lot on and by the time Miriam's old enough to look after 'ersen, you'll be a dried-up old maid.'

Twice, in a matter of days, Polly'd heard the same words, first from Eddie and now from her sister.

Violet twisted herself free and pounded up the stairs.

And as if to give truth to Violet's statement, from the room above came Miriam's plaintive wail as she was disturbed from her sleep.

Twenty-Four

Polly was still sitting by the dying fire when her father came in. She'd unbolted the door again so that he wouldn't question the reason for it.

'Still up, love?' he said as he sat down heavily in the chair opposite her.

'I – I thought you might want a cup of cocoa.'

William stretched his arms above his head. 'No, love, I'm fine. I'm away to my bed. And so should you be. You get up first every morning to get breakfast for all of us. You need your sleep as much as anyone.'

Ever since her row with Violet, Polly had been sitting in the dim light wondering what she should do about her sister. Should she tell William about what had happened? But knowing he'd had a drink or two, she thought it would be best to leave it for a day or so. She didn't want him flying into one of his rages; even a small amount of drink made William volatile. No, she'd leave it for now. Maybe she could find out a little more first.

William stood up and yawned. 'Eddie in, is he?'

'I don't think so, but I'll leave the door on the latch. Night, Dad.' She went into the scullery and listened to her father tiptoeing upstairs. At the same moment, she heard Eddie rattling the door as he came in.

'Dad's just got home,' she whispered in warning.

'Don't make a noise.' And as he stepped into the light, she added, 'Had a good night?'

She wanted to get Eddie on her side; he might know whom Violet was seeing.

Eddie blinked. His elder sister wasn't usually interested in his social life, unless it was to find fault. In fact, he got the distinct impression that she disapproved of almost everything he did.

He shrugged. 'Yeah.' There was a pause and then he added suspiciously, 'Why?'

'Oh nothing. I – I just wondered if you ever saw Violet out with – with her friends?'

Eddie frowned and peered closely at her. 'What's going on, Sis?'

Polly took a deep breath and decided to risk taking him into her confidence. 'When I got home tonight, Violet was in the front room with someone. In the dark. I came in here and whoever it was scarpered. They frightened the life out of me. When I first came in, I thought we'd got burglars.'

Eddie laughed softly. 'Burglars? Us? Don't be daft, Poll. What've we got that'd be worth pinching?'

In the half-light, Polly smiled too. 'That's what I realized when I'd got over the shock.'

''Sides,' Eddie went on. 'Everyone round here knows you're courting a copper. They wouldn't dare.'

There was a pause before Polly asked again, 'So, do you ever see our Vi when she's out? D'you know who her friends are? I mean, she never brings anyone home. Girls or – or boys.' Though she was reluctant to admit it, Polly was forced to accept the fact that her little sister was growing up fast.

Eddie shuffled his feet; something he always did when

he was nervous or caught out doing something he shouldn't.

A warning note crept into Polly's voice as she said, 'Eddie?'

'She's seeing some lad, Poll. That's all.'

'Then why doesn't she bring him home? Dad's never stopped us bringing any of our friends home.' Despite the seriousness of their conversation, she chuckled suddenly. 'Not even Micky Fowler.'

Silence.

'So,' she prompted, 'why doesn't she bring him in? Hasn't she known him very long, is that it? Not ready to meet the whole family, yet she'll skulk about in the front room with him when she thinks no one else 'cept the young ones is at home.'

'Oh, she's known him a long time.' Eddie bit his lip and then muttered. 'I suppose you'll get to know soon enough. He already comes here, Poll. Quite openly. It's Micky Fowler.'

Polly lay awake half the night beside Violet. The girl was sleeping soundly as if she hadn't a care in the world.

Perhaps she hasn't, Polly thought grimly, but just you wait till morning, my girl, then you'll see.

The violent headache that Polly woke up with did nothing to help her temper. The moment Violet appeared, yawning and rubbing her eyes, Polly leapt on her and grasped her shoulders. William and Eddie had already left for work, so there were only Stevie and Miriam sitting at their breakfast to hear.

'Was it Micky Fowler in this house last night?'

'Wha . . . ?' Violet began, but then, shocked into full

wakefulness, she glared back at Polly. 'What's it got to do with you?'

'It's got everything to do with me – if you're bringing God knows who into this house when Dad, me an' Eddie are all out an' only the little ones upstairs.'

'They're not *that* little now. Besides, you're not the head of this house. Dad is.'

Polly released her grip and stood back, her arms folded. She raised her eyebrows and said sarcastically, 'No, I'm not the head of the house, but you'd all be in a fine mess if I upped sticks and walked out, now wouldn't you?'

Violet's lips curled and she looked Polly up and down. Dressed in her workaday clothes, Polly looked a drab creature, she knew. She felt herself cringing under her younger sister's critical eye. 'Wouldn't bother me,' Violet said softly. 'I'd manage.'

'But you don't care about the rest of the family, do you, Violet? You never have. It's always been just about you, hasn't it?'

The girl shrugged, turned away, pulled out a chair and sat down at the breakfast table.

'Well, if you're waiting for me to get your breakfast this morning, you'll be waiting a long time, miss.'

Violet looked up, her eyes narrowing. 'I go out to work and I bring money home. You get something from all of us for the housekeeping. It's your *job* to look after all of us.'

Polly, still standing with her arms folded, tapped her foot on the tiled floor; the floor she scrubbed every other day, keeping the house clean and tidy for the likes of this ungrateful chit sitting at the table expecting to be waited on hand and foot.

'And you think I wouldn't like to go out and get a

job? Earn my own money instead of slaving away here for you lot. And a fat lot of thanks I get for it. I even have to ask everyone's *permission* if I want to go out for an evening.'

'Dad doesn't mind you having Leo here. After all, he's *respectable*, isn't he?'

Deceptively softly, Polly said, 'Are you saying your boyfriend isn't?'

Violet's head shot up. 'Isn't what?'

'Isn't welcome here – or isn't respectable?'

Now Violet hung her head.

Polly – against her own will – felt herself softening. She sat down at the table. 'Vi – is it Micky Fowler you're seeing?'

Slowly, Violet raised her eyes. 'Who – who told you?'

Polly took a deep breath. She didn't like lying, but this time it seemed justified. She wanted Violet to trust her. Suddenly, she had a flash of inspiration. 'When whoever it was here shot out last night, he ran *down* the street, not up. There's no way out down there, only the river. And only the Fowlers and the Hallidays live down there who have boys of the right age. And I knew it wasn't Leo, so I put two and two together and—'

'How very clever of you.' Now Violet lifted her head defiantly. 'And what if it is Micky?'

Polly decided to play into her sister's hands deliberately. 'Micky is Eddie's mate. He's often here. Why are you ashamed to bring him here openly as *your* friend?'

'I'm not ashamed, but I know you don't like him, that's all.'

No, I don't, Polly wanted to say, but she bit back the words.

'You don't like him hanging round with our Eddie,' Violet muttered sulkily, 'so what chance have I got?'

'Because I thought they were getting up to no good together, that's why,' Polly countered.

There were other reasons too. Micky flirted with her, leered at her, and Polly hated it. She'd only ever had eyes for Leo. There was no one else she'd ever wanted – or would want.

But now Micky was seeing Violet. Polly sighed and decided that it would be better for all the family if they knew what Violet was doing. She'd no choice now but to make Micky Fowler welcome in the Longden household. But before she did so, there was something she must warn her sister about.

'A bit of kissing and cuddling with a lad is all right, Vi,' she said seriously, 'but promise me you'll never let him go too far. You know what I mean, don't you?'

Violet flung back her hair and said petulantly, 'Course I do.'

'That's all right then.' Then Polly smiled. 'Ask him to tea on Sunday. We'll make him welcome, Vi, if that's what you want.'

'Really?' Violet couldn't believe what she was hearing.

'Really. And now,' Polly added, getting up, 'you'd better get a move on if you're not going to be late for work. Go and get ready and I'll make your breakfast.' As the younger girl rushed out of the room, Polly muttered, 'As you've made it very clear that it's my job.'

Micky was not the only guest to Sunday afternoon tea. Although Leo was on duty, Roland had called round in the afternoon to chat with William and Polly felt duty bound to ask the kindly man to stay.

So all the family, plus the two guests, sat down. There was an awkwardness at first, but Polly was determined to put everyone at their ease. She had nothing to fear now from Micky. She was walking out with Leo Halliday and the whole street – if not half the neighbourhood – knew it. Added to that, Micky was now seeing Violet and she would not stand for him making eyes at her older sister. So Polly felt much safer.

As she passed round sandwiches and home-made cakes, poured tea and encouraged talk around the tea table, the atmosphere seemed to relax. She caught her father glancing at Micky sitting next to Violet. Across the table, he caught Polly's eye and raised his eyebrows in a silent question. She smiled and gave a tiny nod, but she was not surprised when William frowned.

Her father too, she knew, had doubts about Micky Fowler. But he said nothing and the tea party continued. As they all rose from the table, Roland touched Polly's arm and said, 'May I help with the washing up? I'm quite a dab hand.' He pulled a face. 'I've had to be.'

She smiled kindly at him. 'Then you must have a break from it tonight. Go and sit near the fire with Dad and have a chinwag.' She laughed. 'I think the youngsters have commandeered the front room for a noisy game of charades. Even Micky and Violet are joining in.'

'But you never get a break from the housework, Polly, do you?' Roland said softly.

'Oh, now and again when Leo takes me out.'

Roland's face fell; she couldn't fail to notice it. 'Ah – you're still walking out with Leo, are you? I – I wondered, as he wasn't here tonight.'

'He's on duty.' There was no mistaking the pride in her voice. 'Two to ten today.' She laughed, trying to lighten the atmosphere between them. 'Someone's got to stop the riots when they all come out of church.'

Roland smiled and picked up a tea towel. 'Let me help you. We'll get it done all the quicker and then you can come and sit with us.'

Polly smiled and nodded her agreement. Roland Spicer was such a nice man. It was so sad he'd never married and, now that he was tied to an invalid mother, perhaps he'd never get the chance.

'How old are you, Roland?' With a shock she realized she'd spoken her thoughts aloud. 'Oh, I'm sorry,' she added swiftly. 'That was rude of me.'

Roland smiled and shrugged. 'I don't mind. I'm twenty-nine in September.'

'Are you? You must have been very young to become a foreman when you did.'

He laughed wryly. 'I was. It caused a bit of bother at the time, but you see my dad had been foreman there for years and when he died suddenly – at work, as it happened – I think the boss felt the least he could do was to give me his position. Most folk were fine about it. They'd all liked my dad. Only a couple of the older blokes – Harry Barnes for one – felt they'd been overlooked. You know how it is.'

She didn't, but she could guess.

The evening was pleasant enough, but quiet – dull, almost – and Polly craved Leo's presence. She tried to be a good hostess, but she couldn't help glancing furtively at the clock wondering if Leo would call when he came off duty.

On the stroke of ten o'clock, Roland got up to leave. 'I must see to Mother's cocoa and help her to bed,' he explained.

'I'm sorry about yar mam,' William said. He rose and held out his hand. 'You're welcome here any time,

161

Roland. You were always good to our Poll when she worked at your place and you've been good to us all since. We don't forget kindness, do we, Poll?'

Polly, leading the way through the front room to the door, glanced back and smiled, but she did not add any further words to her father's open invitation; she doubted Roland needed much encouragement to come again – and often.

As she closed the door after him and returned to the warmth of the fire, William knocked out his pipe on the grate. 'That young feller's got an eye for you, our Poll.'

'Oh, Dad, don't.'

William straightened up and looked round at her. 'Whyever not, lass? He'd make a grand husband. He's kind and caring and . . .'

'Dad, I'm walking out with Leo. You know that.'

'Aye, I do. But I'm wondering if you couldn't do better for yarsen. Young Leo dun't seem to be getting on with the job.'

'Dad!' Polly laughed. 'What a thing to say.'

'Well, you know what I mean. You've been walking out with him for what seems like years but has he made his intentions clear yet? Has he asked you to marry him or even to get engaged?' When she didn't answer he went on, 'No, I thought not. Aw, lass, I know you're fond of him, but—'

'No, Dad,' she said quietly. 'Not just "fond". I love Leo. I always have for as long as I can remember. And I know I always will. So you see, even if Leo never asks me to marry him, it wouldn't be fair to marry Roland, now would it? Not to him or to me.'

Twenty-Five

Micky was now a regular visitor to the Longden house-hold and although he was walking out with Violet, Polly still felt his gaze following her about the room and the look in his eyes made her uncomfortable. She was careful never to be alone with him, always keeping Miriam with her when he was around. But Miriam was fast developing a life of her own, young though she still was.

'Can I play out, Poll?' was her constant question during the light evenings in the summer just before she was due to start school. 'Me and Dottie Fowler are friends now. When we start school in September we're going to sit together.'

Polly almost said, 'That'll be for Miss Broughton or whoever your teacher is to decide.' But she bit back the words. She didn't want to put the little girl off the idea of starting school. But her heart sank. Not another friendship between the Longdens and the Fowlers; it was all getting far too cosy for her liking. Even William and Bert had been seen drinking together amicably in the George and Dragon. They hadn't had a fallout at all recently. It crossed Polly's mind that the tragedy that had befallen their city over four years ago now had made people friendlier towards one another, even those who previously would scarcely have passed the time of day.

'I suppose so, but don't get near the river. It's dirty and . . .'

Miriam removed her thumb long enough to say, with a mischievous glint in her dark blue eyes, 'Stevie's gone swimming in the river.'

Polly whirled around. 'He's *what*?'

'Gone swimmin' with the boys from Alfred Street. It's ever so warm, he says and . . .'

But Polly heard no more. She rushed out of the house and down the street, her hair flying loose, her skirts riding up to her knees. At the bottom end of the street, she came to the River Witham flowing lazily through the city's downhill streets. She glanced first to the left and then to the right. Then she saw them; a group of boys splashing in the water near the end of the adjacent street. One or two stood on the bank, ready to dive in and join in the fun.

'No,' she yelled. 'Get out of there.' She scrambled along the bank, holding onto tufts of grass, terrified of slipping into the murky water, of her skirts dragging her under.

As she reached them, panting and red-faced, Stevie was climbing out of the water, standing on the river-bank, dripping and anxious now. Yet the others carried on playing, ignoring Polly's warning shouts and her threats. She reached Stevie, and for the first time ever, she slapped him across the face.

'You – you . . .' She couldn't think of anything bad enough to say to him, to call him. 'Do you want to bring typhoid on us all again? Can't you see how mucky the water is? You haven't the sense you were born with. You're nine, for heaven's sake. You ought to know better.' She grasped his shoulder roughly and began to march him up the street. No way was she going to clamber back along the bank or allow Stevie to get back into the water.

'Poll, you're hurting me. And me feet. I ain't nothing on me feet.'

'I'll hurt you, you little blighter.'

Behind them came the jeers and cat-calls of his friends, but gentle Stevie, still not understanding what he had done that was so wrong, allowed himself to be led away by his irate sister.

In their backyard, she made him strip naked and stand there whilst she threw buckets of icy cold water over him. Then she dragged him into the scullery and washed his hair with carbolic soap. She even made him rinse his mouth out with the soapy mixture until he baulked at the pungent taste.

Then she wrapped him in a towel and sat him by the range, made him some cocoa and sat beside him until his shivering stopped.

'Did you – did you mean it? Will I get typhoid? Will I have – have brought it here?'

Stevie was crying now.

'Have you swallowed any of the river water?'

'I – I dunno.' He hiccuped miserably. 'I might a' done.'

'Well, we'll just have to hope, won't we? Oh, Stevie.' She put her arms around him, her anger dying now, though the fear remained. 'Promise me you'll never go near the river again. You know how I still boil all the water we drink until they get the new water supply to Lincoln working.'

In the previous October, work had begun to bring a supply of water from Elkesley, in Nottinghamshire, but it would be some time yet before it reached the city.

'Was it – was it the water that caused the typhoid then?'

Polly stared at him, but then she realized. He'd only been four when the disease had hit the city, when their mother had died. He couldn't have understood. At the time, she'd been as guilty as anyone of protecting the little boy from the truth.

'Yes,' she said now. 'It was.'

'I'm sorry, Poll. I won't ever do it again.'

'Good boy. And I'm sorry if I embarrassed you in front of all your friends.'

Stevie shrugged. 'I'll tell 'em why tomorrow. They'll understand then why you was so – so mad.'

She smoothed his wet hair back from his forehead. 'You're a good boy usually. It's not often I have to get cross at you, is it?'

Stevie shook his head.

'Now drink your cocoa and forget all about it.'

But it was several days, weeks even, before Polly could stop herself watching the boy for any sign of illness. And Stevie too, though usually quiet and self-contained, was even more subdued and she knew he must be worrying inwardly too.

By September when he returned to school, taking his little sister Miriam by the hand on her first day, the fear had begun to fade, though neither of them ever forgot. And never again did Stevie go swimming in the River Witham.

A year passed by; another Christmas, another New Year and in the April, Polly was another year older.

'Nineteen,' Violet teased her. 'And still no ring on

166

your finger. You'll be an old maid, Poll. I'll mind I'm not still single by the time I'm nineteen.'

'You're only sixteen, Vi,' Polly snapped back. Even she had begun to doubt Leo's intentions as the months passed and he made no offer of marriage. 'You shouldn't be thinking of such things. And you shouldn't be getting serious over any lad. Not yet.'

Violet's face darkened. 'Not over Micky you mean, don't you?' She paused a moment and then added suddenly, 'What is it about him you don't like, Poll?'

Polly avoided her sister's gaze and wriggled her shoulders. 'He's trouble,' she said shortly.

'No, he's not. Not now. Oh, I grant you he was a bit of a tearaway. Him and Eddie both, but after that scare about the chap they work for . . .'

'Vince Norton.'

'Yes, him. But there's been no more trouble, now has there?'

'Well . . .' Polly said slowly.

'And I'm sure,' Violet put in slyly, 'your Leo would soon have told you if there had been.'

Polly glared at her and then said primly, 'Leo doesn't gossip about his work or the people he comes into contact with in the course of his duty.'

Violet pulled a face. 'But he'd've told you if either Eddie or Micky was in trouble, surely.'

Polly was obliged to climb down. 'I suppose so.'

'There you are then,' Violet finished triumphantly. 'They're keeping out of mischief now.'

'Just you mind you do, an' all, our Vi.'

'Oh, I can look after myself, Poll, don't you worry.'

But Polly did worry; she never stopped. She worried about her father and his quick temper. She was fearful of Eddie getting into real trouble. And there was the constant struggle to feed and clothe the family. However was she to afford new shoes for Stevie, who seemed to be shooting up 'like a streak of pump water', as her mother had been fond of saying when her youngsters had a growth spurt?

'Oh, Mam,' Polly still mourned inwardly, 'why did you have to leave us?'

But such moments of despondency and self-pity were rare. Despite the sacrifice of her own dreams, Polly was happy, but that happiness was bound up in one person: Leo.

The months passed, summer came and went and there was another Christmas and a New Year's Eve, the dawning of 1911 when Polly would be twenty in the April. Perhaps he will ask me tonight, Polly thought, as she dressed with care for the New Year's celebrations in their street.

Bert Fowler had obtained some fireworks – no one dared to ask too closely just where or how he'd got them – and there was to be an informal street party around midnight. Everyone would go down to the end of the street and watch Bert set off the fireworks on the riverbank. Even Leo would be there, happy, for once, to ask no questions but to join in the revelry on his evening off.

'Here, Miriam, put this scarf on and borrow my gloves. I don't want you catching cold. Where's Stevie?'

'He's gone already. Poll, will Dottie be allowed to go, d'you think?'

Despite Polly's concern about another bond with the Fowler family, she had to admit that Dottie was a sweet-natured little girl. She and Miriam were firm friends and never seemed to fall out.

'I expect so, though you must promise me you'll go straight to bed as soon as the fireworks are finished and the New Year's in.'

Miriam nodded until her curls shook.

'Come on, then. Is Vi ready?'

'She's gone an' all. There's only us.' Miriam pulled at Polly's hand. 'Oh, do come on. We'll miss the fun.'

When Polly and Miriam stepped into the street, she was surprised by the number of people gathering at the far end near the river. Laughter filled the night air and there was a real feeling of togetherness and of hope for the coming year.

Polly smiled. This was *her* city, *her* people, and it was good to hear the laughter again and feel that everyone was looking towards a better future.

'Come on, let's go and find Vi and the others,' she said as she began to walk down the street with Miriam skipping beside her.

She scoured the crowd, squinting through the darkness for sight of her family. She could see William helping Bert to set up the fireworks. And there was Eddie with his arm around the waist of a girl from Scorer Street, but she couldn't see Violet . . .

Then she saw Leo. He too was scanning the crowd as if he was looking for someone. Her heart missed a beat and when his glance rested on her and held her gaze, he smiled and began to move towards her.

And Polly forgot all about her sister as she moved into Leo's arms.

Twenty-Six

'So, Polly Longden, when are we getting wed, then?'

On the evening of Polly's twentieth birthday the following April, when they were walking home from the theatre – a special treat – Leo at long last asked the question she'd been yearning to hear.

The whole evening had been special and now Polly realized why.

First Leo had taken her to a hotel for a grand meal and then on to the theatre to see 'The Outcast of the Family'. It was the first time she'd been inside Lincoln's Theatre Royal and the thrill of sitting in the plush seats and gaping about her at all the grandly dressed folk had been almost as exciting as watching the performance.

And now, as a finale to a wonderful evening, Leo was proposing. Well, she thought he was.

She giggled nervously and said pertly, 'You haven't asked me yet, sir.'

'D'you want me to go down on one knee in the street?'

'Of course,' she said teasing, not for one moment expecting him to do it.

But there, in the middle of the High Street, Leo turned to her and dropped to one knee. 'Miss Polly Longden, will you do me the great honour of becoming my wife?'

'Oh, Leo, yes – yes – *yes*!'

A short distance along the street, a group of men

were coming out of a pub. Seeing Leo on his knee, one nudged the others and a great guffaw of laughter echoed into the night air.

'By heck, lad, now you've done it. Shackled for life, you are.'

Leo scrambled to his feet and caught hold of Polly's hand. Together they began to run, the raucous laughter following them. But for Polly, though her heart was overflowing with happiness, the laughter had died when she'd seen at the back of the group of men, the devastated face of Roland Spicer.

'Come on, Vi, you're going to be late for work if you don't get up now.'

Polly was still floating on air and bursting to share her news with her sister. But all she got was a low groan and a muffled, 'Leave me alone, I'm ill.'

'Ill?' Fear clutched Polly's heart. Ever since the epidemic and Sarah's death, any sign of illness in a member of the family brought terror to the girl. She pushed the bedroom door wider and approached the bed. Gently, she pulled the covers down and squinted in the half-light of early morning into the pale face huddled beneath the bedclothes.

'I've been sick again.'

'Again? What do you mean – again?'

'It happened yesterday – and the day before. Oh, Poll – ' Violet's eyes were terrified – 'is it the typhoid?'

'No, no,' Polly tried valiantly to make her tone sound reassuring, but inwardly she was as frightened as her sister was. 'You ain't got a headache, have you?'

'N-no.'

'Tummy pains or a cough?'

'No, no.'

'And there ain't a rash?'

Violet shook her head.

Polly bit her lip, staring down at the girl lying wan and lethargic in the bed. 'You'd better see the doctor 'cos I don't know what it is.'

'We can't afford a doctor, Poll, and I can't stay off work neither.' She pulled herself up off the pillows and swung her feet to the floor, but the moment she stood upright she began to retch again. Polly flew to lift the bowl from the washstand and thrust it under her sister's face. But nothing came up and, after a moment, Violet lay back against the pillows.

'Get me a bit of dry toast, Poll. Maybe if I just have something in me stomach.'

A memory stirred in Polly's head. 'Get me a bit of dry toast, love, will you?' It was her mother's voice she was hearing from the past. Polly had been just thirteen and had carried the toast up to her mother's bedroom before going off to school. And then, only weeks later, Sarah had told all the family that she was to have another baby; the baby that had been Miriam.

And now here was Violet asking for dry toast.

'Oh no – no!' Polly whispered as her legs gave way beneath her and she sat down heavily on the end of the bed, staring at Violet.

'What?'

'Toast,' Polly said in a daze. 'You – you feel you want some toast?'

'Yes. What's wrong with that? But if you're too busy to bring me some, then I'll—'

'Oh, Vi, it's not that. It's—. Vi, when did you last have your Auntie Rose?'

'Eh?' Violet looked startled. 'I don't know – weeks ago.'

'How many?'

Violet shrugged. She wrinkled her forehead, trying to remember, but still unconcerned, whilst Polly's fear swelled.

'Vi, has Micky been doing – you know – to you?'

Now the younger girl was puzzled. 'I don't know what you mean.'

Oh Lord, Polly thought. She doesn't know. I should have told her ages ago. If she's pregnant – and I think she is – it'll be my fault because I've left her in ignorance. Not for the first time since their mother's death did Polly feel the burden of responsibility heavy on her shoulders.

Quietly and calmly, she explained how babies were made and as her voice faded away, Violet began to cry hysterically. 'Why didn't you tell me before? Oh, Polly, you should have told me! Micky said it was all right – that I was his girl. He said he'd be careful. I – I didn't know he meant *that*. I thought he meant he wouldn't hurt me.'

'When, Vi? When did he—?'

Between hiccuping sobs, Violet said, 'The first time was New Year's Eve. We was at his place. Everyone else was out in the street, counting down to the New Year. I – I was a bit tipsy . . .' Her voice faded away.

Polly remembered the night so well. Standing in the dark street with Leo's arms around her. He'd worked over Christmas and so had the night off. Together they'd watched the fireworks that Bert Fowler was letting off at the end of the street, watching the bright shower of sparks cascading into the night sky and Leo whispering in her ear. 'I love you, Polly Longden. Happy New Year.'

But now those wonderful memories were tarnished by what Violet was telling her. Whilst Polly had been so happy, Micky Fowler had taken advantage of her naive and innocent sister.

'The *first* time? Do you mean you've let him do it again since? How many times?'

Fresh tears welled and Violet screwed up her face. 'Whenever we was alone somewhere. When you went out with Leo and – and Dad was in the pub and – and . . .'

Violet threw herself against the pillow and wept. Stiffly, Polly rose from the bed and went downstairs.

Gone was her delirious happiness of the previous night. Once more she would carry the blame for the tragedy that had befallen the family.

And this time there'd be the shame to bear too.

Twenty-Seven

'Oh, Mrs Halliday, whatever am I to do?'

Bertha bit her lip, debating whether to tell the distraught girl her own sad little story. Even now the memory of that dreadful day when her grandfather had disowned her was as sharp as if it had happened yesterday. 'What will yar dad do, love? Will he throw her out?'

'I – I don't know.' Tears flooded down Polly's face as much for herself as for her sister.

Bertha pushed a cup of tea across the table and sat down opposite. 'Want me to take a look at her?'

Polly raised her tear-streaked face. 'Oh, would you?'

'Course I will. Better keep it in the family for a bit, eh?'

Fresh tears welled. 'I – I was going to become part of your family. Leo asked me to marry him last night.'

'Aw, lass, that's wonderful. Me an' Seth think the world of you.'

But Polly was shaking her head. 'He won't want to marry me now, will he? I mean, it wouldn't look good for him, would it?'

'Well, there's no denying you've got a bit of trouble coming to your door, but it's happened before and it'll happen again. Mek no mistake about that. But he won't let that stand in his way, if I know my Leo.'

'It's all my fault.'

'*Your* fault? What on earth do you mean, Poll?'

'I – I never told her about – you know – about *it*. Mam told me when I got me Auntie Rose for the first time, but Violet was too young. I should have told her everything when she started, but – but I didn't.'

'You mustn't blame yourself, love. Violet might not have recognized the symptoms of pregnancy, Poll, but she knew well enough how it came about, believe you me, even if she pretends otherwise. Working in that shop with all them girls, she couldn't *not* know. And as for young Micky – ' Bertha snorted – 'he knew just what he was doing. Thought all his birthdays 'ad come at once when he found a willing young lass. Well, he's had his fun, now he'll have to stand by her. I'll see Hetty Fowler and tell her what's what.'

'Oh dear, do be careful, Mrs Halliday. Mr Fowler's got such a temper . . .' Her voice faded away and she stared, wide-eyed, at the woman opposite. 'Oh dear, what'll happen when me dad finds out?' she whispered.

Bertha nodded grimly. 'There'll be a rumpus in this street and no mistake.'

'I'll bloody kill the little tyke.'

William was in a rage – as fierce a temper as Polly had ever seen him. Miriam and Stevie had scuttled upstairs. Violet was sitting huddled in a chair by the fire and Eddie was standing near her, as if to protect his sister, should their father vent his anger on her.

Polly stood on the hearthrug facing her father, though her insides were quaking. He shook his fist at Violet, but then he rounded on Polly. 'This is your fault. Letting her roam the streets at night. And yourn.' He jabbed his finger towards Eddie now. 'Bringing that little bugger into this house in the first place. By, I'll have me say with him – and his father.'

William turned on his heel and slammed out of the house.

'Go after him, Eddie.'

'Not likely. I'm not going to get me nose bloodied by Mr Fowler. He's a brute when he's mad. Worse than Dad and that's sayin' summat.'

'Then I'll go myself,' Polly muttered and rushed out into the warm spring evening after William.

He was striding down the street towards the house on the left-hand side at the end nearest the river, where the Fowlers lived, outrage in every step.

'Dad – Dad,' she cried as she ran after him. 'Don't – please don't.'

'You keep out of this, girl,' he flung back over his shoulder. 'You've done enough. Or rather you haven't done enough to stop it.'

Hurt by his words, Polly slowed to a walking pace. She still followed him, but now she kept her distance as William hammered on the front door and bellowed. 'Fowler, Fowler, come out here. I know you're in there.'

Only minutes earlier the two men – Bert Fowler and William – had been drinking in the pub with their mates. Now William was baying for blood and he wasn't bothered whose it was. Father or son, it made no difference to him, just so long as their name was 'Fowler'.

The door was flung open and Bert's burly figure stood there. 'What's to do, Will?'

'I'll tell you what's to do, Bert,' William spat, shaking his fist at the big man. 'Your lad's got my girl in the family way.'

Bert reached out and grasped William's collar, almost hoisting him up off the ground. 'You what?'

'You're choking me,' William gasped.

'I'll choke ya, ya bleeder, saying things like that about my family. Now, get yarsen away.' He released his grip and William staggered back. 'And we'll say no more about it.'

William was panting, but still he was not about to give in, even faced with the bear-like man in front of him.

'He's got to do right by her, Bert. I'll not see her shamed and do nowt.'

'She should have thought of that before she opened her legs for him.'

Polly gasped at Bert Fowler's crudity and covered her mouth with her hand. Suddenly, Bert glanced towards her.

'You? Is it *you*? Ah well, now, if it's young Polly, that's a different matter.'

'What d'you mean "a different matter"?'

Bert laughed, a deep rumbling sound. 'We all likes Poll and our Micky'd be over the moon to marry *'er*, but I thought she was walking out with the copper, Seth's lad.'

'She is.'

Bert frowned. 'Then what's she doing—?'

'It's not Polly,' William's tone was scathing as if it was preposterous that the other man could even think such a thing about Polly. 'It's Violet.'

'Huh! It would have to be her, wouldn't it? Well, I can tell you now, Will Longden, my lad'll never marry that little trollop. Not in a million years.' Bert laughed cruelly. 'How would he know the little bastard was his anyway?'

William threw himself at the bigger man, his anger

giving him strength. He grasped Bert's waistcoat and hauled him out into the street. Now the two men were locked in battle, slugging it out, blow for blow.

'Dad – no. Stop it! Mr Fowler, please—'

She ran forward and thrust herself between them, but caught a glancing blow from her father's fist, aimed at Bert's jaw.

She screamed and fell to the ground, but both men were so incensed they hardly noticed what had happened. Suddenly, Bert grasped the slighter man around the waist, picked him up and carried him towards the riverbank. He hoisted William up and threw him into the water.

'No, no,' Polly screamed. 'He can't swim. Oh, Dad – *Dad*!' She scrambled up and ran to the riverbank. She could hardly see anything through the dusk, only the black water, but she could hear the splashing and a gurgling as William fought for his life.

Bert stood beside her, searching the murky water and breathing heavily. 'Stupid bugger. He shouldn't have said what he did about our Micky.'

'Save him.' Polly grabbed Bert's arm and tried to push him towards the water. 'He can't swim.' The splashing was less now, as if William had already given up the battle.

Footsteps pounded down the street behind her and then Leo was beside her, flinging off his jacket and plunging into the water. For a moment he floundered and then his head disappeared beneath the surface as he tried to find Will. It seemed an age to Polly, yet it was less than a minute before Leo's head broke the surface. Gasping for air, he hauled William's limp body up and towards the bank. Polly and Bert scrambled down and pulled them out.

'Dad, *Dad*!' Polly shrieked, but her father wasn't moving.

Leo, still panting hard, rolled William over onto his front and then, astride him, began pumping the prone figure on his back. River water gushed from William's mouth and, miraculously it seemed to the terrified girl, her father coughed and spluttered – and began to breathe. Leo ceased his pumping and fell to one side, lying on his back, breathing hard.

As the two men began to recover their breath, Leo sat up. 'Now, what's going on here? I may not be on duty but I'll not have this sort of thing happening under my nose.'

Polly pulled her father to his feet. 'Come on, let's get you home. You'll catch your death out here. You too, Leo.'

'I want to know what's going on,' Leo said stubbornly, though he got to his feet and picked up his jacket.

As Polly dragged her father away from the scene, William, with surprising strength after his ordeal, shook his fist at Bert. 'This ain't finished yet, Bert Fowler.'

'Oh yes, it is,' Leo said firmly, stepping between them and taking William's other arm. 'Whatever it is, it's done.'

And with that he marched William up the street.

Polly cast a last despairing glance at the grim-faced Bert and knew that, whatever Leo said, this wasn't over by a long way.

Twenty-Eight

'I'll see you later,' Leo muttered as he left them outside their door and strode back down the street to his own home.

'See what you've caused?' Polly rounded on Violet still sitting huddled by the fire. 'Shift out the way and let Dad get near the fire. In fact, go to bed. Get out of my sight. Dad nearly drowned 'cos of you. If it hadn't been for Leo . . .'

Violet gave a sob, shot out of the chair and ran upstairs. They could hear her distraught weeping as she went.

Suddenly, the fight seemed to go out of William and he stood on the hearthrug, still dripping the dirty river water.

'Get them wet things off, Dad. I'll fetch the tin bath from the scullery. You'd better have a good wash. No knowing what's in that mucky river.'

She shuddered as she hurried to get the bath, silently praying that her father hadn't caught the dreaded disease from his dip in the River Witham.

She helped her father to bathe, washing his back and his hair for him just as her mother would have done. William was stunned, moving mechanically and hardly bothering to hide his nakedness from his daughter, though Polly kept her eyes averted as best she could.

When he was dry and sitting back in his chair dressed

181

in clean vest and trousers and wrapped in a blanket, Polly made him some hot cocoa and added a generous measure of whisky from the bottle in the sideboard. There had always been a small bottle of the fiery spirit in the house – for medicinal purposes only, Sarah had decreed. Though Polly had always suspected that both her parents took a nip now and again.

'Oh, Poll, what are we going to do?'

It was the same question that Polly had posed to Bertha Halliday and now she gave the woman's answer. 'Our Violet's not the first, Dad, and she won't be the last, so – we deal with it. As a family. Never mind that toe-rag, Micky Fowler. We'll look after her – and her bairn.' She took a deep breath and her voice trembled as she added, 'It's – it's what Mam would have said, isn't it?'

William raised sorrowful eyes and stared at her for a long moment before he said softly, 'Aye, it is, lass. It's what your mam would have wanted.'

As she slipped into bed beside Violet and lay staring into the darkness, Polly realized that in only twenty-four hours her life had gone from the height of happiness to the depths of despair. For she could see that there was no way that Leo would want to marry her now.

'If she's old enough to get herself pregnant, then she's old enough to look after the house, her baby and the rest of the family.' Leo was angry when he found out what the two men had been fighting about. 'It's time you had a life of your own, Polly. A life with me –' he waved his arm to encompass the whole house and everyone in it – 'away from this lot.'

With her whole being, Polly yearned to do just that, but in a small voice she said, 'But it's my fault she's – she's in the family way.'

'*Your* fault? How d'you make that out?'

'I never told her about – about – well, you know what.'

'That's not your job,' Leo began hotly. 'That's her—'

He stopped, appalled at what he'd been about to say, completely forgetting in the heat of the moment that there was no mother in this sorry household and that Polly, young though she was, was still expected to fill Sarah's shoes. That she'd failed in certain aspects was not, to Leo's mind, her fault. But he could see that she was carrying yet another heavy burden of guilt.

He sighed. 'If only me mam had known, she'd have talked to her.'

Polly laughed wryly. 'Talk to Violet? You might as well talk to that brick wall for all the notice she'd take. I did try, Leo, but obviously not hard enough.'

He took her hand in his, his anger dying as he saw how devastated Polly was. 'Chin up, love. We'll think of something. In the meantime, we need to go shopping for a ring. And, I suppose,' he added with a wry smile, 'I ought to ask your father's permission.'

Polly tried to smile too but, at the moment, she couldn't think of any way out and her dream of happiness as Leo's wife, with a family of their own, was fading fast. Would he, with his rigid principles, really want to ally himself to a family who fought, who trod close to the edge of the law at times and who now had an illegitimate baby coming?

'What's going to happen about me dad and Mr Fowler? Are you – are you going to charge them?'

Leo's mouth tightened. 'Not this time, Poll, but I'll have to give them both an official warning. Just 'cos I live in this street doesn't mean I can let folk get away with anything. If me own dad did something, I'd have to run him in. I know that and so does he. It's how it is when you join the police force, Poll. I can't let friends and neighbours make a monkey out of me and they'll just have to understand that.'

Polly shuddered, thinking not of her father but of Eddie. She was sure he stepped close to the edge of the law now and again and if Leo should find out . . .

She made up her mind to have a quiet word with her brother. She couldn't stop him doing whatever he wanted, but she could warn him of the consequences should he be caught. In Eddie's mind, she was sure, he thought that his connection with Leo would protect him. But it wouldn't: Leo had made that very clear.

'I don't think Micky'll marry you, Vi.'

Polly broke the news to her sister the following morning after William and Eddie had gone to work.

Violet raised tearful, red-rimmed eyes. 'Then it's the workhouse, is it?'

'Don't be silly. We'll look after you.'

'What about Dad?'

'He's angry and upset – 'course he is – but he'll stand by you. We all will.'

'Did he say so?'

'Sort of.' Polly bit her lip and then blurted out, 'I reminded him it's what Mam would have wanted.'

Violet smiled tremulously. 'Mam would have half killed me, wouldn't she?'

'Probably,' Polly agreed briskly. 'But then she'd have hugged you and told you it'd be all right.'

'But it won't, will it, Poll? I'm a fallen woman now. Who'd ever want me with a little – little bastard in tow?'

'Violet Longden, don't you ever – *ever* – use that filthy word again in this house. Your baby will be loved and cared for by all of us and don't you forget it.'

Violet sniffled and fresh tears welled in her eyes. 'Why are you so good to me, Poll, when all I've ever done is be horrible and difficult?'

Polly put her arm around Violet's shoulders and gave her the hug she knew their mother would have done. 'Because we're sisters – family – that's why. And families stick together no matter what.'

They were brave words spoken by a heartbroken young girl who faced her own bleak future because of what had happened. And they were words which were to haunt her in the years to come.

'We can still get married, Poll. Maybe in a year or so. By then Violet will be coping with her baby and she can look after the rest of the family too. Stevie's getting a big lad now. He's very sensible for his age, you know. What is he now? Eleven?'

Polly nodded. 'He was eleven a few days after my birthday. We were both born in April.'

'And Miriam—'. Leo smiled. Everybody smiled when they spoke of Miriam. The baby who had never known her mother had grown into a merry six-year-old, the darling of the family. Polly had never spoiled her, but the child was naturally biddable and loving. She was the only one who'd ever dared to climb on William's knee when he came home from work, exhausted and crotchety. But Miriam could always tease a smile out of him.

'Miriam will be another year older,' Leo went on. 'Old enough to do little jobs for Violet. And she'll love there being a little one around the house.'

Polly wasn't so sure. Would Miriam, maybe Stevie too, be jealous of a newcomer who took everyone's attention?

'And we'll mind we get a house close by so that you can come in and help whenever you want to.'

'But I'll go back to work when—'

'Oh no, you won't. I earn quite enough for us both to live on.' He kissed the tip of her nose. 'Besides, you'll have your hands full looking after me.'

'But—'

The dream of becoming a teacher had never quite gone away, not even through the last six years when she'd been forced to care for the family. But now she was being forced to choose between her ambition and the love of her life.

Surely, she could have both . . .

'No buts, darling,' Leo interrupted her daydreams. Then more seriously he added, 'It's not easy being a copper's wife, love. You have to distance yourself a bit from other folks and then there's the shift patterns. I'll be wanting meals at all sorts of funny hours of the day – and the night.'

Polly threw her arms around him and kissed him soundly, as her aspirations were buried beneath her overwhelming love for him. 'It would be wonderful,' she murmured, 'to have my own home and just my husband to care for.'

'Never mind would be. It *will* be,' Leo promised.

Twenty-Nine

The coronation of King George V took place in Westminster Abbey on 22 June 1911, and the country celebrated in various ways over the next few weeks. In Lincoln a sports event was arranged for Saturday, 1 July on the West Common. But to the disappointment of many, especially Stevie and Miriam, who'd looked forward to it ever since Polly had promised she would take them, the event was postponed because of bad weather.

'Why won't you let us go, Polly? It's only rain.'

'It's not on.' Polly ruffled Miriam's hair. 'It's no good going. Nobody'll be there.'

Tears ran down Miriam's cheeks. 'Not never?'

Polly knelt down in front of her little sister, the child who was more like her own than a sibling. She'd cared for her since her birth and felt as if she were her mother. 'Don't cry, ducky. "Postponed" means put off. They say it's going to be next Saturday instead.'

Miriam began to smile through her tears. 'So we can go next week?'

Polly nodded. 'But only if you're good, mind.'

Miriam clapped her hands. 'Oh, I will be, I will be. And Stevie too? He can come?'

'Of course he can. That is . . .' She stopped. No one else in the family knew that at this very moment Stevie had gone in search of a Saturday job with, of all people,

187

Mr Wilmott, the greengrocer on the High Street. Only Polly knew.

'I reckon you'll get short shrift, love,' Polly had said when he'd told her his plans. 'Mr Wilmott got rid of our Eddie because, well, because he didn't want him any more.' She'd no intention of telling Stevie just why Eddie had left the man's employ. Mr Wilmott might tell him himself, of course, but Stevie wasn't going to hear it from Polly's lips.

'But I'm not our Eddie,' Stevie had countered quietly.

Polly had regarded the boy solemnly. He'd grown so much in the last couple of years; she still had trouble keeping him in clothes and shoes. But he looked much older than his eleven years and had a maturity far beyond that age too. Perhaps, she thought, if Mr Wilmott was a fair-minded man he would give the boy a chance and not judge him by his brother's behaviour.

'Stevie'll be back home in a bit,' Polly said now to Miriam. 'And we can ask him.'

But far more important matters were weighing on Polly's mind than the coronation celebrations or even Stevie's job. Violet had no longer been able to hide her condition and she'd been forced to give in her notice at the store.

'For heaven's sake don't wait to be dismissed,' Polly had warned her. 'If you ever want to go back, they'd never have you if you get the sack. They'd remember.'

'They'd never have me back there anyway,' Violet said morosely. 'They'll find out and they'd never employ an unmarried mother, now would they?'

Polly had sighed heavily. 'No, I suppose not.'

'I tell you what, though – ' Violet had brightened visibly as a thought struck her. 'After I've had it, we could pretend it's yours and then I could go back.'

Polly had gaped at her, appalled by such a suggestion. Really, the girl was impossible. Violet had no thought for her sister's reputation and would have happily put the blame on Polly just so that she, Violet, could keep her fancy job.

'Oh no, you don't, my girl. I've given up enough for this family. What on earth would Leo say to such a suggestion and besides, how would you explain an absence from work of about three months at least?'

Violet had pouted. 'I could be ill. I could get Dr Fenwick to write them a letter saying I was – I was suffering from – from – well, he'd think of something.'

'Don't be ridiculous, Violet,' Polly snapped. From being sympathetic at first with her sister's predicament, feeling herself partly to blame, Polly was fast losing patience with her. Since Micky Fowler had refused to marry her – indeed he never came near the house now – and the Longden family had rallied round and promised to look after her, Violet had begun to take advantage of her family's goodness and had returned to her selfish, self-centred ways.

Polly leant closer as she said firmly, 'Doctors don't lie for their patients, Vi.'

Violet stared at her with wide eyes. 'But we *pay* for his services, Poll. Of course he would.'

'No, he wouldn't and don't you ever dare to suggest such a thing to anyone.' She lowered her voice as she added, 'For your information, Dr Fenwick never charged us anything when – when Mam died or Dad was sick. And I've heard it said that he didn't charge a lot of his patients at the time of the typhoid. He's a good man is Dr Fenwick, so don't you go saying such wicked things about him. D'you hear me?'

Violet didn't answer but glowered at her sister as her wonderful idea was torn apart.

The following morning she handed in her notice, telling the head of the millinery department that she had secured a better job.

'Well, I can't think where you've found a better job than at Mawer and Collingham's,' Miss Carr had sniffed.

'It's a smaller emporium.' Violet had elaborated on her own invention, adding slyly, 'I shall have more responsibility than I have here and the – the owner has promised to learn me – to teach me – how to make hats.'

Miss Carr had eyed her sceptically. 'And where is this wonderful place of employment, might I ask?'

'Oh, I couldn't possibly say, Miss Carr. She asked me to keep it completely confidential.' Artfully, Violet leant closer and whispered. 'She wants to get rid of the girl she's got now and she doesn't want her to get to hear that she's being replaced.'

'I – see,' Miss Carr said slowly. 'So you're giving a week's notice, I take it?'

'I'm afraid so,' Violet said regretfully and this feeling was real; she was very sorry to leave her position. She'd thoroughly enjoyed working in the grand store and would miss mixing with a better class of people than she believed her own family to be. And she said as much, adding pertly, 'But if you feel you could give me a reference, Miss Carr, I'd be most grateful.'

'I thought you said you'd already acquired another post.'

'Oh, I have, I have,' Violet said airily and then added flatteringly, 'but a reference from someone like you, Miss Carr, might be so useful in the future.'

'Mm.' The woman regarded her for a moment and then appeared to relent. 'Well, you have been a good and willing worker and whilst you're leaving me in something of a predicament – ' she sighed dramatically – 'how I hate having to train someone new up – it would be churlish of me to refuse you.'

'*Thank you*, Miss Carr.'

As Violet walked home at the end of her final day at the store, carrying the precious letter of recommendation in her handbag, she couldn't help congratulating herself on how she'd been able to dupe the older woman.

And now as Polly tried to comfort Miriam over the postponed outing – a special treat for the Longden family – she was worrying how she was going to manage without Violet's contribution, albeit reluctantly given, to the family's budget.

Stevie, even if he got the job, would only be giving her a few pennies a week, but every little was going to help.

There was a knock at the door and Polly jumped. When she opened it, she found Dottie Fowler there.

'Hello, Polly. Can Miriam play 'cos Mam says we can't go to the cel'brations on the common next week.'

'Of course you can, Dottie. Come on in. You can both play in the bedroom, but don't make a mess up there,' she called after them as they pounded up the stairs.

Polly busied herself making tea for her father when he came home, but she was anxiously listening for Stevie's return.

He came at last, beaming from ear to ear. 'He's given me a chance. A month's trial he said.' His expression sobered and he frowned. 'He said, "So long as you're not like that scallywag of a brother of yourn". What did he mean, Poll?'

Polly sighed. She'd no choice now but to explain it to Stevie. When she had finished, Stevie looked shocked. 'I knew he was a bit of a tearaway. Likes a drink on a Sat'day night and isn't above getting into a fight now and again. But – but I didn't think he – he was a thief.'

'He said he thought it was all right because Mr Wilmott had given us vegetables and fruit that were going off and that he couldn't sell.' She smiled wistfully at the memory of those dark, troubled times and the kindness of the man she hardly knew. 'But Eddie started taking stuff that was still saleable and Mr Wilmott sacked him. He had no choice, but he's a good man to give you a chance. I hoped he would because you're nothing like your brother.'

'No,' Stevie said vehemently, 'I'm not.' He paused and then asked, 'So you don't think I'll be getting any unsaleable stuff? Because, to be honest, I thought that would help us out more'n anything. I mean, I won't get paid much.'

'You'll have to see. But you must only bring home what Mr Wilmott gives you himself.'

Stevie nodded vigorously.

In the middle of the week Leo said, 'I'm taking you out tomorrow night. Violet can stay with the youngsters. She owes you that much.'

Polly clapped her hands like an excited schoolgirl. 'Where are we going?'

Leo tapped her nose playfully. 'You'll see. It's a surprise. But it's not a meal, so have your tea first.'

'Best frock, is it?'

'Absolutely!'

When Leo called for her the following evening, they

walked up the street together arm in arm, declaring proudly to the whole world that they were 'walking out together'. Standing in the doorway, Violet watched them go, scowling and resentful that she was forced to stay in when everyone else was out enjoying a fine, summer's evening. She glanced down the street and saw Micky leaning against the wall of his own home. As he raised his hand to wave, Violet stuck her nose in the air, turned away and flounced back into the house, slamming the door so hard that the sound echoed down the street, reaching, as she'd fully intended it should, Micky's ears.

But Micky Fowler only smiled.

Leo and Polly turned to walk up the High Street.

'We're going to the Corn Exchange. They're showing pictures of the coronation. I thought you'd like to see them.'

Polly beamed. 'Oh, Leo, how lovely.'

For the next hour or so, Polly and Leo sat in the darkness holding hands, watching the jerky scenes of the procession in London on its way to Westminster Abbey.

'It's the King,' she whispered. 'Oh, Leo, look at all his beautiful robes. Is that what they call ermine?'

Leo smiled indulgently at her obvious enjoyment. It warmed his heart to see his Polly so happy. He squeezed her hand, silently vowing that he would always do his best to make her happy for the rest of their lives.

Then came the Royal Naval Review at Spithead with the ships going through a series of, what looked like, to Polly, very complicated manoeuvres. And finally, there was the royal yacht and the King himself.

'He does look very grand,' Polly whispered, 'but so serious.'

'I expect it's a serious business being King,' Leo murmured. 'A lot of responsibilities and they say he has a very strong sense of duty.'

'Just like you, then,' Polly teased and hugged his arm to her.

Later, as they walked home through the dusk, Leo drew her into the shadows, put his arms around her and kissed her long and hard. 'Oh, Poll, let's get married soon. I do love you so. Don't keep me waiting. I know I said a year, but let's do it soon. Please, Polly.'

She kissed him back soundly and whispered, 'Oh, yes, Leo. Yes, please.'

The following Saturday – the day of the postponed coronation festivities – Stevie was due to start his new job.

'Can't you come with us to the cel'brations?' Miriam wailed afresh. Stevie knelt in front of her and took her hands. 'I've got a job with the greengrocer along the High Street and I start today. I'm sorry to miss the fun – I was looking forward to it too – but this is much more important.'

Miriam sniffed and nodded. Young though she was, she already knew that the family had little enough to live on, and she'd also understood that Violet wasn't going to her job at that lovely shop any more, though the little girl did not understand the reason for it. Not yet.

'So,' Stevie was saying, 'you go with Polly and Dottie and bring me back something nice. All right?'

Miriam nodded, her curls bouncing.

So, whilst Stevie, his stomach churning with excitement and a little trepidation, set off to begin his first job, Polly, with Miriam and Dottie skipping along beside her, set off for a day of jollification to celebrate the crowning of the new King.

Thirty

Stevie arrived home that evening, jubilant and bubbling with the success of his first day in proper work and expecting to be greeted by happy faces after their day's outing. He struggled in with a box of half-rotten vegetables, declaring at once, 'Mr Wilmott gave me these, Poll. I promise.' He dumped the box on the table and grinned at the three girls sitting either side of the fireplace. His smile faded.

'What? What's the matter?' When no one answered him, he said again, 'He *did* give me this stuff, Poll. Honest.'

'It's not that, love,' Polly said dully.

'Then – what is it?'

Violet, who hadn't been able to go because her condition was now very noticeable, said, almost with a smug satisfaction, 'There was trouble at the celebrations. A group of louts started a ruckus.'

'They was fighting, Stevie.' Miriam put in, her face still streaked with salty tears. She hiccuped as she added, 'I tried to bring you summat – a balloon, but it got bursted.' Fresh tears welled. 'A horrible boy bursted it.'

Stevie stroked her hair. 'Don't worry about me, love. I'm just so sorry your day's been spoilt.' He glanced again at Polly, raising his eyebrows in question. 'But you're both safe. That's all that matters.'

Polly met his gaze with troubled eyes. 'Yes, *we're* all right.'

'Tell me about it,' Stevie said, sitting down and preparing to listen. He could see that both his sisters were upset and needed to talk about it. 'I heard they held some of the events on Wednesday after last week's postponement. And everything went off all right then. So – what went wrong today?'

'There were *thousands* of people there, Stevie,' Miriam said, her tears drying now she had a willing listener. 'All milling about and hardly any policemen.' She cast a glance at Polly. 'Leo was there. We saw him, but I don't think he saw us. Least, he didn't come and speak to us.'

Violet laughed. 'He wouldn't want to be seen speaking to troublemakers.'

'*We* weren't making any trouble,' Miriam said indignantly. 'But your Micky was. He—'

'That's enough, Miriam,' Polly said as Violet's face fell.

'He's not my Micky any more, it seems,' she muttered.

'What caused the trouble then?' Stevie said, trying to divert the conversation away from Micky Fowler again.

Polly frowned. 'I'm not sure, but someone said it was because they were trying to charge for admission to the grandstand when the sports were supposed to be free for everyone.'

'And the crowd got nasty?'

'Well, just some of them, I suppose. But when a few of them started protesting others joined in and – and it sort of spread. Folks were milling around the winning post and the races couldn't take place properly. The officials seemed helpless.'

'A policeman came on horseback, Stevie,' Miriam put

in. 'And someone – ' here she cast a swift glance at Violet before adding – 'threw a stone, or something, and it hit the horse's head.'

'After that it was just chaos.' Polly took up the tale. 'The crowd flooded onto the course. And more folk started throwing things. They couldn't run the races properly and—'

'And Polly said we should come home. Out of the way.'

'Quite right too.' Stevie squatted down in front of her and took her hands. 'I know it must have been awful to see, but . . .'

'Stevie – Eddie was there.' Polly glanced briefly at Violet before adding, 'With Micky.'

Before she could say more, Miriam cried, 'It was Micky who threw the stone at the horse. We saw him. And our Eddie was with him.'

Horror-struck, Stevie stared at Polly. 'Were they – I mean – did the police – ' he swallowed painfully – 'arrest them?'

Violet screamed. 'Oh no! No! Not Micky.'

Polly and Stevie stared at her.

'Oh, never mind about your *brother*,' Polly said bitterly. 'All you can think about is the lad who's shamed you.'

Violet burst into noisy tears, whilst Stevie said gently, 'Poll, don't have a go at her. It's not her fault.' He paused and then asked hesitantly, 'Did Leo see what happened?'

'I don't know. He could have done.'

'Then, if I was you, I'd expect a visit later.'

*

When William came home, Polly whispered to the family, 'Not a word to Dad. Not yet.' They all nodded agreement and tried to carry on as if nothing had happened, but news travelled fast and bad news, it seemed, even faster.

'Heard there was a bit o' trouble at the racecourse then.' He glanced at Polly and Miriam. 'You both all right?'

'Yes, we're fine,' Polly said swiftly, setting his tea before him. There was no point in lying to him or trying to make out it was nothing much. He'd hear the news all too soon and it would no doubt be reported in the local paper. 'We came away, didn't we, Miriam?'

The young girl nodded and dipped her head so that her long hair hid her face. 'They bursted my balloon,' she muttered.

'What did you say, lass?'

Polly cast a warning glance at her sister. 'Her balloon got burst – the one she was bringing home for Stevie. She's upset about it, that's all.'

At the mention of Stevie William's attention was diverted. 'And how did you get on today, son? All right?'

'Fine, Dad. Mr Wilmott gave me some veg.'

'It's what you're eating now,' Polly put in. 'I cut all the bad bits out, but there was still enough for our teas.'

William nodded. 'Very nice too. He must be a nice bloke that Mr Wilmott. He was very good to us when Eddie worked for him. He must think a lot about our family. I don't know why Eddie ever left him. He'd got a good job there.' Polly held her breath. She'd never told her father the real reason behind Eddie's departure from Mr Wilmott's employ. But William answered his own question. 'Still, I expect he didn't want to be a delivery boy for ever.' He pointed his knife towards Stevie. 'But it's a good start for you, an' all. Just you mind you keep your nose clean and you'll do all right there.'

They ate in silence until they heard the noise of the door opening and Eddie sauntered into the room.

'Hello. Any tea going, Poll?'

Everyone, except William, stared at him. Then Polly, pulling herself together, said, 'Get on with your tea, Miriam.' Sitting beside her, she laid a warning hand on the girl's knee and, when Miriam looked up, put her forefinger to her lips. Then she rose and went into the scullery to fetch the meal she had plated up for Eddie, half-expecting that the food would be wasted; she had not thought to see him come home as though nothing had happened.

But only minutes later the feared and anticipated knock came. Leo, wearing his uniform, stood there.

'Where's Eddie?' he asked bluntly when Polly answered the door. 'And don't try to tell me he's not here because I've just seen him come in.'

Her eyes widened at his brusqueness. No smile of welcome, not even a 'Good evening, Polly.'

'H-having his tea in the kitchen with the rest of us. Why?'

Leo made to step across the threshold, but Polly put up her hand, palm outwards. 'Whoa, there. Just a minute, *Constable*.'

Leo's expression softened a little and she saw the smile quirk at the corner of his mouth. 'I'd just like a word with him, Poll. That's all.'

'Not while you're in your uniform, you don't,' Polly snapped. 'It's official, I presume.'

Leo sighed and said heavily, 'It's official. Please, let me just have a word with him?'

'Why, what's it about?'

'I think you know that only too well, Polly, don't you? You were there. I saw you with Miriam and the Fowlers' girl. You saw what happened. And if you've eyes in your head you'd have seen Eddie, an' all. Alongside the troublemakers.'

'I—'. She was tempted, very tempted, to lie. But she couldn't. It was not in her nature. As she'd said outright to Eddie. 'I'll not tell on you, but I'll never lie for you.' And now the moment she had dreaded was here.

She pulled the door wider and said heavily, 'You'd better come in.'

As she led him through into the kitchen the rest of the family all looked up. Only Eddie calmly continued eating his meal.

'Hello, Leo, lad,' William greeted him. 'What brings you here?'

'Official business, I'm afraid, Mr Longden.' Leo's glance rested on Eddie. 'Could I have a word with Eddie, if you please?'

''Course you can.' William pointed with his knife. 'There he is. Large as life and twice as ugly.'

'Eddie,' Leo began, 'perhaps this'd be better done in private.'

William frowned, sensing that perhaps all was not well. 'You can say anything you have to say in front of us all. There ain't no secrets in this family.'

If only that were true, Polly thought, her heart sinking. If Leo or any of his colleagues had seen Eddie

201

throwing stones, then surely he was about to be arrested?

'Sit down, lad, and tell us what this is all about,' William said.

'I prefer to stand, Mr Longden, thank you.'

'Suit yarsen,' William muttered and carried on eating, blithely unaware of the bombshell that Leo was about to drop.

'Eddie, I saw you on the common today at the celebrations. I saw you amongst the troublemakers and I saw you throw a stone at one of the policemen's horses.'

'Not me, Officer.' Eddie grinned. 'You must have been mistaken.'

'No, I wasn't, Eddie, because Micky Fowler was alongside you. You threw the first one and then he threw a second, the one that actually hit the horse.'

Eddie shrugged, still braving it out. 'Micky has other mates, y'know. It wasn't me.'

'Then can you tell me where you were between the hours of two and four this afternoon?'

Eddie frowned as if trying to remember. 'Out and about, but I didn't go anywhere near the racecourse.'

'You did, Eddie, we seed you,' Miriam piped up before Polly could lay a warning hand on her shoulder.

Eddie glared at his young sister. 'Then you need glasses an' all, our Miriam, 'cos I weren't there. See?'

Miriam quailed beneath his angry look, turned and buried her face in Polly's apron. Absently, Polly stroked the child's hair, but her attention was still on Eddie – and Leo.

'What's been going on?' Now William was getting heated. He stood up and turned to face Leo. 'How dare you come into this house and accuse my son?'

Leo held up his hand. 'Mr Longden, I have come here to warn Eddie, not to arrest him. Not this time, but if any of my colleagues saw him then it'll be out of my hands.' He turned back to face Eddie. 'I'm giving you an official caution, Eddie. I have to do that. You were seen amongst the troublemakers at a serious incident of public disorder.'

'You mean this is going to be recorded?' William said. 'He's going to have a criminal record?'

'No – no, I won't report it, but I am warning him. Any more trouble and I won't have any choice but to take the matter further.'

There was silence in the room as Leo nodded to them all, turned and left the room. No one – not even Polly – saw him to the door.

William sat down heavily. The silence lengthened until at last he asked, 'Were you there, Eddie?'

'Course I was. It was only a bit of fun.'

'I don't call fighting and throwing stones at the horses and jeering and shouting at the police fun,' Polly snapped.

Eddie glowered at her. 'No, well, you wouldn't, would you? Miss Goody-Two-Shoes with a copper for a boyfriend.'

'Fat chance there'll be of that now, I shouldn't wonder,' Polly muttered and, freeing herself from Miriam's clinging arms, she began to stack the dishes, clattering them together in her frustration and anger.

When, oh when, was this family ever going to think of her for once?

Thirty-One

In the July and August of 1911 the city suffered under a heatwave that was affecting the whole country and showed no signs of giving way. Day after day the temperatures soared into the nineties.

'Oh, it's so hot,' Miriam whined. 'Can I go and swim in the river with the others?'

'No, you can't,' Polly snapped, feeling frazzled herself. 'Want to catch typhoid like our mam did?'

The little girl's eyes widened and her lower lip trembled.

Contrite, Polly swept Miriam into her arms. 'Oh, I'm sorry. It's this heat. It's making everyone bad-tempered.' She felt the child's forehead. 'You are hot, aren't you?'

'I keep going to the lavvy and I feel sick,' Miriam wailed.

Now Polly was anxious. Rumour was rife that the hospitals were crowded with children suffering from heatstroke. One or two had even died, Polly had heard, and the thought terrified her.

'Go and lie down on your bed and I'll fetch some water to cool you down. You should keep drinking plenty and I'll sponge you down.'

'Will the water make me poorly, like it did Mam?'

'No, no, not now,' Polly reassured her swiftly. 'The water's quite safe for us to drink. I still boil it anyway.'

What she didn't tell her sister was that there were rumours there might be a shortage of water if this heatwave persisted and there was no rain.

It seemed that Polly and little Miriam were not the only ones made fractious by the heat. William arrived home in a state of excited agitation.

'We're going on strike.'

'What!' Polly stared at him in horror. 'What do you mean?'

'There's a national strike being called.'

'Who by?'

'The Transport Workers Federation.'

'And who are they when they're at home?' Polly slammed his evening meal in front of him, wishing she had the courage to tip it over his head.

Strike indeed! She wished she could go on strike and put her feet up if only for a day. But no, women were expected to carry on with the housework and look after the family, no matter what.

'What it says. It's a collection of several unions that banded together.' William grinned and thumped his fist on the table. 'Gives us more strength. More clout.'

'And who were you thinking of clouting? You'll end up in jail one of these days if you don't stop using them fists of yours. You and Mr Fowler both.'

William sprang up, towering over his daughter. 'You watch your tongue, girl. Just show a bit of respect for your father.'

Polly, all five foot nothing of her, squared up to him. 'I'll show you respect when you deserve it. Strike, indeed. Whatever next?'

Suddenly, William's anger died. He was strangely pensive as he said quietly now, 'You're so like your mam, Poll. That's just what she'd've said. Miriam might

205

look like her, but you've got her spirit. I pity the feller you marry, 'cos he'll never wear the trousers in his own house.'

Accustomed to her father's sudden mood swings, Polly smiled. 'Oh, I think Leo can stand up for himself, don't you?'

William eyed her, gave a grunt and then sat down. 'So – you reckon you're going to marry young Leo, do you? Bring a copper into the family. What d'you reckon our Eddie will think to that?'

'Eddie won't have any say in the matter,' she said sharply. She paused and then asked, 'So what's started all this?'

'You read the papers now, don't you?'

'When I've time.'

'Remember the seamen's strike back in June.'

'Ye-es.'

The seamen had gone on strike in the middle of June, joined by all the workers employed by shipping companies. Under the enormous strain that the strike was causing, by the end of the month the employers had had to give in to the union's demands. The seamen had won their battle and, encouraged by this, a wave of strikes hit Liverpool when the dockers walked out. In support, the seamen again walked out. The unrest had spread to transport workers and now, it seemed, the railway workers were involved.

She'd read all about it in the newspaper, but not for one moment had Polly envisaged trouble coming to Lincoln. This was the sort of thing that happened in other parts of the country, not in her city.

William was sitting gazing into the distance, making no move to start his meal.

'What's the matter, Dad? Aren't you hungry? I know

this heat makes you lose your appetite, but it's your favourite steak and kidney pie.'

'It's not that, Poll. It's just – well – there's going to be trouble. I can see it coming and if there is, then me and your Leo will be on opposite sides of the fence, so to speak.'

Polly stared at him in horror and then sank into a nearby chair as her legs gave way beneath her.

'I just hope you know what you're doing, Dad, that's all. You're getting a mite too friendly with Bert Fowler all of a sudden. He'll lead you astray, he—'

'Don't you think I'm man enough to make up me own mind? I don't need to follow what others say.'

'That's exactly what you are doing—'

'You mind your tongue, girl. I've told you afore, I won't have any cheek from you or else . . .'

Polly stood on the hearth and faced him, her arms folded in front of her. The unrelenting heat was getting to them all, making everyone fractious and quarrelsome. 'Oh aye, or else what, Dad? You'll throw me out? I don't think so. Where'd you be without me to do your cooking, your washing and cleaning the house to say nothing of looking after Stevie and Miriam? And, by the way, she's sick. But I don't expect you've had time to notice that, 'ave ya? Too busy organizing a strike so you can all have a nice few days' holiday.'

'It'll be no holiday, girl, if this goes ahead. There'll be no pay and if the employers—'

'What? What d'you mean, no pay? How do you expect me to feed a family of six on nothing? And there'll be another mouth to feed before long – in case you'd forgotten.'

William shot her an angry look. 'I only wish I could,' he muttered morosely, before adding, 'but the strike won't last long. They'll have to give in eventually.'

'Oh aye. Who? The employers – or the strikers?'

William glared at her again, but this time he made no reply.

'Where are you going?'

Polly grabbed her father's arm as he made for the door.

'Out.'

'I can see that, but where?'

'Nowt to do wi' you.'

'I think it is.'

He whirled round and for a moment she thought he was going to hit her. 'I said,' he muttered through gritted teeth, 'it's nowt to do wi' you.'

'You're going to join the picket line, aren't you?' The railway workers were now on strike and even workers from other trades had joined them. Picket lines were on duty near the level crossings on the High Street. Day after day the hot weather was unrelenting and a feeling of unrest and a strange excitement hung over the city.

'What if I am?'

Polly folded her arms and glared at him. 'Well, if you are, I wash me hands of you. I want nowt to do with any of it.'

For a brief moment William hesitated. Then his frown deepened and he shrugged his shoulders. 'Please yarsen.' He turned away and slammed the door behind him, leaving Polly staring after him.

Thirty-Two

'What's that noise?' Violet asked. 'It sounds like a swarm of bees. Oh, Poll, don't let bees get into the house. I hate bees.'

Polly cocked her head on one side to listen. 'They'll not get in here, Vi, I shouldn't worry.' Then she went to the door and opened it. Returning to the kitchen, she said, 'It looks like there's a lot of people at the top of the road. I'll just go and see what's going on.'

'It'll be the strikers, Poll.'

They exchanged a worried glance. 'And Dad's out there somewhere with them. And Eddie too, more than likely. What if . . . ?'

'You stay here, Vi. I don't think you'd better take your little walk tonight. And don't let either Stevie or Miriam leave the house.'

It was already gone nine o'clock and the two younger children were in bed; Miriam because of her age and Stevie because his work as delivery boy for Mr Wilmott tired him and he went willingly to bed now of his own accord, especially on a Friday night. The following day would be busy, there were always a lot of deliveries on a Saturday.

'Be careful, Poll,' Vi said, her voice quavering with anxiety. 'There might be trouble. Mr Fowler's bound to be there and if they've both been drinking . . .' The suffocating heat was affecting Violet, now nearing the final month of her pregnancy, badly. Only in the cool of late evening when it was dark did she venture out to get some fresh air. But tonight she was going nowhere.

Polly left the house and walked up the street. At the top end, near the High Street, she could see crowds milling about. She hesitated and then, making up her mind, walked on.

As she rounded the corner, she stopped and put her hand out to the nearest wall for support. The High Street was thronged with hundreds of people, mostly men, standing in groups. She edged her way along the wall, trying to find her father or Eddie. Slowly, she made her way along the fringe of the crowd until she came to the Midland station's level crossing, but she could see no sign of either of them. So, she moved on, further up the street until she came to the second level crossing, which served the Great Northern line.

She could see at once what was happening; the crowd were preventing the gates from being opened to allow two waiting trains to cross the High Street.

'This lot aren't all railwaymen,' she muttered. 'There's others here that have nothing to do with the strike. They're just here to cause trouble. Just like at the sports.'

Anxiously, she scanned the faces, searching for her father or Eddie, but now the light was fading and she couldn't pick out anyone she knew. Except Leo. Suddenly, she saw him standing in a group with other officers. She gasped as a senior officer shouted, 'Charge!' and the line of police moved forward, their batons raised.

To Polly's horror, as they reached the milling crowds they began to hit out indiscriminately. Men, a few women, and even one or two youngsters, tried to flee from the whirling sticks. A man fell to the ground, his forehead bleeding. One of the constables was hit on the head by a stone. Women's screams rent the air and men yelled and shook their fists, but the gates were opened and the first train edged its way forward.

Jeering and hooting from the crowd directed at the train driver and his colleagues now drowned the cries of fear. People crowded forward again, but both trains passed over the crossing and gathered speed. No doubt, Polly thought, the driver and his companions were relieved to escape safely.

Now that the trains had gone and the gates were opened once more for road users, Polly thought that the trouble would be over, but just then she heard the sound of breaking glass and saw that a mob of youths were throwing stones and bricks at the signal box. Through the gloom she saw the old signalman duck out of sight as a stone was hurled through the broken window and rattled onto the floor of the box.

Polly turned and hurried away, anxious now for her own safety. Nor did she want to be thought to be taking part in the demonstration that was rapidly getting out of hand. It was bad enough that members of her family were already involved, for amongst the hooligans throwing stones she had, at last, seen Eddie.

As she entered the house and closed the door, she leant against it. But there was no feeling of relief; William and Eddie were still out there in the thick of the commotion. Maybe, even at this moment, Leo was arresting them both.

'Poll? Is that you?' Violet called fearfully from the kitchen.

'Yes, I'm here,' Polly reassured her, moving into the room. 'But it's time you were in bed, Vi. You look done in.'

'How'm I expected to sleep with all that racket going on? What's happening?'

'Some trouble near the Great Northern crossing. There was a crowd of folk trying to stop a couple of trains passing, but the police came and they got through. I think folks are going home now, so off you go to bed and don't worry. I'm sure Dad and Eddie'll be back soon.'

'Did you see them? Are they all right? And Micky? Was Micky there too?'

'I caught sight of Eddie once, but not the others.'

Violet asked no more and heaved herself up out of her chair. 'I'll say goodnight then.'

As Violet mounted the stairs, it was not Micky Fowler or even her father or brother Polly was thinking about.

The image that filled her mind and haunted her sleep that night was the sight of Leo standing with raised baton, ready to charge on his own people.

The following morning Polly went out to do her Saturday morning shopping for the family as usual. She approached the High Street with trepidation, but this morning the streets seemed quiet, certainly more peaceful than the previous night. Stones and broken glass still littered the ground near the signal box that had been attacked, but at both the level crossings on the High Street there were policemen on duty. Pickets hung about the gates, jeering and hooting at the officers from time to time, but the constables ignored them stoically.

'I think the trouble's over,' Polly told Vi when she returned home. 'There's still folk about, but only the strikers and their genuine supporters. It seems quiet now, you know, orderly. I'll cook us a nice meal for tonight and maybe Dad and Eddie will stay at home and keep out of it.'

'Huh! Eddie stay in on a Saturday night? Fat chance!' Violet snorted. 'Nor Dad either. He'll not miss his pint at the George and Dragon.'

'As long as it's nowhere near where the trouble was last night. You know what he gets like when he's had a couple.'

'You'll not stop him if he wants to go and join in the fun.'

Polly rounded on her. 'Fun, you call it? It wasn't fun watching our own folk being charged by the police swinging their batons, I can tell you.'

'You didn't tell me that, Poll,' Violet said reproachfully. 'You made out there wasn't much trouble.'

'I – I didn't want you worrying.'

'What time did Dad an' Eddie come in?'

Polly sniffed with disapproval. 'After midnight and clattering about with no thought for others trying to sleep. It's a wonder they didn't wake Miriam. She's a light sleeper at the best of times.'

'Were they causing trouble?'

Polly hesitated and then sighed. There was little point in lying; Violet would find out soon enough. 'Eddie was chucking stones about, but I didn't see Dad at all. I don't know where he was.'

Violet turned pale. 'You don't think he got arrested? Or – or hurt?'

'Well, he wouldn't have come home if he had, would he?'

'Are you sure he did? I haven't seen sign or sight of him this morning. Only Eddie, who grabbed a bite of breakfast and rushed off out. He wouldn't even speak to me.'

Polly stared at her sister and then ran upstairs. She opened her father's bedroom door and peeped around it.

The sight of the hump beneath the bedclothes and the sound of gentle snoring made her sigh with relief.

'He's still in bed,' she told Vi when she went back downstairs.

'Getting his strength up for another riot tonight, I expect,' Violet said wryly.

'I hope not,' Polly said with feeling.

But Violet's gloomy prophecy turned out to be true; the trouble on the Saturday night proved to be far worse than anything that had happened on the Friday, and was to bring sorrow and shame to the Longden family.

Thirty-Three

William appeared, bleary-eyed, just before dinnertime.

'It's just a sandwich for dinner, Dad, but I'll be cooking a nice meal for us all tonight. It might be cooler then. You will be in, won't you?' She tried to make it sound more like a statement of fact than a question. But her father was having none of it.

'No, I won't. I'm on picket duty tonight. Got to do my shift.'

'You'd do better to be doing a proper shift at work than playing silly buggers with the strikers.'

William glowered at her. 'I aren't no blackleg. And you mind your language, girl. And get me a proper dinner now.'

Polly faced him squarely. 'I'm cooking *tonight*. Not now. Tek it or leave it.'

William growled something unintelligible and glowered all the time he ate the sandwiches she set on the table. He went out of the house without speaking to her again.

The time passed slowly, the day getting hotter and hotter.

'Oh, Poll, I really don't feel well,' Violet moaned restlessly.

'It's the heat. I'll bathe your face and hands. Try and sit quietly, Vi. All this wriggling just makes you even hotter.'

'I just can't get comfortable. I'm the size of a house.'

But there was no escaping the heat; even Miriam, usually so energetic, was lying listlessly on the sofa not wanting to go out to play.

At teatime, when Polly was cooking the tea, the kitchen got hotter and hotter.

'Go and sit in the front room, Vi, with Miriam. How about you play a game of Snap with her? She's bored, poor mite.'

'I'm too hot and uncomfortable. I wish this baby would hurry up and come. Then I could have it adopted and get on with me own life.'

Polly gaped at her. 'Adopted? Oh, Vi, you wouldn't.'

'Why not? I don't want it. And Micky's denying it's even his, meking out I'm some sort of trollop that doesn't even know whose kid it is.' Easy tears filled her eyes.

'But I thought you loved bairns. You were always so good with Miriam when she was a baby.'

Violet grimaced. 'I could always hand her back to you.'

'You'll love your own when it comes,' Polly said softly. 'I know you will.'

Violet shifted uneasily in her seat again. 'Mebbe,' she muttered and then added ominously, 'mebbe not.'

When tea was ready, there was still no sign of William or Eddie. Polly, Violet, Miriam and Stevie, when he came home, ate together, whilst Polly plated up meals for the two missing men.

'What's happening out there?' Violet asked Stevie.

'Not much,' the boy said, eating hungrily. The heat didn't seem to affect Stevie's appetite. 'By heck, Poll, this is good.' He grinned. 'Mr Wilmott's rotting veg comes in handy, doesn't it? It's going off quicker than ever this hot weather. I've brought home another box-ful.' His smile faded as he added, 'He's put boards on the outside of the windows tonight. He reckons there's going to be more trouble.'

Polly and Violet exchanged anxious looks.

'Have you seen Dad or Eddie?'

'Or Micky?' Violet put in.

'No.'

'Why does Mr Wilmott think there might be more trouble tonight? It's been quiet all day,' Polly persisted.

'There's police on duty at both crossings and a few pickets wandering about, but no trouble. Mind you—'

'What?' both girls chorused. Only Miriam sat eating her tea, unfazed by the conversation passing over her head.

'They do say extra county police have been drafted in and they were closing the Great Northern station when I left work.'

'Closing it? At six o'clock on a Saturday evening? Never!'

''S'true. All the lights were turned off. It doesn't half look weird.'

Polly bit her lip worriedly as she cleared away the remnants of the meal and washed up in the scullery. She didn't even try to press-gang Violet into helping her. The girl looked very weary and Polly was concerned about her.

When neither William nor Eddie had come home by ten o'clock, Polly went out to look for them. This time, she vowed, if she could find them she was going to get them to come home even if she had to drag them.

They weren't in the George and Dragon so Polly headed up the High Street, her heart racing. There were people coming from all directions – men, women, youths

217

and even children who, to Polly's mind, should have been safely in bed. There were a few police constables on duty, but they were chatting and exchanging good-natured banter with the pickets. Polly searched up and down the street, determined not to return home before she had found at least one member of her family.

The crowd seemed to be growing by the minute. Surely, she thought, folk should be going home now, not coming out.

It was just past eleven when she noticed lines of policemen marching up the High Street to join those already on duty. Polly gasped as she saw them draw their batons and advance towards the milling crowd, who responded with cat-calling and jeering. The unrest spread like a tidal wave up the street as far as High Bridge.

Suddenly there was a great roar from the crowd. Polly shrank back into a doorway and watched in horror as a line of policemen charged the crowd with batons raised. People fled in all directions, though some gangs of youths stayed to fight. Blow after blow rained down from the police batons and the crowd retaliated by picking up anything to hand and hurling it at the oncoming officers; bottles and bricks flew through the air, smashing onto the ground or finding their mark on a policeman's helmet. The skirmishing continued. The sound of breaking glass shattered the night and cries and yells from both sides grew to a crescendo. The police – far more in number than the city force – charged again and again. Batons flailed and fists flew.

As Polly watched in terror, the rioters, for that was what her fellow citizens had become in a matter of moments, began to attack buildings. Their main target appeared to be the offices of the railway companies, but then they hurled bricks and stones at the shop windows of innocent traders. Street lamps were smashed and now several policemen and a few of the troublemakers were being led or carried away, blood pouring from open wounds.

Polly was close to the railway offices in St Mark's Square when she heard the plaintive wail of two women, clutching the arm of one of the rioters. The man was holding something that was alight at one end.

'No, no, please don't throw it. Our homes will catch fire.'

Polly gasped as she recognized the man with whom the women were pleading. She ran forward, pushing her way through the crowd. 'Dad, what are you doing?'

Before William could answer one of the women grasped Polly's arm. 'Stop him, miss. Please stop him. He's going to set the offices on fire.'

'Oh no, Dad, no!'

'If he does – ' the second woman was in tears – 'our cottages'll likely catch fire. We'll lose our homes.'

Polly hung onto her father's arm. 'Come away, Dad. Come home.'

With a growl, William hit out at her, catching her on the shoulder. 'Leave me be.' But he dropped the lighted missile and disappeared into the crowd. In the darkness, she lost sight of him again.

'Thanks, luv.' One of the women touched Polly's arm. 'But you get yarsen home now, lass, and lock yar door. 'Tain't safe to be out on a night like this. I don't know what's got into folk. Really I don't.'

''Tis the heat. It's made 'em like a lot of madmen,' her companion muttered. 'Come on, Flo, let's get back inside. I reckon we're all right for the moment.'

Polly hurried back into the High Street to try to get

home, away from the terror, when she heard shouting and breaking glass. She squinted through the gloom and saw the dark shapes of youths throwing stones at shop windows and then they put their hands through the shattered glass and snatched the goods from the window displays. She couldn't see what they were taking, not in the dark, but she knew the shops well; boots and shoes, confectionery, clothes, even wine, which would no doubt fortify and fuel the rioters and cause more drunken rampaging through the streets.

She paused, unable to believe what was in front of her; a fat, red-faced woman shouting raucous encouragement to the vandals. Polly bowed her head and hurried on. All around her now was the sound of breaking glass, of shouting and uproar. Figures were running to and fro, hurling bricks and bottles, causing damage and destruction just for the hell of it.

This had nothing to do with the strikers' genuine fight for better conditions, Polly thought. This was an unruly hooligan element that had seized upon the chance to make mischief. And what mischief! Polly was appalled and frightened too. A young woman was no longer safe on the streets on her own at this time of night. She hurried on again, bending her head so as not to be recognized; she didn't want anyone to think she'd been involved in the trouble.

Near the Midland station she could hear a bell being rung and heard more shouting and shrieks of laughter. She paused and looked up in horror at the signal box. Three men had got into the box and were pushing out the window frames and were smashing the inside workings with a lump hammer.

Nearby, the offices of a brewery, housed in railway buildings, were under attack. The windows had been smashed and then, to Polly's horror, she saw a man throw a burning missile through the broken window. Flames soon flickered from inside.

'Fire, fire,' Polly shouted, but her voice was lost in the hubbub. She struggled forward, trying to find someone who would help, but the mob was so dense here she couldn't push her way through. She saw shadows against the blaze, which had now taken hold inside the building. Two men were trying to put it out, but no one else in the crowd moved to help them. They were fighting a losing battle as flames and smoke belched out of the broken windows. The shout went up and Polly saw the glow climbing into the night sky.

Polly watched for what seemed an age, but the fire grew worse and folks stepped back away from the intense heat. At last she heard the noise of an approaching vehicle and heard a clanging bell. A fire engine arrived and the crowd, fearful of being run down, parted to let it through.

The firemen began to tackle the fire amidst shouting from the crowds.

'Let 'em rot.'

'Let it burn.'

'We've shown 'em.'

Slowly, the blaze was brought under control.

She should go home, Polly knew, but she'd still not found Eddie. More than anything now she wanted to find Eddie. She'd found William only to lose him again and having seen his actions with her own eyes, she was disgusted and angry with him.

'He'll have to take his chances,' she muttered. 'He's brought it on himself.'

But Eddie was another matter.

The crowd was thinning; many were slipping away

to their homes, realizing that things were getting out of hand now. The wanton destruction of property and businesses that had nothing to do with the railway companies and the looting from vandalized shops were both criminal offences.

Again, Polly took refuge in a doorway. She knew she should run home as fast as she could, but she couldn't drag herself away. She had to stay; she had to see for herself what was happening.

Thirty-Four

Polly remained half-hidden in the doorway as she heard another sound getting louder, coming closer and closer. The sound of marching feet. She gasped as she saw lines of soldiers marching down the High Street with bayonets fixed and pointing outwards in front of them coming straight towards the crowd. And it seemed to the frightened eyes of the girl that they had no intention of stopping. At the sight of the advancing soldiers, the crowd's raucous shouts and jeering fell strangely quiet as they faced the grim reality. They were no match for armed men and they knew it.

As the soldiers came to a halt a short distance away from where she was standing, Polly saw the officer in charge move to speak to the chief of police. After some discussion, one of the officers stood on a box and addressed the milling crowd. If they didn't disperse immediately, he told them, and go back to their homes, the Riot Act would be read by a magistrate, who was standing beside him. The streets would then be cleared by the military.

A murmuring ran amongst those who heard his message. More and more people began to drift away. As the message was relayed, Polly could see that the gangs of youths were dropping their missiles and slinking away down side streets, the looters still carrying their ill-gotten gains, their defiant laughter ringing through the night.

Polly felt someone grip her arm and a voice whispered in her ear. 'What the hell are you doing out here, Poll?'

'Eddie! Oh, thank God. Are you all right? You're not hurt, are you?'

He was dragging her away towards the corner of their street. 'Come on, we're going home. Now.'

'Where's Dad?'

'I dunno and we're not waiting to find out. Come on, Poll, let's get out of here.'

As they hurried away and turned into their street, Polly asked, 'What on earth are you doing getting involved in all that? It's nowt to do with you.'

Through the darkness, Polly saw his white teeth shining as he grinned. 'You know me, Poll. Always game for a bit of bother.'

'Well, you'd do well to stay out of it. Specially with soldiers charging down the street with bayonets at the ready.'

Eddie's tone was more thoughtful as he said, 'Yes, I could quite fancy a bit of that mesen.'

Polly twisted round. 'What?'

'Bein' a soldier. I reckon that'd suit me.'

Polly groaned. 'Oh, don't joke, Eddie. I've enough with Dad and Leo being on opposite sides. Where's it all going to end?'

Eddie didn't answer her and, as they entered the house and shut the door on the chaos, Polly had the feeling that he might be serious about becoming a soldier.

*

They waited another hour, but William did not arrive home.

'You shouldn't have stopped up, Vi. Not this late. You look dreadful.'

'I feel dreadful.'

'And we should go to bed an' all, Eddie. There's nothing more we can do.'

'D'you want me to go and look for Dad?'

'No, I don't want you involved in any more trouble. You've got away with it so far.' She had the uncomfortable feeling that Eddie might have been involved in the looting. She wondered how many new pairs of boots and shoes, straw hats and bowlers would appear on Vince Norton's stall in the coming weeks. 'Just be thankful and stay out of it now. Please, Eddie.'

'All right.' He rose and made for the staircase, 'I wonder where Micky got to.'

'What?' Violet cried. 'Eddie, come back here. Was Micky with you?'

He turned at the door leading to the staircase. 'Oh yeah. Him and his dad were in the thick of it, alongside our dad, but I lost sight of them and then, when I spotted Polly, all I could think of was getting her home.' He jerked his head. 'I reckon Leo was somewhere amongst the police. So . . .' He shrugged. 'I thought she was better off out of it.'

'But Micky? What about Micky?'

'Don't you worry about him, Vi. He can take care of himself. Micky Fowler won't own up to any trouble he's caused.' He nodded towards her swollen belly. 'He's proved that, hasn't he? Night.'

The two girls, who still shared the same bed, hardly slept for what was left of the night. Violet, hot and uncomfortable, tossed and turned. As it was beginning

225

to grow light, they heard sounds from downstairs and knew their father was home, and as dawn began to filter through the thin curtains, Violet clutched Polly's arm.

'I've got a pain, Poll, and the bed's wet.'

Polly leapt out of bed. 'Let's see.' She threw back the covers to see that Violet's nightdress and the sheet were soaking.

'I reckon your water's have broken.' Just recently, Polly had been asking Bertha for tips about what would happen at the birth.

'Oooh, Poll, it hurts.'

'Bad?'

'Aaah – yes.' Violet cried and writhed on the bed. 'Get Mrs Halliday. Now, Poll.'

'Maybe we should wait a little longer. You're not due yet. It shouldn't be coming now.'

But Violet's next scream of agony and the girl's terrified eyes decided her.

'I'll be as quick as I can, Vi. Hang on . . .'

Polly rushed downstairs, out of the house and down the street still in her nightgown and bare feet.

She banged on the door of the end house and shouted, not caring for once who heard her. Besides, did it matter now? The whole street knew about Violet's baby anyway. There was no way they could have hidden it forever.

'Mrs Halliday, Mrs Halliday. It's our Vi. The baby—'

The door flew open. It was not Bertha standing there, but Leo.

Polly took a step back as she stared at him. He had a bandage round his head and one eye was almost shut, the bruise darkening already. 'Oh, Leo, you're hurt. What—?'

He cut her question short. 'Is it Vi?'

'Yes, she – I think she's in labour.'

'Mam's not here. She's round the corner. Someone's just died and she's gone to lay them out.'

'But Vi's bad. The pain—'

'I'll fetch Mam.' He closed the door, then paused briefly to look down into Polly's eyes, anguish in his own. 'We've got to talk. There's something I have to tell you—'

'I must get back to Vi.'

Leo sighed. 'I'll get Mam.'

Bertha arrived half an hour later. 'She's well on,' she said curtly after a swift examination. Polly bit her lip. Bertha was suddenly no longer the comforting, friendly person she'd always been. There was a constraint between them. Perhaps she was already blaming the Longden family for what had happened to her son in the previous night's skirmish. After all, William was a railwayman. He was one of the strikers and, more than likely, one of the instigators of last night's troubles.

'You – you will stay with her, won't you, Mrs Halliday?'

Bertha returned her gaze steadily. Then she smiled but there was a tinge of sadness in her eyes.

'Of course I will. Now, love, you go downstairs and get some water on the boil.'

Polly turned to go, but first she had to ask, 'Mrs Halliday, what happened to Leo?'

'It was them rowdies last night,' she began angrily. 'He—'

Whatever Bertha had been going to say was cut short by a squeal from the bed. 'It's coming – it's coming – oooh . . .'

*

227

Only forty minutes later, Violet was cradling her baby son in her arms. Flushed and weary from her efforts, she was nevertheless smiling.

'They bring their love with them, don't they?' Bertha remarked as she tidied up the mess of the birth.

Polly moved to the head of the bed and touched the baby's wet head with gentle fingers. 'He's lovely, Vi. Strong and healthy – and lusty,' she added with a laugh as the baby began to bawl.

'He's got a fine pair of lungs, just like his father. I brought him into the world, y'know.' Bertha sniffed. 'Pity he won't do right by you, lass, 'cos we all know that little chap's Micky Fowler's. What you gonna call him?'

'Michael,' Vi said promptly and firmly.

'Oh but—' Polly began but her sister was adamant.

'Michael it is and Michael it'll always be. Never – never,' she insisted, 'Micky.'

Polly shrugged. 'He'll probably get called Mick or Micky at school.'

'But not at home, he won't.'

'Michael Longden.'

'Michael *Fowler* Longden,' Violet insisted. 'I know I can't put Micky's name on the birth certificate as his father, but he's not getting away with it altogether.'

For a moment Polly stared at her, glanced at Bertha and then the two of them burst out laughing. And they laughed even harder when Violet, looking from one to the other, asked, 'What? What have I said?'

As they went downstairs, Polly offered, 'Will you have a cup of tea, Mrs Halliday?'

Bertha accepted gladly. 'I will, love. I didn't get one when I was laying out poor old Mrs Matthews. I came straight here.'

They sat together either side of the table as they drank tea. Bertha smacked her lips. 'By, I was ready for that. Thirsty work seeing 'em off and then bringing another in,' she said as she set her cup down.

Polly chewed her lip before she repeated the question she'd asked before but had not received an answer.

'What happened to Leo? Did he get hurt last night?'

The clouded, anxious look that had lingered on Bertha's face all morning deepened now. 'You saw him. Yes, he got hurt last night and what's more—' Bertha stared at her for a long moment before saying quietly, 'He knows who threw the bottle that hit him. Cut his head badly.' There was a pause before Bertha, her tone tight, added, 'Your dad home, is he?'

'He – he – came in about five, I think.'

Bertha pursed her lips. She nodded but said no more. Soon afterwards, having made sure Violet was all right, she left.

Thirty-Five

Later that Sunday morning Polly could not stop herself from going out into the High Street to see the damage last night's rampaging had caused. Violet was asleep, the baby alongside her, and her father and Eddie had not appeared from their rooms. No doubt they would be startled awake by the baby's cries and realize they were now a grandfather and uncle. Stevie had gone out early and Polly had sent Miriam down to play with Dottie Fowler. She didn't want her little sister seeing all the damage.

'You can tell them Violet's had her baby. A little boy.' Then she added under her breath, 'Not that they'll be interested.'

Polly walked along the High Street, mingling with other curious sightseers who were looking about them and shaking their heads in disbelief.

'That such a thing should happen in our city,' she heard one woman murmur. Polly agreed with her; she was heart-sore to think that such scenes had occurred in her beloved Lincoln and that such devastation had been wrought by some of its own people. As she walked along, stepping over stones, bricks, bottles and broken glass, Polly could see that hardly a window remained whole in any of the shops and offices between the Midland station and the Stonebow. She glanced about

230

her and saw dark stains on the street and knew it to be the blood of someone who'd been injured.

Rumours were rife; she heard snatches of conversation as she moved through the throng. Quiet and peaceable this morning, they were shocked by what they saw in the bright light of day. Some looked shamefaced and Polly guessed they'd been here the previous night, maybe had even taken part in causing the damage that now lay accusingly before them.

She glanced towards the Cornhill, where only a few weeks ago she'd enjoyed the pictures of the coronation, sitting beside Leo, holding his hand. A great wave of sadness overwhelmed her. What would happen between her and Leo now? Her father and brother had been involved; certainly William had for she'd seen it with her own eyes.

As if to deny her thoughts, she heard a man close by proclaiming loudly to anyone who would listen, ''Tweren't the strikers, you know. It weren't the railway workers. They were just mounting a peaceful strike, but gangs of hooligans who'd nothing to do with the railway did all this.' He swept his arm in a wide arc to encompass the damaged buildings, the broken street lamps, the litter of smashed glass, of discarded goods from the shops and the telltale dark stains on the road. 'It was gangs of hooligans did this, that's who,' the man was still insisting. Now he wagged his finger in the air. 'And the police have the names of the ringleaders. They'll be brought to justice. You mark my words.'

Polly's blood ran cold.

She moved on leaden feet towards the Stonebow, where she could see a knot of people gathered around a notice. Polly's heart skipped a beat. Was it a list of the men – the ringleaders – they were seeking? And was William Longden's name on that list?

'It's over!' A woman near the front turned and shouted. 'The strike's been settled.'

Polly pushed her way to the front. The notice, signed by the Town Clerk, stated that he had been notified by the Home Secretary that a settlement in the strike had been reached by unanimous agreement. She turned away, thankfulness flooding through her as she hurried home to break the good news.

William did not believe her.

'I want to hear it for mesen. We're to meet in St Mary's Street this afternoon. If they say it's over, then I'll believe it. Not afore. Them at the Town Hall could put any sort of notice up and we'd not know if it was true.'

'Don't go, Dad, please don't.' Polly begged. 'You'll hear soon enough if it is true.'

William shook off her restraining hand on his arm. 'I'm going. I'll see this through to the end, an' there's nothing you can say to stop me.'

She followed him that afternoon as far as St Mary's Street, where she saw his fellow railway workers congregating. They formed into lines and marched as if in a procession to South Common. Polly followed no further, but returned home to help Violet with the baby.

Saddened by all that happened, Polly was even more distressed that her father hadn't even mentioned the arrival in the world of his grandson.

William returned that evening jubilant that what Polly had already told him was indeed true. 'It's over. You were right, lass, it is over, though they've still got soldiers guarding both level crossings.' He shrugged.

'There's no need now it's settled though. What do they think we are? A bunch of hooligans?'

Polly went to her father and kissed his cheek. 'I'm just glad it's over, Dad. Maybe we can all get back to normal. And now, would you like to come upstairs and say hello to your grandson?'

It was while William was making the acquaintance of Michael Fowler Longden that a loud banging came on the door.

'Now what?' Polly muttered, leaving William leaning over the cot and tickling the baby with his finger.

She opened the door to find Leo standing there with another constable.

'Is your father in, Polly?' Leo said solemnly.

'Yes, he's upstairs with—'

'Will you fetch him down, please?'

Fear flooded through her. Was her worst nightmare about to come true? Had they identified William as being one of the troublemakers? Too late, she realized she could have lied and told them he was out. She'd no choice now but to call him down. She turned away, leaving them standing on the doorstep.

'Dad!' she called up the stairs. 'Can you come down? Leo's here.'

William came downstairs and went to the door. 'Hello, lad. Come away in. And your mate. Cuppa?'

'William Longden,' Leo began formally. 'I'm arresting you on suspicion of causing an affray on the night of Saturday the nineteenth of August, of a breach of the peace and of criminal damage.'

William's mouth dropped open and Polly gasped and

clung to the doorframe for support. Leo was now reciting the official caution and his colleague was already rattling a pair of handcuffs in readiness. Before Polly scarcely had time to take in what was happening, William was being marched up the street in full view of all their neighbours.

'Oh, Leo,' she whispered as she watched them go, 'how could you do this? How could you?'

She went slowly upstairs to the bedroom. 'Dad's just been arrested.'

'Arrested? Whatever for?'

'Causing trouble last night.'

'Did he?'

Polly glanced at her, then looked away without answering. But Violet guessed the truth.

'You *saw* him when you went out, didn't you?'

'Oh, Vi, he was going to set an office on fire and it was close to some cottages. The women who lived there were begging him not to do it. I – I managed to stop him but – ' she rubbed the bruise on her shoulder – 'he hit me before running off.'

'My God!' Violet breathed. 'I know he's got a quick temper, but I never thought he'd do anything like that.'

Polly caught hold of her hand. 'Vi, you mustn't say anything. You mustn't tell a soul.' She tightened her grip. 'Promise me.'

'Of course, I won't tell anyone. D'you think I want to see him in jail?'

Polly shuddered. 'Oh don't, Vi. Please don't say that.'

Violet was eyeing her sister's stricken face. 'Poll,' she asked quietly, 'who arrested Dad?'

Tears sprang to Polly's eyes as she whispered hoarsely, 'Leo.'

Thirty-Six

The following day Polly bought her own newspaper. She didn't want to ask Bertha Halliday if she could read theirs. It gave details of how the agreement to settle the strike had been reached. Representatives of both the workers and the companies had agreed to a Royal Commission being set up to investigate the causes of the discontent. In the meantime, all the strikers were to be reinstated if they reported for work immediately, in which case, the paper said, no action would be taken against them. There were other details that followed, but Polly read no more. She rushed down the street to the Hallidays' home and banged on the door.

'Leo, Leo—' she shouted, but it was his mother who opened the door.

'Where's Leo?'

'In bed asleep. And I'm not going to let you disturb him.'

Polly leant towards her. 'I need to see him now. This is my *father* we're talking about.' She shook the newspaper under Bertha's nose. 'It ses in here that all the workers are to be reinstated if they go back immediately. Dad won't have the chance if he's locked up, will he? You know Leo came to arrest him and carted him off, I suppose? The whole street saw.'

Now Bertha's mouth was a hard line. 'And you saw

Leo's black eye and his head's cut an' all. I bandaged him up mesen, so I know what your dad did to him.'

'Dad? It was *Dad* who injured Leo?'

Bertha nodded grimly. 'Leo tried to tell you when you came to fetch me to your Violet, but you wouldn't listen. Polly, Leo's bent over backwards to keep your family out of trouble, but this time, he'd no choice. He did warn you a few weeks back when there was that trouble at the coronation celebrations and your Eddie was part of it.'

Polly felt her face growing hot. So Leo did not always keep police matters to himself like he'd said. Bertha knew all about Eddie and now she seemed to know about William too – more than Polly knew herself right at this moment.

Bertha sighed. 'All right then, I suppose you'd better see him, though I wish you'd leave it till later.'

But Polly was adamant: she must see Leo at once.

Minutes later, she was sitting in Bertha's kitchen waiting for Leo to appear. He staggered into the room wearing only his pyjamas. Tousle-haired with sleep and with the bandage around his head, he looked like a small boy who'd been in the wars. One eye was still half-closed.

Polly felt a surge of love for him flood through her, but she hardened her heart.

Leo slumped into a chair and rested his arm on the table.

'Why have you arrested my dad, Leo?'

Leo's face was anguished. 'He threw a brick and knocked my helmet off. Then the next thing he lobbed at me – I think it was a bottle – cut my forehead.' He touched the place gingerly and winced. 'Good job

236

Mam's handy with a bandage else I'd likely be in hospital.'

'But you didn't have to arrest him.'

''Course he did,' snapped Bertha, who'd been listening to their conversation. 'What else did you expect him to do? He'd have arrested his own dad if he'd done what yourn's done.'

'And where *was* Mr Halliday when all this was going on?'

'Safely at home where he should have been and where your father – and your brother – *ought* to have been.'

'I'm sorry, Poll,' Leo said heavily. 'There were no other arrests last night, but there will be more.'

A new fear shot through Polly. Eddie? Did Leo know that Eddie had been there too?

'How – how d'you mean?'

'We know the names of the ringleaders. They'll be rounded up and charged.'

Now she rattled the newspaper at Leo. 'But it says here a settlement's been reached—'

'Not exactly,' Leo said, surprisingly gentle now. 'They've agreed to a Commission being set up to look into it. That's all. It doesn't mean the strikers have got what they want. At least, not yet. That'll depend on what the Commission reports.'

'But they're reinstating all the strikers if they go back to work at once. There won't be any more trouble surely?'

Now Leo's face was grim once more. 'We're going to make damn sure there isn't. Another one hundred and fifty soldiers arrived yesterday to help guard the railways. There'll be no more trouble, Poll, I can assure you of that.'

Polly stared at him and then asked softly, 'But how can my dad get his job back if he's locked up in a cell?'

'I'm sorry about that, Poll. But I had to do my duty.'

'Your blasted duty!' Polly raged. She stood up and suddenly felt light-headed. She realized that she'd had nothing to eat since yesterday dinnertime. With the anxiety over her father's arrest, she'd had no tea the previous day. And this morning she'd run out early to get a newspaper. Then the news it contained had quite driven all thoughts of breakfast from her mind. She put her hand to her head and swayed. Concerned, Leo rose and put out his hand.

'Don't – ' Polly gasped. 'Don't touch me.'

'Poll, don't be like that. I – I had to do it. I'd no choice.'

'Yes, you did. *You* needn't have been the one to arrest him.'

Leo's face was bleak but his expression hardened as he asked quietly, 'What sort of an upholder of the law would I be then?'

Polly thrust her face close to his. 'A compassionate one who thought about the girl he's supposed to love.'

'I do love you, Poll, you know I do, but—'

Polly was scarcely aware of Bertha muttering, 'I'll leave you to it,' and quietly leaving the room.

'There shouldn't be any buts between us. Love should be unconditional.' Her voice softened and trembled with the love she felt for him and the overwhelming sorrow that it was slipping away from them.

'And have you always been honest with me, Poll?' he whispered. 'I think you've always known more about Eddie's antics than you've let on.'

Polly glared at him, but now she couldn't answer. The conflict between her love for Leo and loyalty to her

238

family was tearing her apart. At last she muttered, 'I'm going. I've Violet and the youngsters to see to.'

As she turned and moved away towards the door, Leo said, 'I'll see you later, Poll. And I'll let you know what's happening about your dad.'

She whirled around to face him. '*Nothing* would be happening to my dad if it hadn't been for you.'

When she got back home, it was to find Stevie alone in the kitchen, wolfing his breakfast.

'Where's Miriam?'

'Cooing over the baby,' he answered.

Stevie, still blithely unaware of William's arrest, grinned, 'He's a grand little chap, isn't he, even though he's been yelling this past hour?'

'Oh dear, I'd better go up and help her. Maybe Vi's having trouble feeding him.'

She was moving towards the door leading to the staircase when Stevie said, 'I'll be off then.' Stevie had been working extra hours for Mr Wilmott since the start of the school holidays. He stood up and laughed as he asked, 'By the way, where's Dad? Gone off to the picket line already?'

Slowly, Polly turned back to face him. 'Sit down a minute, Stevie love.'

'I can't, Poll. I ought to go.'

'There was a lot of trouble in the city centre on Saturday night.'

'I know all about that. I spent all yesterday clearing up all the glass. They tore down the boards Mr Wilmott put up and still smashed his windows. We had to throw a lot of fruit and veg away. There was glass all over it – at least what didn't get pinched,' he added grimly.

'Stevie – Dad – '. She ran her tongue around her lips. 'Dad was involved in the trouble and – and he – he's been arrested.'

Stevie was suddenly still. '*Arrested!* When?'

Polly nodded. 'Last night. Before you got home.'

'Why didn't you tell me last night?'

'You were so late home, I – I – '

He moved to her and put his arms around her. 'I was helping Mr Wilmott, Poll. He was in a right state about all the mess and everything that the looters had nicked. I had to stay, but I wouldn't have done if I'd known what was going on at home. So – where is he now? Is he going to be charged?'

'I expect so.'

'Then hadn't we better find out where he is and what's going on? Can Leo help?'

Tears filled Polly's eyes as her legs gave way beneath her and she slumped into a chair. She covered her face with her hands and wept.

Stevie touched her shoulder. 'What is it, Poll? Tell me.'

She raised anguished eyes to look up at him as she whispered, 'It was Leo who arrested him.'

Now Stevie too sat down again and took her hands in his. 'Oh, Poll, no.'

They sat together for some moments, clinging to each other's hands for comfort but neither could find any words to say. The thin wail of a hungry baby brought Polly to her feet.

'You go, love. Mr Wilmott'll likely need your help again this morning. Go on.' She gave him a gentle push. 'But don't tell him about Dad. He'll find out soon enough,' she added grimly. 'Everybody will. But we'll keep quiet about it as long as we can.'

240

For the rest of the morning, she helped Violet with the baby. It took a while for the tiny infant to take to the breast, but once he'd got the hang of it he suckled greedily. Violet pulled a face. 'It hurts, Poll.'

'It'll be tender for a bit, I expect, but you'll soon get used to it.'

Easy tears filled Violet's eyes. 'I don't want to get used to it. I never wanted a baby and I still don't.'

Polly stood at the end of the bed and wagged her finger at her sister. 'Now you just listen to me, Vi. It's not this little mite's fault he's been born, so you just love him as he deserves to be loved. I don't want to ever hear you say again that you didn't want him. You hear me, Vi? That's a terrible thing to say. Poor little man.'

'Then you have him. Like I said before, let's pretend he's yours and I can go back to work.'

Polly watched the tiny child, still red and wrinkled from the birth, sucking happily at his mother's breast, quite unaware of the feelings his arrival had wrought. Polly felt an overwhelming tenderness for the helpless infant. She couldn't understand why Violet didn't feel the same. Surely, every mother felt a surge of protective love for her offspring?

But maybe Violet wasn't a natural mother.

In answer to her sister's preposterous suggestion, Polly said quietly, 'He's your baby, Violet. You'll come to love him, I know you will.' And though she tried to put every ounce of confidence into her words that she could muster, she had serious doubts that Violet would ever act like a proper mother should. 'I'm going out for a while,' Polly went on. 'You'll be all right?'

'I suppose so,' Violet muttered morosely.

*

241

As Polly rounded the corner, she was appalled yet again by the devastation that met her eyes. The High Street was quiet now, subdued. There were few people about. Mostly, they were shopkeepers or their employees sweeping up the broken glass and rubble from the damage the marauding hooligans had caused. Policemen were patrolling the streets and seemed to be taking statements from people. Polly walked on slowly, taking in the scene of destruction the violence had left. The brewery offices near the station still smouldered.

As she passed the level crossings and neared the main shopping area, she caught snatches of conversation.

'They've not only smashed me windows,' she heard one shopkeeper complaining to a policeman with a bandage around his forehead beneath his helmet. He had his notebook in his hand and was writing down everything the man was telling him. 'They've been looting in me shop. I've lost no end of stock.'

'Can you give me precise details?'

'Not yet. I'll need to check me stock lists. But don't you worry – I'll let you know, Officer.' The man was angry, waving his arms and shaking his fist, not at the officer attempting to do his duty but at the unknown miscreants who had damaged his property and made off with his stock.

Polly shuddered and walked on, but the scene was the same right along the High Street. Here and there she saw dark patches still staining the roadway, blood. So many had been injured, Leo amongst them. She wondered if anyone had been killed and a tremor of fear ran through her once more. What if her father was accused of being the cause of someone's death?

He could hang for that.

Unable to stand the sight of the devastation, Polly

turned for home, feeling nothing but shame that her father had taken part in such a dreadful event in their beautiful city. As she was about to turn the corner back into her own street, she paused and turned her gaze up to the cathedral, still standing proudly on the hill. But now she fancied the Cathedral of the Blessed Virgin was looking down sorrowfully on her people.

It was one thing, Polly thought, to stand up for your rights, to fight for better conditions of employment and a fair wage, but it was quite another to create havoc and chaos in its cause. Now Polly, once so sure of her beliefs, felt suddenly bereft and very much alone. Her mind – and her heart – were in turmoil. Her father was in a prison cell, the love between her and Leo lay in tatters and now she must again shoulder the responsibility for the rest of her family.

Despite the warmth of the August morning, Polly shivered and ran the rest of the way home, closing the door behind her against the rest of the world.

Thirty-Seven

'Do you know, they've nicked half Mr Wilmott's stock?' Stevie was indignant when he arrived home from work that evening. 'Now we've had time to straighten things up a bit, we can see what's gone.'

'Never! How dreadful.' Polly sighed and shook her head. 'I can hardly believe this is happening. I didn't think there were people like that in our city. Not our beautiful Lincoln.'

Stevie put his arm around her shoulders. Though only eleven, he was already as tall as she was. 'It's not the city's fault, nor most of the people who live here. They didn't want what happened last night any more than we did.'

Polly glanced sideways at him. 'But our dad was one of the ringleaders,' she whispered. 'How are we ever to live it down?'

'I don't know, but we'll have to try. Same as we have to live with Eddie not always being on the right side of the law. They're family, Poll, and we've got to stick by 'em.' He gave her arm a squeeze and went on, 'And talking about family, how's my new nephew doing and have you told Violet about Dad?'

'He's fine and, yes, Vi knows.' Polly bit her lip and then went on haltingly. 'Stevie, she's still saying she doesn't want the baby. I – I thought she'd love him when he came, but all she can think about is herself.'

'That's our Vi.' Stevie laughed wryly. 'Don't worry, Poll. She's maybe feeling a bit low after the birth. I expect it's a difficult thing to go through.'

Polly glanced at him admiringly. He was so sensible for a young boy.

'Perhaps you're right.'

'Where's Eddie? Does he know?'

Polly shrugged. 'I've no idea where he is. He's not been home since Saturday night – well, early Sunday morning when he brought me home. Have you seen him since then?'

'I heard him moving about yesterday morning, but he'd disappeared by the time I came down. I expect he went to see if there was any damage at the market.'

A sudden knock at the door made them jump and they stared, wide-eyed with fear, at each other.

'Do you think that's the police?' Polly whispered.

'I don't know. What shall we do? Pretend no one's here?'

At that moment, the baby chose to start wailing.

Polly grimaced. 'Fat chance of that now. I'd better see who it is.'

She opened the door to find Micky Fowler on the doorstep. He was grinning from ear to ear and carrying a moth-eaten teddy bear. 'I hear tell I have a son.'

'Oh really? Decided to acknowledge it's yours now, have you?'

Micky shrugged. 'I never said any different. That was me dad trying to find an excuse for me not to marry her if I didn't want.'

'Well, you didn't, did you?' Polly snapped.

Micky's face was serious. 'Polly, I only went with your sister because I couldn't have you. You know that—'

'Keep your voice down. I don't want the whole street knowing.'

'I don't mind who knows how I feel about you. How I've always felt.'

'Well, I love my sister – and her little boy. And I won't have her hurt.' Pointedly, she added, 'Not any more than she already has been.'

'So, there's really no chance for us? For you and me, Polly?'

For once she could see that Micky Fowler was serious. Mutely, she shook her head.

He gave a deep sigh and then seemed to square his shoulders. 'Anyway, I'd still like to see me son.'

Polly pulled the door wider open; 'I'll ask her.'

As he stepped inside, Micky said, 'What's she called him?'

Despite all her worries, Polly suddenly found herself smiling impishly. 'Michael Fowler Longden.'

Micky's face was a picture of incredulity and sheer delight and it was the only thing that was to bring laughter into Polly's life in the weeks that lay ahead.

Eddie came home that night, whistling merrily as if nothing had happened.

'Have you heard owt about Dad?'

Eddie blinked. 'Dad? What about Dad? Isn't he here?'

Polly explained and Eddie's jauntiness died instantly.

'Where were you last night? I've been worried sick.'

'I've been with Vince, clearing up the mess and setting his stall up. It was late by the time we finished so I stopped at his place last night.'

'Oh aye,' Polly said grimly. 'Got some nice new stock, have you? Boots and shoes, by any chance?'

Eddie glanced at her, but she noticed that he did not deny it.

'Eddie, have you heard any more news about the strike?' Stevie asked, trying to steer Polly away from asking Eddie too many awkward questions.

'Most of 'em are back at work, but there've been one or two arrests and they say there'll be some more. But I didn't know that Dad was one of them.'

'Have you heard what's going to happen to them?'

'They'll be sent before the magistrates.'

'When?'

Eddie shrugged. 'Tomorrow, mebbe, or the next day.'

Stevie put his arm around Polly's shoulders. 'Don't worry, Poll. He'll be home by the weekend. You'll see.'

On the Wednesday night after the weekend riots, Eddie came rushing in.

'There's a fire in the next street. You can see the flames from here.'

Polly hurried out into the street. Smoke was billowing upwards and flames licked the night sky.

'What's on fire?'

'The motor works.'

'Are the firemen there?'

'Yes.'

'Then we'll stay well out of the way. You too, Eddie.' She gripped his arm. 'Please, listen to me for once.'

'Don't worry, Poll. I'm not stupid. There'll be more arrests after this, specially if anyone's hurt.'

'Is it still to do with the strikes?'

Eddie shrugged his shoulders, but his gaze was still on the flames. Even from here they could smell the smoke and hear the shouts of those trying to put the fire

Margaret Dickinson

out and hear the screams of women afraid for their homes.

'But why now? The strike's settled.'

'Maybe somebody,' Eddie murmured, 'didn't like a member of their family being arrested.'

Polly gasped. 'Oh, Eddie—' she breathed, but before she could say any more, he shook off her hand and went back into the house.

Polly's anxious gaze went back to the glow over the rooftops. 'Please, just don't let anyone get hurt.'

When Polly went to the magistrates' court the following day, she learned to her horror that there had already been one fatality caused by the fire and that another person was in hospital with serious injuries.

She felt so sorry for their families. Brother or not, she thought grimly, if Eddie's had owt to do with the fire, I hope they do come for him. In the meantime, she had to sit and watch helplessly as her father, alongside other men who'd been arrested since, came before the bench. As they stood, crowded together, the charge – the same for all of them – was read out. The language of the law, Polly found, was so stilted and convoluted that she didn't understand exactly what they were being accused of.

'What's it mean?' Polly whispered to the man sitting next to her. 'I don't understand it.'

'Nor do any of us, lass,' he whispered back. 'Why these men? Why've they been singled out, I'd like to know? One of them's me brother and I don't reckon he did owt except support his mates in the strike.'

'Is he on the railway?'

'Nah, none of 'em are. He's just a labourer, but he

likes to stick up for the rights of the working man.' He sniffed. 'And look where that's got him.'

'But – ' Polly began, about to tell the man that her father worked on the railway. But some instinct made her bite her tongue.

It seemed the defendants were being charged with causing riotous behaviour and disturbing the peace. Nothing had been said as yet about the smashed windows, the looting or the fires. But maybe the charge covered a multitude of sins, Polly thought wryly.

As the prosecutor began to speak, it seemed she'd been right; he accused all the defendants of having taken part not only in the noise, shouting and jeering, but also in the violence that had followed, and he pressed the Bench to commit the prisoners to the Assizes for trial.

Witnesses from the police force – several with bruises on their faces or bandages around their heads – were called, but their testimony was what Polly already knew for she'd seen it all with her own terrified eyes. And she'd seen the injured too: members of the public who'd been borne away to the St John Ambulance station and the policemen who'd been the targets of the hostile crowd.

And one of them was Leo.

One by one police witnesses came forward to give details about each prisoner and the reason for their arrest. Most of them had been seen throwing missiles, breaking windows and street lamps and even targeting the police constables. Cautions had been given to one or two of the ringleaders now standing in court, when they'd been advised to go home. But they'd not taken that advice and had continued to cause mayhem.

On and on the evidence went for each prisoner, the details being much the same in each case. And then Leo stepped up. His head was still bandaged and his face was bruised. One eye was half-closed. No one could deny that he'd been injured in the affray.

He gave his evidence against William Longden quietly and it seemed, Polly had to admit, with great sorrow. For a moment her resolve to blame Leo for what was happening to her father wavered. William was guilty of violence, she knew, and Leo was, after all, an upholder of the law. And her father had broken the law . . .

'The accused threw a brick that knocked my helmet off,' Leo was saying. 'Then he threw a bottle that caused a deep cut on my forehead.'

'Is the defendant known to you?'

Leo hesitated, his glance meeting Polly's eyes briefly. She held her breath. Then clearly and firmly, he said, 'Yes. I am walking out with his eldest daughter.'

A surprised murmuring rippled through the courtroom. Even one or two of the other prisoners looked shocked by such a revelation.

The chairman of the magistrates regarded Leo solemnly as he asked, 'And it was you who made the arrest?'

'Yes.' Now Leo's voice was husky.

'Then,' the chairman went on, 'you are indeed to be commended for carrying out your duty under what must be very difficult circumstances.'

Now the expressions on the prisoners' faces had turned to sneers. But William had the grace to hang his head. He didn't look up to meet his daughter's gaze. He didn't even glance at Leo whilst the evidence was being given against him.

The magistrates retired to consider their verdict, then returned to the courtroom to declare that they were satisfied that no genuine striker – no employee of the railway companies – was standing before them and that the prisoners would be sent for trial at the Assizes.

Polly gasped, her gaze seeking out her father. But William steadfastly refused to meet her eyes. She could perhaps understand why her father had lied about his occupation. Maybe he was hoping that by doing so his job would be safe once he was released. What she could not understand was why Leo must have gone along with the lie that her father was not a railwayman.

And that was so unlike the upstanding Constable Halliday, she thought bitterly.

Thirty-Eight

'What's going to happen to Dad?' Violet's voice quavered and Polly glanced at her in surprise. She couldn't ever remember her sister being anxious about anything. Violet went her own way through life and cared for no one except herself.

Polly's mouth set in a grim line. 'He's charged with being one of the main ringleaders. They're being sent for trial. He could have got bail, but where are the likes of us going to find fifty pounds or anyone to stand surety for such an amount? Vi, we'll have to prepare ourselves. He could go to jail.'

Now Violet's eyes widened in horror. 'Jail? But – but what'll happen to us?'

Polly glared at her. She'd been right. All Violet cared about was what might happen to her. At least, Polly thought with a wry smile, she'd had the decency to say 'us', not just 'me'.

When her sister didn't answer at once, Violet asked, her voice rising to a high pitch, 'Will we get turned out of our home?'

'Not if we can keep paying the rent.' Polly was shrewd enough to know that that was all their rent collector would care about. Fall behind and they'd be out on their ear, but keep the payments up regularly and the rent man would turn a blind eye to the fact that the person's name on the rent book was now a jailbird.

'But you and little Michael will be all right.' She paused and then asked gently, 'Has Micky said anything about getting married?'

Violet shook her head.

'Would you, if he asked you?'

Violet wriggled her shoulders. 'I don't know. I suppose so. I don't have much choice, do I, since *you* won't help me. But that's only if he does ask me.'

'You don't have to marry him if you don't love him, Vi,' Polly said softly. 'None of us would expect you to do that.'

Violet's eyes filled with easy tears. She'd been very weepy since the birth of her son, yet Polly was pleased to see that she fed the baby regularly and even seemed to cuddle him lovingly now and again.

'I do love Micky, Polly, that's the trouble, but I'm not sure he loves me.'

Polly felt a shaft of guilt run through her, but this was something she could not share with her sister – nor with anyone. 'I'm sure he's very fond of you, Vi.'

'I suppose it would be better than Michael having horrible names called after him in the street.'

Polly held her breath. Was Vi really thinking of someone else for once, other than herself?

Violet sighed. 'I just feel as if there should be more to life than getting married and having hordes of kids, that's all.'

'Well,' Polly said, getting up to begin preparing yet another meal, 'you know what our mam would have said? You've made your bed, now you're going to have to lie in it.'

Suddenly, Violet began to laugh until the tears ran down her face. Polly eyed her anxiously. Was her sister hysterical? Ought she to slap her face? But Violet dried her tears and looking up at Polly said, 'To tell you the truth, Poll, I quite liked being in bed with Micky Fowler. We had a lot of fun and at least if I did marry him I'd have a licence for it!'

At the beginning of October the city was in a fever of excitement over the celebrations planned for the switching on of the new water supply from Elkesley. Work had begun three years earlier, but now, at last, the pure, clear water was to arrive in Lincoln.

But Polly didn't feel like celebrating. Her father was in prison awaiting trial and her romance with Leo lay in tatters.

How could people forget so quickly? she wondered. But it seemed as if folk were determined to put those dreadful days behind them. They wanted an excuse to go out and enjoy themselves, and the arrival of the new water supply was reason enough.

A special fountain had been built in the Arboretum, where the Mayor would perform the opening ceremony, but Polly shied away from going to the city's park; it held such bittersweet memories for her. So many times she'd strolled there, holding Leo's hand, planning their future together. How could she tread those same pathways knowing there was no future for them now?

'Please, please, please, Polly, can we go?' Miriam begged and even Stevie looked up at her hopefully. 'We've got the day off school specially.'

Polly sighed but relented. She didn't want to spoil the children's fun. They got little enough, for money was tight, and at least this would be free.

But on 4 October – the date set for the festivities – it was raining. Miriam looked out of the window mournfully. 'It's just like that time the coronation sports were postponed.'

'I think the turning on of the water supply will still take place, but I don't know about the entertainment organized for the evening. Still,' Polly said, mustering a brightness she didn't feel, 'let's wrap up well and go and see, eh?'

So, armed with a big, black umbrella that had seen better days, Polly, Stevie and Miriam followed the crowds to the Arboretum and waited for the procession of dignitaries to arrive in the park once a service in the cathedral had finished. The rain fell even more heavily as speeches were made and then the Mayor drank from a silver cup filled with water from a small pipe on the platform.

'Isn't he going to boil it first?' Miriam whispered.

'No, no, he says it's grand.'

Then the Mayor turned the handle that opened the valve to release a spurt of water from the nearby fountain. The jet of water climbed higher and higher into the glowering sky. A cheer rippled amongst the crowd as the Mayor operated another valve that tumbled water over the sides of the fountain, a bubbling cascade of pure, white water. There was a loud boom amongst the trees and Miriam clung to Polly.

'What was that?'

'A maroon being fired,' Stevie said. 'Mr Hopkins told us at school what was going to happen. It signals the official arrival of the new water supply.'

The bangs continued and paper parachutes floated down over the heads of the crowd, bearing tiny Union Jacks. The band of the Territorials began to play and everyone began to sing 'Now Thank We All Our God' and as the hymn came to an end, the cathedral bells chimed, the joyous sound echoing over the city. The crowd cheered and a few wiped their eyes, overcome with the thought that no more would they have to fear the water they drank.

Miriam tugged at Polly's hand. 'Can we stay for the cel'brations? Oh, please, Polly?'

'No, we're going home. I'm soaked now and I don't want you catching a chill.'

Miriam sobbed all the way home, but the little girl's prayers were answered; the evening entertainment was postponed until the following evening, when Polly hadn't the heart to refuse to take her.

'The band from the New Barracks is playing tonight,' Eddie told them. 'Come on, Poll. Let's all go.'

'Wish I could come,' Violet said morosely. 'But I suppose I'm expected to stay here with the baby. *Again!*'

'If you wrap him up warm in the pram,' Eddie suggested, 'he could come, couldn't he?'

Violet stared at him. 'You – you mean you'd be seen out with me?'

Eddie shrugged. 'You're me sister. He's me nephew. I aren't ashamed of you. Besides.' He grinned, teasing her now. 'It'll be dark. Who's to see?'

Violet smiled and punched him lightly on the arm, but she was touched by his words, though she was still unsure what her sister would say. 'Poll?' she asked hesitantly.

Polly regarded her steadily for a moment and then said softly, 'I reckon we've more to be ashamed of now, Vi, than you being an unmarried mother. So get him ready and we'll all go.'

As they left the house that evening when it began to grow dusk, they were determined to lay aside their troubles, just for a few hours. Miriam skipped happily along the pavement, Eddie swaggered with his hands in his pockets, nodding and smiling to folks he knew and Violet pushed her pram proudly.

'Oh, look, do look,' Miriam cried as they entered the park. 'Look at all the pretty lights and the fountain's lit up too.' She clapped her hands as the band began to play. 'It's lovely. Just lovely.'

For an hour or so most of them forgot their troubles, but for Polly there was someone missing. Not their father, for she doubted he would have come anyway, but Leo.

If only Leo was beside her with his arm around her waist . . .

The date for the trial was set for 30 October and on that Monday afternoon, those accused of being the ringleaders in the riots were brought to the courtroom at the Lincoln Assizes. The room was crowded and Polly found herself squashed between a large woman, who needed almost two places, and a miserable-looking man. But she was determined to stay and hear the worst.

After all the defendants had pleaded not guilty, the evidence given was a repeat of the magistrates' court and, hearing it once more, Polly was transported back to that dreadful night. Sitting in the courtroom, she could hear again the tumult, the cries and shouts, hear the breaking glass and smell the smoke.

The speakers droned on. The prosecutor called the witnesses yet again. Leo came and went. She hadn't seen him since that time. Though they lived on the same street, the tension between them persisted. Until the court case was over and the verdict given, it seemed, he did not want to see her.

Polly didn't know whether she was hurt or relieved. She rather thought that Leo might have been told to stay away from her by his superiors until it was all over. If he was known to be 'consorting with a member of a prisoner's family' it might prejudice the case against William. Polly had wondered whether to seek him out on purpose and cause such a complication. It might be the only way to get the case against William dismissed, she'd thought wryly. But what, then, would happen to Leo?

So they had not met. She hadn't even seen Bertha or Seth. It felt as if the Halliday family was steering well clear of the Longdens.

And now the day was here and by nightfall, she believed, she'd know all the answers.

But because the proceedings hadn't started until late in the afternoon, the case went into the next day. Polly was agitated. Why did they have to go through everything again? Everyone had heard it already at the magistrates' court. But then, she realized, the judge and jury had not and they were the ones who had to decide . . .

After the witnesses had all been heard, the prisoners, one by one, proclaimed their innocence.

'I was there,' several admitted when questioned, 'but I was not taking part in the riot.' But the evidence against them said differently.

Polly caught her breath as William stepped up. He listened to the charge against him and waited for the prosecutor to ask him about his part in the violent events of that night.

William squared his shoulders. 'I was there and I was shouting with the rest when the police charged the crowd with raised batons. We – I mean the strikers were making a peaceful protest. We – they . . .'

Oh, Dad, do be careful, Polly crossed her fingers. Mind what you say else you'll give yourself away.

Then William seemed to get a grip on his story. He imagined himself as no longer a railwayman, just an onlooker, an outsider who'd got innocently caught up in a battle that was nothing to do with him.

'They,' he said referring to the strikers, 'have a right to stand up for what they believe in, don't they?'

The prosecutor inclined his head. 'But peaceably, Mr Longden. Peaceably.' There was a pause before William was asked, 'The officer who arrested you, Constable Halliday, says you are well known to him. That you live in the same street. How is it then that you say the constable is mistaken in his identification of you as being the person who threw missiles at him, knocked off his helmet and caused a nasty injury to his forehead?'

William shrugged. 'I don't know. But it wasn't me.'

The prosecutor leaned forward to emphasize his point. 'But the constable is courting your daughter, Mr Longden. Surely he knows you well enough to be able to identify you correctly?'

'It was very dark – the street lamps had been smashed—'

'By you?'

'No, but there was a lot of confusion.'

'There certainly was, Mr Longden,' the prosecutor murmured. 'Of that, we can be sure.'

At last, all the evidence had been given and after a time of consideration, the jury gave its verdict. Two prisoners were found not guilty but the rest, including William, were declared guilty. Polly waited in trepidation for the judge to make his pronouncement. The sentences were handed out individually according to the perceived severity of their actions. Those who had, like William, been unable to raise the bail money had their sentence reduced because of the time they had already spent in jail.

'William Longden. Nine months reduced to six. With hard labour.'

On the last three words, Polly gave a little cry and fell forward. For a few moments she lost consciousness and so missed seeing her father being escorted out of the courtroom to begin his sentence.

Thirty-Nine

They were still reeling from the shock of the sentence imposed upon their father. Polly and Violet sat on either side of the fireplace and stared into the dying fire. Miriam and Stevie had been persuaded to go to bed, but Polly doubted either of them would find sleep easy. Even at six years old – nearly seven – Miriam had understood enough to know that her father had been sent to prison. Only the baby slept peacefully in Violet's arms.

There was silence in the kitchen, the only sound the ticking of the clock – a wedding present to William and Sarah – and the settling of coals in the fire. Brief sparks flared up the chimney illuminating the solemn faces of the two young girls, who sat staring into its glow.

'What would Mam say if she was still here?' Violet whispered.

'I daren't even think about that.'

'D'you think she'd've been able to stop him?'

'Maybe, but I doubt it. You know what a temper he's got. And when he gets a bit of drink in him an' all . . .' Polly's voice faded away.

They both knew only too well.

They sat for a long time until Polly sighed and pushed herself up. 'We'd best get to bed, Vi. Things might look a bit different in the morning.'

'How can they?' Violet cried. 'He's not coming home, is he? Not for six months. And then what? He'll've lost his job and no one's going to give him another. Not now. Not now he's branded a criminal.'

Polly didn't answer; she knew her sister was right. And it might even reflect on the whole family. Would any of them be able to find employment after this? Would they all be classed as troublemakers? She looked down at her sister and, for once, was moved to feel pity for the younger girl. Violet looked stricken and frightened. Polly touched her shoulder and Violet grasped her hand, clinging to it. She looked up, tears filling her eyes. 'Oh, Poll,' she whispered, 'what are we going to do?'

Polly knelt down beside the chair and put her arms around Violet and the baby. 'We'll manage, Vi. Haven't we always? We've got to be strong. You and me. For the younger ones and especially for little Michael here.'

'You're the strong one, Poll. Not me.' It was a rare moment of insight and one of confession, as Violet murmured, 'I'm a selfish cow. I only think of mesen.'

Polly hugged her closer. 'Well, this time, Vi, I'm going to need your help.'

'I'll try, Poll, really I will.'

For a few moments longer, the two sisters cuddled each other, drawing warmth and comfort from the physical closeness. At last Polly said softly, 'Come on, Vi. We must get some sleep – if we can. You take Baby upstairs. I'll lock up and see to the fire.'

Violet was about to mount the stairs when they heard a soft knock. The two girls glanced at each other, their eyes widening in fear. Who on earth was knocking at their door at this time of night?

'You go, Vi, I'll . . .'

'No, I'm not leaving you and don't open it, Poll. Not until you know who it is.'

They crept together towards the door, bending close to listen before Polly called out unsteadily, 'Who – who is it?'

'It's me, Poll. I need to talk to you.' It was the last voice Polly had expected to hear.

In the half light, the two girls glanced at each other.

'He's got a nerve,' Violet muttered and, as Polly reached out to open the door, she added, 'You're never going to let him in?'

'I – I have to, Vi. I must . . .'

'Then you're on your own. I don't ever want to set eyes on Leo Halliday again. Not as long as I live. And if you have owt to do with him, Poll, the same goes for you an' all.'

With that she clasped her baby closer to her and turned for the stairs.

Slowly, Polly opened the door and gestured silently for Leo to step inside. Wordlessly, she turned and went back to sit in the chair by the fire. Uninvited, Leo sat down opposite her.

For several moments he sat just staring at her. Polly refused to meet his gaze. The silence between them lengthened until at last Leo said hoarsely, 'Say something, Poll. Talk to me.'

At last she raised her eyes to meet his troubled gaze and now they stared at each other. 'There's nothing I can say – or do – that's going to alter what you've done.'

'What *I've* done? What on earth do you mean by that?' Now anger crept into his tone.

'You arrested my father and now he's been sent to prison for six months with hard labour. That could kill him.'

'He was breaking the law. Inciting a riot. And he attacked me – an officer of the law – I had to do my duty.'

'Oh yes. Your precious duty. You put that before anything, don't you? You certainly put it before any member of *my* family. You arrested him yourself. You didn't even leave it to one of your colleagues. Do I mean so little to you, Leo, that you can't wait to put a member of my family in jail?'

'Don't be silly, Poll—'

'Silly am I? I haven't forgotten that you've been hounding our Eddie for years. Everything that happens, you come knocking on our door, just to see if it's Eddie. You even thought he'd been involved with painting the lion in the park.'

'Well, wasn't he?' Leo snapped back.

Polly felt the colour tinge her cheeks, but resolutely, she lifted her head and stared him out. 'How would I know?'

'Oh, I think you do, Poll. I really think you know only too well.' His voice was soft now – and sorrowful. 'And if we're talking truth here, I don't think you've always been honest with me.'

'I've never lied to you, Leo.' And she hadn't, though deep in her heart she knew she hadn't always been entirely honest with him. But she'd been protecting her family and who could blame her for that? It seemed, now, that Leo could. 'Well, I don't forget, Leo, and I don't forgive easy either.' She leant closer to him. 'I'd just like to know if it was your father who'd got into trouble, would you have arrested him?'

Leo's face was bleak, but he answered at once. 'Yes, I would.'

Polly blinked, for a moment nonplussed by the swift and firm reply. After a moment she whispered, 'Then what chance have the rest of us got?'

'Poll, I know it's going to be difficult. I'll do what I can to help. I'll—'

Polly stood up suddenly. 'You'll do no such thing. I want nothing to do with you. I don't care if I never clap eyes on you again. You or any member of *your* family. This is my father's house, so you can get out now. You're not welcome here any more.'

He stood up slowly. 'You don't mean that, Poll. We're going to get married, we—'

It took every ounce of Polly's willpower to say, 'There is no "we", Leo. Not any more. Not after what you've done. It's – ' she hesitated briefly before uttering the final word that would end everything; everything she'd hoped for and dreamed of was shattered as she said – 'over.'

Leo shook his head slowly. 'You don't mean it. You *can't* mean it. I love you, Poll, and you love me. I know you do.'

'I did, Leo. I loved you very much, more than you can imagine. But now? Well, at the moment, I don't feel anything much at all.'

He touched her arm, but she flinched away from him as if his touch burnt her.

'You're upset. Of course you are. And you're blaming me. I can understand that, but, given time, you'll see I had to do what I did.'

'No, I'll never see that, Leo. I think you could have helped him. You could have got my dad away, out of the trouble. He'd have listened to you, he—'

Now Leo was getting angry. 'He wasn't listening to

265

anyone. None of 'em were. They were like madmen. Half of 'em were roaring drunk and your dad was one of 'em.'

Now Polly had no arguments left, for she, more than anyone else, knew what her father was like when he'd got a bit of drink in him. And she'd seen for herself William's actions that night. She was bitterly ashamed of him, but still her loyalty to him was strong. She couldn't turn her back on him or the rest of the family; they needed her more than ever now.

Lamely she added now, 'I still think there was summat you could have done.'

'There was nothing, Poll. Nothing at all. I had to do my duty. I had to arrest him.' Bitterly, he added, 'I risked enough by keeping quiet about his real occupation. I knew why your father had said he was a labourer. He wanted to protect the railway workers and – I suppose – his own chances of being reinstated when he comes out of prison.'

'Yes,' Polly whispered, staring at him. 'I thought that too, but – but why, Leo? Why didn't you tell the truth?'

He reached out to touch her, but she shrank from him. With a hopeless sigh, he said heavily, 'I thought it might help him.'

Polly laughed wryly. 'You expect me to believe that when it was you arrested him in the first place?'

'I've told you before – I had no choice about that. He broke the law.'

'But if they find out that you didn't tell them the truth . . . ?' Her voice faded away.

'Then I'll likely be facing some kind of disciplinary action.'

For a brief moment, she felt the familiar surge of love for him; he had tried to do something for her father after all. But then she hardened her resolve and her heart. There was no getting away from the fact that it had been Leo who'd arrested William in the first place. And for that she would never forgive him.

They stood staring at each other and then, with a little shrug, Leo moved towards the door. 'If you won't listen to reason, then I'd better go, but I'm not giving up on you, Poll. I'll never do that.'

As the door closed softly behind him, Polly sank to her knees on the peg rug and bent double. Covering her face with her hands she waited for the tears, for the storm of weeping to envelop her. But no tears came.

Her devastation was too deep for tears.

Forty

'Don't come and see me again, Poll. I don't want you to see me in here.'

Polly had gone up the hill to the prison to visit her father, but when she saw him she wished she hadn't come. He shuffled into the room where prisoners met their visitors, his shoulders hunched, his hair long and unkempt and suddenly grey. His face was gaunt and yellow.

She swallowed. 'Course I'll keep coming, Dad. You can't stop me.'

He smiled weakly. 'Aye, but I can refuse to see you.'

'Aw, Dad, don't do that. Please.'

There was silence between them until he asked, 'How's everyone?'

'Fine,' Polly said brightly. 'And Michael's growing every day. I wish you could see him. He's a lovely little chap and Violet's doing a grand job.' She forbore to add 'now'. The time immediately after the child's birth, when Violet might have rejected the little mite had it not been for Polly, would remain a secret between the two sisters.

'And guess what, Dad?' She knew she was chattering, out of nerves, she supposed. 'Micky keeps coming round to see the baby. He's admitted the baby's his now. So we might hear wedding bells yet.'

William raised bloodshot eyes. 'Bert'll never let him marry our Vi. Not now specially.'

'I don't reckon Mr Fowler'll have any say. You know Micky Fowler, Dad. If he makes up his mind he's going to do summat, he'll do it.'

After a moment's pause, William said, 'D'you think he'd be good to her?'

Polly shrugged. 'I hope so, but Vi's a fiery piece. She'd stand up for herself. And we'd all be around to keep an eye on her and the baby.'

'Not for another five months, I won't,' William said gruffly.

Polly bit her lip, but this time she could think of nothing to say in answer.

'Are you managing, Poll? For money?'

Now Polly plastered a smile on her face and said as brightly as she could, 'Don't you worry about us, Dad. We've managed before and we'll do it again.'

'You know, Poll, I never thought I'd ever hear mesen say it, but I'm glad your mam isn't here to see me like this. It'd've broken her heart, seeing me banged up with all these criminals. Murderers some of 'em. And one or two, you'd never guess it to look at 'em. They're ordinary blokes just like me.'

Polly fought back the tears. She wanted to shout and rage at him. Don't you know you've broken my heart by what you've done?

Because now I can never marry the love of my life.

'Right, Vi, now you're back on your feet, I'll have to see if I can get some work somewhere.'

Violet's head shot up. 'Work? What do you mean you're going to find some work?'

'I have to. We're running out of money. Eddie gives me nearly all his wages now. He's been really good.' She had difficulty in keeping the surprise out of her tone. 'And Stevie hands over every penny of the money he earns on a weekend for Mr Wilmott. And he's still bringing home vegetables and fruit on a Saturday night. But it's still not enough.'

Violet's voice rose. 'You mean you're expecting me to do all the housework? The washing and cooking and cleaning *and* look after Michael.'

'It's what mothers do, Vi. You're no different to anyone else who's had a bairn.'

'Oh yes, I am. I'm only seventeen. I've a right to a bit of life.'

Polly raised her eyebrows. 'Oh, and I hadn't, I suppose, when I took over looking after the family at thirteen?'

Violet pouted. Then suddenly she smiled and put her head on one side. Polly steeled herself; she knew that look. It was Violet's wheedling face.

'Why don't I go back to Mawer and Collingham's? I'd be paid more than you could ever earn. You've been off too long. Nobody'll employ you now.' Slyly, she added, 'Not even dear Roland.'

The Longden family had certainly been shown the truth of the saying that you find out who your real friends are when trouble strikes. The Hallidays were lost to her, but Roland was a frequent and faithful visitor. Out of everyone they knew, only he and Micky Fowler came to the house and Roland brought little gifts, usually food, for the whole family to share.

'I could ask him,' Polly murmured.

'Why won't you let me work instead?' Violet persisted. 'It's doubtful Miss Carr will have found out about the baby and . . .'

'You're the daughter of a jailbird, Vi. She'll have

270

heard about that,' Polly snapped, her patience at an end with her sister's selfishness. 'And your place is with your baby. You're still feeding him yourself. How do you propose to do that if you're serving Lady What's-her-Name with a hat when he gets hungry?'

'He can go onto the bottle.'

'No,' Polly said firmly. 'Breastfeeding's safer for him than on the bottle.'

The two girls exchanged a glance and Violet lowered her gaze; she knew just what Polly meant. And for once she had to agree that her older sister was right.

But Violet had been right about one thing it seemed; no one would give Polly a job and as the money ran shorter and shorter, she was desperate. The shadow of the Union Workhouse loomed large. She began to go without food herself to ensure that the other members of the family never went short. Heartbreak, anxiety and now lack of food, made Polly look thin and tired. Her lovely red hair lost its shine and her eyes were ringed with dark shadows. But every week she trudged up the hill to see William and reassure him that all was well, though the lies were getting harder to make convincing.

'I'm taking you out tomorrow night,' Roland said firmly on one of his visits. 'Dress up in your best black dress, Polly, with that little white lace shawl you wear round your shoulders. You look so pretty in that and we'll go into town. I'll book a table—'

'Oh no, Roland, I couldn't. Everyone will be looking at me and pointing.' Tears sprang to her eyes. 'There goes that jailbird's daughter.'

'Of course they won't. They won't even know who you are. How could they?'

She stared at him, wanting to believe him.

'Dear Polly,' he said gently, taking hold of her cold hands, 'just because everyone in this street – and maybe one or two on either side of you – knows who you are, it doesn't mean the whole city does.'

She understood his reasoning and knew he was right, but she was still afraid to venture out into wider society.

'Besides,' he went on practically, 'people are beginning to forget. They get on with their lives. The strike – and the riots – were dreadful at the time, but memories soon begin to fade. The strikers were reinstated and working conditions for the railwaymen are going to improve.'

'The families of the folks who were killed or injured,' Polly said haltingly, 'aren't ever going to forget, are they? Or forgive.'

'No,' Roland said. 'Of course they won't, but that's the same for all kinds of war. And it was a sort of war, Polly. That's what the seamen called it when they struck in June. But they were standing up for their rights, just like all the transport workers were doing. And they achieved some results. Perhaps not all they wanted, but things are altering, so some good came out of it.'

'You're condoning what they did?'

'I'd never condone the violence that happened here – and in other places – but yes, I agree that it's a working man's right to withdraw his labour in protest if he has a good enough reason.'

'And did they?'

'Did they what?'

'Have a good enough reason?'

'I don't know all the details, but they evidently thought so. It was union backed. It wasn't a wildcat strike.'

'What's that?'

'When workers strike without the backing of their union. Polly, your dad ended up in prison because he helped to incite a riot and even I don't agree with what he did. He'd had a bit too much to drink that Saturday night. I was with him earlier in the George and Dragon. I tried to bring him home – '

Polly hadn't known this.

'But he was too far gone to listen to reason. Him and Bert Fowler both.'

'Bert was with him?'

'Oh yes, but he sidled off when the police began their baton charges. So did Micky and your Eddie.' He sighed. 'Only William was fool enough to carry on throwing bricks and bottles – anything he could lay his hands on.'

'I expect that was when Eddie found me,' Polly murmured, 'and brought me home.'

'You were there? You were out in the streets that night?'

She nodded. 'Yes, both nights. The Friday and the Saturday. Oh, not taking part, of course,' she added hurriedly, in case Roland should think she'd been one of the raucous women shouting encouragement to the rioters. 'I went out to see if I could find Dad and Eddie and – and then, I just couldn't tear myself away. I couldn't believe what was happening.'

'Then thank God Eddie did find you and bring you home, else I might have been visiting you in prison somewhere.'

It was a weak attempt to lighten their conversation, but the effort fell flat.

Polly became aware that Roland was still holding her hands and she eased them gently out of his grasp, but her mind was working quickly now. If she accepted Roland's invitation, at least she would get a decent meal. She felt the colour rise in her face at the thought of how she was using his kindness, but she was desperate, almost faint with hunger some days now.

Roland, however, was blithely unaware of the true reason for the pretty blush on her cheeks as she murmured, 'Thank you, Roland. I will come out with you tomorrow night.'

Forty-One

It wasn't until they were sitting in the fancy restaurant that Roland realized how hungry Polly was. She devoured every course that was put in front of her and cleared each plate of every scrap. At first, when she kept her eyes down and concentrated on the meal, he'd thought it was because she was still anxious about being recognized, that she didn't want eye contact with anyone else in the room. But by the end of the meal, when she sat back with a smile and looked about her, he realized just how famished she'd been.

Fortunately for Polly, this was not one of the places she'd visited with Leo, so there were no poignant memories to spoil her enjoyment. And she even managed, for an all too brief couple of hours, to put thoughts of her father and the concerns of her family out of her mind.

'Oh, Roland, that was wonderful. Thank you.'

He reached across the table and touched her hand. 'We'll do it again, Polly. And soon.'

She smiled thinly, feeling so guilty that she could not share this wonderful food with the rest of her family, but quite unable to refuse the chance of another sumptuous meal.

Over the next few weeks, times were still desperate for the Longdens, but now Roland brought more gifts for the other members of the family too when he realized just how hungry they all must be. And he took Polly out for an evening meal at least once a week. She was not daft and she knew exactly what he was doing and, more worryingly, why he was doing it. But she was powerless to stop him; she needed his help as she had never needed help before. For the sake of her family, she was trapped into accepting succour from a man she knew might be falling in love with her.

She didn't like doing it, but she had no choice.

Just as, a little voice deep inside her reminded her, Leo had had no choice when he had arrested her father for his violent behaviour.

It was July 1912 before William was released, having served the full nine months of his sentence. He might have been out sooner had he not got embroiled in a fight in the prison and lost the reduction in his sentence that the judge had given him.

'Are you never going to learn, Dad?' Polly had hissed at him across the table when she heard about the fight on one of her visits. William would not have admitted it to her, relying on the fact that his daughter would not understand the prison system and would think that a nine-month sentence meant exactly that. He was forgetting entirely that Polly had heard about the reduction to six months given by the judge at his trial. But when he came into the room where she was waiting for him, he was sporting a yellowing bruise around one eye.

'There's this nutcase on our landing and he started a fight when we were on exercise in the yard.'

Polly pursed her lips. 'So I take it you're not going to get out at the end of six months now, like the judge said?'

William glanced at her. So Polly did know. Trust Polly, he thought morosely, but then realizing what a heavy burden she was carrying during his absence, he murmured, 'I'm sorry, Poll. Don't tell 'em at home, will you?'

'I'll have to, Dad. They're all expecting you home in April.'

Now there was another three months to be added on to his sentence. Another three months to try to keep them all out of the workhouse.

The weeks until his release dragged slowly and not only for William but for his family too. The other strikers – those that had not been imprisoned – had been reinstated in their jobs as part of the terms of settlement agreed upon to end the strike. But Polly realized that this would probably not be the case for her father; he would be branded a troublemaker and a jailbird. But at least with him back home, she could go out to work. And yet no one seemed prepared to take her on.

The day she met William coming out of the doors of the jail should have been cause for celebration, but it was not. She was thankful to have him home and yet, in some ways, even more fearful about what would happen next – what he would do next. She'd thought a prison term would sober him, would curb his quick temper, but the fight had proved otherwise. If she had expected a cowed and broken man to emerge, she was mistaken; William Longden would never change. Not even a term in prison with hard labour had altered him.

But nevertheless she was thankful to have him home.

'I hope you're not still seeing that bugger who got me put away,' he said as he sat down in the kitchen.

Polly rounded on him. 'No, I'm not, but if you think you're the innocent in all this, then you can think again. I'll not forgive him for what he did, but I'll not forgive you either for being the cause of it.'

William glowered at her. 'Don't you dare speak to me like that, girl. I'm still master in my own house.'

Polly stood in front of him, her arms folded. 'Are you indeed? Then you'd better get out there and try and find some work.'

Now William blinked. 'Work? What are you talking about? I'll be going back to me work on the railway.'

'I rather think not, Dad. D'you really expect them to take *you* back?'

'You said everyone had got their jobs back.'

'Oh aye, they have.' She leant towards him. 'The ones that didn't get caught for inciting a riot. The ones that didn't get sent to jail.'

He was thoughtful for a moment, before muttering, 'I'll go and see the boss, but first, Poll, you can get the tin bath in out the yard. I want to get the smell of that place off me. I hope you've got me some clean clothes ready?'

'Aye, I have,' Polly said grimly. 'But you just want to be thankful I haven't pawned 'em yet. Nearly everything else has gone.'

He stared at her. 'You've never been tekin' our stuff to the pop shop?'

Now she rounded on him in fury. 'How else d'you think I've managed? There's been very little money coming into this house for nearly a year – ' she couldn't resist the barb – 'in case you'd forgotten.'

Now, for a brief moment, William had the grace to look ashamed and for the rest of the day his sense of shame only grew worse. He returned home from the railway offices, defeat in every line of his thin, hunched shoulders.

'You were right,' he told Polly. 'I'm sacked.'

She sighed. 'I'm sorry, Dad, but it's no more than I expected. Have you seen the union man? Can he help?'

William sat down heavily. 'Doubt he'll want to. But I'll try him tomorrow. Looks like I'm being made a scapegoat.'

'Dad, a lot of people got hurt that night and two men died in a fire that folks say were started by rioters. How're their families going to feel for the rest of their lives, eh? Can't you think about other folks for once?'

'We were only standing up for our rights.'

'Oh aye, your rights! What about those poor fellers that died? What about their rights, eh? They had a right to live, but they lost that because of you and your like.'

'I didn't start any fires, Poll, I—'

'Only because I stopped you.'

He glared at her. 'I didn't start the one at the brewery offices and I was banged up by the time the other one happened. Thanks to your precious boyfriend.'

'He was only doing his duty . . .' Polly stopped in surprise. The words had come out of her mouth of their own volition, as if she'd had no will to stop them.

'Duty, was it? Was it duty to arrest innocent folks and bang 'em up for nine months?'

'You were no innocent. You've brought shame on our family and on our lovely city. It'll be a long time before any of us forget this.' She turned away before he should see the tears in her eyes. 'If we ever do.'

Silent now, Polly dished up the meal she'd made from the half-rotten vegetables which Stevie had brought home the previous Saturday, and, unrepentant, all William said was, 'We got better grub in prison.'

Forty-Two

'Hello, Roland, what brings you here?' William greeted him as he opened the door to a knock. Then he paused and looked closer at Roland's face. 'Summat up, lad? Come away in.'

He ushered their visitor into the kitchen. 'Sit down.'

'Is – is Polly at home?'

William pursed his mouth and shook his head. 'No, she's out job hunting.'

Roland sat down in the chair near the range. 'That's the reason I've come. Well, one of 'em.'

'Oh? Have you got something for her then?'

Roland nodded. 'I've always told Polly that there'd be a job for her back at the factory if ever she—'. He took a deep breath. 'Of course, I haven't mentioned it before because I thought she'd be getting wed.' His voice trailed away and William noticed the anguish in his eyes.

'Well, she's not now,' he said grimly. 'And you know why.'

'Yes.' He paused and bit his lip. 'Mr Longden, I've been coming round here quite a lot while you've been – away. And I've tried to get some work for her at the glue factory when I found out how tough things were for – for the family, but Mr Wainwright wouldn't hear of employing her.'

'Because of me, you mean?'

Roland nodded miserably.

'So has he changed his mind?'

'No, but Mr Wainwright's retired and – and I've been promoted to manager.'

William beamed and slapped him on the back. 'By, this calls for a celebration. We'll have to go to the George and Dragon tonight.' He paused and then asked, 'So now you can employ who you like?'

'That's why I thought I'd come and ask her if she's still looking for work.'

'That's very good of you, Roland. I'm sure she'll jump at the chance. She's been asking round, but there doesn't seem much going at the moment – at least, not what she could do. I suppose she could go into service – she's got a lot of experience in that.' He pulled a wry face. 'But it'd probably mean her living in and we'd miss her here.'

There was silence between them for several moments before William prompted, 'You said that was one of the reasons you'd come round. What's the other?'

'It's my mother. She's in hospital. They don't think it'll be long.'

'Aw lad, I'm sorry.'

Roland tried to smile. 'Thank you, Mr Longden.' Another pause, then he asked, 'Do you think Polly will be home soon?'

William glanced at the clock on the mantelpiece. 'I reckon so. The youngsters'll be coming out of school soon and she always likes to be home then.'

On cue, the door rattled and Polly came in like a whirlwind. 'By heck, but it's blowy today. And it's supposed to be summer. Hello, Roland.' Her face sobered. 'I've just heard about your mam. I am sorry.'

Roland nodded, acknowledging her sympathy but

saying nothing. William heaved himself up out of the chair. 'I think Roland wants to talk to you, Poll, so I'll mek mesen scarce.'

Once alone with Polly, Roland explained swiftly about his promotion and added, 'There's a job going at the factory, if – if you want it.'

Polly's face lit up. 'Really? Oh, Roland, how wonderful.'

'I'm so sorry I couldn't manage it before, but old Wainwright . . .'

'It's all right. I understand.' Then Polly put her head on one side. 'Roland, you're not *making* a place for me, are you?'

'Well—'

'Roland, I don't want to take someone else's place. I don't want you sacking someone—'

'Oh no,' he said swiftly. 'I wouldn't. I mean – I know you wouldn't want me to do that. But I can make a case for an extra pair of hands. Luckily, we're busy just now. And then, when there is a vacancy, I just won't fill it, if you see what I mean.'

Polly wasn't sure she did, but she was grateful to be offered a job. She'd tramped the city all morning and the only offer had been scrubbing floors at a pittance of a wage.

'When do I start?'

'Monday, if you like.'

'I do like. And thank you, Roland. Thank you very much.'

The silence lengthened between them when he made no move to leave.

'Polly,' he said hesitantly at last, 'maybe I shouldn't be saying this now and – and it's just between us. But my mother's not going to live – they've said so. It's only a matter of time and – and when she's gone – I mean, after a suitable time, would you – could you consider marrying me?'

Suddenly he leapt out of his chair and almost threw himself to his knees in front of her. He grasped her hands and looked up beseechingly into her face. 'Polly, I've always loved you. You must know that. I'd do anything to make you happy. And once we were married, you wouldn't have to work. I'd take care of you, I promise. I know – I know you don't love me, but – we're friends, aren't we? And – and I love you so much, Polly.' It was a long speech, probably the longest Polly had ever heard him make, and an impassioned one. But it was one that shocked and embarrassed her. And yet she'd always known that he was fond of her. His eyes had followed her around the room and she would have been stupid not to have noticed the adoration in them. And just lately, when he'd taken her out for a meal each week, she'd seen it more and more. But Roland had always known that it was Leo she loved. Things were different now, though, and Roland was offering her a respectable marriage.

The silence had been so long between them that he prompted, 'Polly, will you at least think about it? Maybe I shouldn't have just blurted it out like that and before my poor mother's even gone. What must you think of me?' Suddenly, he looked embarrassed and ashamed of his own impetuosity. But she couldn't blame him. She could see things from his point of view.

When she'd worked at the factory for the short time before her own mother had died, she'd heard the women talking about the young man who was their foreman.

'Poor old Roland,' they'd said, in their kinder moments. 'Such a dull life he's always had.'

'Why? What d'you mean?' Polly had asked, for even then he'd been some kind of benefactor to her. And this hadn't gone unnoticed by the other women.

'You could liven his life up for him, Polly. He's got his eye on you and no mistake.'

'His father died young and he's been a mother's boy for years,' Nelly Rawdon, a kinder soul than some of the other women at the factory, had told her. 'Even as a little lad, he wasn't allowed to play out in the street with the other lads. And now she's an invalid, he's no life at all.'

'Wish he'd got his eye on me,' one woman had grumbled. 'She always gets the easy jobs.'

'Now, now, Ida. No sour grapes.' Raucous laughter had followed the admonishment, but at only thirteen Polly's face had burned at the suggestion that she was being favoured by the foreman, who seemed, then, to be so much older than she was.

But now, sitting with her hands held tightly in his, her overriding instinct was to pull away. She was angry with Leo, could never forgive him, but she still loved him and was heart-sore at their broken romance. But, she asked herself, though she would never marry Leo, was it fair to marry someone she didn't love just to get a husband, a family and a home of her own? Was it fair on Roland, who was a lovely man? Was it even being fair to her? She needed time to think.

Polly swallowed and made herself squeeze his hands in return. The spark of hope that lit his eyes humbled her.

'Roland, this is so sudden – '. She laughed nervously, realizing she was sounding like some foolish heroine from a romantic novel.

'I know, I'm sorry.' He gave her hands one final squeeze and then pulled away. Standing up, he picked up his cap. 'I've sprung it on you. But, Polly, whatever you decide, I shall understand. I shall always be your friend, if I can't be anything else.' He smiled and then, pulling on his cap, he said with a forced brightness, 'See you on Monday morning, then.'

She nodded as he turned towards the door and left her sitting there, staring into space.

'Dad, I don't know what to do.'

'What about, lass?'

William was sitting in his chair near the range, where he spent most of his time now. He had given up even the pretence of trying to seek work.

'Roland has asked me to marry him.'

'Ah.' He bit down on his empty pipe. There was no money now for tobacco. 'I thought as much when he came the other day.' He paused and then prompted, 'And?'

'Well . . .' She avoided meeting his gaze. 'I – I'm fond of him. He's a nice man, but . . .'

William's tone hardened and he couldn't hide the bitterness as he said, 'But you're still carrying a torch for that copper. Look, Poll, I didn't want any of this to happen, but it has, and we've all got to live with it.'

Polly's head shot up. 'I know, Dad, I know. I'd never marry Leo. Not now, but . . .'

William's eyes softened a little. 'But you can't help how you still feel about him, is that it?'

Miserably, she nodded. 'I hate him – *hate* him – for what he did, but I still can't stop thinking about him, remembering the good times before all the trouble started.' She didn't add, though she was thinking it: and I hate you for your part in it all.

Her father sighed heavily. 'You can't turn your feelings off like a tap, I suppose. Oh, I'm no good at all this sort of talk. You need a woman to talk to.'

The thought lay unspoken between them; you need a mother. But her own mam was gone and now the only other woman who'd been a shoulder to lean on in troubled times, Bertha Halliday, was lost to her too.

'All I know is,' William went on, 'Leo's different to us. Seems to me, he'll always put his job and what he sees as his position, his duty, if you like, before anything else. Before you, before his family – before anything. He's already proved as much, hasn't he?'

'Yes,' she whispered. 'He has.'

'And Roland's a good bloke. He'd be kind to you. He'd look after you.'

'I know, but I don't love him, Dad.'

'I can't help you on that one, Poll. You'll have to make up your own mind.'

'And what about here? Violet's not exactly . . .' She bit her lip, not wanting to tell tales on her sister, yet the girl was showing signs of restlessness already, even though it was only a year since her baby had been born.

'What about Violet?' William snapped. 'She'll have to toe the line. She's brought enough trouble on this house already. Besides, you'll not be far away. Roland only lives in the next street – just round the corner.'

Polly opened her mouth to argue that she might be at work, but Roland had already said she wouldn't need to be. She'd have plenty of time in the day to keep an eye on Violet and the rest of the family.

Then she shook herself. Whatever was she doing?

Already, she was planning her life as Roland's wife when she hadn't even decided to marry him. But his offer was tempting. The man she loved was lost to her; she had to face that. So could she really hope to meet someone else whom she would love like she'd loved Leo? Still loved, if she was honest.

Roland was a good man, a kind man, honest, reliable, hardworking and there was no doubting that he loved her. But was it enough? Wouldn't it always be second best? And was she being fair to him? Not really, but then he was still willing to marry her, knowing full well that she did not love him in the way that he loved her.

For two days Polly pondered his proposal and by the Monday morning when she presented herself at the gates of the factory to start work, she still hadn't come to a decision.

'Mester Spicer ain't here today.' Harry Barnes, whom she remembered vaguely from the time she had worked there before, greeted her. 'His mam died on Saturday.'

'Oh! Er . . .'

'But he left a message with me that you were coming and told me where to set you on.'

Harry Barnes, an older man than Roland, had been one of those who hadn't liked Roland's promotion all those years before. He was a quiet man who rarely smiled, with rounded shoulders and a sallow complexion. 'You'd better come wi' me.' He beckoned her with a grimy finger and turned away. Briefly, he explained what she had to do and then left her to get on with it.

Polly looked about her helplessly. It had been so long since she'd worked here that she'd almost forgotten what to do.

'Well, well, well, if it isn't our little Polly come back to slum it with the rest of us.' But Nelly Rawdon was smiling as she said it. 'It's good to see you, Poll. How've you been?' She moved closer and lowered her voice. 'I was sorry to hear about your troubles. You'll likely get a bit of ribbing, but tek no notice. Now, d'you need me to show you what to do?'

'Oh, please, Nelly. It's been so long.'

But by midday when the workers stopped for their dinner, with the smell of the glue factory permeating her nostrils and clinging to her hair and her clothes, Polly felt as if she'd never been away.

Forty-Three

'I'm so sorry I wasn't there this morning, but there was so much to do to arrange me mother's funeral.' Roland was at their door almost as soon as she arrived home that evening. 'I couldn't do it before today with her dying on a Saturday.'

'Of course not. Come in, Roland. I'll make a cup of tea. Have you had anything to eat today?' She glanced at his pale, stricken face and guessed the answer before he said hesitantly, 'Well, no, not really. There's been so much to do.'

'Then you must stay and eat with us. It's stew tonight – that's if Violet hasn't burnt it to a cinder.'

On the previous Saturday evening, Eddie had tipped a few extra shillings into her lap. 'Just don't ask how I got it,' he'd muttered and had left the room before she could even open her mouth. And though she'd no intention of refusing the welcome windfall, she'd looked down at the coins lying in her apron as if they were thirty pieces of silver.

Polly led Roland towards the hearth. 'Dad'll be in soon. Now you sit there and drink your tea. You must have had a dreadful day.'

'Well, there's one thing that everyone keeps saying to me and I suppose it's true. She's at peace now and she'd been ill for such a long time, I'll have to look on it as a blessing I suppose.'

289

'Yes,' Polly said gently. 'But it's not easy, is it?'

They exchanged an understanding glance before Polly hurried away lest he should read more into her sincere sympathy and start asking her if she'd made up her mind yet about his proposal.

In the scullery there was no sign of Violet or of any meal being prepared. All the vegetables for the stew she'd asked her sister to prepare for the family's evening meal were still sitting on the draining board. With a sigh, Polly set to work.

'Where on earth have you been?'

Violet came home as they were just about to eat, pushing the pram. Michael was screaming with hunger.

'Buying him a birthday present. He's one tomorrow, in case you'd forgotten.'

'Of course, I hadn't. Poor little chap,' Polly murmured picking him up and cuddling him. But it was sustenance the child needed, not cuddles. 'Look sharp, Violet, he's ravenous. Roland's here, so take him upstairs to feed him. I'll bring you anything you need.'

Violet smiled archly at her. 'Who? Roland? Now, who'd've thought you'd be offering me your fancy man?'

'Keep your voice down, Violet,' Polly hissed. 'And don't be so crude and unfeeling. The poor man's been organizing his mother's funeral today.'

Violet had the grace to look ashamed – but only for a brief moment. She plucked Michael from Polly's arms and headed for the stairs. As she passed through the kitchen, she nodded at Roland, murmured his name in greeting and went upstairs.

'Am I in the way?' Roland asked with troubled eyes.

'Of course not.'

Roland followed Polly into the scullery as she prepared the meal. 'Polly, have you had time to think? I
mean, I know maybe this isn't the time, but—'

She was saved from having to answer his question by
the door rattling and Eddie coming in with a cheery,
'Hello.'

Within minutes, William arrived home too. Whilst
Roland couldn't hide his disappointment, Polly felt
relieved.

'You go and sit with Dad and Eddie while I get the
tea on the table and call the young ones in.'

Stevie had passed his twelfth birthday in April and
had left school at the end of the summer term. He was
now working for Mr Wilmott full-time, but he still liked
to play in the street with his mates.

But tonight it seemed the games had gone wrong.

When they came in together, Miriam was in tears.
'Stevie lost my marbles. He said he could beat Joey
Fowler, but he couldn't, an' he's lost them. They was all
I had.' Fresh tears rolled down her grimy cheeks.

'I didn't mean to,' Stevie was red in the face. 'I'm
sorry, Miriam. I reckon Joey cheated, 'cos I'm the best
in our street at marbles. I've always been able to beat
him before.'

'Come and sit on your dad's knee, love.' William
held out his arms. 'Don't cry.' Above her head, he met
Roland's eyes with a wry glance. 'All I'm good for these
days. Drying the little one's tears.'

Roland smiled pensively. 'At least you've got little
ones to comfort, William. I know you've had your
troubles,' he went on softly, 'but in many ways you're a
lucky man. You've a lovely family.'

William was thoughtful for a moment, watching Polly

bustling between kitchen and scullery, Eddie taking off his working boots after his day's work, Stevie leaning against his chair and Miriam, nestling against his chest sucking her thumb. And at that moment, Violet carried his first grandchild into the room and settled him in the battered high chair that had served all William's children and was now still in use for the next generation.

William smiled. 'I suppose I am. As the Good Book says, I suppose I ought to count my blessings.' His smile widened as he met Roland's gaze and said, 'But I understand you want to take one of my "blessings" away from me?'

'Oh, Mr Longden, I wouldn't want you to think that. I'd never stop Polly helping out her family whenever she was needed.'

'I know that, lad, I know that.' William lowered his voice. 'Has she said owt yet?'

Roland shook his head and sighed. 'I know it must be difficult for her.' The two men exchanged an understanding glance. They both knew that there was just one thorn in Roland's happiness.

Leo Halliday.

They sat around the table; Roland seemed one of the family already. The talk was subdued; they were all acutely aware of his recent loss. As Polly stood up to clear away the dishes, there was a loud rapping at the front door.

Eddie stood up suddenly and pushed back his chair. He grabbed his boots from the hearth, his coat from the peg behind the door and fled to the back door. 'Eddie?' Polly began, but her brother was gone.

William said nothing, but frowned as his gaze followed his hastily departing son and, without knowing quite why, Polly was suddenly fearful. 'I'd better see who it is,' she murmured as she went to open the front door reluctantly.

'You!' A startled gasp escaped her lips. He was the last person she'd expected to see.

'Don't think I wanted to come,' Leo said through gritted teeth, 'but I've my duty to do.'

'Oh yes. Your duty. You and your blasted duty. What is it this time?'

'Eddie.'

Polly's heart began to hammer as she stuttered, 'E-Eddie?'

'Is he in?'

'Yes – I mean, no.'

'Polly, you can't go on protecting your family. Eddie's in trouble and this time he'll have to face it.'

'What d'you mean "this time"?'

Leo sighed. 'Poll, Eddie's always in trouble. I've turned a blind eye – and I shouldn't have done really – once or twice, but this time it's more serious. And my sergeant's involved, so there's nothing I can do.'

Polly's lip curled as she said sarcastically, 'Oh, I wouldn't expect you to put your job or your fine reputation as an upholder of the law on the line. Not for a member of *my* family.'

She couldn't miss seeing the hurt in his eyes. 'Oh, Poll, don't be like that. If – if I thought you'd forgive and forget, I'd resign from the police force tomorrow.' There was a brief flicker of hope that died instantly when Polly answered, 'Never. Never in a million years, Leo Halliday.'

She pulled the door open wider with an angry jerk. 'You'd better come in and do your worst.'

She led the way through the front room and into the back kitchen, her mouth tight. As they entered, everyone looked up.

'What's he doing here?' William demanded harshly. Miriam slipped from his knee and reached out her hand towards Stevie. Silently the two youngsters tip-toed away up the stairs to hide in their bedrooms. Young though they still were, they could sense trouble brewing.

Leo set his helmet on the table and sat down without being invited. He pulled his notebook from his pocket. 'I'm investigating the receiving of stolen goods by one of the market traders. And Eddie seems to be caught up in it. I need to talk to him. Where is he?'

Roland stood up. 'I'd best be going, Polly. This is obviously a private family matter.'

Polly put her hand on his arm and looked into his eyes. 'No, stay. You're part of this family now.'

He stared at her for a moment and then caught her hands. 'You mean it?'

'Yes – yes, I do. I'll marry you, Roland.'

But the surge of triumphant revenge she'd expected to feel as she caught sight of the bleak look on Leo's face never came. Instead, she felt hollow inside and soiled as if she had betrayed herself.

But it was done and could not be undone. She'd given her promise and everyone in the room had witnessed the exchange and understood its meaning.

William gave a nod and turned back to Leo. 'Are you calling my son a thief?'

Leo pulled his attention back to the matter with a huge effort. But his voice was hoarse and trembled a little as he said, 'No, Mr Longden, but I think he can help us with our enquiries. Where is he?'

'Out,' William said shortly. 'I don't know where and I wouldn't tell you if I did.'

Leo sighed, stood up. Putting away his notebook, he picked up his helmet. He glanced around at them all, his eyes coming to rest on Polly. 'When you see him, will you ask him to come to the station?' Ominously, he added, 'If he knows what's good for him. If I have to come looking for him again . . .' He left the threat hanging in the air.

As Polly showed him out of the front door again, Leo paused and looked down at her. 'Don't do it, Polly. Please, don't.'

'What I do with my life is no concern of yours. Not now.'

She pushed him out of the door and slammed it behind him. Only then, did she lean against it and allow her tears to fall. 'What have I done?' she whispered to the empty room. 'What *have* I done?'

How could she have been so cruel to the man she still loved, despite everything that had happened? She'd wanted to lash out, to hurt Leo by accepting Roland's proposal in front of him. She'd wanted to see him suffer and she had. But now she was going to bear the consequences of that rash moment for the rest of her life.

A few moments later, scrubbing away any trace of tears, holding her head high and plastering a smile on her face, she returned to the kitchen.

William looked up at her as she came in.

' "Lucky" you called me, Roland?' His face was grim as he muttered again, ' "Lucky", am I?'

Forty-Four

Polly's marriage to Roland took place very quietly in their local church just before Christmas on Miriam's eighth birthday. Roland now had no family, and only William and the rest of the Longden family were at the wedding. But not Eddie.

Eddie had not come home again since the night that Leo had come looking for him and he'd fled the house. Polly anguished for days until a hastily scribbled note arrived.

> *Don't worry about me, Poll. I'll be fine. I'll write when I can.*

Her anxiety lessened but only a little; she still worried constantly about him but tried to put it to the back of her mind. She had a wedding to plan, though there wasn't a lot to do. She couldn't afford a proper wedding dress, though Roland gave her money to buy a new Sunday best dress that would be suitable for her wedding but she could wear afterwards too.

'Mother didn't like unnecessary expense and I'm sure you agree. You're a very sensible girl, Polly.'

Polly had nodded, but a tiny corner of her heart longed for someone to press money into her hand and say, 'Go out and buy the prettiest wedding dress you can find.'

But no, her wedding finery had to be useful.

The church service was brief; Polly scarcely felt married. And then they all went to the George and Dragon, where the landlord had generously provided a few sandwiches for the special day of two of his regular customers. Without William and Roland, and others like them, he would barely scratch a living.

The time Polly had been dreading came all too quickly, the moment when Roland took her home to the rented house that was now in his name. For the first time since Roland had begun his gentle courtship, they were completely alone.

Polly's wedding night was nothing like she had dreamt it would be; she was not in the arms of the man she loved. She was fond of Roland – how could she not be, he had been so kind to her and her family? – but this was nothing like her girlish dreams of ecstasy had been. Roland was nervous and trembling. He was so obviously totally inexperienced. It was over quickly with Roland weeping against her neck and saying over and over, 'I'm sorry, I'm sorry.'

Polly held him close and stroked his hair. But the darkness hid her own tears of loss and desolation.

'Roland, would you mind if my family came here for Christmas?'

'Of course not. It'd be wonderful. We can give them a Christmas to remember.' He put his arms around her. 'You've not had it easy, Polly, and I want to take care of you and if looking after your family too is part of it, then that's fine with me.'

Impulsively, Polly stood on tiptoe and kissed his cheek. He really was such a good, kind man. Perhaps he didn't agree with splashing out on a fancy wedding dress, but he was generous in other ways. 'Thank you, Roland.'

Polly had taken her marriage vows very seriously; she would cherish him and care for him and she would try very hard, every day, to love him as he deserved. But the sort of love she felt for Leo did not come to order.

Despite Eddie's absence, it was a merry Christmas for the Longdens and the Spicers. With more money to spend on Christmas fare, Polly produced a feast fit for royalty and Stevie pronounced that he felt 'FRUTB'.

'Whatever's that mean?' Miriam asked, clutching the new rag doll that Polly had made her.

'Full right up to busting,' Stevie declared, patting his stomach. 'I ain't never felt so full in me life.'

He grinned, happy that he'd been able to make a contribution to the meal. On Christmas Eve he'd arrived at Polly's new home laden with a basket of vegetables and fruit and a small Christmas tree.

'Don't look so worried, Poll,' he'd reassured her as he struggled into the house. 'It's all paid for. Well, some of it, but Mr Wilmott really has given me some decent bits today.' He tipped the contents of the basket onto the table and stood back proudly. 'Will that help, Poll?'

'Oh, Stevie, it's wonderful. *And* a little tree.'

'There's no decorations.'

'Never mind. I'll scatter some cotton wool over it. It'll look like it's snow-covered and if I can find some bits of coloured paper, I could make paper chains.'

'Oh, Miriam's been making some at school. I'll ask her to bring them round.'

And on Christmas Day the family sat around the table in Roland's best front room – a room that had been long unused – lingering over the wonderful meal.

William raised his glass of the beer that Roland had brought home.

'To the Longdens and the Spicers . . .' He began.

'And the Fowlers,' Violet piped up. 'Michael's a Fowler, don't forget.'

William frowned. 'No, he ain't. He's a Longden. That's his name. And you wouldn't have included that bugger's name on the lad's birth certificate if I'd had anything to do with it.'

'Now, now, no squabbling today,' Polly said as she, too, raised her glass. 'Here's to us all, whatever our names are.'

'Aye, well said, Poll.' William's dour expression cleared. 'And here's to a long and happy marriage for the two of you.'

After the remnants of the meal had been cleared away, Polly made up a parcel of food for Violet to take back to the Longdens' home. 'We shan't eat all this, just the two of us. It'll help see you through the week. Now, let's get everyone into some noisy games.'

The house – just for a few hours – was filled with merriment, with Michael at the centre of everyone's attention. He was growing into a lovely boy with dark hair and dark brown eyes and a smile that could soften the hardest of hearts. Even William, who'd never been very good with young children, took the little boy onto his knee and bounced him up and down playing, 'Horsey, horsey, don't you stop.'

They left, close on midnight. William, carrying the now sleeping child, said, 'That were a grand day, Poll. And you, too, Roland.' He stuck out his hand. 'Thanks.'

'You're very welcome, Mr Longden. Thank *you*. This has been the best Christmas this house has seen in a long time.'

As they stood side by side in the doorway, Polly slipped her arm through Roland's, feeling a surge of affection for this man who'd had such a lonely time caring for his ailing and, by all accounts, bad-tempered mother for years.

Tonight, she promised silently, I'll be extra loving . . .

Forty-Five

They settled down after the festivities and, with the New Year, fell into a routine that suited them both; Polly was a good and dutiful wife and she found solace in attacking the dust and grime of years in the little house.

Once again she had left work at the glue factory to become a housewife.

'Now don't you lose touch this time,' Nelly told her.

'You're welcome to come round any time,' Polly invited. 'I'll always be pleased to see you.'

To her surprise, Polly revelled in being able to make a real home. She bought remnants of material from the market and painstakingly stitched new curtains by hand. She paid only coppers for a bundle of scraps of material from the same stallholder to make patchwork cushions.

'You're Eddie's sister, aren't you?' he asked her one day.

Polly looked at him warily, wondering how the man knew her brother and, more frighteningly, what he knew about Eddie.

The big man laughed. 'Don't look so scared, duck. I'm a mate of your brother's. He worked for me for a while.' He stuck out a huge paw of a hand. 'Me name's Albert Thorpe. Folks call me "Albie".' He laughed heartily. 'Too many Berts around here already, so they call me Albie. Pleased to meet you, lass. Eddie was allus talking about you.' Polly put her hand into his to find it almost crushed by a hearty grip. He laughed again. 'Young Eddie was a rascal and no mistake. Got hissen into a bit of bother.' He jerked his thumb over his shoulder towards a thin weaselly looking man. He was standing behind a stall selling cheap jewellery. 'With him yonder – Vince Norton, they call him. We all like a good deal, us market traders, but we like 'em on the right side of the law, see. Now, Vince, he's not above stepping across the line, if you get my meaning. If you ever get owt pinched, you look on Vince's stall a week or two later.' He tapped the side of his nose knowingly. 'Chances are you'll find it there.'

Polly smiled wryly. 'I don't reckon we've got much worth pinching, Mr Thorpe. But thanks for the tip.'

'You keep well away from Vince Norton, duck. He gets the rest of us market traders a bad name. We've tried to get rid of him, but we ain't managed it.' He grinned widely, showing uneven teeth. 'Not yet anyways.'

Polly shuddered, glad that Eddie was now out of the man's clutches.

Albie leant across his stall and lowered his voice. 'You heard from Eddie? I hope he's all right. I liked the lad, even though he was bit of a tearaway.'

'Just – just a brief note after he left. I've heard nothing since.'

The man lowered his voice even further. 'Rumour has it that Eddie's gone in the army. Went up the hill to the New Barracks the very next day after he left home to see what he had to do to join up. Now whether he was able to right there and then, I don't know, but evidently, he saw a sergeant up there who's always trying to find recruits for the regiment. So by the time the peelers caught up with young Eddie, he was signed up so they didn't bother any more. Mind you, your brother didn't do us any favours. We had the peelers sniffing round here for weeks.' He straightened up and laughed again. 'Still, it's all blown over now and the rest of us keep an eye on Vince.'

Polly smiled. She knew a lot of the traders by their first names and mostly they were a good bunch. She – and her mother before her – had been regular customers, especially on a Saturday night when perishable food was sold off cheaply. She could feed the family for the rest of the week for less than half the price it would have cost her in the High Street shops. And Polly still came here. Although Roland earned a good wage and he was generous and trusting with her housekeeping money, she strove to be as thrifty and shrewd as she'd always had to be. The difference was that now she could save a few pennies each week and buy material to smarten up her home.

'So,' Albie said, 'what can I do for you today, love?'

The man's generosity knew no bounds and she staggered home with bundles of fabric remnants that she'd only paid him a few pence for. 'No one else wants 'em, love. No offence, but not all women are as clever with a needle and thread as you must be. And do you need any thicker bits of material for making peg rugs? Now, they are popular so I can't let you have them for nothing.'

'Peg rugs?' Polly said above the mound of material in her arms. 'I – I don't know how to make them.'

'Oh, it's easy. My missus makes 'em by the dozen.' He pointed to two peg rugs displayed at the side of his stall, which seemed to sell anything and everything. 'She makes 'em an' I sell 'em. I could get her to show you how to do it, if you'd like.'

Polly was thinking quickly. They needed new rugs;

the ones in Roland's house were old and full of dust that wouldn't come out, no matter how hard she beat them over the washing line in the backyard. And at home – she still couldn't help but refer to the house her family lived in as home – they were in dire need of new rugs in all the rooms. The task would keep her busy for weeks – months, probably.

'Would she mind?'

'My Selina? Course she wouldn't. She's as much as she can manage to keep me supplied, let alone the few she gets asked to make. Mebbe – if you get good at it – you could help her out.'

Polly smiled doubtfully. 'Maybe.'

'I'll get her to call round. Where do you live?'

Polly gave him Roland's address. 'Why, that's only a couple of streets from us. I'll tell her tonight, so you can expect a visit.'

And so Polly went home with her purchases and set about sorting out all the materials in the spare bedroom. Her mind was busy. There was enough for her to make a new patchwork quilt for their double bed. Her mind shied away from thoughts of what she had to endure in their marital bed.

'Polly – where are you?' It was Violet's voice from below.

'I'm up here. I'll come down.'

She didn't want Violet seeing all the fabric; she'd want Polly to make her a new dress. But when she went downstairs, picked up her nephew and cuddled him, she found that it was far more than a bit of sewing that Violet wanted.

'I'm going mad in that house,' her sister blurted out. 'I don't know how you've stood it all these years. Looking after such an ungrateful lot. And yes, before you say anything, I was one of them. I know that. But I'm no angel. Not like you. You gave up everything for our family. Oh, don't deny it, Poll. We all know how you loved Leo yet you sent him away because of what he did to Dad. You've always put family first, even if it means sacrificing your own happiness.'

'Roland's a good man.'

'I know that.' And then, in a tone more gentle than Polly had ever heard her sister use, Violet said softly, 'But he's not Leo, is he?'

Her unexpected kindness and her understanding threatened to be Polly's undoing. She'd never had any-one she could confide in, except perhaps Bertha once upon a time. She'd never trusted Violet with her secrets. But in that moment she came the closest she would ever come to unburdening herself to her sister. Just in time she remembered Violet's innate selfishness, her spiteful-ness, and the words remained unspoken. Within only a few minutes, she knew she had been right to keep her counsel.

'Anyway, what I came to ask you is, would you look after Michael while I go out to work?'

Polly stared at her. 'But he's only just over a year old. He needs his mother.'

'Nonsense,' Violet said briskly. 'As long as he's fed and changed, what else can a baby need?'

'He needs love, that's what. The same as I tried to give to Miriam after Mam died. The same as I tried to give all of you.'

Violet wriggled her shoulders. 'Like I said, I'm not you. I want more out of life than stuck in a house all day. Housework's just drudgery, Poll.'

Polly smiled. The best thing about having married Roland was that she had her own home now and she lavished all her love and attention on it. She didn't regard cooking, cleaning, washing and ironing as drudgery. Not for a minute. In fact, she loved it. If only . . .

'Besides, we need the money,' Violet went on, knowing that this was the best way to pull at Polly's heartstrings. 'Dad picks up the odd labouring job where they're not too fussy about his murky past, but with Eddie gone and Stevie's money's only a pittance, we're getting desperate.'

Resolutely, Polly turned her attention back to her sister. She sighed heavily. 'I'll have to talk it over with Roland. Make sure he doesn't mind.'

Violet pulled a face. 'It'd only be in the daytime, Poll. He's at work then. It won't interfere with him. In fact – ' Her eyes narrowed. 'You don't even have to tell him.'

'Oh no. Let's not start that. I'm having no secrets from my husband. If I do it – and I'm not saying I will yet – it will have to be with his blessing.' There was a brief pause in which the two sisters regarded one another, each challenging the other. Violet was the first to drop her gaze.

'So – have you got a job?' Polly asked. 'Are you going back to Mawer and Collingham's?'

'No!' Violet snapped. 'Miss Carr heard about Michael and she – ' Violet's cheeks flamed – 'told me they don't employ "fallen women". She actually called me that, Poll. A fallen woman.'

'What are you going to do then?'

'Well . . .' Violet ran her tongue nervously round her lips. 'I was wondering if Roland could find me something.'

Polly gaped at her and then burst out laughing. 'If you were thinking of asking Roland to get you a job, didn't you think he'd ask what was going to happen to the baby?'

'In that case, I wouldn't have asked him, would I?' Violet's tone was impatient. 'But since you're going to tell him anyway.'

'Look, Vi. I don't agree with what you want to do, but if it makes you happy then let me ask him about me looking after Michael first and then – well, we'll see what he says.'

'Oh, Poll.' Violet, her eyes shining, flung her arms around her sister, enveloping Polly and the baby. 'You are good to me. I don't deserve it.'

'No, you don't,' Polly agreed wryly, but she was smiling as she said it.

Roland was reluctant at first.

'But haven't you enough to do, Polly dear?' He glanced appreciatively around him. 'You've got this house looking grand. You cook the most wonderful meals.' He smiled and patted his stomach. 'I'll be putting on weight at this rate.' As Roland was as thin as the proverbial lath, she thought an extra pound or two wouldn't do him any harm. 'I mean,' he went on, 'you go round there to help out most days already, don't you?'

Polly shrugged. 'Yes, but I don't stay all day. Not like I'd have to if I looked after Michael. Mind you, I'd have him here so I could get on with my own work.'

His expression softened. 'But what if we have our own baby?'

Roland's love-making was tender and thoughtful. He never made rough demands on her, but sought her willingness shyly. And his whole attitude towards her was gentle and loving – and grateful. Everything he did was for her and she was humbled by his overwhelming love for her. If only, she thought, she could love him in return.

She was fond of him – very fond – and that fondness was growing into a kind of love. But it was not the exhilarating, tingling, heart-racing love she'd felt for Leo. And sadly, for them both, she didn't think it ever would be. But Roland was a good man and he deserved her devotion. And she knew instinctively that he would be a good father. She hoped that they would have a child of their own. He deserved that much and she knew her own happiness and contentment lay in having children of her own. Her love for them would know no bounds.

'I hope we do,' she told him softly. 'And I'm only prepared to look after Michael if I can. If I find it's too much, I'll tell her. I shall make that plain from the start.'

'Well, as long as you don't overdo it, I don't mind. And don't think you have to get rid of him before I arrive home. I quite like the little chap.' He smiled shyly at her. 'It'll be good practice for me, won't it? I've never had the chance to be around children much.' There was a brief pause before he asked, 'Has she got a job lined up then?'

Polly laughed. 'No. She wondered if there are any jobs going at Cannon's.'

Roland stared at her for a moment and then joined in her laughter. 'Your young sister certainly has a nerve.'

Forty-Six

Violet started work at the glue factory the following week, bringing Michael to Polly's home each morning and collecting him each evening.

'Your Roland's a lovely feller,' she said to Polly at the end of her first week. 'And I'm not saying that just because he found me a job and he's letting you look after Michael. He's been great this week at work, keeping an eye on me and helping me settle in. He even watches that the other women don't get on to me. Mind you,' her eyes glinted. 'I don't need anyone to stick up for me. I can look after mesen.'

'I bet you can,' Polly remarked wryly.

'They're all right – the other women. Quite a good bunch, really.'

Polly nodded. 'Nelly Rawdon will look out for you. Have you met her yet?'

Violet laughed. 'Oh yes. Our Nelly. She's a character and a half, isn't she?'

'Get *her* on your side, Vi, and you'll be all right.'

'Oh, I already have,' Violet said airily. 'She's the ringleader, isn't she? I'd sussed that out by Tuesday. We're bosom pals now, though Ida doesn't like it.'

Polly laughed, enjoying hearing about her former workmates. 'Ida Norton and Nelly have been sworn enemies for years. But you're best with Nelly. She's loud and vulgar, but she's a heart of gold. And she's loyal to her mates. Ida isn't; she's spiteful. She can be a friend one day and fall out with you the next. No, no, you stick with Nelly, Vi, and you'll be all right. Besides, Ida is Vince Norton's wife.'

Violet's eyes widened. 'The bloke that Eddie worked for?'

Polly nodded grimly. 'He all but got our Eddie put in jail. If Eddie hadn't joined the army pretty sharpish, I reckon that's where our dear brother would have ended up.'

Now Violet's eyes narrowed. 'Vince Norton's wife, eh? Well, well, well,' she murmured as she stored away the piece of information, which just might come in handy one day.

'Nelly was asking after you,' she told Polly. 'Course, it's all round the works that Roland's me brother-in-law. Put their backs up a bit until I let 'em know I'm not expecting any favours.'

'Give her my regards. Tell her to come round some-time if she likes. I'd love a good gossip and a catch up.'

Nelly arrived on Polly's doorstep the following Sunday afternoon.

'Not interrupting owt, am I?'

Polly smiled a welcome and threw the door open wide, welcoming the woman into her home.

'Of course not. Roland's having his Sunday afternoon nap in the front room. We can have a good old gossip in the kitchen. That's if you don't mind sitting in the kitchen.' Polly would have loved to have shown off her smart front room with its new curtains and polished furniture, but she was anxious to replace the worn rugs too, before showing it to anyone other than her husband. And Albie's Selina hadn't visited yet to teach her how to make peg rugs.

'I prefer it, duck,' Nelly said, sitting her huge bulk down on one of Polly's kitchen chairs to wait for a cup of tea and a home-made scone with jam and cream. She was already licking her lips as she eyed the plate Polly set before her.

Nelly Rawdon was something of a legend. She was a big woman in all senses of the word and was afraid of no one, man or woman. She made friends easily and enemies just as easily and probably in equal measure, but it was to Nelly folk went if they were in trouble or needed help. She was another Bertha Halliday, but without Bertha's skill and knowledge to bring babies into the world and ease the elderly out of it. Yet she was often to be found at both events, giving moral support and practical help where she could. She knew Bertha well as they ran into each other frequently. They were not particularly friendly, but respected each other for what they did. And Bertha had, on more than one occasion, been thankful for the other woman's larger-than-life presence. Nelly was red-cheeked, with light brown hair that had recently acquired a peppering of grey. Maybe, Polly thought, despite the woman's cheerful smile and laughing eyes, she'd also had anxieties of late. Her husband, Sid, had been arrested a day after William and had served three months 'up the hill' for his part in the riots.

'How's yar dad?' Nelly asked, her mouth full as she bit into the warm scone with relish, jam and cream oozing round her mouth.

'All right. Not working. Hasn't done since – well, you know.'

'Aye, I do. My Sid's the same. Employers don't like ex-cons, do they?'

Polly was silent. She couldn't think of anything to say. Talking about that terrible time brought back all her own heartache.

'So,' she said brightly, 'tell me all the gossip from the factory. And is my sister behaving herself?'

'Oh, she'll be all right. I've kept me eye on her, soon as I found out who she was. Some of the others didn't like it at first, but she's made it clear she's not looking for special treatment from your old man. Mebbe she got the job 'cos of him, but we'd all do the same if we had the chance. No, we don't hold that against her, only if she tried to lord it over us, but she dun't.'

'Good.'

'Mind you,' Nelly went on with a raucous laugh. 'She's a bit of a gal, ain't she?'

Polly looked up sharply. 'What d'you mean?'

'She's a flirt, Poll. Eyes up all the fellers. Married ones an' all. Meks no difference to her.'

'Oh dear.'

'Don't let it bother you, duck. She's not the only one an' she's only havin' a bit of fun. Does she still see Micky Fowler?'

Violet made no secret of the fact that Micky was her baby's father; it was her way of getting back at him for having deserted her. Micky was still around, but he never came to the Longdens' home now, not since the first few months of the baby's life.

Polly shook her head. 'Not that I know of.' Then she smiled wryly. 'But you never know with our Vi.'

The two women gossiped happily until Roland appeared yawning and stretching.

Nelly heaved herself up. 'Now, Mester Spicer, I don't expect you want to see me on a Sunday as well as all week.'

'You're all right, Mrs Rawdon. I'm sure Polly's pleased to see you. Don't rush off on my account.'

'I'd best be going anyway. Sid'll be wanting his tea.'

'How is he?' Roland asked quietly. 'Any luck with work?'

Nelly pursed her lips and shook her head.

'I have tried in the past to get work for him –' Roland glanced at Polly – 'and William at our place, but the boss wouldn't hear of it.' Now he smiled. 'But now I'm in charge I'm watching out for suitable vacancies for them both, though there's nothing at the moment, I'm afraid. Not for men.'

Even Polly hadn't known this.

'That's good of you, Mr Spicer,' Nelly said solemnly. 'I 'preciate it. Still, we manage better than most. Both our lads are in work and they pay their way at home. And as long as my job's safe.'

'Oh, it is, it is, Mrs Rawdon. You're an asset to the workforce.' He chuckled softly and his eyes twinkled. 'I rely on you to keep the other women in line.'

She laughed with him. 'Well, if that's the case, Harry Barnes'd better watch out for his job then. You might want to make me the foreman.'

As Polly walked out of the back door and into the yard to see Nelly off, the older woman turned to her. 'You're making that man really happy, love. It's a pleasure to see him smiling and joking. He never did when his mam were alive. She was an old sourpuss if ever there was one.'

'But she was ill, wasn't she?'

'Latterly, yes. But she was an owd beezum long before that. I knew Maud Spicer all her life and she was always a miserable, whining girl. How she ever got to catch a husband I'll never know, 'cos Roland's dad was

313

a nice bloke. Shame he died so young and poor Roland got lumbered with looking after her. Still, he's happy now. Anyone can see that.' She lowered her voice and bent a little closer. 'I just hopes you are an' all, duck.'

Polly smiled, and to her surprise, was able to answer truthfully, 'Oh yes, Nelly, I'm happy enough.'

Nelly eyed her shrewdly and then gave a brief nod. She understood the meaning behind Polly's words perhaps better than even the girl herself did. Polly had chosen her bed and she was lying in it with a determination to make it work, but that didn't mean that locked away in the depths of her heart there wasn't a yearning for what might have been that would never go away.

Forty-Seven

The next morning there was another knock at the door. Polly, with Michael on her hip, opened it to find a strange woman there, carrying a huge carpetbag. At first she thought it was a gypsy telling fortunes or selling pegs. The woman, with black hair and swarthy skin, was dressed in flowery, flowing garments beneath a moth-eaten fur coat. Bracelets jangled on her wrists and her dark violet eyes caught and held Polly's glance. Before the girl could speak, the woman said, 'I'm Selina – Albie's wife. He said you want to know how to make peg rugs.'

Polly's face brightened. 'Oh, yes, yes. Please come in. Just let me put this little one back in his pen. This is very good of you.'

Michael was now walking well and Polly had penned off one corner of the kitchen to keep the adventurous little boy safe.

Selina stepped in and closed the door behind her. Then she set her bag on the kitchen table and held out her arms towards Michael. 'Don't cage the little fellow up. He'll be all right with us both here to watch him. Long as you've got a fireguard –' She glanced at the range. 'Ah, I see you have. Now, you come to your Auntie Selina . . .'

Michael beamed at his newfound friend and reached for her bracelets. Polly watched in amazement. Michael rarely took to strangers so easily.

'I'll make us some tea first,' Polly offered.

'That'd be nice,' Selina said without looking up. 'I've just come from Albie's stall and I'm fair parched.'

The morning was happily spent – with the occasional break to attend to the little boy or to make another cup of tea – as Selina showed Polly how to make a peg rug. But all the while Selina dandled Michael on her knee, almost as if she didn't want to let him go.

'You can have this proddy, love.'

Polly laughed. 'A what?'

'It's just a pointed tool. Albie made it for me last night to give you. It's just a piece off an old dolly peg whittled to a point. And I've brought you the canvas you need to set you off. You can buy more from Albie. Now, watch me.'

Deftly, Selina showed Polly how to push the small pieces of fabric through the coarse woven canvas. 'Through once like this, then fold it over and into the next hole. See? Your pieces of material should always be cut about half an inch by two inches. And they must all be the same size. Now you have a go.'

Selina was quiet for a moment, watching how her pupil shaped up with her first efforts. 'Course, it's easier if you use a frame to stretch the canvas across. Albie said he'd make you one, if you take to it.'

As dinnertime approached, Selina nodded and said, 'You'll do. Well, I'd best be on me way now.' Reluctantly, she set Michael on the floor and watched him crawl to the heap of cut rags.

'Another cuppa before you go, Mrs Thorpe?'

Selina smiled, her gaze still on Michael. 'Go on, then.'

As it was almost midday, Polly set out scones and cakes too and the two women sat together munching happily and chatting. Michael had curled up on the heap of soft fabric and fallen asleep.

'Give me yar hand,' Selina said suddenly.

Polly was startled but held out her hand obediently. Selina took it and turned it over, palm upwards. She studied the lines for some minutes, whilst Polly became more agitated and almost snatched her hand away. But something held her there, whilst Selina pondered.

'You've a long life-line and – ' She seemed about to say more but stopped abruptly, frowning and tracing the lines on Polly's hand with her finger and turning it this way and that to look at the lines on the sides of her hand as well as those criss-crossing her palm. 'You'll have three children.'

Polly's heart skipped a beat. 'How do you know that?'

Selina smiled secretively. 'Oh, I know, love. Me mother was a fortune teller and a good one too. I haven't quite got that gift, but she taught me to read palms. It's all here, lass,' she glanced up and her dark eyes seemed to bore into Polly's soul. 'It's all in the palm of your hand.'

Meeting that direct, knowing gaze, Polly couldn't doubt her. Selina covered the girl's hand. 'There's dark times coming for all of us, Polly, and you've a lot of trouble and sadness still to come in your life, but be strong and brave. Follow your heart and you will find true happiness. But if you falter, if you're too stubborn to see where your happiness lies, it will elude you forever. Forgive and forget, Polly that's the secret. Forgive and forget.'

Polly couldn't find any words; her heart was beating so loudly and so fast that she was sure Selina must hear it. But the woman patted her hand and stood up. 'And now I really must go. If you want any more help, just send a message by my Albie.'

It took a while for Polly's heart to stop racing and even longer for her to put Selina's strange fortune-telling out of her mind. Picking up Michael when he woke and whimpered to be fed, she tried to make light of the woman's words. 'Three children, eh? Well, I've got one already, haven't I, my pet?'

And as for Selina's advice? Well, she wouldn't ever forget and she would certainly never forgive.

'Much as I like the little chap,' Roland said as he played with Michael, building a castle with a set of old bricks he'd unearthed from the attic, 'are you sure this isn't getting too much for you, Polly? You're looking very white and a bit peaky, love. And Violet's taking advantage. She's out two evenings a week now as well as all day.'

The arrangement had been working well for a year, but in the early months of 1914 Roland was becoming concerned about his beloved wife taking on too much. She ran their house, kept it spotless, and still helped out at her family's home as well as caring each weekday for Michael. Miriam, bright, lovable little girl though she was, spent more time at the Spicers' house than she did in her own home. And at night, Polly would sit making peg rugs or sewing.

She sighed. 'Violet's only young. She deserves a bit of fun now and again.'

'And did you get much fun when you were her age?'

Polly dipped her head and didn't answer. Those were the days when she'd been walking out with Leo. Despite

318

the burden of caring for the family, they'd been the best days of her life. But she couldn't say that and she didn't want her face to betray her.

But Roland answered his own question. 'No, you didn't because you were keeping house for all of them. Polly – '. He bit his lip and hesitated before saying in a rush. 'Polly, I don't like telling tales, but Violet's been seen with Micky Fowler again. I – I thought you ought to know.'

Polly's head jerked up. 'Oh lor'. Not him. Dad'll go mad, if he finds out.'

Roland blinked and looked nervous. 'Did we – did I – ought to tell him?'

'Oh no. I'm not getting in the middle of that, but I will have a word with Vi.'

'Must you? She'll know it's me that's told you.'

'Not necessarily. I see a lot of Nelly now. She comes round most Sunday afternoons. I mean, how did you find out? Did you see them for yourself?'

'No. It was Nelly who told me.'

'There you are then. It's come from Nelly. Violet need never know.'

'Who told you? Who's been spying on me?' Violet's lip curled. 'Roland, I suppose.'

'Roland wouldn't spy on you,' Polly retorted, neatly avoiding answering the question directly. 'It wasn't him saw you together.'

'Who then?' Polly could see her sister's mind was working frantically. 'Ah – I know. Bloody Ida Norton. She saw us. And I bet she couldn't wait to tell Nelly. Spiteful cow! And Nelly, of course, told you.'

This time Polly didn't say anything. Even if Violet

challenged Nelly – and she very much doubted that she would – Nelly Rawdon was quite capable of standing up for herself. She'd give Violet short shrift and no mistake, Polly knew.

'So – are you seeing Micky again?'

Violet wriggled her shoulders. 'Might be.'

'Then you'd better watch out for yourself. I'm not looking after another of your kids, Violet, if you get yourself into trouble again, so there.'

Violet flushed. 'I'm not that daft, Poll. He's not getting his way this time.' She giggled suddenly. 'D'you know, it meks 'em all the keener. That's what Nelly said and it's true. I might even get him to marry me this time.'

Polly's mouth dropped open. 'You – you'd really marry Micky Fowler?'

Violet nodded and said softly, 'I love him, Poll. I always have. I know that now.'

Polly stared at her for a moment, then shrugged her shoulders and turned away before her sister could see the envy in her eyes. 'Oh well,' she said, feigning indifference. 'Whatever makes you happy, I suppose. Though what Dad'll say, I don't know.'

William had plenty to say.

'Over my dead body, girl. You keep away from that Fowler family. Nearly drowned me, Bert did. Have you forgotten? And you want to connect us by marriage?'

Violet's eyes narrowed. 'If we're going to start raking up the past, Dad, then I can do that an' all. You were bosom pals with Bert Fowler when all the trouble was going on. Shoulder to shoulder then, weren't you, on the picket line? But he was a mite cleverer than you were. He didn't get himself arrested and sent to jail.' She leaned towards him as she added spitefully, 'And he's still got his job.'

'That was different,' William glowered, refusing to be side-tracked. 'That was work. But this is family.'

'So, I take it that if I go on seeing Micky – if I marry him – you'll throw me out? Is that it?'

William stared at her for a long moment. 'You can't marry without my permission – you're under age.'

But even this didn't faze Violet. She merely shrugged. 'Then we'll wait till I am.'

'Aye, and spawn another bastard in the meantime?'

Violet's face was set. 'No. That won't happen.'

'Why? What d'you mean?'

'That's none of your business.' Violet turned away. 'Ask your beloved Polly. She'll be glad to explain.'

Forty-Eight

'What did she mean, Poll?'

William was sitting in Polly's kitchen. There was fresh distemper on the walls. Every surface was scrubbed, every pot and pan sparkling and the smell of freshly baked bread made William's mouth water. Not for one moment did he begrudge Polly her happiness as a married woman, but oh, how he missed her at home. Violet was a slovenly housekeeper and with little money coming in now, there was often not enough food to go around them all. With Eddie gone and Stevie only earning a boy's wage, Violet's money could hardly be made to stretch to feed four hungry mouths – five if you counted little Michael. Miriam at nine could do a few tasks about the house; she was a good and willing little thing, but she wasn't old enough to bring money into the home.

Just sometimes in his lonely bed in the darkness of the night, William would wish he'd never got involved with the rioters. He would never voice such thoughts out loud – never have admitted it – but in his heart of hearts he questioned the sense of their actions. He believed every man had to stand up for what he saw as his rights, but he felt guilty that what he'd done had brought injury and heartache to so many, and especially to his own family. In the loneliness of the night, he admitted to himself that his Polly – his bright-haired, feisty lass – had not married the man she truly loved.

And all because of him.

It was taking his beloved city a long time to recover from that dreadful night. It would rise again, he knew, but people had long memories and the bitterness and sorrow would linger for years to come.

Polly sighed as she sat down. She cut a hunk of fresh bread, spread it thickly with butter, added a knob of cheese and pushed it across the table towards her father. He ate hungrily and she felt pity – and anger – flood through her. Pity because she hated to see him – or any of her family – suffering, but anger too because the quick-tempered man had brought it upon himself. He had put his workmates and his principles before the welfare of his family.

Well, damn his principles to high Heaven.

But she voiced none of her thoughts. Instead she managed a wry smile. 'To put it a bit crudely, Dad, she's keeping her legs crossed this time.'

William stopped chewing and stared at her. Then something happened that Polly hadn't seen in a long time. William burst out laughing. He laughed and laughed until he almost choked on his bread and cheese and his eyes watered.

His mirth was infectious and Polly was soon giggling helplessly too. And that was how Roland found them when he came home from work. He washed swiftly in the scullery and came to join them. 'What's all this about then?' He was already smiling, catching their hilarity even though he didn't know the reason for it.

Polly put her hand over his on the table, an affectionate gesture that heartened William. He'd been worried about his eldest daughter, for he'd known full well where her heart really lay and he was sorry that her future happiness had been ruined by the trouble he'd helped to cause. Though he never spoke of it, he knew in his heart of hearts that had it been Polly who'd wanted to make up with Leo, he could have accepted that; but not this. Not Violet and Micky Fowler. His face sobered at the thought and catching his change of mood, Polly's face became serious once more.

'I'll tell you later, Roland. I promise. Dad's come round to talk about Violet.'

'Violet? I can't see how she can have caused so much merriment,' Roland murmured, but it was said without spite. During the time she'd known her husband, and especially since she'd lived with him so closely, she didn't think Roland Spicer had a mean or spiteful bone in his body.

Polly sighed, her laughter gone now as had William's. 'Dad's found out that Violet's seeing Micky Fowler again.'

Roland avoided meeting William's eyes. 'I'm sorry to hear that.' He paused and then asked, 'What are you going to do about it?'

William shrugged. 'Not much I can do, I reckon, except threaten to throw her out. Which I've done and she doesn't seem bothered. I even told her she couldn't marry without my consent, but she just came back at me saying they'd wait till she could.'

Polly was thoughtful. 'Maybe that's the answer. I doubt Micky will wait as long as that.' She bit her lip, wondering if she dare voice what was in her mind. 'There's another thing, though, Dad. I'm not sure if it's right, but if a couple have a child out of wedlock, as they say—'

'A bastard, you mean?' William had no such sensibilities as his daughter. Polly flinched, but did not remonstrate with her father as she had with Violet. Instead, she ignored his remark and pressed on. 'If that same couple eventually marry, doesn't it legitimize the child?'

William stared at her. 'I haven't the faintest idea, Poll. Where did you hear that?'

Polly shrugged. 'Oh, somewhere – I can't remember.' She wasn't about to reveal that she'd been gossiping with Nelly about the matter and she'd said something of the sort.

William sniffed. 'Well, it dun't mek a lot of difference. Everyone knows the kid was born a bastard and that's what it'd always be in their eyes. Even with shotgun weddings, folks always know.' His voice dropped and his eyes had a haunted look. 'Folks have long memories, Poll. They never forget.'

Gently, but greatly daring, Polly said, 'And aren't you doing just the same thing? Bearing grudges against the Fowler family? Oh, don't get me wrong, I've no time for them either. Not any of them – only little Dottie maybe – but if he's Violet's choice, then surely . . . ?' Her voice faded away.

'Micky does have quite a good job now, Mr Longden—'

William's head shot up and he glared at his son-in-law. 'And I don't, you mean?'

Roland flushed as he stuttered. 'No – no – I didn't mean that. Please, I – was just trying to – to help.'

William's anger died as swiftly as it had come. 'Sorry, lad. I'm just tetchy about the subject, that's all. I didn't mean to snap your head off.'

'What I was trying to say is that although he's still working on the market, I understand he's no longer with Vince Norton.'

'Well, that's summat, I suppose,' William grunted and then glanced at Polly. 'What d'you think, Poll? Should we let her go ahead and marry him?'

'Oh, Dad, I don't know.'

'If she did move out, what'd happen to the family?' William said. 'She's not much of a housewife – not like you – but she's better than nowt.'

'Then you'd have to do the housework, Dad.'

The comical look on William's scandalized face brought laughter back into the room.

'You can't go on like this, Polly dear,' Roland said anxiously a few day's later after their conversation with William. 'You'll make yourself ill. You're doing too much. You're keeping this house like a new pin *and* you're going round to your old home every day and doing what Violet should be doing. You're wearing yourself out.'

Polly didn't argue. Instead, she said, 'I saw Mrs Halliday today.'

Roland's head shot up and his hurt gaze searched her face. 'Why?'

Once, there had been true friendship between Polly and the older woman, but since the riots Polly had hardly seen her. The shadow of Leo hung between them. Polly had hurt her son unbearably and even the generous-spirited Bertha Halliday couldn't forgive her any more than Polly was prepared to forgive Leo for arresting her father, thereby being the instigator of William ending up in prison. Maybe, deep down, the woman understood Polly's feelings, but she could never voice it; she would never utter a word against her own son, even though she might secretly question some of the things he'd done in the course of his duty. Since Leo had joined the police force – a fact she'd been very proud of at first – Bertha had found that some of her neighbours avoided her. And it had been even more apparent since the strike and the trouble that had followed. The Longden family was not the only one that couldn't ignore Leo's actions at that time.

So when Bertha opened her door to find Polly standing on her doorstep, she'd been surprised, but pleased. She'd always liked the girl and would have loved to have had her as her daughter-in-law.

Now Polly explained gently to Roland the reason she'd been forced to seek out Bertha's help.

'She's still the local midwife round here, but she doesn't just deliver babies, Roland, she helps young mothers through their pregnancies. Doctors would cost a lot of money and . . .'

Roland closed his eyes and groaned. 'Oh no, don't tell me. Violet has got herself pregnant again.'

Polly was blushing prettily, but still her husband didn't seem to understand what she was trying to tell him. 'No, no, Roland dear. *I* went to see Mrs Halliday about myself, not about Violet.'

Slowly, he raised his head and looked at her as realization began to dawn. It spread across his face, slowly at first and then with a flood of joy that Polly didn't think she'd ever seen on any man's face, not even on Leo's in their happiest moments.

He grasped her hands tightly. 'Oh, Polly, are you sure? Are we really going to have a little one of our own?'

Polly, her eyes shining, nodded and then found herself clasped in his arms. He rocked her to and fro. 'Oh, Polly, my love, my love.'

Forty-Nine

There was no doubting Roland's excitement; he told anyone and everyone who would listen. 'I never thought it would happen to me. I've a lovely wife and now I'm going to be a dad. Can you believe it?'

His listeners would smile indulgently and later would say to each other, 'No, I can't quite believe it, but there you are. And the feller deserves a bit of happiness, when all's said and done.'

Polly's news made William think; perhaps it would be better to allow Violet to marry Micky Fowler. It looked as if they were both determined to do it anyway when Violet was old enough. So there was no good reason to make them wait. And, if Polly was right in what she'd been told, it would make their little boy legitimate. And William was becoming increasingly fond of Michael.

By March William had relented and agreed that Violet could marry Micky Fowler. 'That's if you can get him to the altar, girl. 'Cos I reckon if you don't lift your skirts for him soon, he'll find someone who will.'

But to everyone's surprise, Micky Fowler didn't find another girl. He proposed one night when he was, it had to be admitted, a little worse for the drink, but nevertheless in the cold light of day he didn't try to back out.

Polly, still anxious for her sister, did something she never thought she would ever do; she sought out Micky.

'Are you serious about our Vi?' she asked bluntly. 'Or are you just stringing her along?'

He looked at her for a moment before saying, very solemnly, 'Poll, if I say something to you, will you promise it'll go no further? Not – not even to your husband and certainly never to Violet.'

She wondered what on earth it was he was going to say, but with a brief nod of her head she gave her word.

He sighed and glanced away. 'I've told you before, Poll, it was always you. I think you thought I was joking, but I wasn't. I've never been more serious in my life. It was you I wanted. Still do, if I'm honest.' He gave a quick grin. 'And I'm not often that honest am I?'

Polly was stunned into silence and could only stare at him.

'But when I could see that you only had eyes for Leo – ' He shrugged. 'Well, I gave up and turned to your little sister. Oh, I'm fond of Vi, don't get me wrong. And Michael's a great kid. I'm proud of him, but – ' He bit his lip and scuffed the ground with the toe of his shoe. 'When the riot happened and your dad and mine were in the thick of it, standing shoulder to shoulder for what they believed in, I thought our families might get closer, you know. Then, when you fell out with Leo, I began to hope again. I couldn't help it, Poll. Don't be mad at me. And then you had to go and marry that milksop, Roland Spicer. I couldn't believe it when I heard.' He searched her face. 'Did you do it to spite Leo?'

'No – no,' she cried, finding her voice at last through the shock of what he was telling her. She'd known he'd once cared for her, but she'd never thought he still carried that same feeling after all this time. 'Don't ever say that. Roland is a good man. I – I'm very fond of him.'

'But you don't love him, Poll, do you? Not really.'

'Of course, I do,' she declared hotly, but knew the colour rising in her face belied her words. Pulling her wandering thoughts together, she snapped, 'We're not talking about me, Micky, but about you and Vi. Are you saying you don't really love her?'

He chewed on his lower lip. 'Let's say, Poll, that I love her as much as you love Roland Spicer.'

Polly's blood ran cold. He'd trapped her. If she tried to persuade him not to marry her sister, then he would know she didn't truly love her own husband. And yet how could she let the marriage go ahead if he didn't care deeply for Violet? It was doomed to disaster before it even started. But Micky was not done. He touched her hand lightly and said, 'Don't worry, Big Sister. We'll mek a go of it – me an' Vi. We're from the same mould. You and me – ' he hesitated as if it took him a lot to admit it – 'you and me would never have survived together. You're too good for me. Too honest. It'd've been a nightmare. Better things the way they are. But I'll just say one thing to you, Polly. Though you may not believe me, I love you with all my heart – always have done – and if ever you need a friend, I'll always be there for you.'

She looked deep into his eyes and saw something she'd never thought to see in the eyes of Micky Fowler – sincerity. Then swiftly he was back to being his teasing, flippant self. 'Besides we're going to be brother and sister-in-law, aren't we?'

Despite seeing an unexpected side to Micky's nature, Polly shuddered, fearing for Violet. She turned and walked away, and later she wondered if her mind had been playing tricks on her or if maybe she had dreamt the whole incident.

She really couldn't believe what she'd heard from Micky's own mouth. There had been three men in her life: Leo, whom she had adored, but whom a cruel fate had snatched from her; Roland, who loved her devotedly, but for whom she could only summon a fondness; and now Micky. Micky Fowler, whom she would have said, had anyone asked her, that she hated.

She sighed. Life really was very complicated and most unfair.

Violet and Micky were married very quietly early in April, with the Longdens on one side of the aisle and the Fowlers on the other, glaring at each other.

As they left the church, William and Bert found themselves walking side by side.

'We didn't want this any more than you did, William. I hardly wanted my lad mixed up with a jailbird's family. But I s'pose we've got to make the best of it now, eh? What say we shake hands and let bygones be bygones?'

William stared at him as if he couldn't quite believe his ears. 'You'd have been in jail alongside me if you hadn't slunk away into the night and left the rest of us to take the blame. I saw you smash a shop window, Bert Fowler. Saw it with me own eyes, so don't play the innocent with me.' Then he thrust his face close to Bert's and hissed the same words he'd used to Violet when he'd first learnt she wanted to marry Micky. He'd vowed this day would never happen, but it had. There was nothing he could do about it. But he could and would continue his feud with the Fowler family. 'Over my dead body, Bert Fowler. An' I'll tell you summat else an' all. If that lad of yourn hurts our Vi, it'll be 'im at the bottom of the river next time – an' I'll mind there's no one there to pull 'im out.'

Bert's face darkened. 'Dangerous words, William, dangerous words. If owt happens to my lad, I'll know where to come lookin' then, won't I?'

'Aye, happen you will.'

'Prepared to swing for him, then, a' ya?'

They had reached the church porch and stepped outside. William shook his fist in Bert's face. 'I reckon it'd be worth it if he dun't treat my girl right.'

Bert's mouth twisted. 'And what about your girl treating our Micky right? She's a flighty piece, so I've heard. An' I've never been sure that bairn is really his.'

Before Bert realized what was happening, William had struck him on the mouth. Bert reeled backwards and fell to the ground with William standing astride him. 'How dare you, Bert Fowler? You keep your filthy insinuations to yarsen.'

Bert, holding his mouth, struggled to his feet, whilst William waited, fists clenched, for the retaliation. But it never came.

'Big words, William. Mek sure you know what they mean.'

Bert turned away. He grabbed his wife's arm and hauled her after him. 'We're going, Hetty. And don't you be letting any of the Longdens across my threshold. Only Violet, 'cos she's a Fowler now. Only her and her bairn. You hear me, woman?'

Micky and Violet stood looking on helplessly.

'Well, I aren't going to live at your place, if that's how he feels,' Violet said. 'You can come to ours.'

Polly, carrying Michael in her arms, moved forward and handed the child to Violet. Avoiding meeting Micky's eyes, she said, 'I don't reckon that's a good idea, Vi. Best try to find a place of your own. Start as you mean to go on.'

She could feel Micky's gaze upon her as he said slowly, 'Polly's right, love. I'll sort summat out, but come to ours just till I do.'

'No,' Violet said firmly in a tone that brooked no argument. 'You do what you want, but I'm going home.'

Polly risked a swift glance at Micky's face and had to stifle her laughter when she saw the look of horror on his face and heard him splutter, 'But it's our wedding night. I've waited months – '

Violet smiled up at him coquettishly. 'Then you'd better find somewhere for us to live pretty quick, hadn't you?'

And with that, she hitched Michael onto her hip and marched down the road, leaving Micky and her own family staring after her.

It was Roland who broke the stunned silence. 'Micky, there's a spare room at our place. You – you and Violet could have it for – for tonight. That'd be all right, wouldn't it, Polly?'

'I – er – ' Polly was stunned. She'd believed that Roland had no time for the Fowlers, and especially Micky, like the rest of them.

Micky looked uncomfortable but he recovered enough to say, 'That's kind of you, but – '

'Roland, dear,' Polly put her hand on his arm. 'I don't think—'

But for once Roland was decisive. 'We can't let a young newly married couple spend their wedding night apart. We can let them have the house to themselves.

We can go and stay at your father's house. Just for tonight. And then tomorrow, I'll go with Micky and try to help him find somewhere for them to live. In fact, I might already know of somewhere, but I'd need to find out.'

Micky – and Polly – were both looking relieved. Polly couldn't forget Micky's declaration of his feelings for her. And Micky was wishing heartily that he'd never said a word to her. But he pulled himself together and said, 'That's very generous of you, Roland. I'll gladly take up your offer – if Vi's willing.' He pulled a comical face. 'But as you've seen my *wife* has a mind of her own.'

Now that Roland had fully explained his solution, Polly was happy to go along with it. They'd be in the spare room – not in the bed she shared with Roland – and she would be at home. Impulsively, she said, 'And I'll look after Michael for you. In fact, why don't you make it two nights – until Monday morning when you've to go to work?'

'That's kind of you, Polly. If Violet agrees, we will. And thank you.'

Violet jumped at the chance. Polly and Roland hurriedly packed the few belongings they would need and Micky and Violet did the same.

'It'll be just like a honeymoon,' Violet said. 'Your Roland is such a nice man. I hope you know how lucky you are to have him, Poll.'

'He is,' Polly agreed, neatly avoiding answering the last part of the question. 'Look, Vi,' she said as she helped Violet carry the bundle of belongings to the house that was now her home, 'none of us were happy about you marrying Micky. But you have. It's done, so now you must try and keep him in line. It looks as if you're not afraid to stand up to him.'

'I'm not, Poll.' Violet's forehead wrinkled. 'But I'm no romantic fool either. I know he's difficult and I know too that he's going along with everything I say just because he wants to – well, you know. That's what this is all about. He reckons he's waited long enough and he's not going to wait another minute.' She laughed wryly. 'That's men for you.'

Polly said nothing, thinking of her own wedding night, of Roland's shyness, his tentativeness and his consideration for her.

She blotted out the thought of what a wedding night with Leo might have been like and tried to concentrate on the problems she could foresee for her sister. She hoped she was wrong, but she had the horrible feeling she wasn't.

Fifty

But Polly's new brother-in-law was full of surprises. The very next day – Sunday morning – he set off with Roland in search of the man who might have a property to rent out. He walked with a newfound swagger, whistling cheerfully. He was a married man now, with a pretty little wife – even if she did have a sharp tongue at times – and he was with his son. Micky had decided to acknowledge Michael as his own and for the last few months had made no secret of the fact. Everyone believed it anyway; Violet had made sure of that from the start and in his heart of hearts he knew it to be true. He'd only gone along with what his father had said to avoid being trapped into a hasty marriage. But recently, realizing that there really was no chance with Polly, he'd grown very fond of Violet, and Michael was a boy to be proud of. Besides, it was time he settled down.

Roland's contact had had a flat available until the previous week.

'I'm sorry, mate, I've let it. The folks are moving in tomorrow.' He pondered a moment and then said, 'Have you asked Albie? Him what runs the material stall in the market.'

'I know Albie,' Micky said at once. 'I work on the markets. Why?'

Roland nodded too. 'And Polly knows both him and his wife.'

'He rents out two rooms in his house. There's only him and his missus. They never had no kids and I reckon their last lodgers have just left. See him.'

As they walked away, Micky muttered, 'I don't reckon Albie will want owt to do wi' me. I ain't got a good name round the market.'

'Oh dear,' Roland murmured. 'Perhaps we'd better go on looking then.'

They did, but when dusk began to fall, they trudged home without having found any other leads towards getting the newly married couple a place of their own.

'Mebbe we could stay at yours, Roland? Vi could help Polly and they could still look after the rest of the family together.'

Roland was doubtful. He liked to see the best in people, but he was not stupid. He'd seen the looks that Micky gave Polly, had seen the flash of desire in them at rare moments when Micky thought no one else was watching. To his relief, though, he'd seen Polly turn away in disgust and knew that, whatever Micky's feelings for her were, they were certainly not reciprocated.

'It'd be better if you could find a place of your own. After all, it's not as if there's just the two of you. There's Michael too.'

At the thought of his son, Micky smiled. 'D'you know, Roland, I wouldn't admit it to everyone, but he's the best part of all this. At last I get to live with my son.'

'So you do acknowledge he's yours, then?'

Now Micky shoved his hands in his pockets and had the grace to look ashamed. 'I was scared, Roland. We were both so young and me dad – well – he said I should deny it. But I reckon it was more to get at

William than anything else. He wanted to see the Long-dens brought down. He's always thought the whole family's too high and mighty.'

Roland said nothing for they had reached the Long-dens' home to find Polly and Violet waiting with a hot meal for them and anxious questions.

Micky related the events of the morning and, to Roland's surprise, left nothing out.

'I could ask Selina – Albie's wife – if you like,' Polly offered. 'We've become quite friendly.'

Micky shrugged. 'Wouldn't mek no odds, Poll. Albie'd have the final say and it'd be a "no".'

Polly regarded him thoughtfully for a moment and then said, 'No harm in asking. If they do say no, it'll be no more than you're expecting.'

Micky pulled a face.

'Maybe it would be best if you asked Albie, love,' Roland suggested. 'You know him well too, don't you?'

As they finished their meal and Violet spooned the last of Michael's dinner into his mouth, Polly promised, 'I'll go first thing tomorrow morning. And as long as Roland doesn't mind, you can stay here a night or two longer. We're all right at Dad's.'

She would never have admitted it out loud, but she was quite enjoying being back with Stevie and Miriam; she still missed the youngsters.

Early the next morning Polly approached the market nervously.

'Hello, lass,' Albie greeted her. 'Now I'm glad I've seen you. I've got some lovely bits of material for you. Perfect for rug making.' He grinned at her. 'But maybe you've got all you want now?'

Polly smiled weakly.

Albie peered at her. 'Summat wrong, duck?'

'Er – not exactly. But I've come to ask you something and I'm afraid you're going to say no.'

'Spit it out then.'

'It's about my sister and – and Micky Fowler.'

'Oh – him!'

His tone didn't sound promising and Polly's heart sank.

'They're looking for a place to live. Just – just rooms or a small flat or house. And Roland heard that you let out a couple of rooms in your house.'

Albie regarded her thoughtfully. 'There's a babby, ain't there?'

'Yes. Michael. He'll be three in August, but he's a good little chap.'

'It's not that, Polly.' Albie sighed heavily and there was sorrow in his eyes.

'It's Micky, isn't it?'

'No. Actually it's not him either, though I do have me doubts about that young man.'

There was a pause whilst Polly waited impatiently. She bit her lip to stop herself saying, 'What then?'

Albie let out a deep sigh. 'It's the kiddie – '

As Polly opened her mouth to defend her nephew, Albie put up his hand. 'Oh, I don't doubt what you say, but you see, duck, it'd be heart-breaking for my missus to have a little 'un about the place. We – we desperately wanted children, Polly, but it never happened and it's been a great sadness to us all these years. I'd've taken a risk on Micky – really I would – but I couldn't do that to my Selina.'

'Of course not,' Polly said huskily. She turned away, nodding her thanks.

Both of them forgot all about the remnants of material which Albie had carefully put on one side for her.

Violet and Micky spent one more night at Polly and Roland's home, whilst they again stayed with William, Stevie and Miriam.

Just before her bedtime Miriam climbed on Polly's knee and wound her chubby little arms around her older sister's neck. 'Have you come home, Polly? I miss you. Violet never gives me cuddles like you do, or tells me bedtime stories. She's always too busy.'

'Huh! I don't know what with, the house is a tip,' William groused. 'And the meals she cooks, well, I've seen stray cats turn their noses up at the leftovers.'

Polly hugged Miriam to her. 'You can come round to our house any time you like for a cuddle and a story.'

'Can I come and live with you?'

'No, no, your home is here with Dad and Stevie. But Violet, Micky and Michael are going to get a home of their own, so you'll have to help Dad around the house. And when you're a bit older, you can learn to cook.'

'I can make gingerbread men now. Mrs Halliday showed me.'

Polly was startled and glanced at her father. William moved uneasily in his chair and avoided her gaze.

'Miriam goes down the road to see her sometimes,' he muttered.

Polly nodded, not in the least surprised that Bertha Halliday held no grudges against the innocent young girl. The only people to blame for her son's unhappiness were Polly, and William for being the cause of his daughter's refusal to forgive and forget.

Fifty-One

Polly was back in her own home and cleaning vigorously. Violet and Michael were back at the Longdens' home and Micky had been banished to the Fowlers' house – much to his disgust.

Polly was singing cheerfully at the top of her voice and scrubbing her scullery floor when she thought she heard a sound. She stopped to listen and then it came again. Someone was knocking at the door.

She threw her floor cloth into the bucket and pulled herself up. As she did so a wave of nausea overwhelmed her and she clutched the edge of the sink to steady herself. This was the third time it had happened in as many days and she'd felt very queasy each morning. But at least now she knew the reason. She staggered to the back door to open it.

To her surprise, Selina Thorpe was standing there.

'Good lord, girl. You look as white as a sheet. Let me help you to a chair.'

Whilst Polly leant back and closed her eyes, Selina made herself at home by finding everything she needed to make a cup of tea. When at last she sat down opposite and regarded the girl steadily, she said, 'Albie told me your sister's looking for a place.'

Polly drank the hot tea gratefully and nibbled the biscuit Selina had put in her saucer. The nausea began to subside a little.

'She is, but – ' She hesitated.

Selina nodded. 'I know what he told you, but he got it wrong.' Although there was still a deep sadness in the woman's eyes, she was smiling. 'I've learned to live with it, Polly. And do you know, I'd love to have a little one about the place. If we get to know each other, I'd like nothing better than to look after him whilst Violet goes out to work – if she wants to, that is, now she's got a husband to look after her.' Selina pulled a face. 'Though she'd do well not to rely on that scallywag too much.'

'Oh, but – '

'I know you look after little Michael for her, but – ' Selina's smile broadened. 'If I'm not mistaken, and I'm not often wrong, one of those kiddies I said you'd have one day, is already on its way.'

Polly's cup rattled in its saucer as her hand trembled. She stared at Selina.

'How on earth did you know?' Was the woman really a witch as some of the folks around here called her? 'I'm not far on yet. I'm not even showing.'

'Oh, I know,' the older woman said and the two women laughed together. 'I bet your hubby's tickled pink, ain't he? Now,' Selina went on briskly, 'about Violet. Albie and me are prepared to give it a go. We suggest a month's trial for both sides. At the end of the month, if it's not working out for either of us, then they can find somewhere else.'

'Really? Are you sure? I mean Micky's not exactly Albie's favourite person. There's been some trouble at the market, hasn't there?'

'Oh, several times,' Selina said airily. 'But Albie's prepared to give Micky a second chance. The lad got in with Vince Norton when he was young and got led astray. It's easy done. The market folk are good people, Polly, in general but you always get the odd bad apple. Maybe, given the chance, Micky will mend his ways. If not . . .'

She said no more, but the threat left hanging in the air was obvious.

Second chance? Forgive and forget? Such words haunted Polly. Why was it she was so steadfast in her hatred of Leo? Why couldn't she have given him a second chance? But it was too late now; she'd made her bed and she would have to lie in it.

Resolutely, she looked to the future, counting the days to when she would hold her own child in her arms.

'I wish we could hear news of Eddie,' William said mournfully. Polly was at home, ironing for the family with an old blanket spread on the table and two flat irons heating alternately on the hob.

'He's probably abroad, Dad. Well out of harm's way. He's best where he is.' Under her breath, she added, 'Wherever that is.'

She too longed to hear news of Eddie. Despite the trouble he'd always caused her, he was still her brother and she cared about him and hoped he was well and happy.

'There's talk of war, you know. Ever since that Archduke or whatever he was and his wife got assassinated at the end of June, they reckon there's going to be a war.'

'It won't involve us, will it?'

William shrugged. 'They reckon it might.'

'And who's "they"?'

'Fellers in the pub.'

'Oh, a lot of drunks. I wouldn't take any notice of what they say.'

He cast her an angry glance. 'It's in the papers, an' all.'

Polly pursed her lips and slammed her iron down harder on the shirt she was ironing as if to make her point. She wanted to say, 'You'd do better to try and find some proper work than worry about politics over which you've no control.' But she held her tongue.

'Roland, is there going to be war?'

Polly still read the paper every day now that she had her own and she'd read for herself the talk of war in the press. But she'd wondered if it was eager reporters trying to make the headlines. Roland's anxious eyes answered her question without him needing to speak a word. Polly clutched her throat. 'And – and will we be involved?'

'This country may be, but I don't know about us personally.'

'But – but Eddie? If – if he is in the army, then – then – ?'

Roland nodded solemnly. 'Yes, I'm afraid he would be.'

By the time Polly's baby was due in early August, the war clouds were gathering over Europe. Roland and Polly spent the August Bank Holiday quietly; the hot weather made her uncomfortable.

'We could go to the park if you feel able,' Roland suggested tentatively. Polly was sitting in their kitchen, wiping the beads of perspiration from her forehead. 'It might be cooler there.'

'I don't think I could walk that far, Roland.' She smiled. 'Besides, what would me mam have said about me walking out in public when I'm the size of an elephant?'

Tentatively, Roland put his hand protectively over her swollen belly. 'You look beautiful, Polly dear.'

Polly grimaced. 'To you, maybe, but then I'm carrying your son.'

Roland chuckled. 'You're sure it's going to be a boy then?'

Polly shifted in her chair, trying to find a comfortable position. 'I'm sure,' she said tartly. 'Only a boy would cause me so much discomfort. And besides, Selina said it was going to be a boy.'

'And you trust Selina's gift?'

Polly chuckled. 'Implicitly!' And they laughed together.

'Not long now, though,' Roland comforted. 'When did Mrs Halliday –' there was still a change, a constraint, in Roland's tone whenever he mentioned the name Halliday – 'say the baby would come?'

'Second week in August, she thought, but he could come any time now.' She sighed and moved restlessly again. 'I just wish he'd hurry up and get it over with.'

Roland got up and went to fetch a cooling drink for her, and for the rest of the day he watched her with anxious eyes. He, too, wished it was all over.

Polly woke with a start; the sky was just beginning to lighten over the rooftops. She reached out and gripped Roland's arm, waking him at once.

'What is it?'

'I think you'd better fetch – someone. Maybe – Nelly

Rawdon.' Despite that pain that was coming in regular waves now, she was still sensitive to Roland's feeling. He wouldn't want Leo's mother in his house and certainly not delivering his child.

But Roland was generous to the last.

'You've been seeing Mrs Halliday,' he said as he swung his legs to the floor and began to dress hastily. 'So Mrs Halliday it shall be.'

'But – '

'No buts, Polly. She's the best – you've always said so – and I want the best for you and – and for our baby. Whoever that person might be.'

As another contraction racked her, Polly argued no more.

Leo opened the door to Roland's urgent knocking. For a brief moment they stared at one another, shocked to come face to face.

'It's Polly,' Roland blurted out at last. 'It's the baby.'

'I'll get Mother,' Leo said and turned away to shout up the stairs. 'Mam, it's Mr Spicer. Poll – Mrs Spicer's gone into labour.'

Roland heard Bertha's voice. 'I'll be as quick as I can. Tell him the usual . . .'

Leo turned round and came back to the door.

'The usual,' Roland asked. 'What's that?'

'Get plenty of water on the boil and cover the bed with old sheets and towels. I expect Poll – your wife . . .' he hesitated, 'will have got everything ready. You'd best get back to her.' He stuck out his hand. 'Good luck.'

After a moment's hesitation, Roland took the proffered hand and shook it. 'Thank you,' he said simply before turning away and running back up the street. He paused only to rap on the Longdens' door and to tell William, who was already up and about, what was happening.

'Owt I can do, lad, you just let me know. Mebbe we're best out of the way, so if you want to go to the pub later . . .'

'I'll see,' Roland said as he hurried away. Talking about wetting the baby's head already was a mite too early to his mind.

Despite their differences, Bertha came at once to the house and stayed with Polly until the baby – a boy, as Polly had expected – fought his way, kicking and screaming, into an uncertain world.

When it was all over and the baby was nestling in her arms, Polly watched Bertha moving around the bedroom, tidying away all traces of the birthing before she allowed the new father into the room.

'Mrs Halliday, thank you for coming. It – it can't have been easy for you.'

Bertha blinked at her. 'What? Oh – that? No, Polly, it's not that. I'm not one to bear grudges, specially where there's an innocent little life concerned. No, it's – it's summat else.'

'What?' Polly felt a sudden fear and her tone was harsher than she'd intended as she demanded, 'Tell me.'

'You won't have heard – ' Bertha smiled, but the anxiety did not quite leave her eyes – 'but war's been declared today. Germany marched into Belgium, and so we're at war.'

'How d'you know?'

Bertha lifted her plump shoulders. 'Oh, the papers get news through very fast these days, don't they? Telegraph or summat, but the city's buzzing with the news and our Leo—'

The stab of fear made Polly tremble and the baby in her arms began to whimper.

'There, there,' she said absently, but her mind was on Leo. When she should have been concentrating on her newborn son and her husband still waiting impatiently outside the door to see them both, Polly was thinking about her lost love, the man she told herself every day she hated.

'What about him?' she whispered.

Bertha came to the end of the bed and said in a low voice. 'He's talking about enlisting. Joining up. The whole city's in a fervour of patriotism.' Her face was bleak. 'Oh, Polly, I don't want my lad going.'

'But surely, he's needed here. He's a policeman,' Polly said unnecessarily. As if any of them were likely to forget it.

'They're calling for volunteers. It seems they'll take anyone who wants to go.'

Polly felt a fresh shaft of dread. 'Anyone?'

Bertha nodded miserably. There was silence between the two women as they stared at each other. And they both knew, in that shared moment, that their terror was for one man and only one man.

Leo.

Fifty-Two

'He's wonderful, Polly. You're so clever.'

'Well, you had a bit to do with it, Roland dear.' Polly was striving to be extra nice to her husband, though in his joy and pride at the birth of their son she doubted he would have noticed her quiet mood. And if he had, the kindly man would undoubtedly put it down to her preoccupation with the tiny baby. They were both trying not to let the shadow of war spoil what should have been the happiest day of their married life.

But there was no cause for concern over Jacob, who fed greedily and yelled lustily. And it wasn't as if Polly hadn't had the caring of tiny babies before; with both Miriam and more recently with Michael, she was an old hand and suffered none of the uncertainties and nervousness of many a first-time mother.

That she couldn't glory in her baby son was her own fault; she couldn't forget that any day now Leo might be marching off to war.

As the days passed, her fears lessened a little. There was no word from Mrs Halliday and she called in every so often to check on mother and baby. The subject wasn't mentioned between them again and yet both women knew it was uppermost in both their minds each time they met.

The papers were already full of war news. Polly tried

to close her mind to it, but it kept intruding into her life.

'Polly, Polly – ' Her sister came charging in through Polly's back door, dragging Michael with her.

'Vi – whatever's the matter?'

Not more trouble, she thought. Vi and Micky seemed settled at Albie's. Their trial month had passed long ago and both sides had declared themselves happy with the arrangement. Indeed, Selina had taken a liking to Violet and even more of a one to the little boy. She happily offered to look after Michael whilst Violet went out to work.

'Polly's got plenty on now with her little one,' Selina told Violet. 'Until she's better from her confinement, at least, let me look after him. If she wants him back then, well . . .' But there was no doubting the reluctance in her tone and Violet had smiled as she'd related the incident to her sister.

Albie, too, it seemed had been as good as his word. He'd given Micky the promised second chance and was taking an interest in the young man's work on the market, even offering him work on his own stall. 'I could do with someone I can trust to look after me stall when I goes buying,' he'd said, eyeing Micky severely. 'Now, lad, a' you that person?'

Micky, unusually solemn, had nodded. 'I am, Mr Thorpe. I know I was wild a few years back, but I'm a married man now.' He'd puffed out his chest. 'I've got responsibilities. Besides,' he'd grinned, suddenly more like the cheeky young feller of old. 'What's it they say about "doing you-know-what on your own doorstep"?'

Albie had roared with laughter. 'Now, none of that language here, m'lad. But I'll give it a go. My missus has taken to that little wife of yours and the bairn.' His eyes had clouded briefly. 'I wasn't sure about you moving in with us, I have to be honest, but it seems to be working out nicely all round.'

So Polly was a little irritable when Violet burst into her home as she was peacefully feeding Jacob. 'What on earth are you getting in such a flap about, Vi?'

'It's Eddie. He's come home. I mean – on a visit. He's come to say goodbye.' Violet flung herself to her knees and buried her face in Polly's lap, dislodging the baby from suckling at his mother's breast. Jacob at once set up a plaintive wail but Violet was oblivious as she cried, 'Oh, Poll, he's going to war.'

Polly felt the blood drain from her face as she put her arm around Violet and the two sisters hugged, each one supporting the other. At last they drew back.

'You've got to come, Poll. Dad's in tears, begging and pleading with him not to go. I've never seen me dad in such a state. It's not as if he's even talked that much about our Eddie lately.'

'I think it was a relief when our dear brother went away, Vi,' Polly said grimly. 'I know it was for me. Eddie was in with a bad crowd and goodness knows where he might have ended up if he hadn't joined the army. In prison, more than likely. I thought going into the army was the best thing he ever did. But now I'm not so sure.' She paused and the two sisters looked at each other again, dread in their eyes. 'I'll come straight away.'

Polly hardly recognized her brother. He'd grown taller and filled out, his shoulders and chest broad, narrowing to his waist, and then strong, sturdy thighs. And he looked so smart in his uniform. He'd aged in his face too, as if he'd seen the world – or a good part of it – and a slice of life that was totally different from the one he'd known. But his grin was as cheeky as ever and his eyes, still as full of mischief and daring, twinkled at her. He held out his arms. 'Polly – I do believe you've grown an' all. I hardly recognized our Vi and her a married woman. And you too, so I hear? But to Roland Spicer of all people. What happened to everybody's favourite copper, then? I really thought you'd make it up with him after all the dust had settled.'

There was an awkward silence before Polly, avoiding his questioning gaze, said shortly, 'It didn't work out.'

Eddie shrugged and let the matter drop – for the moment. But he intended to find out what had gone wrong. He wanted to know everything that had happened to his family whilst he'd been away.

'Tell him, Poll,' William spoke up from his chair by the fire, the chair where he spent most of his days now.

Polly glanced at her father, not quite sure what it was she was supposed to say to her brother.

'Tell him he's not to go.'

Eddie sighed. 'I've been trying to explain it to him, Poll, but he's not listening. I'm a soldier now. I can't get out of the army even if I wanted to, specially not now. And, besides, I don't want to. It's a good life.'

She gazed at him, drinking in the sight of this stranger standing tall and proud in front of her – she knew that army life had been the making of him. She'd been right after all; it had been the best thing he'd ever done. And yet . . .

Polly took a deep breath. 'Is it true you've – you've got to go to war? Abroad? Maybe – maybe to the Front?'

There was a sudden fire in his eyes and a straightening of his shoulders as if he relished the idea, couldn't wait to go. 'I'm with the First Battalion of the Lincolnshire Regiment. We've been stationed in Portsmouth and we're one of the first battalions to go.'

William groaned and Eddie put his hand on his father's shoulder. 'There's no need to worry, Dad. It'll be over by Christmas. That's what they all say.'

Of course it wasn't over by Christmas; indeed the fighting was getting worse.

The Longden family had had to come to terms with Eddie's commitment and they'd done their best to make his brief leave happy and memorable. On the day he left they'd all shed tears; even Stevie, who considered himself a grown-up at fourteen, had tried to hold back the tears but had failed. Only Eddie was genuinely cheerful.

There was one brief moment that caught at Polly's heart as he hugged her and whispered in her ear, 'Look after 'em, Poll. But then, I don't really need to ask, do I? 'Cos I know you always will.' He'd drawn back and held her at arm's length looking down into her eyes, for a brief moment deadly serious and seeing far more in the depths of her eyes than she intended him to see. Whilst he'd been home, he'd learned all about what had torn the two young lovers apart. Now his voice dropped even lower so that she almost missed the words. 'Even if it means sacrificing your own happiness, you'll look after them, though I'm not sure they deserve it.' Her brother knew her too well – even though he hadn't been around much over the last few years. He cleared his throat and added, 'Try to be happy, Poll, as happy as you can be. Roland's a good chap.'

She'd nodded, unable to speak for the tears filling her throat. And the unspoken words lay between them.

But he's not Leo.

*

As before, they heard nothing from Eddie for weeks on end. And now they worried more than ever before. But they were not the only ones. All over the city men and boys as young as sixteen were enlisting, urged on by the patriotic fervour sweeping through the streets into pubs, homes and places of work.

Polly kept herself busy, trying to keep her mind off thoughts of Eddie – and Leo. But she'd heard no more from Bertha Halliday.

Caring for her husband and child, and seeing that her father, Stevie and Miriam were all right too, left Polly little time. And at night she was far too exhausted to lie awake for long. But it was in the early hours of the morning that the fear struck and woke her from her sleep. Then she would lie staring into the darkness until a pale dawn, or her baby's cries, reminded her that it was time to rise and begin another day.

If only, she mourned, things had been different. If her mother hadn't died, if she'd been able to follow her dream and become a teacher. And, most of all, if she'd become Leo's wife. How very different her life might have been.

Fifty-Three

'Come and sit down to your tea, Roland dear. It's all ready. Hard day?' Polly bustled about the kitchen, setting his evening meal before him. Jacob was soundly asleep in his cot upstairs. Seven months old now, he'd been sleeping through the night for a while and was growing into a strong, sturdy infant. Already he could sit up on his own.

Roland sat down heavily and silently placed a tiny white feather on the table.

'Get that mucky thing off the tea table—' she began and then was suddenly still, staring terror-struck at the offending feather. The gravy boat she was holding slipped from her grasp and smashed to the floor, splashing the hot liquid on her legs and spilling over the new peg rug she had only just finished making. But neither she nor Roland seemed to notice; she wasn't even aware of the scalding pain. They were both staring, transfixed, at the white feather.

'Oh no,' she breathed. 'Not that. Not that.' She dragged her gaze away and looked at Roland, sitting with his shoulders hunched, his face pale and frightened.

'Who? Not them bitches at work? Surely not? Ida? Was it Ida?' She knew it wouldn't have been Nelly. Nelly was her friend and it had been she who'd told Polly of the white feathers being handed out at the factory to men who were fit enough and the right age to enlist.

Slowly, Roland shook his head and said hoarsely,
'No, it wasn't any of them. Surprisingly, because I
expect I'm not popular with all of 'em. No.' He sighed
heavily. 'It was a woman in the street. There's a band
of them, marching up and down the High Street and
handing out these – these badges of cowardice.'

'Roland, no!' She dropped to her knees beside him.
For the first time her concern was wholly and totally for
him. 'You're not a coward. Take no notice. You're not
to allow them to – to shame you into volunteering.
Besides,' she went on with a surge of fresh hope, 'you're
too old, aren't you?'

He gave a wry smile. 'No, love. I'm not. I'm thirty-
four and that's not too old to – to become cannon
fodder.'

'Roland, don't.'

At his words, her fears were back. All of them and
now with an added worry: Roland too, might enlist.

He continued at his work for another two weeks,
two weeks in which he became a changed man. He was
quiet and withdrawn, locked in a world of his own
private terrors where even Polly couldn't reach him.
At last she could stand the anxiety no longer and she
sought out the one woman she knew would understand.
Carrying Jacob in her arms, she knocked with trembling
fingers, fearing that it might be Leo who came to the
door.

She breathed a sigh of relief when it opened and
Bertha stood there. Surprise flitted across the woman's
face, but she held the door wider, silently inviting Polly
into her home once more.

'Is – is Leo here?'

'No, love. Did you want to see him?'

Polly's head dipped. Of course she wanted to see him;

she always wanted to see him. To drink in the sight of him and hold him close in her heart. But she couldn't say the words. She must never again say those words. Instead she blurted out, 'Has he – has he enlisted?'

The lines in Bertha's face sagged. 'Not yet.'

Polly searched her face. 'But he's going to, isn't he?'

'So he reckons.'

'I – I think Roland's going too. He was given a white feather in the street two weeks ago and he's been so quiet and withdrawn since. Oh, Mrs Halliday . . .' Suddenly, tears overwhelmed her.

Bertha put her arms around her and drew her against her ample, comforting bosom. Sensing his mother's distress, Jacob began to whimper. 'There, there, Poll. Give the bairn to me. You're such a brave lass. Don't give way now. We've got to be strong. All of us.'

But Polly couldn't stem the flow of her misery. All the years of hurt welled up. She'd had to keep her family going after the death of her mother, through the humiliation of her father's imprisonment and then, worst of all, she'd been forced to turn her back on the man she loved, the only man she would ever love. She was very fond of Roland – fond enough never to hurt him. But he wasn't Leo. And no one, however good and kind and upstanding, could ever replace the love of her life.

'Sit down and I'll make us a cup of tea.' It was Bertha's answer to all troubles, whatever they were. She settled the child on Polly's knee and whilst Bertha busied herself, Polly mopped her face on her apron. By the time Bertha set the hot, sweet tea in front of her, Polly had stopped weeping.

'Now, love,' Bertha said firmly, 'it's high time you an' me put our differences behind us. We're facing far more serious worries than we've ever had in the past.

Oh aye,' she added swiftly, before Polly could say anything, 'I know yar dad going to prison was bad enough, but this – ' Bertha sighed and shook her head – 'is summat else.'

Polly didn't answer immediately, but she knew the woman was right. William had brought all his troubles on himself. She could see that now.

The older woman's voice was laden with anxiety and a sorrow that, although it was yet to come, she knew was inevitable. 'We're going to lose a lot of men from our city. Fathers, husbands and – and sons. It's started already. You've seen the casualty lists, haven't you?'

Polly nodded, her throat too tight to speak.

'We've got to face it, lass,' Bertha went on. 'They're going to go whether we like it or not and there's nowt we can do to stop them. Not mothers, wives nor – nor sweethearts.' Then disbelief crept into her tone. 'Why, they're even making out that any woman who doesn't encourage her man to go is being unpatriotic. Well, Polly, if it's being unpatriotic not to want my lad to get killed – ' now there was vigour surging back into Bertha's voice – 'then I am.' She thrust her head forward across the table, as if defying Polly to argue with her. 'And I'll stand up in front of anyone and say me piece if I have to. There's nobody more loyal to King and Country than me and mine, but I can't see the sense in going to fight someone else's war. Can you?'

Polly smiled wanly as she felt the courage seeping back into her tortured mind. 'No, Mrs Halliday, I can't. But then, I don't understand rightly how it's all come about. Roland tried to explain it to me, but I can't understand why some foreign Archduke getting killed makes half the world go to war.'

'It's all to do with alliances,' Bertha scoffed. 'Alliances, indeed. They're not worth the paper they're written on.'

'But why are *we* in the war? That's what I don't understand.'

'Me neither, lass, but like I say, it's all to do with promises we've made to other folks – other countries. Why we can't keep ourselves to ourselves and mind our own business, I don't know.'

Bertha fell silent, realizing she was treading on dangerous ground. If she said more, it might sound as if she was harking back to the riot and all the trouble that had caused. But Polly's mind was too filled with her present worries to notice.

Heavily she said, 'Then there's nothing we can do?'

'I'm sorry, lass, but I don't think there is.'

And there wasn't. Ironically, Roland and Leo enlisted in the Lincolnshire Regiment on the same day in April.

'I've done it, Polly.' Roland said when he returned home and sat down heavily in his armchair near the range. 'I've joined up.' His tone was flat, completely devoid of any of the excitement that had been in Eddie's demeanour. Her brother hadn't been able to hide his enthusiasm for the cause and his keenness to 'get up and at 'em'. He'd been excited at the prospect, but Roland had been forced into it because he didn't want to be branded a coward or thought unpatriotic.

Polly sank into the chair opposite him. For a brief moment anger surged through her, overwhelming the fear. She pursed her mouth. 'So you think more of being a hero than you do of taking care of your wife and son, do you?'

His face was bleak. 'Aw, Poll, don't say that. Please don't say that. You know how much I love you and little Jake . . .'

'His name's *Jacob*,' she muttered through gritted teeth, trying to latch on to anything that would take her mind away from the dread growing in her breast.

She heard Roland's heavy sigh of disappointment, but she couldn't bring herself to comfort him; she was too angry. Why, oh why, did responsibility always fall so heavily on her? Wasn't it enough what she'd had to suffer in her young life already?

Evidently not, for at Roland's next words a dread such as she'd never experienced before in her life, flooded through her and twisted her insides into knots.

'Polly, love, there's something else you – you ought to know. Leo Halliday was there at the same time as me. He's enlisted an' all.'

Polly and Bertha stood side by side on the station platform waving off the two men. Polly forced herself to turn to the right, where she could see Roland's head poking out of the carriage window towards the end of the train. She dared not risk a glance towards the front, where she knew Leo was waving from another carriage. Bertha was waving her handkerchief frantically, trying to catch her son's attention.

'He's seen us, Poll. Give him a wave.'

But Polly kept her back resolutely turned and waved again to Roland, blowing him a kiss and holding a squealing Jacob aloft so that her husband might catch a last sight of his son.

The whistle sounded, doors banged and the train huffed and puffed and drew out of the station in a cloud of steam. Polly turned slowly, keeping her gaze fixed on Roland.

As they made their way out of the station, Bertha said reproachfully, 'You could have waved him off, Polly. You could at least have waved goodbye to Leo an' all.'

Fifty-Four

Left alone in the terraced house with only Jacob to care for, Polly's days were long and lonely. To make matters worse, a few days after Roland and Leo had left to start their basic training, the newspapers were full of reports on a British spring offensive near Ypres. And now the soldiers were facing a new and deadly weapon: chlorine gas. Roland and Leo wouldn't be involved in that particular battle – they'd still be training, but Polly shuddered and threw down the paper in disgust. Eddie might be there, though. He might be facing not only bullets and shells, but also the dreadful gas that attacked the lungs of anyone who breathed it in and led to a slow and painful death. She was almost tempted to stop reading the news. The lists of casualties and the graphic descriptions of life in the trenches at the Front just caused her more heartache. She'd have to find something else to do to take her mind off things.

The following morning she put Jacob into the perambulator and walked round the corner to the Thorpes' home two streets away.

When she opened the door, a look of fear flitted across Selina's face and she invited her visitor in with obvious reluctance. 'You've come to take him away, haven't you? You – you want Michael back? Well, I suppose it was going to happen once you got back on your feet after having little Jacob.'

'What?' Polly stared at her uncomprehendingly for a moment before she understood. 'Oh no, Selina, no. It's not that. In fact, it's exactly the opposite.'

Now it was Selina's turn to look mystified.

Polly smiled. 'I was wondering if you'd think about looking after Jacob as well. D'you think you could manage two?' Polly was babbling, but then she saw Selina's eyes light up with joy.

'Manage? Of course I could manage.' Selina clasped her hands together. 'Oh, Polly, I'd love it. That's if – if you'd trust me with him.'

'I wouldn't be here if I didn't. It's not that I don't enjoy looking after him – I do. To tell you the truth, I'm not sure I'm doing the right thing. I might find I miss him too much, but . . .'

Selina, ever intuitive, finished Polly's sentence, 'You haven't enough to do now your hubby's gone and you want to go back to work.'

Polly gaped at her. 'How – ?' she began, but then she stopped and smiled. Of course Selina knew. 'Just a little part-time job somewhere. I – I want to be able to talk to adults now and again.'

'You can always come round here,' Selina began, then laughed at herself. 'Hark at me, trying to talk myself out of looking after your lovely little boy.'

Polly chuckled inwardly, feeling more light-hearted than she had done in weeks. She didn't say what was in her mind: that talking to Selina would be little better than trying to converse with Jacob. Selina's whole world was bound up in Michael. Polly wondered if Albie ever got fed up of hearing Selina's daily report on the child's antics when he came home tired after a long day at the market.

'Have you got something in mind then?'

363

Polly shook her head. 'Not really. I don't want to go back to the factory – I know that.' She still blamed the women there for Roland enlisting. She was sure there'd been whispers that had affected him, even though he'd denied it. And besides, with Violet still working there, it might make things difficult for her sister. Violet had carved out her own niche amongst the other women workers and Polly didn't want to upset things.

'I was talking to some of the other mothers,' Selina went on and again Polly hid her smile. She talked as if Michael really was her child. 'Some of them have little jobs when their youngsters are at school. You might ask around. Best place to catch them is when the bairns are coming out of school. Most of them congregate near the school gate.'

Polly beamed at her. 'I never thought of that. What a good idea.'

Her heart was beating faster as she pushed the heavy perambulator that had served so many children in the Longden family towards the school. As Selina had said, there were several young mothers gathered outside the gates chatting to each other whilst they waited.

Polly hovered near a group of three young women who looked not much older than she was. She hesitated to interrupt as one of them was in full flow. She stood listening, not wanting to be thought to be eavesdropping, but unable to drag herself away.

'. . . and I said to him, how can you give up a good job like you've got to go and be shot at by the Huns? And leaving me with three children to bring up on my own? But would he listen? No. So he's gone. And it's not only me he's left . . .' She nodded towards the school building. 'What about all the youngsters he taught? They need him nearly as much as his family. And he loved his job, loved being a teacher. I can't understand him, really I can't.'

'It's the shame of being thought a coward,' one of the other women put in. 'My Tom'd be off like a shot. In fact, he got as far as the medical but he was turned down. Now he's as miserable as sin 'cos he reckons everyone's pointing the finger at him.'

'What's he do? Any good at teaching, is he? Because they're crying out for teachers now.' Again the woman whose husband had volunteered nodded towards the school just as they heard a bell sound in the distance, saw the doors burst open and a flood of running children come surging across the playground.

Polly's heart had skipped a beat and then begun to thud so loudly she was sure the three women must hear it.

Teachers! They were looking for teachers. She ran her tongue around her lips that were suddenly dry with excitement. She hadn't even needed to ask about a job. Overhearing what the woman had said had given her an idea.

Miriam came skipping towards her. 'I didn't know you was coming to meet me today, Poll.'

Miriam, at ten, was trusted to walk home on her own from school now, but Polly felt guilty when she realized she hadn't given her young sister a thought. Her mind had been filled with possibilities . . .

Polly smiled down at her as Miriam bent over the pram. Her mind worked quickly. 'I was wondering if you'd just mind Jacob for me for a few minutes while I have a word with Miss Broughton.'

Startled, Miriam looked up. 'Why? Is it about me? Am I in trouble?'

'Heavens, no, darling. Whatever gave you that idea?'

Miriam shrugged. 'Just wondered why you'd come to see Miss Broughton, that's all.'

'It's not about you, I promise.' She paused and then asked again, 'So will you look after Jacob for me?'

'Can I wheel him round the playground?'

'I expect so.'

Leaving Miriam chattering happily to the child, Polly walked slowly across the schoolyard. Her heart was pounding, but determination led her on. She pushed open the door leading into the school, the door she had entered so many times as a child, for this was the school she'd attended. It squeaked as it swung open; she remembered the sound so well that it felt as if she were coming home.

She walked along the familiar corridor, her feet taking her, almost of their own accord, towards her old classroom. Would Miss Broughton still be there in the very same room after all this time?

Polly stopped outside the door and peered through the glass panel into the room. She caught her breath. Seated on the high chair behind the tall desk, she saw the woman who had been her teacher, mentor and, yes, friend for most of the time she had spent within these walls.

Miss Broughton hadn't changed so very much. The dark hair, still drawn back into its familiar bun at the back of her head, was streaked with grey now, but her figure in the navy blue dress with its white collar and cuffs was still trim. She was bending over an exercise book on her desk, gently chewing her bottom lip. Polly smiled. How well she recalled the teacher's little habit when she was concentrating.

Strangely nervous as she realized just how important

366

the next few minutes might be, Polly tapped on the door and then opened it.

As Miss Broughton raised her head and saw who her visitor was, she smiled. 'Polly, my dear. How nice to see you. Please – come in.'

Automatically, without really thinking what she was doing, Polly moved towards the desk directly in front of the teacher, the desk where she'd sat in her final months at school and which she'd hoped to occupy for so much longer than she'd been able.

She sat down at the double desk and folded her hands on the ink-stained surface. She glanced around the familiar room. It was just the same: the blackboard and easel, the list of tables – she could almost hear the children chanting them. Two times two is four, two times three is six . . . The pegs where they hung their coats in winter and the big black stove at the back, around which all the children clustered on cold winter mornings. The years faded away; it was as if she'd never left as she gazed up into the face of the woman she'd admired so much. Miss Broughton, from her lofty chair, smiled down at her.

'How are you, Polly? Surely, you've not come about enrolling your little boy yet.' Her smile broadened and her eyes crinkled with laughter lines. She'd been a wonderful teacher, strict when it was needed but also kind and fun-loving. She'd made the lessons so enjoyable. She'd instilled most of her pupils with her own love of learning, and school for Polly and her classmates had never been the place that many a youngster dreaded.

'You – you know about my little boy?'

'Oh yes, Polly. I try to keep up with what most of my pupils are doing with their lives even after they have left my charge.' Her face clouded for a moment. 'I was so

367

sorry when you had to leave school, Polly, and the reason for it. And it must have been difficult for you, having to take on caring for your family at such a young age and to give up your own plans.'

'It – it was good of you to come when – when Mam died,' Polly said huskily as she remembered that awful time when she'd lost not only her mother, but also her hopes and dreams. Even after she'd been obliged to leave school and work in the glue factory, Polly had always harboured the hope that one day – somehow – she'd be able to achieve her ambition of becoming a teacher. But after her mother's death her hopes had crumbled to dust. She could never have dreamt that it would take a war to offer her that chance again.

But she was leaping ahead, she told herself sternly. Perhaps Miss Broughton would not be able to help her.

And then, unwittingly, Miss Broughton touched on an even more bitter memory. 'But you're married and with a little boy. You're happy now.'

It was a statement rather than a question, but it opened the raw wound of her broken romance with Leo. She shied away from giving a direct response and said, 'Roland – my husband – has enlisted.'

There was a pause during which Miss Broughton watched her one-time star pupil before saying softly, 'I'm sorry to hear that, but please,' she added hastily, 'don't tell anyone I said so. We're supposed to be terribly patriotic here. We have to be, whatever our own thoughts might be. So many children's fathers have gone to war, we have to make them feel that it's all worthwhile.'

'But you don't think it is?'

Miss Broughton avoided meeting her gaze as she sighed. 'I believe in the right to defend ourselves if attacked, but we haven't been. At least, not yet. Oh, it's difficult to explain. I'm not even sure of my own feelings sometimes.'

'But you must understand all the political reasons that started it. I don't, I'm afraid. Roland tried to explain it all, but it's beyond me.'

Miss Broughton smiled. 'I'm not surprised and I don't mean that as an insult to your intelligence, Polly. I think it's beyond a lot of us. And the losses . . .' She stopped, suddenly realizing what she had been about to say might distress Polly. Swiftly, she changed the subject. 'So what does bring you to see me?'

Polly took a deep breath. 'I've too much time on my hands with only Jacob to look after now that Roland has gone. Too much time to think – to brood. I've got a good friend who looks after Violet's little boy. You knew Violet had a baby, I suppose?'

Miss Broughton nodded.

'She's married now. To the father and they're really trying to make a go of it. You remember Micky Fowler?'

The teacher's mouth tightened. 'Indeed I do.'

Polly chuckled. 'He was a right little tearaway at school, wasn't he?'

Now Miss Broughton's eyes twinkled too. 'That's a polite way of putting it. Go on.'

'He's settled down a lot and they've found lodgings with the Thorpes – you know Albie Thorpe on the market?'

Miss Broughton nodded and Polly continued, telling her former teacher everything that had happened to her family over the last few years. She left nothing out, not even the terrible time of her father's involvement in the riots and his subsequent imprisonment. Polly felt Miss Broughton's eyes watching her the whole time. She saw the sympathy there but still, even when she came back to the present, the teacher had not guessed the reason for her visit.

'I need something to do. Selina – Mrs Thorpe – is willing to have Jacob. In fact, she jumped at the chance. She just loves children and she can't have any of her own. Anyway, she said if I came to the school gates at coming-out time, the other mothers might know of part-time work going. I don't want to go back to the glue factory,' she added swiftly.

'And did they know of anything?'

Polly gazed up at Miss Broughton for a long moment before she said hesitantly, 'Not – exactly, I didn't ask them, because – because I heard three of them talking. One of them was saying that her husband had just joined up and – and that he was a teacher – ' Now the words were tumbling over themselves in her eagerness. 'And with him and others going, the schools are crying out for teachers and you know that's what I always wanted to do.'

Miss Broughton stared at her for a moment and then clasping her hands together she leant towards her. 'Polly, dear, you can't just become a teacher like that . . .'

'I know. I know that, but I wondered if there was any way I could come and work at the school. Perhaps I could help the little ones with their reading or – or their sums or just read them stories whilst the teacher is busy with another group. You know, like you used to get me to read to the younger ones when you were busy with something else.'

Miss Broughton smiled and murmured, 'I remember.' She had always taught a class of mixed age groups and teaching different levels of ability had been taxing. She had often relied upon the help of the older, brighter children like Polly.

'We are very short of staff now, it's true. Mr Ellis – he's the headmaster now—'

'What happened to Mr Hopkins?'

'He retired two years ago and Mr Ellis took his place. He's young and go-ahead. We're all a bit worried that he might volunteer too, but we keep telling him that he's needed here . . . Look, I'll have a word with him, Polly, but I can't promise anything.'

Polly beamed. She had the utmost faith in Miss Broughton.

Fifty-Five

For the next few days Polly waited on tenterhooks, unwilling to look for work elsewhere in case it spoilt her chances of being employed at the school. Since the idea had first come to her outside the school gates, the desire to become a teacher had blossomed once more until it became an obsession. But the days grew into a week and then two and there was still no news from Miss Broughton.

Towards the end of the third week, when Polly had almost given up hope, a note addressed to her in Miss Broughton's neat sloping handwriting arrived at her home, delivered by one of the schoolchildren who lived nearby. Polly tore it open, dreading to read the words that would destroy all her hopes. But instead, to her joy, Miss Broughton had written:

> *I'm so sorry not to have been in touch before, but there have been some recent developments at the school which were not entirely unexpected, but which have altered things slightly. So, if you can come to see me one afternoon this week after school, I will explain.*
>
> *Yours sincerely, Celia Broughton*

Celia. Polly had never known her teacher's name, but seeing it at the bottom of the page, written personally to her, made her feel special, as if the teacher was treating her as an equal. Whatever the outcome of their meeting would be, it gave Polly a warm glow.

Leaving Jacob with Selina, she was waiting outside the school gate the very next afternoon, long before the bell was due to ring. Again she eavesdropped unashamedly on the same three women whom she'd overheard talking previously.

'Have you heard?'

'What?'

'He's gone?'

'Who's gone?'

'The head, Mr Ellis. He's only gone and volunteered.'

The other two women – including the one whose teacher husband had already enlisted – groaned.

'Silly man. What on earth are they going to do now?'

'Bring back some old feller out of retirement, I wouldn't wonder.'

Polly's heart plummeted. This would be what Miss Broughton wanted to tell her. Mr Hopkins would be coming back to take the younger man's place. And he was an old stick-in-the-mud. He wouldn't entertain the idea of a young woman with no training and no education beyond the leaving certificate level being anything more at the school than a cleaner! Well, Polly thought, her chin jutting out resolutely, there was no shame in that. She'd be proud to be a cleaner at the school if it meant she could be close to the children, could help to look after them and maybe one day . . .

The bell interrupted her thoughts and, once again, she waited until all the children and their mothers had left. This time Miriam skipped towards her, hand in hand with Dottie Fowler.

'Hello, Poll. Me an' Dottie are going to the park.'

Polly nodded. 'Be careful then. Mind you stay to-gether.'

She waved the two girls off as she pushed open the squeaking door and made her way with dragging feet to Miss Broughton's classroom.

Polly knocked and opened the door and then stopped in surprise. A young, fair-haired woman was seated at Miss Broughton's desk. She looked up and smiled, her cheeks dimpling prettily. 'You must be Polly. Miss Broughton's expecting you.' She slid off the high chair and came towards Polly, who was still hovering in the doorway. 'Come, I'll show you to her office.'

'Office?' Polly repeated stupidly, now completely be-wildered as she followed her along the corridor. The young teacher chuckled. 'Oh yes, Miss Broughton has her own office now. Here we are . . .'

'But – but this is the headmaster's – ' Polly began, but was cut short by the teacher knocking on the door and being bidden to enter.

The young woman opened the door and ushered Polly inside, but did not enter herself. As she pulled the door shut again, she whispered, 'Good luck.'

Polly stood on the carpet in front of the huge desk that in her mind had always belonged to Mr Hopkins. On the very few occasions she'd been summoned to his forbidding presence, she'd stood on this very spot, ner-vously casting about her mind for whatever misdemean-our she might have committed. And the same feeling overwhelmed her now. But there was no need for her to feel like a schoolgirl in trouble any more. She was a grown woman – a married woman – with a child of her own. And yet she couldn't rid herself of the feeling until Celia Broughton looked up from the papers on her desk, smiled a welcome and gestured towards a chair set in front of the desk.

'Polly, how are you?'

'I – I'm fine, thank you.'

Polly perched on the edge of the chair and waited.

'I'll come straight to the point,' Celia said and Polly's heart sank. That was what people always said when they had bad news to impart. 'As I said in my letter, there have been some changes here and things have happened very quickly. Mr Ellis has enlisted and he's gone already.' She sighed. 'We all tried to dissuade him, but he wouldn't listen.' Her face fell into lines of sadness and Polly knew she was fearful for her colleague. It was the same dread that Polly carried with her every minute of every day.

Celia was speaking again. 'I've been put in charge temporarily, though I have applied to be allowed to continue as headmistress for the duration of the war. Whether my application will be successful, I don't know as yet. In the meantime, I have discussed the problem of staffing at this school with someone in authority. The situation was bad enough before Mr Ellis went, but now –' she spread her hands helplessly – 'it's deplorable. Anyway,' she continued more briskly, 'I mentioned you to him and I've now received written permission from him that I may take you on as a pupil teacher for a trial period.'

Polly gasped, her mouth dropped open and her eyes were shining, but before she could speak Miss Broughton went on. 'You do realize that this is only happening because of the war, Polly. In ordinary circumstances, it might not have been possible, particularly as you're a married woman with a child, but in the situation we're facing, we must utilize young women like yourself who have promise.' She smiled. 'I gave him such a glowing report – I hope you're not going to let me down.'

'Oh, Miss Broughton, I won't. I promise I won't. I'll work so hard . . .'

'I know you will, Polly. And this could be the start you need and – deserve. You will need to do some studying in your own time, but I can guide you with that. There's just one thing I must ask you: what would happen if your child were ill? Would you feel willing to leave him in Mrs Thorpe's care? And, perhaps more to the point, would she mind?'

'I'll have to ask her, but I don't think so. Little Michael – Violet's boy – had chickenpox a while back and Violet never stayed off work. Not once.'

'Mm.' Celia eyed her uncertainly. 'But Violet's Violet.' How well Miss Broughton remembered all her pupils, Polly thought with a flash of amusement. 'It might be different for you.'

Polly took a deep breath. 'I have to be honest with you, Miss Broughton. If he was seriously ill – which I hope he won't be – but if he was, then I would want to take time off. I can't deny that. I wouldn't trust anyone else, not even Selina, to look after him if he needed his mother.'

Celia regarded her solemnly for a moment and Polly held her breath. Were her dreams to be snatched away once more? But then the acting headmistress smiled. 'That's the sort of answer I'd hoped you'd give. I wouldn't want any teacher of mine to be uncaring towards her own sick child. Now, Polly, when could you start? You'd be with Miss Miller, who brought you to my office. She's not much older than you and is just out of training, so I think you would get on very well together. She's taken over my class temporarily, but when we get everything sorted out, she'll be teaching the infants and I think that's where you could be most useful. Miss Miller is young, bright and enthusiastic with plenty of new ideas. Learn from her, Polly, and you won't go far wrong.'

Polly felt as if she was walking on air as she made her way to collect Jacob.

Almost in a daze, she told Selina, 'I'm to start as a trainee pupil teacher at the school on Monday.'

'Aw, lass, that's wonderful.' Selina clapped her hands and smiled delightedly, though Polly wasn't quite sure whether Selina's pleasure was for her or for herself that she would have another little one to care for. Polly smiled; whatever the reason, the result was the same: this could be the start of her being able to achieve her ambition. But Polly was grounded enough to realize that she still might never become a real teacher. In the meantime the war had given her an opportunity she'd never dared to hope for, that she could never have foreseen happening.

It was the only thing she had to be thankful to the war for.

But the war had not only given Polly an opportunity, it also gave William a second chance.

When she arrived at the Longdens' home that same evening, it was to find William in a state of excited agitation. Stevie was grinning and Miriam was dancing round the table. Polly was about say, 'So, you've heard then,' when she realized that her own news would not generate such obvious joy.

'The union man came round this morning and told

me if I went and saw the boss, there might be a possibility he'd take me back.'

'There's so many joining up, Polly,' Stevie explained, but it was said without censure, he was just stating the obvious fact. 'They're getting short-staffed.'

But even the implication behind his son's words could not dampen William's pleasure.

'And?' Polly looked at her father enquiringly.

He took a deep breath. 'So I went and saw Mr Christian. Christian by name and Christian by nature, that man is.'

Polly pursed her lips before they should say what was in her mind: That's not what you used to say about him. You used to call him all the names you could lay your tongue to in the old days. But she kept silent.

'We had a long talk and he said if I gave him my word that there'd be no more troublemaking, then he'd take me back. In my old job in the goods department an' all, Poll. And I can start tomorrow.'

Polly beamed. 'Dad, that's wonderful. I'm so pleased for you. Perhaps we can really start to put the past behind us.'

They sat down to an evening meal that Miriam and Stevie had prepared between them, but Polly did not impart her news tonight. This was William's moment and she did not want to take anything away from him.

Tomorrow would be soon enough to tell her family of her own good fortune.

Fifty-Six

Nancy Miller proved to be as sweet-natured as her looks implied. The children in her charge adored her and Polly, too, quickly became fond of her. Theirs was a working relationship that soon developed beyond the classroom into a firm friendship, though in school they were both careful to stick to the proprieties demanded of them.

'You're a natural teacher,' Nancy told her as they sat together in the empty classroom eating their sandwiches during the dinner break. 'You should apply for proper training.'

Polly pulled a face. 'I don't think they'd take me, would they? I'm a married woman with a child. I've only been able to do this because of the war and because I have such good care for my little boy. In normal times . . .' She said no more, but Nancy nodded sympathetically. 'I know, but perhaps the war will change all that. Maybe, even after it's over, there might be a way. You could go to the Lincoln Training College. That's where I went. You wouldn't be far from home then.'

'I doubt it. When the men come back, the women who've taken on all their jobs while they're away will have to go back to the kitchen.'

Nancy's face was solemn. 'Yes, but how many men are going to come back, Polly?'

*

Polly's joy at embarking on what she hoped would turn out to be the fulfilment of her dreams was tempered by the news from the Front and guilt swept over her in waves. How could she revel in her achievements when they'd only come about through such tragic circumstances?

The casualty lists continued in the newspapers and a cloud of despair hung over the whole city as family after family lost a loved one; sometimes even more than one member of the same family was killed. Fathers, brothers, sons and friends, who, caught up in the fever of patriotism, had enlisted together, trained together, were posted together and even died together. These became known as the 'Pals' battalions. And so many families mourned two or three at once and every street commiserated with one another when bad news came.

Polly still went to her old home every day after school, pushing Jacob in the perambulator. Although Miriam, now aged ten, was doing her best to care for her father and brother Stevie, she was still very young to take on the responsibility of looking after the household. And Polly was determined that the fate she'd suffered as a young girl should not fall upon her little sister. So, despite her work at the school, which, although she found it exhilarating, was also tiring, she still made the effort to go to her father's house every evening. At weekends she spent most of each day there.

The Longden family settled into a routine, but it could not be called a happy one. When a printed postcard with the sentences that did not apply to him scratched out arrived from Eddie or a longer letter from Roland came, the family felt a surge of relief. But when the days stretched into weeks, and there was no word from either of them, the whole family became anxious and jittery and tempers were frayed. And Polly had the added burden of her secret fear: she couldn't talk to anyone about Leo. Not even Bertha. Though they still bumped into each other in the street now and again, and Polly dared to enquire after Leo, she could not unburden the secrets of her heart.

So the months passed. Violet was an affectionate, if careless, mother but a happier one because she could go out to work. Selina was in heaven with two little boys to care for. And Polly was following her ambition, yet she never forgot the reason why this had come about. Every day she prayed that this terrible war might come to an end, even though it might also mean the end of her dreams.

Another Christmas, subdued for everyone, came and went and the New Year of 1916 dawned with still no sign of an armistice.

'Will Eddie come home, d'you think?' Miriam had asked hopefully.

Polly had sighed. 'They do get leave, but they don't always have enough time to get back to this country. Sometimes they do,' she added, trying not to dash the young girl's hopes completely. 'We'll just have to wait and see.'

But neither Eddie nor Roland had appeared in time for Christmas. Nor did Leo and so Polly's private anxiety continued. If only there was someone she could talk to, someone she could trust. She couldn't speak to anyone about it, not even Selina, in case she should let a word or a gesture slip in front of Violet.

But Polly had reckoned without Selina's intuitive gifts.

One cold, dark evening when Polly called at Selina's home to pick up Jacob, Selina opened the door and gestured her inside.

'Jacob's having a little nap upstairs. Don't disturb him yet, Polly. And Michael can play on the rug with his toy farmyard. Have you time for a cuppa?'

Polly nodded, shivering as she stepped gratefully into the warm kitchen. 'I'd love one, Selina.'

'Sit down and get yourself warm.'

Polly sat by the fire, drawing off her gloves as Michael tipped his toy animals out of a box onto the rug.

When she'd made the tea, Selina sat down on the opposite side of the fireplace and regarded Polly steadily.

'How are you coping, Polly?'

Polly looked up sharply, almost spilling her tea into the saucer, but the woman's gaze never flickered.

'I – I – ' Polly forced a smile. 'All right. I love the work at the school. I can't thank you enough for . . .' Her voice trailed away as Selina shook her head.

'I know that. But how are you – inside? There's the worry of your family, I know. Your husband and brother. But – ' She paused and her glance flickered briefly to Michael as if deciding how much the young boy might or might not understand of their conversation. 'There's your fears for someone else too. Someone you can't speak of. I know it's hard for you, Polly dear, and if you ever feel the need to talk, just know that I'm here.' Selina smiled a little wistfully. 'You'd be surprised how many secrets I hold. Some because folks feel they can confide in me, others – well, because I just know, I suppose.' She held Polly's gaze again. 'And I know how you're hurting deep inside.'

Polly's cup rattled in the saucer as her hands began

to shake. Tears ran down her face. Selina rose quickly and took the tea from her. Polly covered her face with her hands and rocked backwards and forwards.

'It's all right, Michael,' she heard Selina say softly. 'Auntie Polly's just a bit upset, that's all.'

Polly gulped back her tears and let her hands fall. 'I'm so sorry. Michael, don't worry. I'm fine.'

Michael looked up at her, his face solemn, his eyes wide. She ruffled his hair. 'You play with your toys.'

Above his head, the two women exchanged an understanding look. 'Any time you want to talk,' Selina murmured. 'I'm here.'

'Thank you,' Polly whispered.

But then Selina dropped the bombshell that Polly had not been expecting. 'Stevie's sixteen in April, isn't he?'

Polly nodded.

'Do you realize,' Selina said slowly, 'that he can enlist at that age? And probably will.'

Polly gaped at her in horror. 'No, no. He's not old enough. It's eighteen, isn't it?'

'Officially, I believe so.' Again the violet eyes watched Polly. 'But if boys lie about their age, the army sometimes doesn't enquire too closely . . .'

Fifty-Seven

For the next two months, until his sixteenth birthday in April, Polly watched Stevie closely. But he gave no sign of wanting to enlist; indeed he displayed little interest in the progress of the war. He still worked for Mr Wilmott, still took home unsaleable vegetables on a Saturday night and went out with his friends at the weekend. And Stevie, Miriam told her, always arrived home at a reasonable hour and was helpful about the house too. Unlike Eddie – and Violet, for that matter – at the same age, Polly couldn't help thinking.

His birthday came and went and still he seemed settled. Conscription had been brought in in January, and at the beginning of May new rules were approved by Parliament. Polly devoured the item in the daily newspaper. The Prime Minister had stated that recruitment rallies all over the country had still failed to gain enough volunteers for the army. Now the ages of conscription would be between eighteen and forty-one. Polly gasped as she read the words; her father was only forty-five. He was safe for now, but what if they extended the age range yet again?

'I don't think I'd have to go, Poll,' William tried to reassure her. 'Working on the railway is classed as important work for the war effort. No, I think they've already got everyone they're going to get from this family. 'Cept of course, Micky. He'll likely be called up now.'

On 1 July the British and French began an offensive in Picardy near the River Somme. From the very first day the casualty numbers were catastrophic. And now, when she visited her old home, she saw to her horror that Stevie was scouring the papers for news of the war.

Stevie, the merry, outgoing one who always had a smile on his face, became quiet and withdrawn. Polly watched him anxiously and questioned Miriam. 'Does he talk about – about joining up?'

'We don't talk about it at home, Poll. It upsets Dad. It reminds him Eddie's out there and his son-in-law, to say nothing of – ' Miriam bit her lip and glanced away before muttering, 'others too.'

At twelve, Miriam was having to grow up quickly, just like Polly had had to do, but for a different reason. Polly sighed. She'd have given anything to see her little sister having a happy, carefree childhood.

So, though she'd feared it, it came as no surprise when a solemn-faced Stevie knocked at her door late one night.

'What is it?' she asked at once, pulling him inside. 'It's not Eddie, is it?'

Stevie, his shoulder hunched, his hands thrust deep into the pockets of his coat, shook his head. 'No, no. It's me.'

Polly gasped and her eyes widened. 'Oh no, you haven't done it, have you? You haven't enlisted?'

Stevie nodded. 'I've got to go, Poll. I can't be the only one left at home.'

'But you're not old enough. You're only sixteen. Why did they take you?' She stared at him, but knew the answer before he uttered the words.

'I told them I was seventeen, nearly eighteen. And they believed me.'

Polly snorted. 'Well, they would, wouldn't they? You're tall for your age and – and they want anyone they can get.' She touched his arm. 'Oh, I didn't mean that like it sounded. But they shouldn't be taking you. You're too young.'

Her eyes filled with tears. Polly didn't often cry, but this was too much. Her little Stevie going to war, into a carnage that was so horrific that the men who came home injured or on a brief leave refused to talk about it even to their families.

Stevie and Miriam had seemed like her children. She'd brought them up and the two of them had never caused her a moment's worry or disappointment. She'd hardly ever had to chastise them and she could only remember that one time, when Stevie went swimming in the river, that she'd been angry with him. He'd been her pride and joy; they both had. And now he was going to become cannon fodder.

'Oh, Stevie, don't go. Please, don't go.' She rested her head against his shoulder and wept, embarrassing the young boy.

'I've got to now, Poll. I've taken the King's shilling.'

Her head snapped up. 'I'll go and see them tomorrow. I'll go up to the barracks and bang on the door until they let me in. I'll tell them you're only sixteen. They'll listen to me. I'll *make* them listen to me.'

'I – I didn't enlist at the barracks.'

'Then where? Tell me!' She gripped his arms until her fingers dug into his flesh, but Stevie was mutinous.

'I'll find out,' she threatened. 'If you don't tell me, I'll find out.'

But Stevie steadfastly refused to tell her and when she rushed to her old home early the following morning it was to find that Stevie had already left.

'He volunteered a week ago,' William told her sadly. 'But he didn't tell us until he knew he was actually going and it'd be too late to stop him.'

'I'm still going up to the barracks. I'll tell them . . .' She stopped, staring in amazement at her father. She'd thought she could count on his support. Surely he didn't want his younger son to go to war, but William was shaking his head. 'Don't do that, Poll. Don't make him look a fool in front of his superiors. It wouldn't be fair.'

'But he's only . . .'

'I know, I know. He's only sixteen and to you and me, Poll, he's still a lad. But to the army he's a man now. And there's nowt we can do about it.'

'You sound as if you don't want to.'

William smiled sadly. 'Oh, part of me does, Poll. Part of me wants to do exactly what you're suggesting, but the other part . . .' He stopped and his face took on a dreamy, faraway look.

'The other part?' Polly prompted.

'The other part of me is that damned proud of him, I'm envious.'

'*Envious?*'

'Yes, envious. I'd give anything to be marching off to war with me head held high because, even if he does get killed, he'll be a hero. His name will be feted and remembered forever.'

'He'll likely get blown to pieces and never found, just buried beneath the mud and forgotten.'

'Aye, aye, mebbe that's what will happen – the first bit anyway. But as for being forgotten, you're wrong there, Poll, because our war heroes are never, ever going to be forgotten. We'll make sure of that.'

Fifty-Eight

Only two weeks after Stevie had gone the news they had all been dreading came to the Longden household.

One Saturday morning towards the end of July Polly wheeled a sleeping Jacob round to her old home.

'You'll soon be too big for this pram,' she murmured. At almost two, the child was growing fast. He was sturdy and could walk well now, but he still liked a sleep in his pram and Polly hadn't the heart to wake him when it was time to see if Miriam needed any shopping. Polly enjoyed the walks into the city with her sister on a Saturday morning and later on, towards evening, they'd sometimes go again to pick up the best bargains in the market.

It was just beginning to rain, so she pulled the pram through the door and left Jacob in the quiet of the front room.

As she stepped into the kitchen, she found her father slumped in his chair by the fire, still holding the dreaded telegram in his hands. Miriam was standing beside him, her arm around his neck, her head resting on his shoulder. She was weeping silently, the tears flooding down her cheeks.

'Oh no!' Polly clutched at the doorframe for support as her legs threatened to give way beneath her. '*No!*'

She eased the piece of paper out of her father's fingers and read the stark message.

DEEPLY REGRET INFORM YOU THAT CORPORAL EDWARD
LONGDEN, 1ST BATTALION, THE LINCOLNSHIRE REGIMENT,
DIED OF WOUNDS, 20TH JULY 1916. THE ARMY COUNCIL
EXPRESS THEIR SYMPATHY.

Eddie was dead. There was no hope to cling to that
he was merely missing, believed killed; the wording was
definite. Perhaps later they would receive a letter telling
them in more detail what had happened to him, but
there could be no doubt.

William lifted sorrowful eyes to the photograph on
the mantelpiece of Eddie in his uniform taken just before
he'd been sent abroad.

'At least we can be proud of him, Poll. He turned his
life around by joining the army. God knows what might
have become of him if he hadn't.'

'He might still be alive,' Polly couldn't help saying
bitterly.

'Aye, lass, he might. But he might have brought more
shame on this family than it's already had to deal with.
He might have ended up in prison.' The unspoken words
hung heavily between them. Like I did. William cleared
his throat and said strongly, 'Better to die a hero's death
defending his country. *I'm* proud of him anyway.'

Polly was thoughtful for a long moment before saying
quietly, 'Yes, Dad, and so am I, but all these fellers
dying – it just seems such a terrible waste of young
lives.'

'It is, Poll. But what's the alternative? Someone's got
to fight for freedom. Someone's got to fight the Kaiser.'

Polly said no more, she didn't argue because she
couldn't. She still didn't understand how – and why –
this dreadful war had come about. And she was sure
that countless others throughout the city and beyond

389

didn't understand it either. All they knew was that when their country called for them they had to go and do their duty. Just as Eddie had; just as Leo and Roland and even Mr Ellis had. And now the first loss to touch their family had happened. And who would be the next? Her husband?

Or Leo?

On her way back home, some inner intuition made her pause at the corner. On a sudden impulse, she turned the pram around and headed back down the street to the house at the very end and knocked on the door. It was a long time being answered and she almost fled. And then the door opened slowly and Bertha stood there.

It only took a glance at the woman's face for Polly to realize that she, too, had had terrible news. For the second time in a matter of hours, Polly breathed, 'No, oh no!'

'Come in, lass,' Bertha said heavily. 'And bring the little 'un with you.'

Polly scooped a protesting Jacob out of the pram and followed Bertha inside. She cuddled him against her and the child soon quietened.

'What's happened?'

'We had a telegram, love. Just like your dad's had. Delivered at the same time, it was.'

'What does it say?' Though she feared the answer, she had to know.

'Missing, presumed killed,' Bertha said flatly. 'But we all know what it really means.'

Polly clutched at the tiny hope. 'No – no, it doesn't, Mrs Halliday. It means what it says. He's missing. Ours was different. It said 'died of wounds'. I reckon Eddie must have been in a field hospital or somewhere, so they know he – he's really dead. But Leo – there's still hope for him.' She touched Bertha's arm. 'Don't lose hope, Mrs Halliday. I couldn't bear it if you lose hope.'

'Aw, lass, I know you don't want to face it any more than I do, but we've got to be realistic. You've seen them casualty lists in the papers. Longer and longer they're getting every day. And they get blown to smithereens and nobody ever knows where they are. Or – or they find bodies and don't know who they are.' She shuddered and wiped her eyes with the corner of her apron. 'We might never know, Poll, what's happened to him.'

Polly's chin jutted out with determination. 'Well, I'm not going to believe it until you get it in black and white that he's dead.'

Even in her overwhelming sadness, Bertha couldn't help smiling wistfully at the young girl's steadfast conviction. 'If your belief will keep him alive, love, then he's nowt to fear. Oh, Poll, you still love him, don't you?'

They gazed at each other until Polly said softly, 'I've never stopped.'

They all had to try to carry on with their lives as best they could. Polly found solace in her work at the school. So many children came into the classroom – even the very youngest – with solemn, bewildered faces. They were mirroring their mothers' distress. Some knew that their father was never coming home again; others could not understand and yet caught the feeling of hopelessness and despair that pervaded their home, their street, their city. And even at school the children could not escape hearing about the war when Miss Broughton had to tell them that Mr Ellis, their headmaster, had been killed in action.

The printed cards that the soldiers were given to send home, deleting the sentences that did not apply to them, continued to arrive regularly from Roland and often he wrote a longer letter. Polly strove to be thankful. Every Sunday she prayed for the safe return of her husband, for her little brother Stevie and now she could not stop herself from adding a fervent prayer for Leo. 'Just let him be safe. Dear Lord, just let him be safe.'

William went to work each day, determined not to let slip the second chance he'd been given. Miriam, who was growing up to be the image of her mother, Sarah, worked diligently at school and, with Polly's help, did her best to look after her father. Perhaps, of all of them, Miriam missed Stevie the most. He'd always been willing to help her about the house and he'd made her laugh. But at least he was still in England and he even got home on leave occasionally. Miriam lived for those days.

Michael started school in the September. Polly collected him from Selina's when she took Jacob, walked to school with him and back again each afternoon when she collected her own little boy. The arrangement worked well for everyone.

As for Violet, she continued to go merrily on her own sweet way. Even when Micky was called up it scarcely left a ripple on the surface of the life Violet had carved out for herself. Only Polly worried for him.

'I'm glad really, Poll. I don't want to be the only one not to go,' he'd told her. 'Keep an eye on our Vi, for me, won't you? And take care of yarsen.'

Polly had nodded, her throat too full of tears to be

able to speak. They'd already lost Eddie, Roland was out there somewhere and Leo was missing. And Stevie had now been sent to gunnery school and, young though he was, would no doubt be sent to the Front soon enough.

How was she to bear it?

Fifty-Nine

Every unexpected knock at the door these days filled Polly – and, she was sure, countless other women like her – with dread. Another Christmas had passed and, as not one of their men had come home on leave yet again, it had hardly been a celebration. The adults had done their best to make it a happy day for the two young boys, but their own enjoyment was clouded by anxiety. Even Violet seemed on edge, as if she'd rather be anywhere but in their old home with her family.

One Friday evening in early January, when Polly had just put Jacob to bed and was sitting with her feet on the fender almost dropping asleep after a busy week, a soft knock sounded on the back door.

'Surely not the telegraph boy at this time of night,' she murmured, but even so she was unable to prevent the shiver of fear running through her. As she went to answer the knock, she heard the sound of a crying child and quickened her step, flinging open the door.

Selina stood there with Michael clinging to her hand. 'Is your Vi here?'

'Here?' Polly repeated stupidly, but automatically reached out to draw her nephew into the warmth. 'No. Isn't she with you? Oh, sorry, that was a silly question, else you wouldn't be looking for her.'

Selina stepped over the threshold, closed the door behind her and moved towards the fireplace, stretching out her hands towards the warmth of the fire. 'Oh, Polly, maybe I should have told you before –' She paused and bit her lip.

Polly sat down and Michael leant against her knee and rested his head against her shoulder. His loud crying had stopped, but he still hiccuped softly.

'My, you're getting a big boy now.' Polly looked at him in concern. His face was red and blotchy with tears, but it was more than that. She felt his forehead with the flat of her hand.

'He's burning up.'

'He's not well, Polly. Hasn't been for a day or two. I tried to tell Violet last night when she came in – eventually.'

'What do you mean "eventually"?'

'I don't like telling tales, Polly, and I don't mind looking after Michael. Even my Albie's taken to the little chap and doesn't mind him being with us. But –' Again, she bit on her lower lip.

'Tell me, Selina,' Polly said gently.

The words came out in a tumble. 'She's been staying out late for three or four weeks now. At first she made out she was doing overtime at work, but I know that's not true because the girl across the street from us works there an' all and – and I asked her.'

'So where's she been going?'

Now Selina avoided meeting her gaze and merely shrugged.

'Maybe she's got another little job in the evenings,' Polly suggested, trying to cling to the hope that Violet was innocent of the suspicion growing in her mind. 'Like – like cleaning or something.' She knew that the school cleaners and no doubt office cleaners and the like had to work in the evenings when the buildings were empty.

'Then why hasn't she told me if it's something innocent like that?'

'Innocent? What do you mean "innocent"?'

Selina looked uncomfortable.

'Come on, Selina, if there's something you're not telling me . . .'

'She's been seen in the pubs,' Selina blurted out. 'With – with other fellers.'

'In pubs?' Polly was shocked. 'And – and with another man?'

Sadly, Selina corrected her. 'Men, Polly. Plural.'

'Oh my!' Polly breathed, dismayed and disgusted beyond words. 'But you saw her last night? You told her that Michael wasn't well?'

Selina nodded.

'And?'

'She just shrugged it off saying it was probably nothing. But, Poll, you can see the little chap's feeling poorly?'

Polly put her arms about him and, big though he now was, she pulled him onto her lap and rocked him, biting back the words that Selina should not have brought him out in the cold night air. Instead, she said, 'He'd best stay here tonight.' Her tone hardened. 'And I'll see Vi tomorrow.'

A look of relief flooded Selina's face. 'Do you want me to bring anything round for him? More clothes or bedding?'

Polly shook her head. 'We'll manage. I'll put him in my bed for tonight and see how he is in the morning.'

Selina rose. 'I'll come round first thing. And I won't sleep a wink, I know I won't.' Gently, she touched Michael's hair, but the boy was already asleep against Polly. 'I'll see myself out, Poll.'

'Thank you, Selina, and if you see Vi – ' Polly's tone hardened – 'tell her I want a word.'

By the morning, thankfully, Michael was much better. His fever had gone and he was bouncing about on Polly's bed.

'Well, you look better this morning.' Polly smiled at him with relief. 'Are you hungry?'

Jacob was standing up in his cot stretching out his arms to Polly. She lifted him out and carried him downstairs, with Michael following.

'Yes, please, Auntie Polly. Can I have bacon, egg *and* fried bread? Selina always makes me fried bread. I love fried bread.'

For the first few weeks after Michael had started at the school where she now taught, Polly had kept an eye on him, but her nephew had settled in quickly and there'd been no need for her to keep a close watch on him. Now she castigated herself for not noticing the previous day that he was unwell. Still, he seemed bright as a button this morning and was hungry. That was a good sign, unless . . .

The dark memories flooded into her mind; Sarah demanding a cooked breakfast that had undoubtedly helped to cause her death. Michael hadn't got typhoid, just a childish fever that was soon over, but Polly could never quite rid herself of the fear.

'I think you'd be better with something lighter this morning. Perhaps some milky porridge?'

The boy's face fell. 'Aw, Auntie Polly . . .' Then, impishly, he smiled. 'All right then, as long as you'll take me and Jacob to the park this afternoon.'

Polly knew when she was beaten.

Selina arrived as they were finishing breakfast.

'Oh, thank goodness he's better,' she said with heart-felt relief as she gathered the little boy into her arms. 'I've been so worried.'

'He's fine.' Polly smiled. 'Thank goodness. As it happens, Violet was right, but it still doesn't excuse her from leaving him with you when he was poorly.'

'I don't mind that, Poll. But I didn't know what to do.'

'Where is she? I'd've thought she'd have come with you this morning to see how he is.'

Selina was suddenly agitated. 'She doesn't know about Michael being worse. I don't know where she is. She – she didn't come home at all last night.'

Polly stared at her, for once quite bereft of words.

Sixty

'How's Vi?' William asked when he sat down at the table that same evening as Polly settled Jacob in the high chair. 'Has she heard from Micky?'

'How would I know?' Polly replied shortly, her lips pursed with disapproval. 'My sister doesn't confide in me. Never has.'

She still hadn't been able to speak to Violet; the young woman had been missing all day. And now Polly, as was her custom at the weekend, had come to her old home to cook an evening meal for her father and Miriam.

Polly was tired; she hadn't slept well, waking frequently through the previous night to check on Michael. The long walk to the park and back and now her anxiety – and anger – with her sister were making her irritable.

William cast her a puzzled glance but, as Polly set the plate of food in front of him, he lost interest and picked up his knife and fork.

Serving Miriam and Jacob, Polly was about to sit down herself when a loud banging sounded on their front door.

Polly felt the colour drain from her face and her limbs trembled. It sounded urgent – and serious.

Jacob, frightened by the sudden noise, began to wail.

'Who on earth – ?' William began and then he noticed

399

Polly's terrified face. Sighing heavily, he pulled himself up and went to answer the door. It was not the dreaded telegraph boy standing there but the bulky figure of Bert Fowler.

'That daughter of yourn is no better than she should be. There's rumours, Will, an' I won't have it. Not when my lad – 'er husband – is fighting for his country. Now, where is the little trollop? And where's my grandson?'

Polly held her breath. Oh, not again, she sighed inwardly: not another fallout between the two men that might result in the police being called.

She hurried to the door and grasped her father's arm and tried to pull him back, tried to push herself between the two men.

'It's all right, Poll,' William said, with surprising calm. 'I ain't going to rise to it this time.' But he faced up to the other man squarely. 'Bert, I don't want no more trouble. Just come in, man. Have a bite with us and let's talk this out, 'cos at the moment, I haven't a clue what you're on about.'

Bert Fowler blinked. He'd been ready for fisticuffs, but it seemed William Longden had lost his fight.

'Oh – er – well,' he stuttered, completely taken unawares, 'all right then.'

With amazing meekness, the big man stepped across the threshold and took a place at their table.

'Tea, Mr Fowler?' Polly offered. Though she was pleased that a brawl in the street had so far been avoided, she was still wary and trying to do everything she could to diffuse the tense atmosphere.

'Anything to eat left for Bert, Poll?' William began, but Bert shook his head.

'Thankee kindly, but I've just 'ad me tea, though what our Hetty was telling me while I was having it hasn't done me digestion any favours. But I won't say no to a cuppa, lass.'

'You'll excuse me if I carry on wi' mine then?' William said, picking up his knife and fork again, whilst, with wide eyes, Jacob regarded the stranger who'd appeared suddenly in their midst. Miriam carried on eating and helping her little nephew to spoon his meal into his mouth as if nothing was happening.

Polly placed a cup of tea in front of their visitor and sat down again, but she did not resume eating; she guessed what was coming and her appetite had suddenly deserted her.

'There's a rumour going around that your Violet's seeing another man. In fact, Will, more than one.'

William's fork was suspended halfway between the plate and his mouth as he stared at Bert. Slowly he put his fork down. 'What did you say?'

'I said – ' Bert began but William cut him short.

'I heard you.' He stood up suddenly, knocking over his chair so that it fell to the floor with a clatter. 'How dare you insult – ?'

Polly leapt to her feet and stood in front of her father. 'Dad, don't. I've heard the rumours too.'

'What?' William's face darkened. 'Then you should have told me, girl. This is your fault.'

Suddenly, the years fell away and she was a young girl again, being blamed for her mother's death, for Eddie's rebellious ways and even for Violet's unwanted pregnancy. It was a wonder she didn't get the blame for her father landing himself in prison, she thought.

Surprisingly, Bert defended her. 'It's not Polly's fault, Will. She's got her own troubles and responsibilities.' He nodded towards Polly, who was still standing between them. 'You should be proud of this lass, of all she's done for you over the years, not blaming 'er for summat that's nowt to do wi' her. There's only one person at fault and that's your Violet. If she was mine, I'd have taken the strap to her years ago.'

'Well, your Micky's no angel, so your strap didn't do much good, did it?'

The two men glared at each other and Polly's heart sank. Pushing aside her own hurt at her father's words, she tried again. 'Dad, sit down. Let's talk this out and decide what we ought to do.'

Reluctantly, William sat down and now he too pushed his unfinished meal aside. Only Miriam and Jacob continued to eat as if nothing was amiss, though Miriam cast anxious glances at Polly.

'So, come on, let's hear it then?'

'That Mrs Thorpe they live with,' Bert began, 'looks after young Michael and – '

'I know all that,' William snapped testily. 'But what's this about Violet?'

'Some of me mates are saying that she's going into pubs, flirting with the fellers there and – '

'A' you saying she's – she's a tart?' William was on his feet again, fists clenched. 'Cos if you are – '

'Dad, sit down, do, and hear Mr Fowler out.'

'No, Will, I'm not saying that. At least,' Bert added ominously, 'not yet.'

'You'd better not be saying any such thing about a daughter of mine. She'll likely be having a bit of fun, that's all. Pretty lass, our Violet. You can't blame her.'

'I can, Will, and I do. She's a married woman with a bairn. She should be at home looking after him and waiting for her husband, not gallivanting out half the night.'

The whole night, if truth be told, Polly thought

bitterly, relieved that at least Bert didn't seem to know that bit. Just you wait, our Vi, she thought, till I get my hands on you!

She was waiting for her sister at Selina's home late that night. By arrangement with Mr and Mrs Thorpe, she'd brought Jacob round to stay the night too and now both children were asleep in Violet's double bed whilst Polly sat near the dying embers of the fire in her sister's sitting room.

As she heard the back door open quietly, Polly was reminded how it had been years before, when she'd sat up late, waiting for her wayward sister to sneak home in the early hours. That had been bad enough, but this was far more serious. Violet was a married woman with a child.

Polly tiptoed to the door and the moment Violet had closed it softly behind her, Polly pounced on her, clapping her hand over her sister's mouth to stop her cry of surprise waking the household. Even so, Violet gave a muffled shriek and grappled with her unknown assailant.

'Shut up, Vi,' Polly spat through gritted teeth. 'It's me.'

At once Violet ceased her struggling, but as Polly relaxed her hold, her sister wrenched herself away. 'What do you think you're doing? Grabbing me like that?'

Polly stood with her arms folded now. 'And what do you think *you're* doing? Staying out till all hours. All night sometimes, so I hear.'

In the soft light from the fire, the two sisters glared at each other. 'Oh, Selina been telling tales, has she?'

403

'Actually, no. She's been covering for you, though she shouldn't have done. No, it was Micky's father.'

Violet's eyes widened and, even in the half-light, Polly saw the colour flush her face. 'Mr – Mr Fowler? He – he told you?'

'He told *Dad*.'

'Oh heck!'

'Yes,' Polly said grimly. 'You might well say, "Oh heck!"'

Violet wriggled her shoulders – a habit Polly knew so well when she'd been caught out. 'I'm not doing any harm. I'm only having a bit of fun. Cheering up the soldiers a bit, that's all.'

'Oh aye. That's what they call it, do they? Bringing comfort to the troops?'

Violet hung her head, unable to deny the accusation in Polly's words.

'Oh, Vi, Vi. What if you get pregnant when your husband's away? Everyone will know it's not his and . . .'

'He's not going to come back, is he, Poll?' Violet whispered. 'None of 'em are. Eddie's gone for certain. Roland and Micky are out there and Stevie soon too, I shouldn't wonder.' She met Polly's gaze as she added softly, 'And your Leo's missing.'

Even after all this time Violet referred to him as if he still belonged to her sister. And, deep in Polly's heart, he did.

She swallowed the lump in her throat at the mere thought of the danger Leo was in. Resolutely, she kept her mind on Violet. 'It's got to stop, Vi. You can't carry on like this. The rumours are getting round about you. And if Bert Fowler's heard them you can bet it'll be round half the city by the end of the week. Telling Bert

Fowler anything is better than putting an advert in the *Chronicle*.'

Violet sighed. 'They're all such nice boys, Polly. So lost and frightened. They don't talk about it much, but you can see it in their eyes. A haunted look.' She shuddered. 'It's horrible, Poll. Just horrible.'

Polly was thoughtful then bluntly she asked, 'Is it really because you want to help them forget, even just for a short time? Or is it because – because you're missing a – a man?'

Violet gaped at her sister. 'By heck, Poll, you don't half give it straight, don't you?'

Polly pursed her mouth. 'It's the way I've always been. I'm not likely to alter now. Well?'

For once in her life, Violet had to be honest. 'Both,' she said abruptly. Her eyes were bleak. 'I miss his arms around me, whispering silly nonsense. I miss him loving me. I miss the laughs we had, an' all. Micky's not such a bad 'un, Poll.'

'I know that now, Vi,' Polly said softly, 'but that's all the more reason why you shouldn't be unfaithful to him. You're taking such a risk. If he finds out, he'll half kill you.' She sniffed and added, 'If his dad doesn't get to you first. And besides, he'll make sure Micky *does* get to know the very next time he comes home on leave. Then what?'

'Ah, yes,' Violet said slowly, 'Mr Fowler. Now how am I going to deal with him?'

'And Dad,' Polly warned. 'Don't forget Dad.'

Polly never found out what Violet had said to either of the two men, but somehow she'd lied her way out of a very tricky situation. Somehow she must have made them believe that she was entirely innocent. She stopped going out in the evenings unless it was in the company of a group of women from work. 'If I've got Nelly and the rest of 'em to vouch for me, even Ida Norton's wicked tongue won't be able to spread gossip. I reckon it was her told Micky's dad.'

'However did you convince Mr Fowler?' Polly asked. 'Dad I can understand. You always could twist him round your little finger, but Mr Fowler?'

Violet grinned impishly and tapped the side of her nose. 'Never you mind, our Poll. Let's just say a pretty girl in tears and pining for her brave soldier husband works wonders on a man like him.'

Polly chuckled, unable to quell a reluctant admiration for her scheming sister. Really, Violet was the limit. She was relieved, but it didn't stop Polly from keeping a watchful eye on Violet's waistline for the next few weeks.

Sixty-One

At the beginning of April, just before his seventeenth birthday, and when the papers were full of the news that America had entered the war, Stevie arrived home on embarkation leave.

'Oh, you've grown so,' Polly cried, hugging him. 'And you look so smart. We must get a photograph of you in your uniform.'

Stevie grinned. 'You'll have a row of us on your mantelpiece soon.' He glanced at the shelf above the range in Polly's kitchen. Roland sat in pride of place in the centre, solemn and with a look of panic that he'd been unable to hide. To one side was Eddie – a black ribbon draped across the top of the frame. On the other side stood a more recent one of a grinning Micky. All the families she knew who had loved ones in the fighting made sure they had photos of their men in uniform, even if they had to scrape the money together to pay the photographer.

His gaze still on the pictures, Stevie put his arm about her shoulders. Softly, he said, 'There's one missing, isn't there, Poll, but I expect you can't put that one up, can you?'

Polly gasped and stared up at him. He was taller than she was now. He rested his cheek against her hair and sighed heavily. 'Oh, Poll, how I wish things could have been different for you.'

407

She touched his cheek with gentle fingers. 'Just – just take care of yourself. That's all I ask.'

And so now there were four photographs of men in uniform arranged along Polly's mantelpiece, but the missing face was the one that filled her thoughts the most.

There was still no news of Leo and though Polly dared not be seen visiting Bertha too often, the two women now met whenever they could. Sometimes Bertha would contrive to be passing the school gate – even though she had no excuse to be meeting a child – when she thought Polly would be leaving for home. With Michael walking between them, no one could guess that there was more between them than two former neighbours chatting.

'Any word?' Polly would whisper, but her heart would sink as Bertha shook her head yet again.

'You'd think we'd hear summat, wouldn't you? But there's been nothing since that telegram. "*Missing, presumed killed.*" You'd've thought they'd have had the decency at least to let us know when he actually went missing. I don't even know where he was. It could've been anywhere in France for all I know.'

'He was with the Seventh Battalion, wasn't he? Part of Kitchener's army. Like Roland. And – and Stevie joined the same battalion later.'

Bertha eyed her shrewdly. 'Is he out there an' all now? Little Stevie?'

Polly smiled wistfully. Everyone still called him 'little Stevie', remembering the bright-eyed, laughing boy. She nodded, her voice husky as she murmured, 'Yes, he came home on leave just before they – they were going. He said he'd keep an eye out for Roland and Micky.'

'Funny they've never been home on leave, Polly. Several of the fellows I know of – even those abroad – do get home, though I have to admit 't ain't often.'

Haltingly, Polly explained. 'Roland said in one of his letters that he didn't want to come home. He was afraid that, if he did, he wouldn't go back.'

Bertha turned to her in surprise. 'He actually put that? In a letter?'

Polly nodded.

'Well, I'm amazed it got past the censor. They read all their letters, you know? And ours to them.'

Polly giggled. 'I bet some of them between sweethearts and wives and husbands make interesting reading.'

Bertha chuckled too. 'I can imagine. Poor devils – it's all they've got to cling on to.' She paused and then asked, 'What about Micky? Hasn't he had a chance to come home?'

Now Polly laughed aloud. 'Oh, who knows with Micky Fowler?'

Bertha joined in the laughter but then her expression sobered. 'Perhaps it'd've been better for your Vi if he had come home once in a while.'

Polly shot her a look. So, Bertha had heard the rumours too.

'Still,' the older woman continued, 'mebbe it'll soon be over now the Yanks have come in.'

There had been great hopes that when the might of the United States arrived the war would soon be over, but it dragged on into another year.

'Nineteen eighteen,' Polly moaned as they attempted to celebrate another New Year. 'It'll soon have been going four years come August. Whenever is it going to end?'

Stevie wrote regularly and often, trying to allay his

family's fears. Roland wrote spasmodically now and Polly wondered at the change. When he'd first been sent abroad the letters had arrived frequently. Micky – as might be expected – only managed a pre-printed postcard every so often. Violet still went out in the evenings, but now she was careful never to give anyone cause to spread gossip about her. Polly was surprised; she'd thought her rebellious sister wouldn't have cared. Whether Violet was wary of her father or of her father-in-law – perhaps both – Polly didn't know, but she hoped it was because Vi genuinely didn't want to hurt Micky. Whatever the reason, Polly began to relax a little where Violet was concerned.

'I'll keep me eye on her, duck,' Nelly promised when she visited Polly on a Sunday. 'Don't be too hard on her. She's young and it's difficult for the lasses with their menfolk away.'

So Polly tried to immerse herself in the life of the school. Surrounded by the children, whose resilience to all the bad news they must be aware of even at their tender ages she admired, she fought to put her own worries to the back of her mind.

But even at school the war kept intruding. The teachers were always alert to any sign of distress in the children, realizing at once when bad news had arrived at their home. One morning in June Polly came to school to find Nancy sitting at the teacher's desk in her classroom with swollen eyes and a stricken look on her face.

'Oh, Nancy, what is it?' Polly put her arm around Nancy's shoulders.

Hoarsely, the young woman whispered, 'It's Bob.'

Polly was mystified. 'Bob? Who's Bob?'

'A – a soldier I – I know. I'd been writing to him. He lived up-hill. With his parents.' The explanation was halting and painful. 'He was with the Second Battalion. He'd joined the army before the war. You know, like your brother.'

Perhaps not for the same reason, Polly thought, but she said nothing.

'I've known him for years. I met him when I was at the college, but just recently it'd – it'd become – more.'

'Has he been killed?'

Nancy nodded. 'His parents had a telegram yesterday. His father came round to tell us last night. Oh, Polly, he's their only son – their only child. They're heartbroken.'

Polly hugged her tightly and then said, 'You should go home – just for today,' she added swiftly as Nancy began to protest. 'I'll go and find Miss Broughton.'

So, before the children could see their teacher, Polly sought permission for Nancy to go home and, for the rest of the day, she took charge of the class with one or two visits from the head teacher to see that she was coping.

But Polly was in her element. This was what she wanted to do with her life, but she knew she must not get too hopeful; when the war was over things might change. If Roland came home – and she prayed that he would – she would have to go back to being a housewife and mother. But for the moment, she would enjoy the brief freedom to follow her dreams.

During the August school holidays Polly took the opportunity to clean her house from top to bottom. Jacob, now four, helped her, sweeping and dusting and shaking the rugs. He was more of a hindrance, but Polly enjoyed the time with him and felt a flash of guilt that perhaps she had put her own ambitions before the needs of her son. But he was a merry little boy, happy, it seemed, with either his mother or Selina.

And it was good for him, Polly told herself, to have a man's presence in his life. Albie Thorpe was a stand-in for the father whom Jacob could not remember.

One hot evening Polly had put her son to bed, had bathed and washed her hair and was drying it in front of the fire in the range that always burned, winter and summer, when a soft knock sounded at the front door.

When Polly opened it, she felt as if she'd been dealt a blow in her midriff that had knocked the breath out of her. She stood and stared at the man standing there. He was tall, but now he stooped a little, leaning heavily on a stick. His face was gaunt and his eyes haunted, with the same expression she'd seen in the soldiers walking the city streets – soldiers who'd survived the trenches but whose lives had been scarred forever by the horrors they had witnessed and the wounds they bore. He was still in his uniform, his jacket hanging loosely on his thin frame.

They stared at each other for what seemed like an age until at last she whispered his name, like the answer to a prayer. 'Leo. Oh, Leo.'

His lips moved but no sound came out. He just stood there, staring at her, drinking in the sight of her like a thirsting man in the desert who comes to an oasis.

Polly gathered her scattered wits. 'What am I thinking? Come in, come in.'

Leo found his voice at last. 'No, no, I'll not intrude.'

Gently, she said, 'You're not intruding. There's no one here but me and Jacob. And he's in bed.'

At the mention of her son's name, Leo's expression softened a little and some of the horror left his eyes.

They sat on either side of the table and looked at each other again. Tentatively, Leo stretched out his hand, palm upwards and, without a second's hesitation, Polly put hers into his warm, strong grasp.

'Now I'm really home and safe,' he whispered hoarsely.

'Oh, Leo, Leo,' she murmured. It was all she could say. Her heart was overflowing with gratitude that, though he was obviously wounded, his life had been spared. They sat in silence for a long time. Words were not needed; at least, not at the moment. There was so much to say, so much that had to be said, but not just now. Not in the moment when he'd come back from hell – when he'd come back to her.

'Where've you been?' she asked at last. 'Why have we heard nothing from you or even about you?'

He shook his head and sighed. 'I don't really know myself what happened. When I was wounded – I think we were being shelled, but I can't remember clearly – I was taken to a first aid post then to a field hospital. At least, that's what I've been told since, but I was out cold. For a while they thought I was dead.' He smiled wryly. 'In fact, one of the orderlies in the field hospital told me that they'd put me with the dead and it was only because a sharp-eyed orderly heard me groan that I was found.'

'Oh, Leo!'

'Anyway,' Leo went on, trying to make light of it, 'when I eventually came to my senses, I was being transported to a hospital back at the coast. By this time all my belongings had gone and I'd no identification on me.'

413

'What? Stolen, you mean?'

'No, no,' Leo sought to reassure her hastily. 'At least, I don't think so. I think everything had been lost when – when we were blown up.'

'Go on.'

'Well, my head was injured.' He touched his right temple just above the faint scar that he still bore from the injury her father had inflicted upon him. 'And – for a while – I couldn't remember a thing. Not even my name. So, for several weeks, months actually, no one knew who I was – including me.'

'But it's been two *years*, Leo.'

'As soon as I got my memory back, I wrote home, but it seems Mam never got my letters. I've been writing ever since of course, even though I've been back at the Front.'

'The Front?' Polly's voice was a high-pitched squeak of indignation. 'They sent you back to the Front? But your leg? How could you fight with an injured leg.'

'I didn't – I mean, that injury wasn't caused then. This is just recently. At Amiens. By the way, I saw Stevie briefly.'

'Oh, Leo, is he all right. Is he in danger?'

'Polly, darling, I can't lie to you. Of course, he's in danger, but he was fine when I saw him. And he's in very good spirits. In fact, his sergeant told me that Stevie's the one who keeps everyone's spirits up, even though he's so young.'

'He shouldn't be there. He was only eighteen in April just gone. He shouldn't even be out there yet.'

'I know, I know.'

She gazed at him, still hardly able to believe he was actually sitting in front of her, safe if not completely sound.

'And this injury?'

Now he smiled broadly. 'This is a Blighty wound. I'll be taking no more part in the war, Poll.'

'Thank God,' she breathed and lifted his hand to her lips to kiss it gently.

Sixty-Two

'Poll – is it too late for us?'

They'd been sitting together for hours as the darkness closed in around them. It was late now, but Leo made no attempt to leave.

She stared at him. 'What – what d'you mean?'

His grasp tightened on her hand. 'I want us to be together.'

'But – but I can't. There's Roland. I – I can't *leave* him, Leo.'

'Yes, you can. It's happened to a lot of the fellers I was with. They got letters from home telling them their wives or sweethearts had found someone else.'

'And you're asking me to do that to Roland?' she whispered hoarsely.

'One thing I've learnt out of this lot,' he said grimly, 'is to grab your happiness wherever and whenever you can. Life's too short, Poll.'

She gazed at him, seeing a different side, a new side to the man she'd always loved and still did. But this war had changed him; he was harder, more selfish and seemed to have totally abandoned his own principle of always trying to do what was right.

She held his hand between hers. 'Roland is a good, kind man. I couldn't do that to him, Leo.'

'But you don't love him. You never have,' he said harshly. 'You love me.'

'I – I can't deny that,' she said sadly. 'And worse still, I think Roland has always known that too. I *do* love him, but in a very different way from the way I love you.'

Now he reached out with his other hand too and gripped both of hers in a surprisingly strong hold considering his weakened state. 'Then just let me love you, Poll. Let me make love to you. Roland need never know. No one will ever know. Poll, I need you so desperately. I need your arms around me. I need to know I'm alive.'

For a moment she wavered. Her heart overflowed with love and pity for him. Leo, whom she'd always loved with all her heart and still did, was asking her – begging her – to go upstairs with him. Into the bed she'd shared with Roland, the bed where Jacob had been conceived and where she'd given birth to him.

She felt as if her heart was breaking; it was a physical pain she would not have believed possible. She tried to pull away, but he held her fast.

'He'd never know. I swear I'd be careful. I – I wouldn't let you get pregnant.'

Pregnant! With Leo's child. The longing threatened to overwhelm her. To feel his hands caressing her; to know he loved her, needed her and then to plant his seed within her. To bear him a child. It was what she'd always dreamed of; it was still what she dreamed of in the darkness of the long, lonely nights.

Yet, somehow, very gently and with great sorrow, she found the strength to pull her hands from his grasp. 'I – can't, Leo. I can't betray my husband in such a way.'

Whilst she struggled with her own desire, she was shocked at the change in Leo. The Leo she knew and loved would never have asked such a thing of her. How

417

this dreadful war had changed them all. Some, like Micky Fowler, had proved he had a better side to his disreputable character and even Roland, diffident and shy, had found the bravery to enlist and do his duty. But the man sitting before her, who'd always put duty above everything else, had left his high principles buried in the mud of Flanders.

He sat slumped in the chair, broken and defeated. He looked so forlorn, so utterly without hope, that Polly almost relented. Her arms ached to hold him. Her breath quickened as she imagined the feel of his arms about her, the touch of his lips on hers, searching, demanding and then . . .

She closed her mind to what that would, inevitably, lead to. She couldn't let it happen; she wouldn't let it happen. She would never forgive herself.

Leo raised unhappy eyes to gaze at her. 'I – I'd better go,' he said heavily. 'If your father got to hear I'd been here . . .'

'It's all right. He's over all that now.'

Leo frowned. 'Over what?'

'The – the trouble.'

He blinked, as if that dreadful time now seemed a million years ago, obliterated by the vast horror of the war. 'Oh yes, that.'

There was a long silence until he asked softly, 'But are you, Poll?'

'Am I what?'

'Over it?'

Polly sighed, releasing all the long-held resentment, letting go of all the bitterness. It was a sigh of forgiveness.

'It's taken a war – *this* war – to make us realize just how futile fighting is. Dad thought he was doing right,

418

standing up for what he believed in. But nothing's worth men losing their lives over. And lives were lost back then and they shouldn't have been. No more than all the thousands that have been lost and are still being lost every day.'

'We have to defend ourselves, Poll? As a nation, we have to.'

'I know that – but we shouldn't start the trouble.'

'We didn't – well, not with the war, I mean.'

She frowned. 'I'm not quite sure how – or why – the war started, Leo. I never understood it at the time and I still don't. All I know is that a generation of fine young men has been wiped out and a generation of young women has been left to remain spinsters the whole of their lives. They'll never be wives and mothers. They'll never know the joy of holding their babies. We've not lost one generation but the next and the next and so on. No, this war has taught me a lot, Leo. And Dad too. He's mellowed. He's not the fiery, quick-tempered man he was.'

A smile, so long unused, quivered on his mouth. 'You haven't changed, my lovely Polly. You're still as feisty as ever.'

She put her head on one side, her eyes twinkled and she smiled, really smiled for the first time in a long time. 'Oh yes, every bit. When it comes to defending those I – I love, I most certainly am. But – ' the smile faded and she became very serious again – 'I have learned, finally, to forgive. My father's been given a second chance. They were short-handed on the railway because of the war and they took him back.'

'So it was only because of the shortage of workers?'

'At first, yes, but he's behaving himself because he knows that if he causes trouble again he'll be out, and out for good next time. Of course, they all know what he did. Folks don't always forget, but they do seem to have forgiven him. Even his employers – and that's really something. He always was a good worker – no one has ever said otherwise. And now his boss has made his job permanent. He's promised Dad that even when the war ends, there'll still be a job for him.'

Leo's face clouded. '*If* it ever ends.'

'It must,' Polly said simply. 'It has to.'

'But how many more lives are going to be lost before it does?'

To that Polly had no answer.

Sixty-Three

With Fate's cruel irony, on the last day in September when news came that the Allies had broken through enemy lines and were 'sweeping all before them along the whole Western Front', the national newspapers also reported that Spanish flu had spread into Europe and even to America. China and India had been hit badly by the disease, with millions reported dead, and now it was said that more US servicemen had died of the flu than had been killed in the war. Civilians, weakened by the privations of war, were succumbing to it in their thousands.

By mid-October, the flu was rife throughout Britain. Reading the news, Polly shuddered. Another dreadful disease was about to hit their city.

On the last Friday morning of the month, a solemn-faced Nancy met Polly as she arrived at the school. Polly's heart leapt in fear. There had been a quiet rejoicing amongst the staff at the school the previous day, with news that the war could soon be over. The children were caught up in the fever of excitement that had rippled through the classrooms, so much so that it had been difficult to maintain discipline, a most unusual occurrence in Celia Broughton's school.

'What is it? What's happened? It's not your brother, is it?' Polly whispered so as not to be heard by the children clattering into the classroom. Nancy's younger

421

brother had been called up a few months earlier and had been sent abroad recently.

Nancy shook her head. 'No, no, he's fine. As far as we know. Mother had a letter last week. Of course . . .' Her voice faded away, but Polly knew what she meant. Even though the arrival of a letter heartened and reassured the families that their loved one had been safe and well at the time of writing, no one could be sure that in the days since, something hadn't happened to them. Relief was always tempered by a renewed fear of what might be happening now, at this very minute.

'It's not that,' Nancy was saying. 'Miss Broughton has received notice to close the school until at least a week on Tuesday because of the influenza. It might be for even longer than that. Another teacher has sent word this morning that she's ill, and fewer and fewer children are coming each day. It's getting worse, Polly.'

Nancy's eyes met Polly's. The two young women were of a similar age and could both remember the typhoid epidemic. Although this was a different cause, the fear sweeping through the city was the same.

Polly sighed. 'I suppose they're right. What's going to happen?'

'Miss Broughton is dismissing everyone this morning.'

Polly nodded. She would miss her work at the school, but she knew the decision was the right one.

But despite such precautions, the disease spread and reached their own streets, and once again Leo's mother, Bertha, was in great demand, going from house to house helping to nurse the sick without regard for her own health.

'I can't stop her,' Leo told Polly. He'd taken to calling round and Polly hadn't the heart nor, if she were truthful, the desire to stop him. Let the neighbours gossip, she told herself. She had nothing to be ashamed of and she would tell Roland herself if he came home.

When he came home, she repeated to herself. *When* Roland came home. The guilt swept through her. She wasn't feeling the joy, the excited anticipation that she should have been at the thought that her husband was coming home. There was none of that thankfulness that there'd been when Leo had appeared on her doorstep, wounded but safe. Polly closed her eyes and groaned. She couldn't help her feelings; she was a wicked, wicked woman, she told herself, but she vowed that Roland would never know, would never guess.

For Roland's survival meant the end of the innermost secret longing of her heart: a future with Leo.

The war was over and the city paused to celebrate. There was revelry throughout the streets, though the jubilation was tempered by the memory of all those sons, husbands and fathers who would never be coming home again.

'So.' Leo regarded her solemnly. 'Roland's coming back.' They were standing together outside Polly's family home watching the children shrieking and laughing in the street. Despite the grey skies of the November day, everyone had come out of their houses and an impromptu street party was developing.

Polly widened her smile. 'Yes, isn't it wonderful? I had a letter only last week, so I'm sure he's still safe.'

'I'm sure he is,' Leo said softly. 'I *hope* he is, Polly, truly I do. I want you to believe that and I – I'm so sorry for what I said to you – how I acted – when I first came home. It was despicable and I hate myself for it.'

Polly glanced up at him. He looked so much better now. His face had filled out and his limp was less pronounced, but the haunted look in his eyes was still there and she knew the horrors he'd seen would never fully leave him. He and thousands like him would never forget this terrible war and the suffering it had caused.

'Please don't,' she said softly. 'You weren't yourself.'

And he hadn't been, not her proud, conscientious, principled Leo. And though his devotion to duty had split them apart, she'd always in her heart of hearts admired him for it.

'Thank God you were strong enough for both of us, Poll.'

'It's over, Leo. Forgotten. No one else knows what passed between us and they never will. Not from me anyway.'

'Nor me,' he murmured with a heartfelt promise. 'But what about the wagging tongues? Just look at Hetty Fowler over there. She can't take her eyes of us. There's a juicy bit of gossip in the making right here, Poll.'

Polly chuckled and waved. 'Come on, let's go across and talk to her. That'll stop her in her tracks.'

'Eh?' Leo looked scandalized. 'Talk to the Fowlers? I thought you were sworn enemies.'

Polly laughed again, throwing back her head with a loud, joyous sound. 'Not if you look at my dad and Bert Fowler leaning against each other over there. I don't know who's going to fall down first.'

Leo, seeing the sense in her suggestion of confounding the gossips to their faces, pushed himself off the wall where he'd been leaning, laughing as he did so. 'Well, if one of them falls down the other'll go down an' all.'

They made slow progress down the street until they came near to Hetty standing in her own doorway, a shawl pulled tightly round her shoulders. 'They could a' picked a warmer day to call an armistice,' she greeted them, but Polly ignored her grumbles.

'It's a wonderful day, though, Mrs Fowler, whatever the weather. And your Micky's coming home. And our Stevie too.'

'Aye, he is, thank the good Lord. And your man –' the woman glanced at Leo as she asked the question – 'is he safe?'

'Yes, yes, he is. Roland,' Polly stressed the name deliberately, 'will be coming home too.' She sobered as she added, 'We've been lucky really in this street. Only – only our Eddie.'

'Aye, I was sorry about that, lass.' Hetty's tone softened. 'I reckon you've had more'n your fair share of trouble an' I wouldn't have wished that on you. He were a bit of a rascal, your Eddie, but he were no worse than our Micky.' She laughed. 'I reckon they egged each other on.'

'More than likely, Mrs Fowler.'

The careworn woman glanced at Leo with a hint of sauciness in her eyes, almost a girlish coquetry from her youth that must have caught Bert Fowler's eye long, long ago. 'I shouldn't be saying all this in front of our local copper, now should I?'

'I'm no longer a copper, Mrs Fowler,' Leo said seriously and there was more than a hint of regret in his tone. 'I can't go back into the force.'

'Then I'm sorry to hear that, lad. Real sorry, 'cos we all knew, if we're honest about it, that you was only doing your duty as you saw it. And, most of the time, you were right.' Polly felt the woman's eyes upon her, but she avoided meeting her gaze as Hetty added, 'Even my Bert said you were one of the fairest coppers we had around here, and that was summat coming from our Bert.'

'Indeed it was, Mrs Fowler,' Leo murmured. 'Thank you.'

There was a pause whilst the three of them still stood together watching the youngsters playing and in the midst of them all, lifting her skirts and skipping with the rest of them, was Violet.

'Aye, an' it'll be a good thing when our lad does get home. I reckon your Violet's been missing him, Polly.' Was there a hint of accusation or even sarcasm in the woman's tone? Polly chose to ignore it and said simply instead, 'She has, Mrs Fowler. We'll all be glad to see the boys home.'

But as she said the words, she did not dare to meet Leo's gaze.

Sixty-Four

Although the gunfire had ceased in November, it took weeks for all the soldiers to come home and some were still required to stay abroad. Happily, Roland was not one of them and Polly was at the railway station one cold, blustery January day to meet him.

Although she'd prepared herself to see change in him – just as she'd seen in Leo – she scarcely recognized the man who staggered off the train. Roland was thin and stooping. He looked physically shattered as well as mentally: there was that same haunted look in his eyes that she could see in each and every one of the men arriving home, the very same look she'd seen in Leo's eyes.

Leo had been so very different from the young man who'd gone away, yet he was mending now. She must help Roland to do the same. She pushed her way through the throng to reach him and flung her arms about him, anxious to demonstrate just how thankful she was to have him home.

'Roland, oh, Roland,' she cried, hugging him.

She felt him stiffen beneath her embrace. 'Don't make a scene, Polly. Let's get home.'

She drew back, strangely hurt by his abrupt rebuff. 'Of course,' she said meekly. 'Is – is there anything I can help you with? Carry anything.'

'Huh! I've been carrying it for nearly four years. Another hour or so won't matter.'

427

They walked out of the station and turned to the left, walking down the High Street towards their own street. They walked in silence; Roland didn't seem to want to talk and Polly, for once in her life, was lost for words. She didn't know how to treat this stranger.

As they turned the corner into their street, Polly said, 'Jacob can't wait to see you. He's grown into such a wonderful little boy. I have a job to keep pace with his clothes and shoes . . .' She was babbling now, strangely nervous. She'd never been nervous of anyone before and certainly never of sweet, gentle Roland. But now she didn't know what to do or to say. 'I've got a special tea waiting for you. And your favourite for afters. A trifle.'

'You shouldn't have been splashing out on fancy meals, Polly. Things are going to be tight now. I doubt I'll get my job back at the factory and—'

'Oh, I've got a job. We'll manage.'

It was the wrong thing to say entirely. Roland frowned.

'You're working? Back at Cannon's?'

'No, no. They were short of teachers, so I'm a pupil teacher – sort of – at the primary school just down the road. The one Michael goes to . . .' She was babbling again, the words tumbling from her lips, trying to explain. She could feel his disapproval even before he said a word. 'Miss Broughton – my old teacher – she's headmistress there now.'

'A woman? As head? What happened to Mr Ellis?'

'He – he enlisted.'

'And?'

'He was killed. On the Somme.'

Roland's only reply was a grunt. As he struggled through the front door with all his kit, Polly stood helplessly by, not daring to offer again to assist him. He dumped everything on the floor of the front room and went through to the kitchen.

'A cuppa wouldn't go amiss. That's if you're not too busy. Where's Jacob?'

'At Selina's. She – she'll bring him round later. About four.'

'Who's Selina?'

'Selina Thorpe. She looks after Jacob. Michael too when Vi and I are at work.'

'Shouldn't you be at work today?'

'Yes – no – I got the day off to meet you.'

'You needn't have bothered.'

He took off his coat and flung it over the back of a chair and then sat down beside the range, holding out his hands to the warmth. Polly hurried to make a pot of tea.

'Would you like something to eat? We could have proper tea if you like. We needn't wait for Jacob.'

'No, a cuppa will be fine just now.'

They'd scarcely begun to drink their tea when a knock sounded at the front door. At the sudden noise, Roland jumped and his hands began to tremble, spilling the tea into the saucer. His eyes were wide and fearful.

'I'll see who it is,' Polly said, placing her own cup down but making no remark on Roland's reaction. She didn't even draw attention to it by offering to take away his cup. She merely rose and went to the door to admit whoever was knocking. A moment later she returned.

'Leo's come to see you. He knew you'd be on the afternoon train.'

Leo limped into the room and went straight towards Roland, stretching out his hand in welcome.

'It's good to see you home, Roland. How are you?'

Roland glanced up and then at the proffered hand.

There was a long pause. Polly held her breath until, slowly, Roland put his hand into Leo's. 'Not bad, I suppose.' Another pause before he asked – and it sounded grudging – 'And you?'

'A wound in the leg that's not healing properly.'

'Sit down, Leo,' Polly murmured. 'Cup of tea?'

'Thanks, Poll. I won't say no.' He turned back to Roland so that he would not feel excluded. 'Mam's out such a lot, helping folks ill with this wretched flu.'

'It's here, then, is it?' Roland turned accusing eyes on Polly. 'You never said.'

'I – I didn't want to worry you.'

To her surprise, Roland lifted his shoulders in a shrug, as if he wouldn't – or couldn't – have cared one way or the other. And now he didn't even ask if she or Jacob – or anyone else they knew – had had it. But Polly answered his unspoken question.

'We've all been fine, but they closed the school at the end of October for a month when the attendance was so poor. Several of the teachers had the illness too.' She grimaced. 'The situation's not much better now, but at least the school's open again.'

'You'll have to be careful, Roland,' Leo said seriously. 'In a weakened state, you might pick up the infection easily.'

'Who says I'm weak?' Roland snapped.

Leo raised his eyebrows. 'I didn't say "weak", old chap. I said "weakened". We all are when we first get home. It's been a long haul and it's taken its toll on every one of us.'

There was an awkward silence until Leo, feeling it, rose. 'I'll go then. I just wanted to see how you are. I'll let you get settled in. I'll see myself out, Poll. Don't you get up.'

430

After they had heard the door close behind him, there was a long silence in the room, the only sounds were the ticking clock and the crackling fire. Polly waited, her heart beating painfully.

At last Roland said morosely, 'He seems to be at home here.'

'He calls now and again to see if we're all right,' Polly said, making her tone casual, but determined to be truthful with him from the start. 'We've all had to pull together. It's been hard and the flu has made things even worse.'

'So, you're – friends again with Leo Halliday, are you? All forgiven and forgotten, is it?'

Polly sighed. 'The war's altered things, Roland. My dad's changed. He's mellowed and only too pleased to be back at work on the railway. But you knew all that. I told you in my letters.'

'You didn't tell me about Halliday making himself at home here.'

Polly faced him squarely, thankful that she was able to look him in the eyes and say honestly, 'He came as a friend, Roland, and nothing more. And now I'll get tea ready. Jacob will be in very soon.'

She got up and turned away, the matter at an end as far as she was concerned. But she was very much afraid that it wasn't finished with for Roland.

Sixty-Five

The only one amongst those who had returned to their small community so far and who did not seem changed by their experiences in the war was Micky Fowler.

He returned home, sweeping Violet off her feet and swinging her round in a bear-hug embrace.

'He couldn't wait to get me home and up the stairs,' Violet told Polly a few days later, giggling deliciously. She patted her stomach. 'I reckon I'll have another little 'un in there already. I hope it's a girl. How about Roland? I bet he won't leave you alone either.'

Polly smiled thinly and did not answer. Luckily, Violet, caught up in her own happiness, didn't seem to notice. The truth was that Roland hadn't touched Polly since he'd come home, hadn't once made love to her, or even kissed her.

And now there was no one in whom she could confide. Bertha, for such intimate conversations, was lost to her. And Violet was certainly not one to keep such a confidence. She'd considered Selina, but dismissed the idea. No, Polly thought, this I must bear alone. Perhaps he just needs time. But as the days went by Roland's attitude did not improve. He hardly spoke to either Polly or Jacob and the boy left for Selina's each morning with a sober, puzzled look on his face.

Despite Roland's obvious disapproval, Polly kept her

job at the school. Walking to Selina's one morning with Jacob, she tentatively broached the subject of his father's sullen attitude. 'He's had a bad time, love. He'll come round in time. What – what do the other boys say about their fathers?'

Jacob shrugged. 'Some's all right – like Uncle Micky. But one or two of them have said their dads have changed.' He looked up at her. 'Was Daddy different before, then?'

With a shock, Polly realized that Jacob had no memory of Roland; he couldn't remember the real man.

As they parted, Polly ruffled her son's hair. 'He was a good, kind, gentle man before the war. But try not to worry about it. He'll come around when he's been home a bit. We'll just have to be patient, that's all.'

But it was very difficult to be patient when Roland sat by the fire day after day, making no effort to rouse himself. It reminded Polly sharply of the time after her mother's death when her father had acted in the same way and then again after he'd come home from prison. Perhaps William was the one to pull Roland out of the depths of despair. After all, it had been Roland himself who'd helped William in much the same way.

'Dad?'

'Hello, Poll. You've heard then? Thought you wouldn't be long coming round.' William laughed.

Polly frowned. 'Heard? Heard what?'

William flung open the door into the kitchen. 'Just look who's home!'

The young man who rose from the chair was still in his army uniform. Tall and broad and grinning from ear to ear. He stretched his arms wide. 'Here I am, Poll, safe and sound. Not a scratch.'

Polly gasped and then flew across the room to hug

him so tightly he begged for mercy. 'Stevie, oh, Stevie. Thank God you're safe.'

The room was filled with laughter, with them all talking at once, until Miriam said, 'Sit down, Poll. I'll make a cuppa.'

At fourteen, Miriam was growing into a beauty so like the mother she'd never known. But unlike Sarah she was placid and dreamy, though Polly had to admit she kept the home spotless and cooked good, wholesome meals for her father. And what was more the young girl seemed quite content to stay at home and care for him; she had none of Polly's driving ambition.

They sat there laughing and talking and drinking tea and Polly quite forgot the reason for her visit. It wasn't until Stevie began asking about the others who'd come back that she remembered just why she'd sought out her father.

'We've been lucky, really, when you think about it. Roland and Micky are home and now so's Stevie. Oh, I know we lost our Eddie and that has been dreadful, but some families have lost several members. One woman I know of lost her husband and two sons. Poor woman. How will she ever get over that?'

The merriment in the room died and then Stevie asked quietly, 'How's Roland, Sis?'

Polly sighed. 'Not good, I'm afraid.'

'Was he wounded?'

Polly shook her head. 'Yes and no. No physical wound as such, but he said he got a whiff of gas once and it's affected his lungs a bit. But he's changed. His personality, I mean. Very changed.' She glanced at William. 'Dad, you remember how he used to come round here when you were – well – feeling down?'

Solemnly, William nodded. 'I do. But for Roland, I might still have been sat here feeling sorry for mesen and being a burden to you, lass.'

Polly took a deep breath, 'Well, d'you think you could do the same for him now? Come and talk to him. Take him out to the pub now and again.'

'Course I will, lass. You should have said summat afore.'

Polly shrugged helplessly. 'I thought he might come out of it when he'd been home a bit, but he's not doing well.'

'I'll come and see him an' all,' Stevie offered. 'He might feel he can talk to me about it all. If he wants to, that is.'

'I don't know that he will. He won't tell me anything.'

For a brief moment there was that same haunted look in Stevie's eyes too as he said quietly, 'We don't like talking about it to our families.' But then with the resilience of youth, he banished the bad memories and said, 'But if he wants to talk – if it'd help – then I don't mind.'

Polly returned home to find the house in darkness and Roland in bed, pretending to be asleep.

She crept beneath the sheets and snuggled close to his back for warmth, but when he edged away from her touch, she was left staring dry-eyed into the darkness, feeling as if, once more, it was her fault.

If it hadn't been for Stevie and Micky Fowler – Micky, of all people, she couldn't help thinking – Polly didn't know what she'd have done. William failed to prise

Roland out of his chair to go to the pub, though he did visit regularly and did his best to chat normally and draw the morose man out of himself.

'I can't get through to him,' William told Polly after one such visit. 'I reckon he's still back in them trenches, seeing all the dreadful sights in his mind's eye.'

'I know, Dad, but thanks for trying.' She patted his arm and tried to smile.

Strangely, it was Stevie and Micky who had the greatest effect. They got him to talk to them and even got him out to the pub once.

'You'd have thought he wouldn't want to talk to them, being soldiers,' Polly had confided in Nancy during one lunch break. Nancy's brother had come back too, though he was badly wounded and still in hospital down south. Nancy had visited him once, taking two days off school. She'd come back sober-faced and anxious but with the reassurance that he would live. 'But he'll be crippled for life. They've – they've amputated his left leg.'

'Oh, Nancy.' Polly had hugged her swiftly. 'I'm so sorry, but at least your parents – and you – will have him home.'

Tears had filled Nancy's eyes and Polly knew she was thinking of Bob. Bob was one of the many, many thousands who would not be coming home.

'But Micky bounced into the room and slapped him on the back as if the last four years hadn't happened,' Polly told her now. 'And then Stevie was nearly as bad.' She smiled 'Or good, according to how you look at it.'

'And what did Roland do?'

'Nothing really. He frowned a bit, but he didn't snap at them like he does at me.'

'He can't really, can he? They've been through

436

exactly what he has and yet they're dealing with it.' She hesitated before saying gently, 'Do you think you might be pandering to him a bit too much? You know, treating him with kid gloves when perhaps all he needs is to be treated normally? Just like they're doing.'

Polly was thoughtful. 'Perhaps you're right. I suppose I have been treating him differently, but – *he's* different, Nancy.'

Nancy touched her arm. 'I know, I know,' she said softly. 'But why not give it a try, eh? It can't make matters worse.'

But it did. When Polly went home that night, she breezed into the house and greeted Roland cheerfully.

'What have you got to be so happy about? Ah, but I'm forgetting. You haven't existed in freezing mud for four years, living with the thought of getting your head blown off any second. You haven't slept with rats as big as cats sleeping under your armpits or with lice crawling all over you.'

Polly stopped and stood very still. Then slowly she came towards him and sat down in the chair opposite him. She stared at him. He avoided her gaze, but still he groused. 'You've no idea what hell it was out there. You, with your comfy, safe little job and your family all around you. Even your *friend* has come back.'

She didn't insult him by pretending she didn't know who he meant. Instead she said sorrowfully, 'But my brother didn't.'

For a moment, there was a brief flash of apology in Roland's eyes, but it was not voiced and it was gone in an instant.

Polly pulled in a deep breath. 'Tell me what you want me to do, Roland. How you want me to be, to act, and I'll do it.'

'Just leave me alone. That's all I want. I don't want you or Jacob or your blasted family coming round here. And most of all you can keep *him* away.'

'Leo? Has he been here again?' The words were out of her mouth before she could stop them.

Roland's lip curled. 'So you do know who I mean. Been coming here regularly, has he? Been *comforting* him have you?'

Polly sprang to her feet, her green eyes blazing. 'There's nothing between me and Leo.'

'But he's been coming here, hasn't he? Before I came back. Bert Fowler was here yesterday and he told me, so don't deny it.'

'I'm not trying to. Yes, he's been here as a *friend* and nothing more, Roland. I told you that when you first came home. And if you can't or won't believe me, then there's nowt I can do.' In her anger, Polly slipped back into the dialect of her childhood. 'I was always honest with you, Roland, and I'll be truthful now. I've always been fond of you. You're a good, kind man and, since we married, I've come to love you. Oh, mebbe in a different way to the way I loved him, I'll not lie to you, but I do love you and I admire the way you volunteered when it was totally against your gentle nature to go killing others. I didn't agree with you – I didn't agree with anyone going – but I could see that you all felt you had to do your duty.'

There it was again, that principle that had brought so much pain into her young life.

'And while you were away, Roland, I was a good and faithful wife to you. Perhaps the only thing I've done that you don't like is to find myself a job – the one I've always wanted and one that I do not intend to give up as long as they still want me. So there you have it.

And you can choose who you want to believe. Me –
your wife – or the gossips like Bert Fowler. It's up to
you.'

She made as if to turn away, but he sprang up
suddenly, with an agility he'd not shown he still pos-
sessed. He grabbed her arm and swung her round to
face him. 'Don't you turn your back on me, woman,' he
yelled. 'And don't tell me what I can or can't do. I *will*
be master in my own house. You will leave that job and
do as I say.'

Polly stood very still, his fingers biting into her flesh.
Her heart was beating fast and her knees were trembling. She was frightened of him. Sweet, kind, gentle
Roland had come back from the trenches a different
being. Beaten and cowed, weakened and withdrawn,
she could have understood and treated him with gentle-
ness, but this roaring stranger she had not expected.
Whilst she quaked inside, she jutted out her chin and
faced him with an outward show of strength and fear-
lessness.

'I will not,' she said quietly, 'give up my job at the
school. I love being with the children and besides – '
she thrust her face closer to his – 'we need the money.'

Roland still held her with his left hand and now he
raised his right arm and slapped her hard across the
face.

Sixty-Six

'How did you get that bruise on your face?' Leo demanded as he met her one afternoon outside the school. All around them children laughed and shrieked as they chased each other, released from the confines of the classroom.

'You shouldn't be here. If we're seen together . . .'

'What?' He frowned. 'You don't mean – ' he pointed to the purple mark on her left cheek – 'he did that to you because of me?'

She bowed her head, afraid to look at him, afraid to meet the tender concern in his eyes, terrified that she would lose control completely and throw herself into his arms. 'Not – not really.'

'Then it did have something to do with me. Be honest with me, Poll.'

She sighed. 'We were arguing – about all sorts of things. Yes, you came into it a bit. Bert Fowler had been to see him and he'd said something about you visiting me, and knowing Bert he would only have had to insinuate something by the tone of his voice for Roland to be suspicious.'

'But there's nothing to suspect – more's the pity.' He paused and when she didn't speak he went on, 'So, didn't you tell him we're just friends and no more?'

'Of course, though I don't think he believed me. But it wasn't that – ' she touched her cheek – 'that caused this. It was when I refused to give up my job here. He wants to be master in his own house, he said. I mean, he never wanted me to work after we married and I didn't, but now . . . Leo, I need this job. I need to get out each day and, like I told him, we can do with the money. He's not working – not even making any effort to find work.'

'But it'll still be hurting his pride, Poll, that you're now the breadwinner.'

'Then why won't he try to find something? Micky's gone back to the market, Stevie's working for Mr Wilmott again and even you, who've been wounded, have found work.'

Leo had not been able to go back into the police force, his injury prevented that, but his superiors at the station had found employment for him in a civilian post. 'You'll be useful to us because of your background knowledge,' his inspector had told him. 'It's all been approved. You're to work in the records office.'

It wasn't what Leo had joined the force to do, but it was better than nothing and certainly better than being thrown on the streets as had happened to so many returning 'heroes'. In time, he came to enjoy the work; it kept him in touch with all the arrests made, the problems solved and life out there on the city streets in general, even though he was forced to experience it vicariously.

But now it was Polly who concerned him.

'Leave him, Poll. Come to me. I don't care about the gossips, about the scandal.'

Polly smiled sadly. 'But I do, Leo. Besides, it's my duty to stay with my husband and care for him – no matter what. And we have a child together. I have a duty to Jacob too.'

441

And now the tables were turned; it was Polly who saw the long, lonely road ahead of duty and loyalty to the vows she'd made before God.

Wordlessly, Leo stared at her and then he turned and walked away. She watched him go. His shoulders were hunched with disappointment and anxiety, his limp more pronounced. She watched him disappear into the gloom of the winter's afternoon, but Leo did not look round. Not once.

By the middle of March the national newspapers were reporting that the number of deaths in England and Wales was exceeding the number of births, due to the influenza epidemic.

On the last Friday in March Polly staggered home in the late afternoon carrying two heavy shopping bags, shivering and with a violent headache. She knew at once what was afflicting her.

She opened the door and leant wearily against the doorframe, but she did not step inside. 'Roland,' she called weakly. 'Roland!'

After a few moments he appeared but at once she held up her hand, palm outwards. 'Don't come near me. I have the flu. Tell Jacob to put some of his clothes into a bag and go straight round to Selina's. She'll have him. And you too. You go too. She'll take you, I know.'

'Don't be ridiculous, Polly. Don't stand there getting chilled, come on in.'

'Not until you've both left,' Polly said stubbornly.

'Jacob can go, but I'm going nowhere.' He turned and shouted to his son. Jacob came running in from the backyard and Polly heard Roland telling him what he'd to do.

'But what about Mam?'

'I'll look after your mam. Now go, hurry. She's standing outside and won't come into the house until you've gone.'

Within minutes Jacob had thrown a few clothes and belongings into a bag and was scuttling out of the door. He paused briefly to say, 'Mam?' but she waved him away. 'Be a good boy for Selina,' she gasped. 'As long as I know you're safe . . .'

Only when she'd seen him run up to the top of the street, turn and wave to her and then disappear round the corner, did she step into the house. She sank into a chair by the range, shivering uncontrollably and almost crying with the pain in her head and her limbs. 'Oh, Roland, please, go too. You'll catch it and you're not strong . . .'

'I'm going nowhere,' he repeated.

She leant back and closed her eyes; she no longer had the strength to argue.

For three days Polly lay in bed, delirious, sweating and shivering and with the worst headache she'd every known in her life. Her breathing was rasping and pain-ful, every muscle in her body seemed to ache.

'Don't lift me feet, Roland,' she moaned. It was the weirdest feeling.

'I'm not touching your feet.' She heard his voice as if from a long way off. Once she fancied she saw Dr Fenwick at the side of the bed. But that was foolish. It was only flu she had, there was no need for the doctor.

She felt a cooling flannel on her forehead that brought momentary relief, but she'd no idea who it was sitting beside her. In her delirium, she called out for her mother. 'Mam, oh, Mam,' and Eddie, believing him to be still alive and lastly, Leo. In her delirium, she called for Leo and, though he knew that she was unaware of him sitting beside the bed and didn't even realize what she was saying, it was a shaft through Roland's heart.

On the morning of the fourth day, she woke up and stared up at the familiar face standing beside the bed. 'Mrs Halliday.'

'Aye, lass, it's me and glad I am to see you recognize me today.' Bertha put her cool hand on Polly's forehead and, even though she'd not known at the time, she recognized the touch and knew who had been sponging her burning forehead at the height of her illness. 'You're on the mend now, but there was a time we thought we were losing you.' Bertha leant closer and lowered her voice. 'And I've two of 'em to deal with worrying theirsens silly about you, not to mention your dad and the bairns. Been trooping up here every day they have.' She sniffed her disapproval and said, 'Mind you, done 'em all a power of good to realize just what they'd be missing if they lost you. Anyway,' she said brightly, 'you're back with us now and I've strict instructions from Dr Fenwick on how to look after you, so you'll be seeing my ugly face around here for a few more days yet.'

Polly smiled weakly and tried to sit up, but the effort was just too much and she fell back against the pillows as a fit of coughing seized her.

It was several more days before Polly felt able to get out of bed and sit in a chair, wrapped in shawls and a blanket.

'You've been one of the lucky ones,' Bertha told her. 'No complications. A nasty cough, but it's not pneumonia.'

She didn't feel lucky; the illness had been dreadful, but she knew what Bertha meant. She was still alive and she would recover. So many in the city had not.

'Is Jacob all right? He hasn't caught it, has he?'

'Not so far, duck. Selina's looking after him. She'd have been a great mother.' Bertha shook her head and sighed. 'Life's so unfair, ain't it?'

Polly closed her eyes and breathed a sigh of thankfulness and then she heard Bertha hesitantly say the words she dreaded to hear. 'But your Roland's gone to bed early. He's not feeling too good.'

'Oh no, no!' Polly whispered.

Sixty-Seven

The following morning, when Roland did not come into the bedroom to bring her breakfast as he'd been doing each morning whilst she'd been ill, Polly dragged herself out of bed and went to the spare room where he'd been sleeping. She opened the door and held her breath. He was lying in the bed, his face bathed in sweat and he was threshing from side to side, muttering in delirium. Though still weak herself, Polly dressed and went downstairs on legs that threatened to give way beneath her at any second. She filled the kettle with water that gushed, pure and safe, from the tap now and set it on the hob.

'Fluids,' she murmured to herself. 'He must have plenty of fluids.'

Minutes later she was mounting the stairs again carrying a warm drink and a bowl of lukewarm water with which to bathe his face.

'No, no,' he was writhing and shouting when she entered the bedroom and sat down beside the bed. 'It'll go off. Get away, get away!'

She bathed his face and his hands, speaking softly and soothingly to him. 'There, there, Roland, dear. Do try to be calm. You'll do yourself no good. Now, try to sit up and drink this.'

But they were both so weak – Roland couldn't raise himself and she couldn't lift him – that between them they spilt the liquid all over the bedclothes. Polly, with

fear and weakness, was close to tears and when a knock
sounded at the front door about mid-morning, she
didn't think she'd ever been so glad to see anyone in her
life.

'Oh, Mrs Halliday, he's got the flu. Roland's got it
now.'

'Aye, I thought as much last night when I left,' Bertha
said, stepping fearlessly across the threshold and making
for the stairs. 'Doctor's on his way. I knew that'd be
what you'd want.'

'Oh yes, yes. Thank you.'

Bertha pulled herself up the steep stairs, saying, 'You
sit by the fire and rest, duck. You're not fit yourself. I'll
see to him.'

'But . . .'

'No buts, lass. I've seen it all before and he'll not
know a lot about it.'

'He's rambling,' Polly called up after her as Bertha
reached the top. 'He thinks he's back in the trenches.'

Bertha turned briefly and looked down at her solemnly. 'Aye, I know. That's what a lot of them that's
come back and caught the flu have been doing, but, God
willing, he'll pull through.'

But Bertha's optimism was misplaced, Roland deteri-
orated steadily.

On the fourth day of his illness and whilst Polly grew
stronger, Roland grew weaker.

Dr Fenwick came downstairs. 'My dear, I have to be
honest with you. He's sinking. His lungs were damaged
in the war, so I understand, and he's got pneumonia. If
there's anyone who'd want to see him, then – you
should send for them at once.'

'Oh no,' she breathed and sat down suddenly. Her
legs, still weak from her own illness, gave way beneath

her. She stared at the doctor with wide, frightened eyes. 'There's – there's Jacob, but the infection . . . ?'

'I think it's a risk you'll have to take, my dear.'

'I – I'll send word to Mrs Thorpe's.'

As the doctor picked up his bag, he said, 'He's no longer delirious, Polly, so whatever he says to you now, you can believe it. He's – er – asking to see Leo Halliday.'

'Leo?' Polly was startled.

'Yes. He asked specifically if I would ask Mrs Halliday if Leo would come to see him.'

He left by the front door leaving Polly, open-mouthed, gaping after him.

Bertha, arriving only moments after the doctor's departure, found her still sitting in the chair by the fire, gazing into space. 'Poll? What is it?'

'He – Roland – has asked to see Leo.'

Bertha nodded. 'I know. Dr Fenwick's just told me. I passed him on my way in.' She paused and searched Polly's face. 'Do you want me to ask him to come?'

'I – I don't know. I mean, I don't want Leo to catch it, but . . .'

'Leo's stronger now and they've been going down like flies with it at the station. I don't think that'll worry him, but I think he'll wonder what Roland wants.'

'So do I,' Polly said shortly.

Selina brought Jacob home at dinnertime, wide-eyed and frightened. He'd now been away from home for over two weeks and whilst either Selina or Albie had brought him to the door every evening to ask first his father how his mother was and then, recently, to ask her after Roland, he'd never been allowed to come into the house. But Selina had explained to him very gently that his father was seriously ill and that he must be a brave boy and go up to see him.

'Mam,' he said, coming to stand beside her knee and leaning his head on her shoulder, 'is Daddy – is he going to die?'

Polly took a deep breath and realized that she should not lie to her son. He was a solemn four year old who'd already been surrounded by grown-ups talking of death almost daily. As she stroked his hair, Polly breathed a sigh of great sadness and yet it was tinged with relief. There was sadness because Jacob would now never get to know his father and yet there was relief too that the young child would not suffer the deep grief and desolation that so many children had experienced in losing a dearly loved father.

'He's very, very poorly, Jacob. I want you to go into the bedroom and stand near the door so he can see you. Can you do that, d'you think?'

The boy nodded and Polly took him by the hand and led him upstairs.

Roland was calmer than he'd been since the illness had struck. Beads of sweat still stood out on his forehead, but he was no longer delirious. His breathing was laboured and painful, but he turned his head to look at his son, a ghost of a smile lingered on his cracked lips.

'Look after your mam, Jacob. Be a good boy for her.' The effort to speak brought on a fit of coughing that racked his body. Jacob pulled his hand from his mother's grasp, turned and ran down the stairs.

'Jacob . . .' Polly started after him but a noise from the bed made her turn back.

'Let – him – go,' Roland gasped out between coughs. 'The sickroom – is no place for a boy.'

At last the spasm subsided and Roland lay back against the pillows, exhausted and with his eyes closed.

Polly moved to the bedside and began to sponge his face. 'I'm so sorry, Polly, for how I behaved when I came home. It was – unforgivable.'

'Nothing's unforgivable, Roland dear. Don't fret. Just rest.'

'I can't rest. I mustn't. There are things I need to say – to do. I must see Leo. Why doesn't he come?'

He was becoming distressed again and Polly knew she had no choice but to give way to him. 'But why d'you want to see him, Roland?' She didn't add: Him of all people?

'I want to see him, Polly. Please, indulge me in this one thing. I'm begging you.'

'All right. I'll send for him, if you'll try to rest.'

He was calmer at once, as if he knew she would keep her promise and that Leo would come. She bathed him again and plumped his pillows before going downstairs. Jacob was sitting on Selina's lap, tears running down his face.

'I thought I should wait, but I'll take him home, if you think it best, Polly.'

Polly tried to smile at her son as she said softly to Selina, 'I think it'd be best. Thank you.'

'Come along, my poppet. Let's go and see Uncle Albie on his stall. He might let you help him for a while.' She smiled at Polly. 'He likes helping at the market.'

Polly nodded, her throat too full to speak. Was he going to follow in his Uncle Eddie's footsteps and be a market trader? She just hoped that he wouldn't fall in with a bad lot like Eddie, but with Albie Thorpe as his mentor that was unlikely.

The house was quiet when they'd gone – unnaturally so. Polly was restless. There was nothing else she could do for Roland except bathe him and give him fluids. Her own strength was returning gradually, but she was overwhelmed with fear and guilt. She'd brought the infection into their home and, in his weakened state, Roland had succumbed to it. And now he was going to die. The doctor had implied as much. And then there was Roland's insistence that he wanted to see Leo.

Why? What on earth did he want to say to him?

There was a soft knock at the door and Leo was standing there. 'Is it true? Is Roland asking to see me?'

She nodded and held the door open for him to enter. 'He's in the little bedroom at the back. It's – it's where he was sleeping whilst I was ill and he's been too ill to move him back to the front room.' Her voice broke. She covered her face with her hands and swayed.

Leo grasped her arms to steady her, but she shook him off. 'No, no, don't,' she whispered, almost as if she was afraid Roland might suddenly appear downstairs and see them together. 'Just – just go up to him. See what he wants. I'll wait here.'

She sat down and it seemed an age before Leo appeared again. She'd heard the low murmur of their voices from the room above, but she'd not been able to hear what was being said.

When Leo came back into the kitchen, she twisted round to ask, 'What did he say? What did he want?'

Leo sat down. 'I'm not going to tell you everything, Poll. Not now. Maybe one day I will, but not now. It wouldn't be right. Suffice to say two things: one, we've made our peace and two, he's asked me to stay here with you until – ' he pulled in a deep breath – 'until the end.'

Polly gave a sob and covered her mouth with her hand, staring at him with tear-filled eyes. 'It's all my fault,' she gulped. 'If I hadn't been so stubborn about keeping on me job, I wouldn't have caught the flu and he wouldn't have got it neither.'

'Poll, you have to stop blaming yourself for everything that happens. The infection's been rife through the city. Unless you both – all three of you, if it comes to that – locked yourselves away in isolation for several months, you couldn't have escaped it. Now,' he said more firmly, 'who is there who'd like to see him? Jacob's been, hasn't he?'

Polly nodded.

'What about his family?'

'There's no one.'

'Your family then? They're fond of him, aren't they?'

'Yes, but they might not want to because of catching it.'

But Polly was wrong: they all came. Trooping up to the bedroom and coming down again solemn-faced or in tears like Violet and Miriam. Even Micky came, bringing a scared Michael. But the seven-year-old went upstairs, clinging to his dad's hand.

It was as if Roland had waited to see them all; he'd hung on to say whatever he'd wanted to say to Leo and now it was left to Polly to sit by his bedside and hold his hand until peace came to him. She was the only one he wanted in the room, though he was safe in the knowledge that Leo was downstairs ready to help Polly.

He couldn't talk very much; already he was exhausted and the telltale rattle had begun in his throat.

Hearing it, Polly clung to his hand, willing him to fight, willing him to get better. But the brave soldier – the gentle man who should never have gone to war – could not win this battle. At three o'clock in the morning he slipped quietly away.

Polly went downstairs and hearing the door opening, Leo stood up and held his arms out to her in comfort. Without a moment's hesitation she went to him and allowed him to enfold her into his strong embrace. She laid her head against his shoulder and wept.

Sixty-Eight

More people attended Roland's funeral than Polly had expected. Her family were all there, of course, but she had not thought that Nelly and Ida and several others from the factory would attend. But they all remembered him as a well-liked and respected foreman – and latterly manager – who'd always treated them fairly and even stood up to the employers on their behalf on occasion. They'd missed Roland when he'd volunteered, for his place had been taken by Harry Barnes, a boss's man, as Nelly called him, who'd made the workers' lives a misery.

Selina and Albie came to take care of Jacob, and even the Fowler family came, and several from the street where Roland had lived all his life made up the congregation. There were three men, still in uniform, who'd served at the Front with Roland. Somehow they'd heard of his death and had travelled from London and Liverpool to attend. Polly couldn't think how they'd got to know, until one of them said that Leo had got in touch with them. Nancy Miller and Celia Broughton were there too. Though neither of them had known Roland, they came to support Polly and Jacob. And right at the back of the church Polly noticed Bertha, Seth and Leo slipping into a pew at the last moment.

After the interment in a chilly, windswept cemetery, they returned home, where Polly, with Violet's help, had laid on a spread for anyone who came back to the house. It seemed as if most of them had, relishing the prospect of a warming cup of tea and a bite to eat. They crowded into the terraced house, standing with cup and plate balanced in their hands whilst they chatted in desultory tones.

'He was such a good son to that mother of his. God rest her soul,' Nelly Rawdon said, clasping Polly's cold hand in hers. 'But she didn't deserve such devotion. She was a miserable old bat, though I shouldn't speak ill of the dead.'

'And you've got a lovely son to remember him by.' Ida nodded and then added, with deceptive nonchalance, 'But I 'spect you won't be on your own forever. Pretty young widow like you.' She glanced around Polly's front room as if searching for a particular young man.

'Ida,' Nelly chided warningly. 'This ain't the time nor the place for your speculations.'

Polly smiled weakly and vowed silently that no one should ever hear a word spoken against Roland and certainly not from her lips. The man who'd come home from the war had not been the real Roland and she would never tell anyone what had happened behind the lace curtains of their home. Only Leo knew and she wanted it to stay that way.

'Michael, take Jacob upstairs and play with him would you? There's a love,' Violet, handing round sandwiches and cakes, said, 'I'll fetch you down when everyone's gone.'

'But, Mam, we're hungry,' the boy began.

'Go on with you,' Violet pushed him towards the stairs. 'There'll be plenty left for you and Jacob, I promise. Now take the little lad out of this.'

'Do as yer mam ses, Michael,' Micky said. 'And I'll take you and Jacob to the park later.'

'Can we play football, Uncle Micky?' Jacob piped up and when promised they could, both boys clattered up the stairs.

'What fine boys they are, Micky,' Ida said, sidling up to him. 'You must be so proud of your son.' There was a definite accent on the word *your*, but Micky only grinned and assured her that he certainly was and of his little wife, who'd coped so magnificently whilst he'd been away fighting.

Ida began to say something, but Nelly broke in saying loudly, 'Aye, she were a little trooper. Worked like a good 'un, she did at the factory, even though she'd been used to better things in that fancy shop in the High Street. But for all that, she was soon one of us, weren't she, Ida?' Nelly dug a sharp elbow into Ida's ribs. 'Vi could stand up to old misery guts, Harry Barnes, even better than us lot who've been there years. She's a way with her, all right.'

Ida was nodding vigorously. 'Aye, she certainly had, specially with all the . . .'

'Right, Ida Norton, time you and me was going home.' Nelly almost snatched the plate out of Ida's hand and grasped her arm in one smooth movement. 'Bye, Micky. Glad to see you back, lad, safe an' sound. Now, don't you go catching this flu, will yer?'

Micky winked at Nelly and grinned. He was fully aware of the tales that Ida Norton would have liked to tell him about Violet's antics whilst he'd been away. He'd heard them all from his dad or the fellers in the pub. But he didn't care. He'd been to hell and back in the trenches and he'd survived without serious injury. Whatever Vi had been up to in his absence didn't unduly worry him; she was still here waiting for him and as ready and willing for his loving as she'd ever been.

He looked across the room at Polly. At her white, drawn face and thought yet again how lovely she was and how life had dealt her a rough deal. He'd never understood why she'd married Roland, good man though he'd been, but now maybe she'd have a chance at real happiness given a decent interval. He hoped so. Deep in his heart, he still loved her and he always would, but that was a secret that only he and Polly shared. But he'd watch out for her; he would always watch out for her.

When they'd all gone except for Violet, Micky and Leo, Polly loaded two plates with sandwiches and cakes and called the boys down.

'I'd best be going too, Poll.' Leo put his hands on her shoulders as footsteps clattered down the stairs. 'If there's anything I can do – anything at all – just let me know. Promise, now.'

Polly nodded. 'I will and – and thank you, Leo.'

As the front door closed behind him, Violet said softly, 'He still loves you, you know. I don't think he's ever stopped.'

'Not now, Vi,' Polly whispered. 'Now's not the time.'

It seemed to those around her, to those who loved and cared about her, that it was never going to be the right time for Polly to face up to the love that still existed between herself and Leo.

Roland's will, made before he'd left for the Front, had left all his worldly goods to Polly. Her name was now on the rent book and she had a little money in the bank. But a week after Roland's funeral she returned to school and the job she loved. She buried herself in work and caring for Jacob.

She saw little of Leo and that was how she wanted it. The riots and their consequences had faded into the past. Her father had regained his job and was holding on to it even after the war had ended, for many of those who'd enlisted had not returned or had come back so badly maimed they could not take up their old employment. And the bitter memories were fading, if not quite forgotten. That time was rarely spoken of now, for a greater, more widespread catastrophe had overtaken their city, one that had left countless families mourning loved ones.

Even Polly had forgiven Leo for his part in her father's arrest and imprisonment and, it seemed, so too had William.

In midsummer of 1919 he came to Polly's home one evening after work.

'Hello, Dad,' she said, surprised to see him on the doorstep. Her face clouded. 'Something wrong?'

'Now, lass, why would you always be thinking summat's wrong?'

She smiled wryly. 'Well, I'm not very often honoured by a visit from you without an invitation, am I? Are Stevie and Miriam all right?'

'They're fine. And Miriam's turning into a wonderful little housewife. She looks after us a treat.' He smiled slowly at her. 'Almost as good as you did, Poll.'

'Oh, I'm sure she's better than ever I was.'

William shook his head and said seriously, 'No, Poll, no one could have done a better job than you – not even your poor mam, God rest her soul. I never realized it at the time, but you had such a heavy burden to bear and I didn't help you like I could have done – like I *should* have done. I wasn't a very good dad, Poll, I know that. Yar mam always kept me on the straight and narrow, but after we lost her, well, I went a bit wild. You did your best, but no one could have expected a slip of a girl to keep me in check.' He looked straight at her and held her gaze. 'What I'm trying to say to you, love, is that whatever happened to me was me own fault. It wasn't yours and – it wasn't Leo's neither. The lad was only doing what he had to: his duty. It's time to move on. It's time you made it up with him, Poll.' He leaned across the table towards her. 'D'you know summat, lass, that lad has never had another girl. Not even after you upped and married Roland. He's always loved you – and he still does. And – ' he leant back in the chair again – 'if I'm not mistaken, you still love him.'

As she opened her mouth to speak he put up his hand, 'And don't try to deny it, Poll, 'cos I won't believe you and neither will anyone else who's got eyes in their heads.'

Quietly, she said, 'I wasn't going to, Dad, but it's not even six months since Roland died and – and . . .' Her head drooped.

'And?'

Hoarsely, she whispered, 'I can't stop blaming myself for Roland's death.'

'Eh? What on earth d'you mean? He died of the flu, like a good many more.'

'He caught the flu from me, Dad. I brought it into this house – to a man weakened by the war – and he caught it from me.'

'Oh, Polly, Polly, why must you go on blaming yourself for everything? It wasn't your fault you caught flu and he got it too. He could have got it anywhere.'

'But he wanted me to give up working at the school,

stay at home and look after him and Jacob, but I – I disobeyed him.'

'Disobeyed him?' William was genuinely puzzled, then his expression cleared. 'Oh, I see it. You're thinking of your marriage vows, eh? Promising to love, honour and obey. Is that it?'

When Polly nodded, he laughed wryly. 'Well, a lot of us men'd give our eye teeth to have our wives remember that particular bit of the service, lass. And I include your mam in that, an' all. Sarah? Obey me? That's a laugh!'

Despite the seriousness of their conversation, a smile twitched at Polly's mouth. 'She was a strong woman, wasn't she?'

William nodded. 'She was. And you're very like her, Polly. You've had it tough in your young life, but I've never heard one word of complaint pass your lips. You've just got on with it. And now you've to do it again. But this time you must think of yourself. What you want. And if it's Leo Halliday – and he still wants you – then you have my blessing.' He heaved himself up from the chair. 'That's all I've got to say, lass.' As he passed by her on his way out, he touched her shoulder. Quietly, in a voice that was not quite steady, he said, 'You deserve a bit of happiness, Poll. Real happiness.'

He left her sitting deep in thought in the dusk of a summer's evening, watching the shadows lengthen in the backyard.

Sixty-Nine

It was the summer holidays, so there was no school. Her time was filled with caring for Jacob and cleaning the house from top to bottom. She threw out all the old musty bedlinen, tablecloths and curtains that Roland's mother had stored for years in cupboards and ottomans.

'Hello, duck, what brings you here?' Albie greeted her and Jacob. 'Now then, Jacob, me lad. We aren't half missing you, me and the missus.' He winked at Jacob. 'We'll be glad when school starts and yar mam lets us look after you again.'

Polly smiled at him. 'You're very good to us, Albie, but Jacob starts school in September.'

When she saw the big man's face fall, she knew that he'd enjoyed having Jacob to care for almost as much as Selina had.

'Aw, that's a pity. My Selina'll miss you summat rotten.' His face brightened. 'But mebbe yar mam'll let you come round and see us after school, eh? Now, what can I do for you?'

'I'm after some new material, Albie. I've been having a clear-out and we need some new curtains and cushions and, oh, all sorts of things, don't we, Jacob?'

The boy nodded solemnly. 'Mam's going to sew me some new sheets for my bed.'

'You've got a sewing machine then?'

Polly laughed. 'Good Heavens, no! I do it all by hand.'

'It'll take you weeks and you'll likely strain your eyes.'

Polly sighed. 'Well, I've plenty of time on my hands. Once Jacob's in bed, there's – there's nothing else to do.' Her voice trailed away and Albie couldn't help noticing the wistfulness in her tone.

'Mmm.' The big man was thoughtful. 'You need a machine if you're going to do all that sewing, lass. Tell you what, you nip over to Vince's stall. I know he's got a nice little Singer sewing machine there.'

Polly's eyes widened and reading the meaning in them Albie laughed. 'It's all right. All above board, 'cos I know where it came from. An' you tell him I sent you and he'll treat you right, else he'll have me to answer to.'

'But I don't know how to use one, Albie.'

'Oh, that's no problem. Selina'll show you.' He chuckled and nodded towards Jacob. 'And it'll give her an excuse to see this little chap.'

Polly approached Vince Norton's stall, feeling an unaccustomed nervousness.

'Hello, Poll, what you doin' here?' Micky popped up from behind the stall and grinned at her.

'I – er – Albie tells me Vince has got a sewing machine for sale.'

'That's right. Why, d'you want it?'

'Er – well – yes. I think so.'

'Going to take in sewing as well as teaching kids their A, B, C and wiping snotty noses?'

Polly pursed her lips primly. 'Behave yourself, Micky Fowler, else I'm off. Besides, what are you doing on

Vince's stall? I thought you didn't work for him any more? I thought you've been with Albie since you came back?'

Micky sobered at once. 'I am, an' I mean to keep me job with him, but we all help each other out now and again and Albie sent me across here this morning. Now let's see if we can find this machine . . .'

Later than evening, Micky struggled to Polly's home with the sewing machine. He set it on the table.

'Albie says Selina'll come round in the morning and get you going.'

Polly fingered the curve of the wooden case lovingly.

There was silence between them until Polly looked up and found Micky watching her. 'Are you all right, Poll?' he asked softly.

She forced a smile. 'I'm fine.'

He sighed and shook his head. 'You can't fool me, Polly. I've known you – and loved you – for a long time. Remember?'

'Micky, don't. Please don't.'

'It's all right, I'm not going to embarrass you. I just want you to be happy, Poll. That's all. Once, I was as jealous as hell of Leo and the way you loved him, but now I'd give anything to see you happy with him. Why don't you – ?'

She put up her hand as if to ward him off and said yet again, 'Please don't, Micky.'

He said no more, but after he'd gone Polly was left feeling even more lonely and unsettled.

Everyone was telling her that she and Leo should make up, but since Roland's death the one person who'd been nowhere near her was Leo.

*

It was the end of September when he finally came to see her, almost six months after Roland's death.

'How are you, Poll? Though I don't really need to ask. I've been kept well informed.'

'Really? Who by?'

He gave a sideways grin. 'Oh, just about everybody you could think of.' He ticked them off on his fingers. 'My mother for a start, then your dad, Violet – even Micky. And Stevie and Miriam weren't to be left out either, and then there's been – '

'Stop, stop!' She put her hands over her ears, laughing. When she lowered them she was serious again. 'But I did wonder why you didn't come yourself.'

He sat down uninvited as he said quietly, 'I thought it best. I had to wait a decent interval, Poll – you know that – and I'm sure you feel the same. But now it's time we had a good talk and – ' he took a deep breath – 'and I told you what it was that Roland said to me.'

Slowly, she sat down too and waited, her fingers twisting in her lap.

'He was so very sorry for what had happened between you when he first came home after the war and, by the end, Poll, he was the old Roland.'

She nodded as tears constricted her throat.

'All his concern was not for himself but for you and for Jacob. He regretted that he hardly knew his son and that too, he said, had been his own fault. He could have come home on leave a few times, and when the war ended he could have made more effort, he said, to get close to the boy, but he'd been so wrapped up in his own depression that he'd no thought for anyone else. Not you, not Jacob – not anyone.'

Still Polly said nothing.

'But, like I say, at the end there he was thinking of

464

you both. He – he told me that you'd been a wonderful wife to him, even though he'd always known that you couldn't love him in the same way that he loved you. But he said you'd devoted yourself to him and to making him happy.'

Polly gave a sob and pressed her hand to her mouth.

'He knew that you loved someone else. He – he knew you loved me and all he wanted was for you to be happy after he'd gone. He asked me if I still cared for you and I told him I still loved you with all my heart and I always would.'

Tears now ran down Polly's face, but Leo went on, ' "Then marry her with my blessing and take care of my son," he said.'

Polly buried her face in her hands and wept openly. Now Leo moved across the space between them and knelt by her side. 'Polly, my dearest, darling Polly, will you marry me?'

For some time, Polly could not speak and then she heard herself saying, 'I can't, I can't.'

'Why not, darling? You do still love me, don't you?'

'You know I do.'

'Then why? Are you afraid of the gossips, because – ?'

'No, no. I – I just feel so guilty that I brought the flu to the house, that he caught it off me.'

'Oh, darling.' Leo was actually laughing, confident he could allay her fears, but they were far too deeply embedded to be brushed away so lightly.

The guilt of years, the blame she'd carried for most of her young life, would not allow Polly to let herself be happy. She could forgive others, but she couldn't forgive herself.

Seventy

'You're being ridiculous,' Violet stormed at her. 'You'll
lose him for good if you don't watch out. Even Leo
won't wait for ever. How he's waited this long for you,
I don't know. I'd have found mesen someone else years
ago.'

Polly smiled weakly, but still Violet couldn't persuade
her. None of them could.

Nelly had her say too. 'If you're bothered about the
Hetty Fowlers and the Ida Nortons of this world, then
you can forget them, duck. We all know them for what
they are.' She snorted with laughter. 'Even Bert knows
what his wife's like. Why, he said to me the other night
in the pub, "When do you reckon there's going to be
wedding bells, then?" Now would he say that if half the
neighbourhood weren't expecting it? *And* wanting it for
you and Leo.'

But Polly could not be persuaded. At last, when
they'd all tried, Selina said calmly, 'Why don't you go
up to the cathedral? It's a lovely place to sit and think.
Or go to a service on Sunday, if you like. We'll have
Jacob.'

Polly smiled. The woman would do anything to get
Jacob to herself for an hour or two.

As she went home that evening, she paused at the end
of her own street and looked up at the cathedral. She'd
always wanted to see inside, but life had been so hectic

she'd never made the time; now she felt drawn to it, felt the need to see for herself inside the building that stood guard over the city.

She lay awake that night, a strange feeling of excitement that she couldn't explain keeping sleep at bay. She didn't fall asleep until dawn was already creeping through the new curtains that now hung at her window, thanks to Selina's tuition with the sewing machine.

And once again, she decided, she would take the older woman's advice.

Polly went alone and told no one. Jacob was playing happily at the Thorpes' house and didn't even ask where she was going, though she thought that Selina guessed.

She walked along the High Street and climbed Steep Hill, the cathedral drawing her closer and closer. At last she stood in the square, staring up at the majestic building. She'd never been this close before, never even been to the top of the hill. She'd known it was big, but it towered into the sky, reaching up to heaven, Polly thought fancifully. She passed slowly through the archway and approached the huge door. From the interior, she could hear singing. She hesitated; she didn't want to intrude upon a service. She just wanted to see inside, to sit a while and think.

A man in clerical garb came to the door. 'Come in, my child. You're very welcome.'

'Is there a service going on? I don't want . . .'

'No, no. It's only choir practice. You'll not disturb them, I promise.'

She stepped into the cool vastness and looked about her in awe.

'Your first time?' the man asked gently. When she

467

nodded, he chuckled. 'It does take your breath away, doesn't it? Now, can I help you at all?'

Polly shook her head. 'I – just came to see it.'

'Then have a good look around, my dear, but if you need someone to talk to, I'm here.'

'Thank you,' she whispered and the sound seemed to echo all around her.

Polly wandered through archways and along the worn flagstones. She stepped into St Hugh's choir and marvelled at the intricacy of the carved dark wooden stalls. She caught her breath at the magnificent rose windows, the smaller stained-glass windows and the stone effigies. She even searched for the imp – a stone gargoyle – and found him sitting cheekily at the top of a pillar. Then she sat down in the nave and stared around her at the vast splendour. She'd never imagined it would be so beautiful and regretted all the years that had passed when she'd revered the cathedral from afar but had never made the effort to visit it.

She sat there for a long time, listening to the choir singing, until the cold seeped through her clothes and began to chill her. And then, without really forming proper words, proper sentences, she began to pray. It was more a feeling that crept into her, a sensation of peace enveloping her. The burden of guilt she'd carried for years slowly rolled away. Just as she had found it in her heart to forgive others, she felt herself forgiven and, most of all, she could forgive herself.

At last she walked outside and lifted her face to the sky. She closed her eyes and revelled in the warmth of the bright September day. When she opened them and began to walk towards the archway leading to the top of Steep Hill, she saw a familiar figure leaning against the stone wall. She caught her breath and her steps faltered. He made no move, but his gaze was fastened on her face. Oblivious of everyone around them, Polly walked slowly towards him until she stood only a few feet away. Then she lifted her chin and said, 'I love you, Leo Halliday. And, yes, I will marry you.'

He pushed himself off the wall, strode towards her and swept her into a crushing embrace, raining kisses on her upturned face. She laughed and clung to him, returning his kisses.

Gone were all her doubts, gone was all the misery of the past few years. Laughing, and with their arms around each other, they walked to the top of the hill and paused to look down over the city.

'We've all been through so much,' Leo murmured, sweeping his arm wide as if to embrace the city they both loved. 'But we're the lucky ones. We've survived. We'll never forget those we've lost, but we've so much to look forward to now.' He turned towards her and cupped her face with both his hands. 'And we'll never let anything or anyone come between us ever again.'

'No, we won't,' Polly breathed, her face alight with a newfound joy at the thought of the happiness to come.

Loved *Forgive and Forget*?

Now you can buy Margaret Dickinson's classic Fleethaven novels for JUST £3.99* EACH

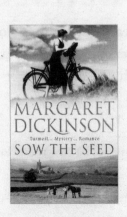

Plough the Furrow   Sow the Seed   Reap the Harvest

* £1 postage and packaging costs to UK addresses, £2 for overseas

To buy the books with this special discount, simply phone 01256 302699, quoting 4RH as your discount code

Offer expires 1st March 2012

This offer is subject to availability of stock and applies to paperback editions only

FOR MORE ON

MARGARET DICKINSON

sign up to receive our

SAGA NEWSLETTER

Packed with **features, competitions, authors'** **and readers' letters** and **news of exclusive events,** it's a 'must-read' for every Margaret Dickinson fan!

Simply fill in your details below and tick to confirm that you would like to receive saga-related news and promotions and return to us at **Pan Macmillan, Saga Newsletter, 20 New Wharf Road, London, N1 9RR.**

NAME Iman Kehal

ADDRESS _____

_____

_____ POSTCODE _____

EMAIL _____

☐ *I would like to receive saga-related news and promotions (please tick)*

You can unsubscribe at any time in writing or through our website where you can also see our privacy policy which explains how we will store and use your data.